Can You Forgive Her?
Vol. I

by

Anthony Trollope

Double 9
BOOKS

Can You Forgive Her?
Vol. I
by Anthony Trollope

ISBN: 978-93-61154-82-9

Published by

DOUBLE 9 BOOKS

2/13-B, Ansari Road
Daryaganj, New Delhi – 110002
info@double9books.com
www.double9books.com
Tel. 011-40042856

This book is under public domain

ABOUT THE AUTHOR

Anthony Trollope was an English novelist and government official during the Victorian era. His best-known works include the Chronicles of Barsetshire, a series of novels set in the fictional county of Barsetshire. He also authored novels about politics, social issues, and gender, among other topics. Trollope's literary fame plummeted in his final years, but he regained some popularity by the mid-twentieth century. Anthony Trollope was the son of barrister Thomas Anthony Trollope and Frances Milton Trollope, a novelist and travel writer. Despite being a brilliant and well-educated man and a Fellow of New College, Oxford, Thomas Trollope failed at the Bar because of his nasty temper. Farming ventures proved unproductive, and he missed out on an expected bequest when an elderly childless uncle remarried and had children. Thomas Trollope was the son of Rev. (Thomas) Anthony Trollope, rector of Cottered in Hertfordshire, and the sixth son of Sir Thomas Trollope, 4th Baronet. The baronetcy was later passed down to the descendants of Anthony Trollope's second son, Frederick.

CONTENTS

CHAPTER I
MR. VAVASOR AND HIS DAUGHTER

Whether or no, she, whom you are to forgive, if you can, did or did not belong to the Upper Ten Thousand of this our English world, I am not prepared to say with any strength of affirmation. By blood she was connected with big people,—distantly connected with some very big people indeed, people who belonged to the Upper Ten Hundred if there be any such division; but of these very big relations she had known and seen little, and they had cared as little for her. Her grandfather, Squire Vavasor of Vavasor Hall, in Westmoreland, was a country gentleman, possessing some thousand a year at the outside, and he therefore never came up to London, and had no ambition to have himself numbered as one in any exclusive set. A hot-headed, ignorant, honest old gentleman, he lived ever at Vavasor Hall, declaring to any who would listen to him, that the country was going to the mischief, and congratulating himself that at any rate, in his county, parliamentary reform had been powerless to alter the old political arrangements. Alice Vavasor, whose offence against the world I am to tell you, and if possible to excuse, was the daughter of his younger son; and as her father, John Vavasor, had done nothing to raise the family name to eminence, Alice could not lay claim to any high position from her birth as a Vavasor. John Vavasor had come up to London early in life as a barrister, and had failed. He had failed at least in attaining either much wealth or much repute, though he had succeeded in earning, or perhaps I might better say, in obtaining, a livelihood. He had married a lady somewhat older than himself, who was in possession of four hundred a year, and who was related to those big people to whom I have alluded. Who these were and the special nature of the relationship, I shall be called upon to explain hereafter, but at present it will suffice to say that Alice Macleod gave great offence to all her friends by her marriage. She did not, however, give them much time for the indulgence of their anger. Having given birth to a daughter within twelve months of her marriage, she died, leaving in abeyance that question as to whether the fault of her marriage should or should not be pardoned by her family.

When a man marries an heiress for her money, if that money be within her own control, as was the case with Miss Macleod's fortune, it is generally well for the speculating lover that the lady's friends should quarrel with him and with her. She is thereby driven to throw herself entirely into the gentleman's arms, and he thus becomes possessed of the wife and the money without the abominable nuisance of stringent settlements. But the Macleods, though they quarrelled with Alice, did not quarrel with her *à l'outrance*. They snubbed herself and her chosen husband; but they did not so far separate themselves from her and her affairs as to give up the charge of her possessions. Her four hundred a year was settled very closely on herself and on her children, without even a life interest having been given to Mr. Vavasor, and therefore when she died the mother's fortune became the property of the little baby. But, under these circumstances, the big people did not refuse to interest themselves to some extent on behalf of the father. I do not suppose that any actual agreement or compact was made between Mr. Vavasor and the Macleods; but it came to be understood between them that if he made no demand upon them for his daughter's money, and allowed them to have charge of her education, they would do something for him. He was a practising barrister, though his practice had never amounted to much; and a practising barrister is always supposed to be capable of filling any situation which may come his way. Two years after his wife's death Mr. Vavasor was appointed assistant commissioner in some office which had to do with insolvents, and which was abolished three years after his appointment. It was at first thought that he would keep his eight hundred a year for life and be required to do nothing for it; but a wretched cheeseparing Whig government, as John Vavasor called it when describing the circumstances of the arrangement to his father, down in Westmoreland, would not permit this; it gave him the option of taking four hundred a year for doing nothing, or of keeping his whole income and attending three days a week for three hours a day during term time, at a miserable dingy little office near Chancery Lane, where his duty would consist in signing his name to accounts which he never read, and at which he was never supposed even to look. He had sulkily elected to keep the money, and this signing had been now for nearly twenty years the business of his life. Of course he considered himself to be a very hardly-used man. One Lord Chancellor after another he petitioned, begging that he might be relieved from the cruelty of his position, and allowed to take his salary without doing anything in return for it. The amount of work which he did perform was certainly a minimum of labour. Term time, as terms were counted in Mr. Vavasor's office, hardly comprised half the year, and the hours of weekly attendance did not do more than make one day's work a week for a working man; but Mr. Vavasor had been appointed an assistant commissioner, and with every

Lord Chancellor he argued that all Westminster Hall, and Lincoln's Inn to boot, had no right to call upon him to degrade himself by signing his name to accounts. In answer to every memorial he was offered the alternative of freedom with half his income; and so the thing went on.

There can, however, be no doubt that Mr. Vavasor was better off and happier with his almost nominal employment than he would have been without it. He always argued that it kept him in London; but he would undoubtedly have lived in London with or without his official occupation. He had become so habituated to London life in a small way, before the choice of leaving London was open to him, that nothing would have kept him long away from it. After his wife's death he dined at his club every day on which a dinner was not given to him by some friend elsewhere, and was rarely happy except when so dining. They who have seen him scanning the steward's list of dishes, and giving the necessary orders for his own and his friend's dinner, at about half past four in the afternoon, have seen John Vavasor at the only moment of the day at which he is ever much in earnest. All other things are light and easy to him,—to be taken easily and to be dismissed easily. Even the eating of the dinner calls forth from him no special sign of energy. Sometimes a frown will gather on his brow as he tastes the first half glass from his bottle of claret; but as a rule that which he has prepared for himself with so much elaborate care, is consumed with only pleasant enjoyment. Now and again it will happen that the cook is treacherous even to him, and then he can hit hard; but in hitting he is quiet, and strikes with a smile on his face.

Such had been Mr. Vavasor's pursuits and pleasures in life up to the time at which my story commences. But I must not allow the reader to suppose that he was a man without good qualities. Had he when young possessed the gift of industry I think that he might have shone in his profession, and have been well spoken of and esteemed in the world. As it was he was a discontented man, but nevertheless he was popular, and to some extent esteemed. He was liberal as far as his means would permit; he was a man of his word; and he understood well that code of by-laws which was presumed to constitute the character of a gentleman in his circle. He knew how to carry himself well among men, and understood thoroughly what might be said, and what might not; what might be done among those with whom he lived, and what should be left undone. By nature, too, he was kindly disposed, loving many persons a little if he loved few or none passionately. Moreover, at the age of fifty, he was a handsome man, with a fine forehead, round which the hair and beard was only beginning to show itself to be grey. He stood well, with a large person, only now beginning to become corpulent.

His eyes were bright and grey, and his mouth and chin were sharply cut, and told of gentle birth. Most men who knew John Vavasor well, declared it to be a pity that he should spend his time in signing accounts in Chancery Lane.

I have said that Alice Vavasor's big relatives cared but little for her in her early years; but I have also said that they were careful to undertake the charge of her education, and I must explain away this little discrepancy. The biggest of these big people had hardly heard of her; but there was a certain Lady Macleod, not very big herself, but, as it were, hanging on to the skirts of those who were so, who cared very much for Alice. She was the widow of a Sir Archibald Macleod, K.C.B., who had been a soldier, she herself having also been a Macleod by birth; and for very many years past—from a time previous to the birth of Alice Vavasor—she had lived at Cheltenham, making short sojourns in London during the spring, when the contents of her limited purse would admit of her doing so. Of old Lady Macleod I think I may say that she was a good woman;—that she was a good woman, though subject to two of the most serious drawbacks to goodness which can afflict a lady. She was a Calvinistic Sabbatarian in religion, and in worldly matters she was a devout believer in the high rank of her noble relatives. She could almost worship a youthful marquis, though he lived a life that would disgrace a heathen among heathens; and she could and did, in her own mind, condemn crowds of commonplace men and women to all eternal torments of which her imagination could conceive, because they listened to profane music in a park on Sunday. Yet she was a good woman. Out of her small means she gave much away. She owed no man anything. She strove to love her neighbours. She bore much pain with calm unspeaking endurance, and she lived in trust of a better world. Alice Vavasor, who was after all only her cousin, she loved with an exceeding love, and yet Alice had done very much to extinguish such love. Alice, in the years of her childhood, had been brought up by Lady Macleod; at the age of twelve she had been sent to a school at Aix-la-Chapelle,—a comitatus of her relatives having agreed that such was to be her fate, much in opposition to Lady Macleod's judgement; at nineteen she had returned to Cheltenham, and after remaining there for little more than a year, had expressed her unwillingness to remain longer with her cousin. She could sympathize neither with her relative's faults or virtues. She made an arrangement, therefore, with her father, that they two would keep house together in London, and so they had lived for the last five years;—for Alice Vavasor when she will be introduced to the reader had already passed her twenty-fourth birthday.

Their mode of life had been singular and certainly not in all respects satisfactory. Alice when she was twenty-one had the full command of her own fortune; and when she induced her father, who for the last fifteen years had lived in lodgings, to take a small house in Queen Anne Street, of course she offered to incur a portion of the expense. He had warned her that his habits were not those of a domestic man, but he had been content simply so to warn her. He had not felt it to be his duty to decline the arrangement because he knew himself to be unable to give to his child all that attention which a widowed father under such circumstances should pay to an only daughter. The house had been taken, and Alice and he had lived together, but their lives had been quite apart. For a short time, for a month or two, he had striven to dine at home and even to remain at home through the evening; but the work had been too hard for him and he had utterly broken down. He had said to her and to himself that his health would fail him under the effects of so great a change made so late in life, and I am not sure that he had not spoken truly. At any rate the effort had been abandoned, and Mr. Vavasor now never dined at home. Nor did he and his daughter ever dine out together. Their joint means did not admit of their giving dinners, and therefore they could not make their joint way in the same circle. It thus came to pass that they lived apart,—quite apart. They saw each other, probably daily; but they did little more than see each other. They did not even breakfast together, and after three o'clock in the day Mr. Vavasor was never to be found in his own house.

Miss Vavasor had made for herself a certain footing in society, though I am disposed to doubt her right to be considered as holding a place among the Upper Ten Thousand. Two classes of people she had chosen to avoid, having been driven to such avoidings by her aunt's preferences; marquises and such-like, whether wicked or otherwise, she had eschewed, and had eschewed likewise all Low Church tendencies. The eschewing of marquises is not generally very difficult. Young ladies living with their fathers on very moderate incomes in or about Queen Anne Street are not usually much troubled on that matter. Nor can I say that Miss Vavasor was so troubled. But with her there was a certain definite thing to be done towards such eschewal. Lady Macleod by no means avoided her noble relatives, nor did she at all avoid Alice Vavasor. When in London she was persevering in her visits to Queen Anne Street, though she considered herself, nobody knew why, not to be on speaking terms with Mr.. Vavasor. And she strove hard to produce an intimacy between Alice and her noble relatives—such an intimacy as that which she herself enjoyed;—an intimacy which gave her a footing in their houses but no footing in their hearts, or even in their habits. But all this Alice declined with as much consistency as she did those other struggles which her old cousin made on her behalf,—strong, never-flagging, but ever-failing efforts to induce the girl to go to such places of worship as Lady Macleod herself frequented.

A few words must be said as to Alice Vavasor's person; one fact also must be told, and then, I believe, I may start upon my story. As regards her character, I will leave it to be read in the story itself. The reader already knows that she appears upon the scene at no very early age, and the mode of her life had perhaps given to her an appearance of more years than those which she really possessed. It was not that her face was old, but that there was nothing that was girlish in her manners. Her demeanour was as staid, and her voice as self-possessed as though she had already been ten years married. In person she was tall and well made, rather large in her neck and shoulders, as were all the Vavasors, but by no means fat. Her hair was brown, but very dark, and she wore it rather lower upon her forehead than is customary at the present day. Her eyes, too, were dark, though they were not black, and her complexion, though not quite that of a brunette, was far away from being fair. Her nose was somewhat broad, and *retroussé* too, but to my thinking it was a charming nose, full of character, and giving to her face at times a look of pleasant humour, which it would otherwise have lacked. Her mouth was large, and full of character, and her chin oval, dimpled, and finely chiselled, like her father's. I beg you, in taking her for all in all, to admit that she was a fine, handsome, high-spirited young woman.

And now for my fact. At the time of which I am writing she was already engaged to be married.

CHAPTER II
LADY MACLEOD

I cannot say that the house in Queen Anne Street was a pleasant house. I am now speaking of the material house, made up of the walls and furniture, and not of any pleasantness or unpleasantness supplied by the inmates. It was a small house on the south side of the street, squeezed in between two large mansions which seemed to crush it, and by which its fair proportion of doorstep and area was in truth curtailed. The stairs were narrow; the dining-room was dark, and possessed none of those appearances of plenteous hospitality which a dining-room should have. But all this would have been as nothing if the drawing-room had been pretty as it is the bounden duty of all drawing-rooms to be. But Alice Vavasor's drawing-room was not pretty. Her father had had the care of furnishing the house, and he had intrusted the duty to a tradesman who had chosen green paper, a green carpet, green curtains, and green damask chairs. There was a green damask sofa, and two green arm-chairs opposite to each other at the two sides of the fireplace. The room was altogether green, and was not enticing. In shape it was nearly square, the very small back room on the same floor not having been, as is usual, added to it. This had been fitted up as a "study" for Mr. Vavasor, and was very rarely used for any purpose.

Most of us know when we enter a drawing-room whether it is a pretty room or no; but how few of us know how to make a drawing-room pretty! There has come up in London in these latter days a form of room so monstrously ugly that I will venture to say that no other people on earth but Londoners would put up with it. Londoners, as a rule, take their houses as they can get them, looking only to situation, size, and price. What Grecian, what Roman, what Turk, what Italian would endure, or would ever have endured, to use a room with a monstrous cantle in the form of a parallelogram cut sheerly out of one corner of it? This is the shape of room we have now adopted,—or rather which the builders have adopted for us,—in order to throw the whole first floor into one apartment which may be presumed to have noble dimensions,—with such drawback from it as the necessities of the staircase may require. A sharp unadorned corner projects itself into these would-be noble dimensions, and as ugly a form of chamber is produced as any upon which the eye can look. I would say more on the subject if I dared to do so here, but I am bound now to confine myself to Miss Vavasor's room. The monstrous deformity of which I have spoken was not known when that house in Queen Anne Street was built. There is to be found no such abomination of shape in the buildings of our ancestors,— not even in the days of George the Second. But yet the drawing-room of which I speak was ugly, and Alice knew that it was so. She knew that it was ugly, and she would greatly have liked to banish the green sofa, to have re-papered the wall, and to have hung up curtains with a dash of pink through them. With the green carpet she would have been contented. But her father was an extravagant man; and from the day on which she had come of age she had determined that it was her special duty to avoid extravagance.

"It's the ugliest room I ever saw in my life," her father once said to her.

"It is not very pretty," Alice replied.

"I'll go halves with you in the expense of redoing it," said Mr.. Vavasor.

"Wouldn't that be extravagant, papa? The things have not been here quite four years yet."

Then Mr. Vavasor had shrugged his shoulders and said nothing more about it. It was little to him whether the drawing-room in Queen Anne Street was ugly or pretty. He was on the committee of his club, and he took care that the furniture there should be in all respects comfortable.

It was now June; and that month Lady Macleod was in the habit of spending among her noble relatives in London when she had succeeded in making both ends so far overlap each other at Cheltenham as to give her the fifty pounds necessary for this purpose. For though she spent her month in London among her noble friends, it must not be supposed that her noble friends gave her bed or board. They sometimes gave her tea, such as it was, and once or twice in the month they gave the old lady a second-rate dinner. On these occasions she hired a little parlour and bedroom behind it in King Street, Saint James's, and lived a hot, uncomfortable life, going about at nights to gatherings of fashionable people of which she in her heart disapproved, seeking for smiles which seldom came to her, and which she excused herself for desiring because they were the smiles of her kith and her kin, telling herself always that she made this vain journey to the modern Babylon for the good of Alice Vavasor, and telling herself as often that she now made it for the last time. On the occasion of her preceding visit she had reminded herself that she was then seventy-five years old, and had sworn to herself that she would come to London no more; but here she was again in London, having justified the journey to herself on the plea that there were circumstances in Alice's engagement which made it desirable that she should for a while be near her niece. Her niece, as she thought, was hardly managing her own affairs discreetly.

"Well, aunt," said Alice, as the old lady walked into the drawing-room one morning at eleven o'clock. Alice always called Lady Macleod her aunt, though, as has been before explained, there was no such close connexion between them. During Lady Macleod's sojourn in London these morning visits were made almost every day. Alice never denied herself, and even made a point of remaining at home to receive them unless she had previously explained that she would be out; but I am not prepared to say that they were, of their own nature, agreeable to her.

"Would you mind shutting the window, my dear?" said Lady Macleod, seating herself stiffly on one of the small ugly green chairs. She had been educated at a time when easy-chairs were considered vicious, and among people who regarded all easy postures as being so; and she could still boast, at seventy-six, that she never leaned back. "Would you mind shutting the window? I'm so warm that I'm afraid of the draught."

"Would you mind shutting the window?"

"You don't mean to say that you've walked from King Street," said Alice, doing as she was desired.

"Indeed I do,—every step of the way. Cabs are so ruinous. It's a most unfortunate thing; they always say it's just over the two miles here. I don't believe a word of it, because I'm only a little more than the half-hour walking it; and those men will say anything. But how can I prove it, you know?"

"I really think it's too far for you to walk when it's so warm."

"But what can I do, my dear? I must come, when I've specially come up to London to see you. I shall have a cab back again, because it'll be hotter then, and dear Lady Midlothian has promised to send her carriage at three to take me to the concert. I do so wish you'd go, Alice."

"It's out of the question, aunt. The idea of my going in that way at the last moment, without any invitation!"

"It wouldn't be without an invitation, Alice. The marchioness has said to me over and over again how glad she would be to see you, if I would bring you."

"Why doesn't she come and call if she is so anxious to know me?"

"My dear, you've no right to expect it; you haven't indeed. She never calls even on me."

"I know I've no right, and I don't expect it, and I don't want it. But neither has she a right to suppose that, under such circumstances, I shall go to her house. You might as well give it up, aunt. Cart ropes wouldn't drag me there."

"I think you are very wrong,—particularly under your present circumstances. A young woman that is going to be married, as you are—"

"As I am,—perhaps."

"That's nonsense, Alice. Of course you are; and for his sake you are bound to cultivate any advantages that naturally belong to you. As to Lady Midlothian or the marchioness coming to call on you here in your father's house, after all that has passed, you really have no right to look for it."

"And I don't look for it."

"That sort of people are not expected to call. If you'll think of it, how could they do it with all the demands they have on their time?"

"My dear aunt, I wouldn't interfere with their time for worlds."

"Nobody can say of me, I'm sure, that I run after great people or rich people. It does happen that some of the nearest relations I have,—indeed I may say the nearest relations,—are people of high rank; and I do not see that I'm bound to turn away from my own flesh and blood because of that, particularly when they are always so anxious to keep up the connexion."

"I was only speaking of myself, aunt. It is very different with you. You have known them all your life."

"And how are you to know them if you won't begin? Lady Midlothian said to me only yesterday that she was glad to hear that you were going to be married so respectably, and then—"

"Upon my word I'm very much obliged to her ladyship. I wonder whether she considered that she married respectably when she took Lord Midlothian?"

Now Lady Midlothian had been unfortunate in her marriage, having united herself to a man of bad character, who had used her ill, and from whom she had now been for some years separated. Alice might have spared her allusion to this misfortune when speaking of the countess to the cousin who was so fond of her, but she was angered by the application of that odious word respectable to her own prospects; and perhaps the more angered as she was somewhat inclined to feel that the epithet did suit her own position. Her engagement, she had sometimes told herself, was very respectable, and had as often told herself that it lacked other attractions which it should have possessed. She was not quite pleased with herself in having accepted John Grey,—or rather perhaps was not satisfied with herself in having loved him. In her many thoughts on the subject, she always admitted to herself that she had accepted him simply because she loved him;—that she had given her quick assent to his quick proposal simply because he had won her heart. But she was sometimes almost angry with herself that she had permitted her heart to be thus easily taken from her, and had rebuked herself for her girlish facility. But the marriage would be at any rate respectable. Mr. Grey was a man of high character, of good though moderate means; he was, too, well educated, of good birth, a gentleman, and a man of talent. No one could deny that the marriage would be highly respectable, and her father had been more than satisfied. Why Miss Vavasor herself was not quite satisfied will, I hope, in time make itself appear. In the meanwhile it can be understood that Lady Midlothian's praise would gall her.

"Alice, don't be uncharitable," said Lady Macleod severely. "Whatever may have been Lady Midlothian's misfortunes no one can say they have resulted from her own fault."

"Yes they can, aunt, if she married a man whom she knew to be a scapegrace because he was very rich and an earl."

"She was the daughter of a nobleman herself, and only married in her own degree. But I don't want to discuss that. She meant to be good-natured when she mentioned your marriage, and you should take it as it was meant. After all she was only your mother's second cousin—"

"Dear aunt, I make no claim on her cousinship."

"But she admits the claim, and is quite anxious that you should know her. She has been at the trouble to find out everything about Mr.. Grey, and told me that nothing could be more satisfactory."

"Upon my word I am very much obliged to her."

Lady Macleod was a woman of much patience, and possessed also of considerable perseverance. For another half-hour she went on expatiating on the advantages which would accrue to Alice as a married woman from an acquaintance with her noble relatives, and endeavouring to persuade her that no better opportunity than the present would present itself. There would be a place in Lady Midlothian's carriage, as none other of the daughters were going but Lady Jane. Lady Midlothian would take it quite as a compliment, and a concert was not like a ball or any customary party. An unmarried girl might very properly go to a concert under such circumstances as now existed without any special invitation. Lady Macleod ought to have known her adopted niece better. Alice was immoveable. As a matter of course she was immoveable. Lady Macleod had seldom been able to persuade her to anything, and ought to have been well sure that, of all things, she could not have persuaded her to this.

Then, at last, they came to another subject, as to which Lady Macleod declared that she had specially come on this special morning, forgetting, probably, that she had already made the same assertion with reference to the concert. But in truth the last assertion was the correct one, and on that other subject she had been hurried on to say more than she meant by the eagerness of the moment. All the morning she had been full of the matter on which she was now about to speak. She had discussed it quite at length with Lady Midlothian;—though she was by no means prepared to tell Alice Vavasor that any such discussion had taken place. From the concert, and the effect which Lady Midlothian's countenance might have upon Mr.. Grey's future welfare, she got herself by degrees round to a projected Swiss tour which Alice was about to make. Of this Swiss tour she had heard before, but had not heard who were to be Miss Vavasor's companions until Lady Midlothian had told her. How it had come to pass that Lady Midlothian had interested herself so much in the concerns of a person whom she did not know, and on whom she in her greatness could not be expected to call, I cannot say; but from some quarter she had learned who were the proposed companions of Alice Vavasor's tour, and she had told Lady Macleod that she did not at all approve of the arrangement.

"And when do you go, Alice?" said Lady Macleod.

"Early in July, I believe. It will be very hot, but Kate must be back by the middle of August." Kate Vavasor was Alice's first cousin.

"Oh! Kate is to go with you?"

"Of course she is. I could not go alone, or with no one but George. Indeed it was Kate who made up the party."

"Of course you could not go alone with George," said Lady Macleod, very grimly. Now George Vavasor was Kate's brother, and was therefore also first cousin to Alice. He was heir to the old squire down in Westmoreland, with whom Kate lived, their father being dead. Nothing, it would seem, could be more rational than that Alice should go to Switzerland with her cousins; but Lady Macleod was clearly not of this opinion; she looked very grim as she made this allusion to cousin George, and seemed to be preparing herself for a fight.

"That is exactly what I say," answered Alice. "But, indeed, he is simply going as an escort to me and Kate, as we don't like the rôle of unprotected females. It is very good-natured of him, seeing how much his time is taken up."

"I thought he never did anything."

"That's because you don't know him, aunt."

"No; certainly I don't know him." She did not add that she had no wish to know Mr. George Vavasor, but she looked it. "And has your father been told that he is going?"

"Of course he has."

"And does—" Lady Macleod hesitated a little before she went on, and then finished her question with a little spasmodic assumption of courage. "And does Mr. Grey know that he is going?"

Alice remained silent for a full minute before she answered this question, during which Lady Macleod sat watching her grimly, with her eyes very intent upon her niece's face. If she supposed such silence to have been in any degree produced by shame in answering the question, she was much mistaken. But it may be doubted whether she understood the character of the girl whom she thought she knew so well, and it is probable that she did make such mistake.

"I might tell you simply that he does," said Alice at last, "seeing that I wrote to him yesterday, letting him know that such were our arrangements; but I feel that I should not thus answer the question you mean to ask. You want to know whether Mr. Grey will approve of it. As I only wrote yesterday of course I have not heard, and therefore cannot say. But I can say this, aunt, that much as I might regret his disapproval, it would make no change in my plans."

"Would it not? Then I must tell you, you are very wrong. It ought to make a change. What! the disapproval of the man you are going to marry make no change in your plans?"

"Not in that matter. Come, aunt, if we must discuss this matter let us do it at any rate fairly. In an ordinary way, if Mr. Grey had asked me to give up for any reason my trip altogether, I should have given it up certainly, as I would give up any other indifferent project at the request of so dear a friend,—a friend with whom I am so—so—so closely connected. But if he asked me not to travel with my cousin George, I should refuse him absolutely, without a word of parley on the subject, simply because of the nature and closeness of my connection with him. I suppose you understand what I mean, aunt?"

"I suppose I do. You mean that you would refuse to obey him on the very subject on which he has a right to claim your obedience."

"He has no right to claim my obedience on any subject," said Alice; and as she spoke Aunt Macleod jumped up with a little start at the vehemence of the words, and of the tone in which they were expressed. She had heard that tone before, and might have been used to it; but, nevertheless, the little jump was involuntary. "At present he has no right to my obedience on any subject, but least of all on that," said Alice. "His advice he may give me, but I am quite sure he will not ask for obedience."

"And if he advises you you will slight his advice."

"If he tells me that I had better not travel with my cousin George I shall certainly not take his advice. Moreover, I should be careful to let him know how much I was offended by any such counsel from him. It would show a littleness on his part, and a suspicion of which I cannot suppose him to be capable." Alice, as she said this, got up from her seat and walked about the room. When she had finished she stood at one of the windows with her back to her visitor. There was silence between them for a minute or two, during which Lady Macleod was deeply considering how best she might speak the terrible words, which, as Alice's nearest female relative, she felt herself bound to utter. At last she collected her thoughts and her courage, and spoke out.

"My dear Alice, I need hardly say that if you had a mother living, or any person with you filling the place of a mother, I should not interfere in this matter."

"Of course, Aunt Macleod, if you think I am wrong you have quite a right to say so."

"I do think you are wrong,—very wrong, indeed; and if you persist in this I am afraid I must say that I shall think you wicked. Of course Mr. Grey cannot like you to travel with George Vavasor."

"And why not, aunt?" Alice, as she asked this question, turned round and confronted Lady Macleod boldly. She spoke with a steady voice, and fixed her eyes upon the old lady's face, as though determined to show that she had no fear of what might be said to her.

"Why not, Alice? Surely you do not wish me to say why not."

"But I do wish you to say why not. How can I defend myself till the accusation is made?"

"You are now engaged to marry Mr. Grey, with the consent and approbation of all your friends. Two years ago you had—had—"

"Had what, aunt? If you mean to say that two years ago I was engaged to my cousin George you are mistaken. Three years ago I told him that under certain conditions I would become engaged to him. But my conditions did not suit him, nor his me, and no engagement was ever made. Mr. Grey knows the history of the whole thing. As far as it was possible I have told him everything that took place."

"The fact was, Alice, that George Vavasor's mode of life was such that an engagement with him would have been absolute madness."

"Dear aunt, you must excuse me if I say that I cannot discuss George Vavasor's mode of life. If I were thinking of becoming his wife you would have a perfect right to discuss it, because of your constant kindness to me.

But as matters are he is simply a cousin; and as I like him and you do not, we had better say nothing about him."

"I must say this—that after what has passed, and at the present crisis of your life—"

"Dear aunt, I'm not in any crisis."

"Yes you are, Alice; in the most special crisis of a girl's life. You are still a girl, but you are the promised wife of a very worthy man, who will look to you for all his domestic happiness. George Vavasor has the name, at least, of being very wild."

"The worthy man and the wild man must fight it out between them. If I were going away with George by himself, there might be something in what you say."

"That would be monstrous."

"Monstrous or not, it isn't what I'm about to do. Kate and I have put our purses together, and are going to have an outing for our special fun and gratification. As we should be poor travellers alone, George has promised to go with his sister. Papa knows all about it, and never thought of making any objection."

Lady Macleod shook her head. She did not like to say anything against Mr. Vavasor before his daughter; but the shaking of her head was intended to signify that Mr. Vavasor's assent in such a matter was worth nothing.

"I can only say again," said Lady Macleod, "that I think Mr. Grey will be displeased,—and that he will have very great cause for displeasure. And I think, moreover, that his approbation ought to be your chief study. I believe, my dear, I'll ask you to let Jane get me a cab. I shan't have a bit too much time to dress for the concert."

Alice simply rang the bell, and said no further word on the subject which they had been discussing. When Lady Macleod got up to go away, Alice kissed her, as was customary with them, and the old lady as she went uttered her customary valediction. "God bless you, my dear. Good-bye! I'll come to-morrow if I can." There was therefore no quarrel between them. But both of them felt that words had been spoken which must probably lead to some diminution of their past intimacy.

When Lady Macleod had gone Alice sat alone for an hour thinking of what had passed between them,—thinking rather of those two men, the worthy man and the wild man, whose names had been mentioned in close connection with herself. John Grey was a worthy man, a man worthy at all points, as far as she knew him. She told herself it was so. And she told herself, also, that her cousin George was wild,—very wild. And yet her thoughts were, I fear, on the whole more kindly towards her cousin than towards her lover. She had declared to her aunt that John Grey would be incapable of such suspicion as would be shown by any objection on his part to the arrangements made for the tour. She had said so, and had so believed; and yet she continued to brood over the position which her affairs would take, if he did make the objection which Lady Macleod anticipated. She told herself over and over again, that under such circumstances she would not give way an inch. "He is free to go," she said to herself. "If he does not trust me he is quite free to go." It may almost be said that she came at last to anticipate from her lover that very answer to her own letter which she had declared him to be incapable of making.

CHAPTER III
JOHN GREY, THE WORTHY MAN

Mr. Grey's answer to Alice Vavasor's letter, which was duly sent by return of post and duly received on the morning after Lady Macleod's visit, may perhaps be taken as giving a sample of his worthiness. It was dated from Nethercoats, a small country-house in Cambridgeshire which belonged to him, at which he already spent much of his time, and at which he intended to live altogether after his marriage.

Nethercoats, June, 186—.

Dearest Alice,

I am glad you have settled your affairs,—foreign affairs, I mean,—so much to your mind. As to your home affairs they are not, to my thinking, quite so satisfactorily arranged. But as I am a party interested in the latter my opinion may perhaps have an undue bias. Touching the tour, I quite agree with you that you and Kate would have been uncomfortable alone. It's a very fine theory, that of women being able to get along without men as well as with them; but, like other fine theories, it will be found very troublesome by those who first put it in practice. Gloved hands, petticoats, feminine softness, and the general homage paid to beauty, all stand in the way of success. These things may perhaps some day be got rid of, and possibly with advantage; but while young ladies are still encumbered with them a male companion will always be found to be a comfort. I don't quite know whether your cousin George is the best possible knight you might have chosen. I should consider myself to be infinitely preferable, had my going been upon the cards. Were you in danger of meeting Paynim foes, he, no doubt, would kill them off much quicker than I could do, and would be much more serviceable in liberating you from the dungeons of oppressors, or even from stray tigers in the Swiss forests. But I doubt his being punctual with the luggage. He will

want you or Kate to keep the accounts, if any are kept. He
will be slow in getting you glasses of water at the railway
stations, and will always keep you waiting at breakfast.
I hold that a man with two ladies on a tour should be
an absolute slave to them, or they will not fully enjoy
themselves. He should simply be an upper servant, with
the privilege of sitting at the same table with his mistresses.
I have my doubts as to whether your cousin is fit for the
place; but, as to myself, it is just the thing that I was made
for. Luckily, however, neither you nor Kate are without
wills of your own, and perhaps you may be able to reduce
Mr. Vavasor to obedience.

As to the home affairs I have very little to say here,—in
this letter. I shall of course run up and see you before you
start, and shall probably stay a week in town. I know I
ought not to do so, as it will be a week of idleness, and yet
not a week of happiness. I'd sooner have an hour with you
in the country than a whole day in London. And I always
feel in town that I've too much to do to allow of my doing
anything. If it were sheer idleness I could enjoy it, but it is
a feverish idleness, in which one is driven here and there,
expecting some gratification which not only never comes,
but which never even begins to come. I will, however,
undergo a week of it,—say the last seven days of this
month, and shall trust to you to recompense me by as much
of yourself as your town doings will permit.

And now again as to those home affairs. If I say nothing
now I believe you will understand why I refrain. You have
cunningly just left me to imply, from what you say, that
all my arguments have been of no avail; but you do not
answer them, or even tell me that you have decided. I shall
therefore imply nothing, and still trust to my personal
eloquence for success. Or rather not trust,—not trust, but
hope.

The garden is going on very well. We are rather short of
water, and therefore not quite as bright as I had hoped;
but we are preparing with untiring industry for future
brightness. Your commands have been obeyed in all things,
and Morrison always says "The mistress didn't mean this,"
or "The mistress did intend that." God bless the mistress is
what I now say, and send her home, to her own home, to
her flowers, and her fruit, and her house, and her husband,
as soon as may be, with no more of these delays which

are to me so grievous, and which seem to me to be so unnecessary. That is my prayer.

Yours ever and always,

J. G.

"I didn't give commands," Alice said to herself, as she sat with the letter at her solitary breakfast-table. "He asked me how I liked the things, and of course I was obliged to say. I was obliged to seem to care, even if I didn't care." Such were her first thoughts as she put the letter back into its envelope, after reading it the second time. When she opened it, which she did quickly, not pausing a moment lest she should suspect herself of fearing to see what might be its contents, her mind was full of that rebuke which her aunt had anticipated, and which she had almost taught herself to expect. She had torn the letter open rapidly, and had dashed at its contents with quick eyes. In half a moment she had seen what was the nature of the reply respecting the proposed companion of her tour, and then she had completed her reading slowly enough. "No; I gave no commands," she repeated to herself, as though she might thereby absolve herself from blame in reference to some possible future accusations, which might perhaps be brought against her under certain circumstances which she was contemplating.

Then she considered the letter bit by bit, taking it backwards, and sipping her tea every now and then amidst her thoughts. No; she had no home, no house, there. She had no husband;—not as yet. He spoke of their engagement as though it were a betrothal, as betrothals used to be of yore; as though they were already in some sort married. Such betrothals were not made now-a-days. There still remained, both to him and to her, a certain liberty of extricating themselves from this engagement. Should he come to her and say that he found that their contemplated marriage would not make him happy, would not she release him without a word of reproach? Would not she regard him as much more honourable in doing so than in adhering to a marriage which was distasteful to him? And if she would so judge him,—judge him and certainly acquit him, was it not reasonable that she under similar circumstances should expect a similar acquittal? Then she declared to herself that she carried on this argument within her own breast simply as an argument, induced to do so by that assertion on his part that he was already her husband,—that his house was even now her home. She had no intention of using that power which was still hers. She had no wish to go back from her pledged word. She thought that she had no such wish. She loved him much, and admired him even more than she loved him. He was noble, generous, clever, good,—so good as to be almost perfect; nay, for aught she knew he was perfect. Would that he had some faults! Would that he had! Would that he had! How could she, full of faults as she knew herself to be,—how could she hope to make happy a man perfect as he was! But then there would be no doubt as to her present duty. She loved him, and that was everything. Having told him that she loved him, and having on that score accepted his love, nothing but a change in her heart towards him could justify her in seeking to break the bond which bound them together. She did love him, and she loved him only.

But she had once loved her cousin. Yes, truly it was so. In her thoughts she did not now deny it. She had loved him, and was tormented by a feeling that she had had a more full delight in that love than in this other that had sprung up subsequently. She had told herself that this had come of her youth;—that love at twenty was sweeter than it could be afterwards. There had been a something of rapture in that earlier dream which could never be repeated,—which could never live, indeed, except in a dream. Now, now that she was older and perhaps wiser, love meant a partnership, in which each partner would be honest to the other, in which each would wish and strive for the other's welfare, so that thus their joint welfare might be insured. Then, in those early girlish days, it had meant a total abnegation of self. The one was of earth, and therefore possible. The other had been a ray from heaven,—and impossible, except in a dream.

And she had been mistaken in her first love. She admitted that frankly. He whom she had worshipped had been an idol of clay, and she knew that it was well for her to have abandoned that idolatry. He had not only been untrue to her, but, worse than that, had been false in excusing his untruth. He had not only promised falsely, but had made such promises with a deliberate, premeditated falsehood. And he had been selfish, coldly selfish, weighing the value of his own low lusts against that of her holy love. She had known this, and had parted from him with an oath to herself that no promised contrition on his part should ever bring them again together. But she had pardoned him as a man, though never as a lover, and had bade him welcome again as a cousin and as her friend's brother. She had again become very anxious as to his career, not hiding her regard, but professing that anxiety aloud. She knew him to be clever, ambitious, bold,—and she believed even yet, in spite of her own experience, that he might not be bad at heart. Now, as she told herself that in truth she loved the man to whom her troth was plighted, I fear that she almost thought more of that other man from whom she had torn herself asunder.

"Why should he find himself unhappy in London?" she said, as she went back to the letter. "Why should he pretend to condemn the very place which most men find the fittest for all their energies? Were I a man, no earthly consideration should induce me to live elsewhere. It is odd how we differ in all things. However brilliant might be his own light, he would be contented to hide it under a bushel!"

And at last she recurred to that matter as to which she had been so anxious when she first opened her lover's letter. It will be remembered how assured she had expressed herself that Mr. Grey would not condescend to object to her travelling with her cousin. He had not so condescended. He had written on the matter with a pleasant joke, like a gentleman as he was, disdaining to allude to the past passages in the life of her whom he loved, abstaining even from expressing anything that might be taken as a permission on his part. There had been in Alice's words, as she told him of their proposed plan, a something that had betrayed a tremor in her thoughts. She had studiously striven so to frame her phrases that her tale might be told as any other simple statement,—as though there had been no trembling in her mind as she wrote. But she had failed, and she knew that she had failed. She had failed; and he had read all her effort and all her failure. She was quite conscious of this; she felt it thoroughly; and she knew that he was noble and a gentleman to the last drop of his blood. And yet—yet—yet there was almost a feeling of disappointment in that he had not written such a letter as Lady Macleod had anticipated.

During the next week Lady Macleod still came almost daily to Queen Anne Street, but nothing further was said between her and Miss Vavasor as to the Swiss tour; nor were any questions asked about Mr.. Grey's opinion on the subject. The old lady of course discovered that there was no quarrel, or, as she believed, any probability of a quarrel; and with that she was obliged to be contented. Nor did she again on this occasion attempt to take Alice to Lady Midlothian's. Indeed, their usual subjects of conversation were almost abandoned, and Lady Macleod's visits, though they were as constant as heretofore, were not so long. She did not dare to talk about Mr. Grey, and because she did not so dare, was determined to regard herself as in a degree ill-used. So she was silent, reserved, and fretful. At length came the last day of her London season, and her last visit to her niece. "I would come because it's my last day," said Lady Macleod; "but really I'm so hurried, and have so many things to do, that I hardly know how to manage it."

"It's very kind," said Alice, giving her aunt an affectionate squeeze of the hand.

"I'm keeping the cab, so I can just stay twenty-five minutes. I've marked the time accurately, but I know the man will swear it's over the half-hour."

"You'll have no more trouble about cabs, aunt, when you are back in Cheltenham."

"The flies are worse, my dear. I really think they're worse. I pay the bill every month, but they've always one down that I didn't have. It's the regular practice, for I've had them from all the men in the place."

"It's hard enough to find honest men anywhere, I suppose."

"Or honest women either. What do you think of Mrs. Green wanting to charge me for an extra week, because she says I didn't give her notice till Tuesday morning? I won't pay her, and she may stop my things if she dares. However, it's the last time. I shall never come up to London again, my dear."

"Oh, aunt, don't say that!"

"But I do say it, my dear. What should an old woman like me do, trailing up to town every year, merely because it's what people choose to call the season."

"To see your friends, of course. Age doesn't matter when a person's health is so good as yours."

"If you knew what I suffer from lumbago,—though I must say coming to London always does cure that for the time. But as for friends—! Well, I suppose one has no right to complain when one gets to be as old as I am; but I declare I believe that those I love best would sooner be without me than with me."

"Do you mean me, aunt?"

"No, my dear, I don't mean you. Of course my life would have been very different if you could have consented to remain with me till you were married. But I didn't mean you. I don't know that I meant any one. You shouldn't mind what an old woman like me says."

"You're a little melancholy because you're going away."

"No, indeed. I don't know why I stayed the last week. I did say to Lady Midlothian that I thought I should go on the 20th; and, though I know that she knew that I really didn't go, she has not once sent to me since. To be sure they've been out every night; but I thought she might have asked me to come and lunch. It's so very lonely dining by myself in lodgings in London."

"And yet you never will come and dine with me."

"No, my dear; no. But we won't talk about that. I've just one word more to say. Let me see. I've just six minutes to stay. I've made up my mind that I'll never come up to town again,—except for one thing."

"And what's that, aunt?" Alice, as she asked the question, well knew what that one thing was.

"I'll come for your marriage, my dear. I do hope you will not keep me long waiting."

"Ah! I can't make any promise. There's no knowing when that may be."

"And why should there be no knowing? I always think that when a girl is once engaged the sooner she's married the better. There may be reasons for delay on the gentleman's part."

"There very often are, you know,"

"But, Alice, you don't mean to say that Mr. Grey is putting it off?"

Alice was silent for a moment, during which Lady Macleod's face assumed a look of almost tragic horror. Was there something wrong on Mr. Grey's side of which she was altogether unaware? Alice, though for a second or two she had been guilty of a slight playful deceit, was too honest to allow the impression to remain. "No, aunt," she said; "Mr. Grey is not putting it off. It has been left to me to fix the time."

"And why don't you fix it?"

"It is such a serious thing! After all it is not more than four months yet since I—I accepted him. I don't know that there has been any delay."

"But you might fix the time now, if he wishes it."

"Well, perhaps I shall,—some day, aunt. I'm going to think about it, and you mustn't drive me."

"But you should have some one to advise you, Alice."

"Ah! that's just it. People always do seem to think it so terrible that a girl should have her own way in anything. She mustn't like any one at first; and then, when she does like some one, she must marry him directly she's bidden. I haven't much of my own way at present; but you see, when I'm married I shan't have it at all. You can't wonder that I shouldn't be in a hurry."

"I am not advocating anything like hurry, my dear. But, goodness gracious me! I've been here twenty-eight minutes, and that horrid man will impose upon me. Good-bye; God bless you! Mind you write." And Lady Macleod hurried out of the room more intent at the present moment upon saving her sixpence than she was on any other matter whatsoever.

And then John Grey came up to town, arriving a day or two after the time that he had fixed. It is not, perhaps, improbable that Alice had used some diplomatic skill in preventing a meeting between Lady Macleod and her lover. They both were very anxious to obtain the same object, and Alice was to some extent opposed to their views. Had Lady Macleod and John

Grey put their forces together she might have found herself unable to resist their joint endeavours. She was resolved that she would not at any rate name any day for her marriage before her return from Switzerland; and she may therefore have thought it wise to keep Mr. Grey in the country till after Lady Macleod had gone, even though she thereby cut down the time of his sojourn in London to four days. On the occasion of that visit Mr. Vavasor did a very memorable thing. He dined at home with the view of welcoming his future son-in-law. He dined at home, and asked, or rather assented to Alice's asking, George and Kate Vavasor to join the dinner-party. "What an auspicious omen for the future nuptials!" said Kate, with her little sarcastic smile. "Uncle John dines at home, and Mr. Grey joins in the dissipation of a dinner-party. We shall all be changed soon, I suppose, and George and I will take to keeping a little cottage in the country."

"Kate," said Alice, angrily, "I think you are about the most unjust person I ever met. I would forgive your raillery, however painful it might be, if it were only fair."

"And to whom is it unfair on the present occasion;—to your father?"

"It was not intended for him."

"To yourself?"

"I care nothing as to myself; you know that very well."

"Then it must have been unfair to Mr. Grey."

"Yes; it was Mr. Grey whom you meant to attack. If I can forgive him for not caring for society, surely you might do so."

"Exactly; but that's just what you can't do, my dear. You don't forgive him. If you did you might be quite sure that I should say nothing. And if you choose to bid me hold my tongue I will say nothing. But when you tell me all your own thoughts about this thing you can hardly expect but that I should let you know mine in return. I'm not particular; and if you are ready for a little good, wholesome, useful hypocrisy, I won't balk you. I mayn't be quite so dishonest as you call me, but I'm not so wedded to truth but what I can look, and act, and speak a few falsehoods if you wish it. Only let us understand each other."

"You know I wish for no falsehood, Kate."

"I know it's very hard to understand what you do wish. I know that for the last year or two I have been trying to find out your wishes, and, upon my word, my success has been very indifferent. I suppose you wish to marry Mr. Grey, but I'm by no means certain. I suppose the last thing on earth you'd wish would be to marry George?"

"The very last. You're right there at any rate."

"Alice—! sometimes you drive me too hard; you do, indeed. You make me doubt whether I hate or love you most. Knowing what my feelings are about George, I cannot understand how you can bring yourself to speak of him to me with such contempt!" Kate Vavasor, as she spoke these words, left the room with a quick step, and hurried up to her own chamber. There Alice found her in tears, and was driven by her friend's real grief into the expression of an apology, which she knew was not properly due from her. Kate was acquainted with all the circumstances of that old affair between her brother and Alice. She had given in her adhesion to the propriety of what Alice had done. She had allowed that her brother George's behaviour had been such as to make any engagement between them impossible. The fault, therefore, had been hers in making any reference to the question of such a marriage. Nor had it been by any means her first fault of the same kind. Till Alice had become engaged to Mr. Grey she had spoken of George only as her brother, or as her friend's cousin, but now she was constantly making allusion to those past occurrences, which all of them should have striven to forget. Under these circumstances was not Lady Macleod right in saying that George Vavasor should not have been accepted as a companion for the Swiss tour?

"Sometimes you drive me too hard."

The little dinner-party went off very quietly; and if no other ground existed for charging Mr. Grey with London dissipation than what that afforded, he was accused most unjustly. The two young men had never before met each other; and Vavasor had gone to his uncle's house, prepared not only to dislike but to despise his successor in Alice's favour. But in this he was either disappointed or gratified, as the case may be. "He has plenty to say for himself," he said to Kate on his way home.

"Oh yes; he can talk."

"And he doesn't talk like a prig either, which was what I expected. He's uncommonly handsome."

"I thought men never saw that in each other. I never see it in any man."

"I see it in every animal—in men, women, horses, dogs, and even pigs. I like to look on handsome things. I think people always do who are ugly themselves."

"And so you're going into raptures in favour of John Grey."

"No, I'm not. I very seldom go into raptures about anything. But he talks in the way I like a man to talk. How he bowled my uncle over about those actors; and yet if my uncle knows anything about anything it is about the stage twenty years ago." There was nothing more said then about John Grey; but Kate understood her brother well enough to be aware that this praise meant very little. George Vavasor spoke sometimes from his heart, and did so more frequently to his sister than to any one else; but his words came generally from his head.

On the day after the little dinner in Queen Anne Street, John Grey came to say good-bye to his betrothed;—for his betrothed she certainly was, in spite of those very poor arguments which she had used in trying to convince herself that she was still free if she wished to claim her freedom. Though he had been constantly with Alice during the last three days, he had not hitherto said anything as to the day of their marriage. He had been constantly with her alone, sitting for hours in that ugly green drawing-room, but he had never touched the subject. He had told her much of Switzerland, which she had never yet seen but which he knew well. He had told her much of his garden and house, whither she had once gone with her father, whilst paying a visit nominally to the colleges at Cambridge. And he had talked of various matters, matters bearing in no immediate way upon his own or her affairs; for Mr. Grey was a man who knew well how to make words pleasant; but previous to this last moment he had said nothing on that subject on which he was so intent.

"Well, Alice," he said, when the last hour had come, "and about that question of home affairs?"

"Let us finish off the foreign affairs first."

"We have finished them; haven't we?"

"Finished them! why we haven't started yet."

"No; you haven't started. But we've had the discussion. Is there any reason why you'd rather not have this thing settled."

"No; no special reason."

"Then why not let it be fixed? Do you fear coming to me as my wife?"

"No."

"I cannot think that you repent your goodness to me."

"No; I don't repent it;—what you call my goodness? I love you too entirely for that."

"My darling!" And now he passed his arm round her waist as they stood near the empty fireplace. "And if you love me—"

"I do love you."

"Then why should you not wish to come to me?"

"I do wish it. I think I wish it."

"But, Alice, you must have wished it altogether when you consented to be my wife."

"A person may wish for a thing altogether, and yet not wish for it instantly."

"Instantly! Come; I have not been hard on you. This is still June. Will you say the middle of September, and we shall still be in time for warm pleasant days among the lakes? Is that asking for too much?"

"It is not asking for anything."

"Nay, but it is, love. Grant it, and I will swear that you have granted me everything."

She was silent, having things to say but not knowing in what words to put them. Now that he was with her she could not say the things which she had told herself that she would utter to him. She could not bring herself to hint to him that his views of life were so unlike her own, that there could be no chance of happiness between them, unless each could strive to lean somewhat towards the other. No man could be more gracious in word and manner than John Grey; no man more chivalrous in his carriage towards a woman; but he always spoke and acted as though there could be no question that his manner of life was to be adopted, without a word or thought of doubting, by his wife. When two came together, why should not each yield something, and each claim something? This she had meant to say to him on this day; but now that he was with her she could not say it.

"John," she said at last, "do not press me about this till I return."

"But then you will say the time is short. It would be short then."

"I cannot answer you now;—indeed, I cannot. That is I cannot answer in the affirmative. It is such a solemn thing."

"Will it ever be less solemn, dearest?"

"Never, I hope never."

He did not press her further then, but kissed her and bade her farewell.

CHAPTER IV
GEORGE VAVASOR, THE WILD MAN

It will no doubt be understood that George Vavasor did not roam about in the woods unshorn, or wear leathern trappings and sandals, like Robinson Crusoe, instead of coats and trousers. His wildness was of another kind. Indeed, I don't know that he was in truth at all wild, though Lady Macleod had called him so, and Alice had assented to her use of the word.

George Vavasor had lived in London since he was twenty, and now, at the time of the beginning of my story, he was a year or two over thirty. He was and ever had been the heir to his grandfather's estate; but that estate was small, and when George first came to London his father was a strong man of forty, with as much promise of life in him as his son had. A profession had therefore been absolutely necessary to him; and he had, at his uncle John's instance, been placed in the office of a parliamentary land agent. With this parliamentary land agent he had quarrelled to the knife, but not before he had by his talents made himself so useful that he had before him the prospects of a lucrative partnership in the business. George Vavasor had many faults, but idleness—absolute idleness—was not one of them. He would occasionally postpone his work to pleasure. He would be at Newmarket when he should have been at Whitehall. But it was not usual with him to be in bed when he should be at his desk, and when he was at his desk he did not whittle his ruler, or pick his teeth, or clip his nails. Upon the whole his friends were pleased with the first five years of his life in London—in spite of his having been found to be in debt on more than one occasion. But his debts had been paid; and all was going on swimmingly, when one day he knocked down the parliamentary agent with a blow between the eyes, and then there was an end of that. He himself was wont to say that he had known very well what he was about, that it had behoved him to knock down the man who was to have been his partner, and that he regretted nothing in the matter. At any rate the deed was looked upon with approving eyes by many men of good standing,—or, at any rate, sufficient standing to help George to another position; and within six weeks of the time of his leaving the office at Whitehall, he had become a partner in an established firm of wine merchants. A great-aunt had just then left him a couple of thousand pounds, which no doubt assisted him in his views with the wine merchants.

In this employment he remained for another period of five years, and was supposed by all his friends to be doing very well. And indeed he did not do badly, only that he did not do well enough to satisfy himself. He was ambitious of making the house to which he belonged the first house in the trade in London, and scared his partners by the boldness and extent of his views. He himself declared that if they would only have gone along with him he would have made them princes in the wine market. But they were men either of more prudence or of less audacity than he, and they declined to walk in his courses. At the end of the five years Vavasor left the house, not having knocked any one down on this occasion, and taking with him a very nice sum of money.

The two last of these five years had certainly been the best period of his life, for he had really worked very hard, like a man, giving up all pleasure that took time from him,—and giving up also most pleasures which were dangerous on account of their costliness. He went to no races, played no billiards, and spoke of Cremorne as a childish thing, which he had abandoned now that he was no longer a child. It was during these two years that he had had his love passages with his cousin; and it must be presumed that he had, at any rate, intended at one time to settle himself respectably as a married man. He had, however, behaved very badly to Alice, and the match had been broken off.

He had also during the last two years quarrelled with his grandfather. He had wished to raise a sum of money on the Vavasor estate, which, as it was unentailed, he could only do with his grandfather's concurrence. The old gentleman would not hear of it,—would listen with no patience to the proposition. It was in vain that George attempted to make the squire understand that the wine business was going on very well, that he himself owed no man anything, that everything with him was flourishing;—but that his trade might be extended indefinitely by the use of a few thousand pounds at moderate interest. Old Mr. Vavasor was furious. No documents and no assurances could make him lay aside a belief that the wine merchants, and the business, and his grandson were all ruined and ruinous together. No one but a ruined man would attempt to raise money on the family estate! So they had quarrelled, and had never spoken or seen each other since. "He shall have the estate for his life," the squire said to his son John. "I don't think I have a right to leave it away from him. It never has been left away from the heir. But I'll tie it up so that he shan't cut a tree on it." John Vavasor perhaps thought that the old rule of primogeniture might under such circumstances have been judiciously abandoned—in this one instance, in his own favour.

But he did not say so. Nor would he have said it had there been a chance of his doing so with success. He was a man from whom no very noble deed could be expected; but he was also one who would do no ignoble deed.

After that George Vavasor had become a stockbroker, and a stockbroker he was now. In the first twelve months after his leaving the wine business,— the same being the first year after his breach with Alice,—he had gone back greatly in the estimation of men. He had lived in open defiance of decency. He had spent much money and had apparently made none, and had been, as all his friends declared, on the high road to ruin. Aunt Macleod had taken her judgement from this period of his life when she had spoken of him as a man who never did anything. But he had come forth again suddenly as a working man; and now they who professed to know, declared that he was by no means poor. He was in the City every day; and during the last two years had earned the character of a shrewd fellow who knew what he was about, who might not perhaps be very mealy-mouthed in affairs of business, but who was fairly and decently honourable in his money transactions. In fact, he stood well on 'Change.

And during these two years he had stood a contest for a seat in Parliament, having striven to represent the metropolitan borough of Chelsea, on the extremely Radical interest. It is true that he had failed, and that he had spent a considerable sum of money in the contest. "Where on earth does your nephew get his money?" men said to John Vavasor at his club. "Upon my word I don't know," said Vavasor. "He doesn't get it from me, and I'm sure he doesn't get it from my father." But George Vavasor, though he failed at Chelsea, did not spend his money altogether fruitlessly. He gained reputation by the struggle, and men came to speak of him as though he were one who would do something. He was a stockbroker, a thorough-going Radical, and yet he was the heir to a fine estate, which had come down from father to son for four hundred years! There was something captivating about his history and adventures, especially as just at the time of the election he became engaged to an heiress, who died a month before the marriage should have taken place. She died without a will, and her money all went to some third cousins.

George Vavasor bore this last disappointment like a man, and it was at this time that he again became fully reconciled to his cousin. Previous to this they had met; and Alice, at her cousin Kate's instigation, had induced her father to meet him. But at first there had been no renewal of real friendship. Alice had given her cordial assent to her cousin's marriage with the heiress, Miss Grant, telling Kate that such an engagement was the very thing to put him thoroughly on his feet. And then she had been much pleased by his spirit at that Chelsea election. "It was grand of him, wasn't it?" said Kate, her eyes brimming full of tears. "It was very spirited," said Alice. "If you knew all, you would say so. They could get no one else to stand but that Mr. Travers, and he wouldn't come forward, unless they would guarantee all his expenses." "I hope it didn't cost George much," said Alice. "It did, though; nearly all he had got. But what matters? Money's nothing to him, except for its uses. My own little mite is my own now, and he shall have every farthing of it for the next election, even though I should go out as a housemaid the next day." There must have been something great about George Vavasor, or he would not have been so idolized by such a girl as his sister Kate.

Early in the present spring, before the arrangements for the Swiss journey were made, George Vavasor had spoken to Alice about that intended marriage which had been broken off by the lady's death. He was sitting one evening with his cousin in the drawing-room in Queen Anne Street, waiting for Kate, who was to join him there before going to some party. I wonder whether Kate had had a hint from her brother to be late! At any rate, the two were together for an hour, and the talk had been all about himself. He had congratulated her on her engagement with Mr. Grey, which had just become known to him, and had then spoken of his own last intended marriage.

"I grieved for her," he said, "greatly."

"I'm sure you did, George."

"Yes, I did;—for her, herself. Of course the world has given me credit for lamenting the loss of her money. But the truth is, that as regards both herself and her money, it is much better for me that we were never married."

"Do you mean even though she should have lived?"

"Yes;—even had she lived."

"And why so? If you liked her, her money was surely no drawback."

"No; not if I had liked her."

"And did you not like her?"

"No."

"Oh, George!"

"I did not love her as a man should love his wife, if you mean that. As for my liking her, I did like her. I liked her very much."

"But you would have loved her?"

"I don't know. I don't find that task of loving so very easy. It might have been that I should have learned to hate her."

"If so, it is better for you, and better for her, that she has gone."

"It is better. I am sure of it. And yet I grieve for her, and in thinking of her I almost feel as though I were guilty of her death."

"But she never suspected that you did not love her?"

"Oh no. But she was not given to think much of such things. She took all that for granted. Poor girl! she is at rest now, and her money has gone, where it should go, among her own relatives."

"Yes; with such feelings as yours are about her, her money would have been a burden to you."

"I would not have taken it. I hope, at least, that I would not have taken it. Money is a sore temptation, especially to a poor man like me. It is well for me that the trial did not come in my way."

"But you are not such a very poor man now, are you, George? I thought your business was a good one."

"It is, and I have no right to be a poor man. But a man will be poor who does such mad things as I do. I had three or four thousand pounds clear, and I spent every shilling of it on the Chelsea election. Goodness knows whether I shall have a shilling at all when another chance comes round; but if I have I shall certainly spend it, and if I have not, I shall go in debt wherever I can raise a hundred pounds."

"I hope you will be successful at last."

"I feel sure that I shall. But, in the mean time, I cannot but know that my career is perfectly reckless. No woman ought to join her lot to mine unless she has within her courage to be as reckless as I am. You know what men do when they toss up for shillings?"

"Yes, I suppose I do."

"I am tossing up every day of my life for every shilling that I have."

"Do you mean that you're—gambling?"

"No. I have given that up altogether. I used to gamble, but I never do that now, and never shall again. What I mean is this,—that I hold myself in readiness to risk everything at any moment, in order to gain any object that may serve my turn. I am always ready to lead a forlorn hope. That's what I mean by tossing up every day for every shilling that I have."

Alice did not quite understand him, and perhaps he did not intend that she should. Perhaps his object was to mystify her imagination. She did not understand him, but I fear that she admired the kind of courage which he professed. And he had not only professed it: in that matter of the past election he had certainly practised it.

In talking of beauty to his sister he had spoken of himself as being ugly. He would not generally have been called ugly by women, had not one side of his face been dreadfully scarred by a cicatrice, which in healing, had left a dark indented line down from his left eye to his lower jaw. That black ravine running through his cheek was certainly ugly. On some occasions, when he was angry or disappointed, it was very hideous; for he would so contort his face that the scar would, as it were, stretch itself out, revealing all its horrors, and his countenance would become all scar. "He looked at me like the devil himself—making the hole in his face gape at me," the old squire had said to John Vavasor in describing the interview in which the grandson had tried to bully his grandfather into assenting to his own views about the mortgage. But in other respects George's face was not ugly, and might have been thought handsome by many women. His hair was black, and was parted in the front. His forehead, though low, was broad. His eyes were dark and bright, and his eyebrows were very full, and perfectly black. At those periods of his anger, all his face which was not scar, was eye and eyebrow. He wore a thick black moustache, which covered his mouth, but no whiskers. People said of him that he was so proud of his wound that he would not grow a hair to cover it. The fact, however, was that no whisker could be made to come sufficiently forward to be of service, and therefore he wore none.

The story of that wound should be told. When he was yet hardly more than a boy, before he had come up to London, he was living in a house in the country which his father then occupied. At the time his father was absent, and he and his sister only were in the house with the maid-servants. His sister had a few jewels in her room, and an exaggerated report of them having come to the ears of certain enterprising burglars, a little plan was arranged for obtaining them. A small boy was hidden in the house, a window was opened, and at the proper witching hour of night a stout individual crept up-stairs in his stocking-feet, and was already at Kate Vavasor's door,— when, in the dark, dressed only in his nightshirt, wholly unarmed, George Vavasor flew at the fellow's throat. Two hours elapsed before the horror-stricken women of the house could bring men to the place. George's face had then been ripped open from the eye downwards, with some chisel, or house-breaking instrument. But the man was dead. George had wrenched from him his own tool, and having first jabbed him all over with insufficient wounds, had at last driven the steel through his windpipe. The small boy escaped, carrying with him two shillings and threepence which Kate had left upon the drawing-room mantelpiece.

George Vavasor was rather low in stature, but well made, with small hands and feet, but broad in the chest and strong in the loins. He was a fine horseman and a hard rider; and men who had known him well said that he could fence and shoot with a pistol as few men care to do in these peaceable days. Since volunteering had come up, he had become a captain of Volunteers, and had won prizes with his rifle at Wimbledon.

Such had been the life of George Vavasor, and such was his character, and such his appearance. He had always lived alone in London, and did so at present; but just now his sister was much with him, as she was staying up in town with an aunt, another Vavasor by birth, with whom the reader will, if he persevere, become acquainted in course of time. I hope he will persevere a little, for of all the Vavasors Mrs.. Greenow was perhaps the best worth knowing. But Kate Vavasor's home was understood to be in her grandfather's house in Westmoreland.

On the evening before they started for Switzerland, George and Kate walked from Queen Anne Street, where they had been dining with Alice, to Mrs. Greenow's house. Everything had been settled about luggage, hours of starting, and routes as regarded their few first days; and the common purse had been made over to George. That portion of Mr.. Grey's letter had been read which alluded to the Paynims and the glasses of water, and everything had passed in the best of good-humour. "I'll endeavour to get the cold water for you," George had said; "but as to the breakfasts, I can only hope you won't put me to severe trials by any very early hours. When people go out for pleasure it should be pleasure."

The brother and sister walked through two or three streets in silence, and then Kate asked a question.

"George, I wonder what your wishes really are about Alice?"

"That she shouldn't want her breakfast too early while we are away."

"That means that I'm to hold my tongue, of course."

"No, it doesn't."

"Then it means that you intend to hold yours."

"No; not that either."

"Then what does it mean?"

"That I have no fixed wishes on the subject. Of course she'll marry this man John Grey, and then no one will hear another word about her."

"She will no doubt, if you don't interfere. Probably she will whether you interfere or not. But if you wish to interfere—"

"She's got four hundred a year, and is not so good-looking as she was."

"Yes; she has got four hundred a year, and she is more handsome now than ever she was. I know that you think so;—and that you love her and love no one else—unless you have a sneaking fondness for me."

"I'll leave you to judge of that last."

"And as for me,—I only love two people in the world; her and you. If ever you mean to try, you should try now."

CHAPTER V
THE BALCONY AT BASLE

I am not going to describe the Vavasors' Swiss tour. It would not be fair on my readers. "Six Weeks in the Bernese Oberland, by party of three," would have but very small chance of success in the literary world at present, and I should consider myself to be dishonest if I attempt to palm off such matter on the public in the pages of a novel. It is true that I have just returned from Switzerland, and should find such a course of writing very convenient. But I dismiss the temptation, strong as it is. *Retro age, Satanas*. No living man or woman any longer wants to be told anything of the Grimsell or of the Gemmi. Ludgate Hill is now-a-days more interesting than the Jungfrau.

The Vavasors were not very energetic on their tour. As George had said, they had gone out for pleasure and not for work. They went direct to Interlaken and then hung about between that place and Grindelwald and Lauterbrunnen. It delighted him to sit still on some outer bench, looking at the mountains, with a cigar in his mouth, and it seemed to delight them to be with him. Much that Mr. Grey prophesied had come true. The two girls were ministers to him, instead of having him as their slave.

"What fine fellows those Alpine club men think themselves," he said on one of these occasions, "and how thoroughly they despise the sort of enjoyment I get from mountains. But they're mistaken."

"I don't see why either need be mistaken," said Alice.

"But they are mistaken," he continued. "They rob the mountains of their poetry, which is or should be their greatest charm. Mont Blanc can have no mystery for a man who has been up it half a dozen times. It's like getting behind the scenes at a ballet, or making a conjuror explain his tricks."

"But is the exercise nothing?" said Kate.

"Yes; the exercise is very fine;—but that avoids the question."

"And they all botanize," said Alice.

"I don't believe it. I believe that the most of them simply walk up the mountain and down again. But if they did, that avoids the question also. The poetry and mystery of the mountains are lost to those who make themselves familiar with their details, not the less because such familiarity may have useful results. In this world things are beautiful only because they are not quite seen, or not perfectly understood. Poetry is precious chiefly because it suggests more than it declares. Look in there, through that valley, where you just see the distant little peak at the end. Are you not dreaming of the unknown beautiful world that exists up there;—beautiful, as heaven is beautiful, because you know nothing of the reality? If you make your way up there and back to-morrow, and find out all about it, do you mean to say that it will be as beautiful to you when you come back?"

"Yes;—I think it would," said Alice.

"Then you've no poetry in you. Now I'm made up of poetry." After that they began to laugh at him and were very happy.

I think that Mr. Grey was right in answering Alice's letter as he did; but I think that Lady Macleod was also right in saying that Alice should not have gone to Switzerland in company with George Vavasor. A peculiar familiarity sprang up, which, had all its circumstances been known to Mr. Grey, would not have entirely satisfied him, even though no word was said which might in itself have displeased him. During the first weeks of their travelling no word was said which would have displeased him; but at last, when the time for their return was drawing nigh, when their happiness was nearly over, and that feeling of melancholy was coming on them which always pervades the last hours of any period that has been pleasant,—then words became softer than they had been, and references were made to old days,—allusions which never should have been permitted between them.

Alice had been very happy,—more happy perhaps in that she had been a joint minister with Kate to her cousin George's idle fantasies, than she would have been hurrying about with him as her slave. They had tacitly agreed to spoil him with comforts; and girls are always happier in spoiling some man than in being spoiled by men. And he had taken it all well, doing his despotism pleasantly, exacting much, but exacting nothing that was disagreeable. And he had been amusing always, as Alice thought without any effort. But men and women, when they show themselves at their best, seldom do so without an effort. If the object be near the heart the effort will be pleasant to him who makes it, and if it be made well, it will be hidden; but, not the less, will the effort be there. George Vavasor had on the present occasion done his very best to please his cousin.

They were sitting at Basle one evening in the balcony of the big hotel which overlooks the Rhine. The balcony runs the length of the house, and is open to all the company; but it is spacious, and little parties can be formed there with perfect privacy. The swift broad Rhine runs underneath, rushing through from the bridge which here spans the river; and every now and then on summer evenings loud shouts come up from strong swimmers in the water, who are glorying in the swiftness of the current. The three were sitting there, by themselves, at the end of the balcony. Coffee was before them on a little table, and George's cigar, as usual, was in his mouth.

"It's nearly all over," said he, after they had remained silent for some minutes.

"And I do think it has been a success," said Kate. "Always excepting about the money. I'm ruined for ever."

"I'll make your money all straight," said George.

"Indeed you'll do nothing of the kind," said Kate. "I'm ruined, but you are ruineder. But what signifies? It is such a great thing ever to have had six weeks' happiness, that the ruin is, in point of fact, a good speculation. What do you say, Alice? Won't you vote, too, that we've done it well?"

"I think we've done it very well. I have enjoyed myself thoroughly."

"And now you've got to go home to John Grey and Cambridgeshire! It's no wonder you should be melancholy." That was the thought in Kate's mind, but she did not speak it out on this occasion.

"That's good of you, Alice," said Kate. "Is it not, George? I like a person who will give a hearty meed of approbation."

"But I am giving the meed of approbation to myself."

"I like a person even to do that heartily," said Kate. "Not that George and I are thankful for the compliment. We are prepared to admit that we owe almost everything to you, — are we not, George?"

"I'm not; by any means," said George.

"Well, I am, and I expect to have something pretty said to me in return. Have I been cross once, Alice?"

"No; I don't think you have. You are never cross, though you are often ferocious."

"But I haven't been once ferocious, — nor has George."

"He would have been the most ungrateful man alive if he had," said Alice. "We've done nothing since we've started but realize from him that picture in 'Punch' of the young gentleman at Jeddo who had a dozen ladies to wait upon him."

"And now he has got to go home to his lodgings, and wait upon himself again. Poor fellow! I do pity you, George."

"No, you don't;—nor does Alice. I believe girls always think that a bachelor in London has the happiest of all lives. It's because they think so that they generally want to put an end to the man's condition."

"It's envy that makes us want to get married,—not love," said Kate.

"It's the devil in some shape, as often as not," said he. "With a man, marriage always seems to him to be an evil at the instant."

"Not always," said Alice.

"Almost always;—but he does it, as he takes physic, because something worse will come if he don't. A man never likes having his tooth pulled out, but all men do have their teeth pulled out,—and they who delay it too long suffer the very mischief."

"I do like George's philosophy," said Kate, getting up from her chair as she spoke; "it is so sharp, and has such a pleasant acid taste about it; and then we all know that it means nothing. Alice, I'm going up-stairs to begin the final packing."

"I'll come with you, dear."

"No, don't. To tell the truth I'm only going into that man's room because he won't put up a single thing of his own decently. We'll do ours, of course, when we go up to bed. Whatever you disarrange to-night, Master George, you must rearrange for yourself to-morrow morning, for I promise I won't go into your room at five o'clock."

"How I do hate that early work," said George.

"I'll be down again very soon," said Kate. "Then we'll take one turn on the bridge and go to bed."

Alice and George were left together sitting in the balcony. They had been alone together before many times since their travels had commenced; but they both of them felt that there was something to them in the present moment different from any other period of their journey. There was something that each felt to be sweet, undefinable, and dangerous. Alice had known that it would be better for her to go up-stairs with Kate; but Kate's answer had been of such a nature that had she gone she would have shown that she had some special reason for going. Why should she show such a need? Or why, indeed, should she entertain it?

Alice was seated quite at the end of the gallery, and Kate's chair was at her feet in the corner. When Alice and Kate had seated themselves, the waiter had brought a small table for the coffee-cups, and George had placed his chair on the other side of that. So that Alice was, as it were, a prisoner. She could not slip away without some special preparation for going, and

Kate had so placed her chair in leaving, that she must actually have asked George to move it before she could escape. But why should she wish to escape? Nothing could be more lovely and enticing than the scene before her. The night had come on, with quick but still unperceived approach, as it does in those parts; for the twilight there is not prolonged as it is with us more northern folk. The night had come on, but there was a rising moon, which just sufficed to give a sheen to the water beneath her. The air was deliciously soft;—of that softness which produces no sensation either of warmth or cold, but which just seems to touch one with loving tenderness, as though the unseen spirits of the air kissed one's forehead as they passed on their wings. The Rhine was running at her feet, so near, that in the soft half light it seemed as though she might step into its ripple. The Rhine was running by with that delicious sound of rapidly moving waters, that fresh refreshing gurgle of the river, which is so delicious to the ear at all times. If you be talking, it wraps up your speech, keeping it for yourselves, making it difficult neither to her who listens nor to him who speaks. If you would sleep, it is of all lullabies the sweetest. If you are alone and would think, it aids all your thoughts. If you are alone, and, alas! would not think,—if thinking be too painful,—it will dispel your sorrow, and give the comfort which music alone can give. Alice felt that the air kissed her, that the river sang for her its sweetest song, that the moon shone for her with its softest light,—that light which lends the poetry of half-developed beauty to everything that it touches. Why should she leave it?

Nothing was said for some minutes after Kate's departure, and Alice was beginning to shake from her that half feeling of danger which had come over her. Vavasor had sat back in his chair, leaning against the house, with his feet raised upon a stool; his arms were folded across his breast, and he seemed to have divided himself between his thoughts and his cigar. Alice was looking full upon the river, and her thoughts had strayed away to her future home among John Grey's flower-beds and shrubs; but the river, though it sang to her pleasantly, seemed to sing a song of other things than such a home as that,—a song full of mystery, as are all river songs when one tries to understand their words.

"When are you to be married, Alice?" said George at last.

"Oh, George!" said she. "You ask me a question as though you were putting a pistol to my ear."

"I'm sorry the question was so unpleasant."

"I didn't say that it was unpleasant; but you asked it so suddenly! The truth is, I didn't expect you to speak at all just then. I suppose I was thinking of something."

"But if it be not unpleasant,—when are you to be married?"

"I do not know. It is not fixed."

"But about when, I mean? This summer?"

"Certainly not this summer, for the summer will be over when we reach home."

"This winter? Next spring? Next year?—or in ten years' time?"

"Before the expiration of the ten years, I suppose. Anything more exact than that I can't say."

"I suppose you like it?" he then said.

"What, being married? You see I've never tried yet."

"The idea of it,—the anticipation. You look forward with satisfaction to the kind of life you will lead at Nethercoats? Don't suppose I am saying anything against it, for I have no conception what sort of a place Nethercoats is. On the whole I don't know that there is any kind of life better than that of an English country gentleman in his own place;—that is, if he can keep it up, and not live as the old squire does, in a state of chronic poverty."

"Mr. Grey's place doesn't entitle him to be called a country gentleman."

"But you like the prospect of it?"

"Oh, George, how you do cross-question one! Of course I like it, or I shouldn't have accepted it."

"That does not follow. But I quite acknowledge that I have no right to cross-question you. If I ever had such right on the score of cousinship, I have lost it on the score of—; but we won't mind that, will we, Alice?" To this she at first made no answer, but he repeated the question. "Will we, Alice?"

"Will we what?"

"Recur to the old days."

"Why should we recur to them? They are passed, and as we are again friends and dear cousins the sting of them is gone."

"Ah, yes! The sting of them is gone. It is for that reason, because it is so, that we may at last recur to them without danger. If we regret nothing,—if neither of us has anything to regret, why not recur to them, and talk of them freely?"

"No, George; that would not do."

"By heavens, no! It would drive me mad; and if I know aught of you, it would hardly leave you as calm as you are at present."

"As I would wish to be left calm—"

"Would you? Then I suppose I ought to hold my tongue. But, Alice, I shall never have the power of speaking to you again as I speak now. Since we have been out together, we have been dear friends; is it not so?"

"And shall we not always be dear friends?"

"No, certainly not. How will it be possible? Think of it. How can I really be your friend when you are the mistress of that man's house in Cambridgeshire?"

"George!"

"I mean nothing disrespectful. I truly beg your pardon if it has seemed so. Let me say that gentleman's house;—for he is a gentleman."

"That he certainly is."

"You could not have accepted him were he not so. But how can I be your friend when you are his wife? I may still call you cousin Alice, and pat your children on the head if I chance to see them; and shall stop in the streets and shake hands with him if I meet him;—that is if my untoward fate does not induce him to cut my acquaintance;—but as for friendship, that will be over when you and I shall have parted next Thursday evening at London Bridge."

"Oh, George, don't say so!"

"But I do."

"And why on Thursday? Do you mean that you won't come to Queen Anne Street any more?"

"Yes, that is what I do mean. This trip of ours has been very successful, Kate says. Perhaps Kate knows nothing about it."

"It has been very pleasant,—at least to me."

"And the pleasure has had no drawback?"

"None to me."

"It has been very pleasant to me, also;—but the pleasure has had its alloy. Alice, I have nothing to ask from you,—nothing."

"Anything that you should ask, I would do for you."

"I have nothing to ask;—nothing. But I have one word to say."

"George, do not say it. Let me go up-stairs. Let me go to Kate."

"Certainly; if you wish it you shall go." He still held his foot against the chair which barred her passage, and did not attempt to rise as he must have done to make way for her passage out. "Certainly you shall go to Kate, if you refuse to hear me. But after all that has passed between us, after these six weeks of intimate companionship, I think you ought to listen to me. I tell you that I have nothing to ask. I am not going to make love to you."

Alice had commenced some attempt to rise, but she had again settled herself in her chair. And now, when he paused for a moment, she made no further sign that she wished to escape, nor did she say a word to intimate her further wish that he should be silent.

"I am not going to make love to you," he said again. "As for making love, as the word goes, that must be over between you and me. It has been made and marred, and cannot be remade. It may exist, or it may have been expelled; but where it does not exist, it will never be brought back again."

"It should not be spoken of between you and me."

"So, no doubt, any proper-going duenna would say, and so, too, little children should be told; but between you and me there can be no necessity for falsehood. We have grown beyond our sugar-toothed ages, and are now men and women. I perfectly understood your breaking away from me. I understood you, and in spite of my sorrow knew that you were right. I am not going to accuse or to defend myself; but I knew that you were right."

"Then let there be no more about it."

"Yes; there must be more about it. I did not understand you when you accepted Mr. Grey. Against him I have not a whisper to make. He may be perfect for aught I know. But, knowing you as I thought I did, I could not understand your loving such a man as him. It was as though one who had lived on brandy should take himself suddenly to a milk diet,—and enjoy the change! A milk diet is no doubt the best. But men who have lived on brandy can't make those changes very suddenly. They perish in the attempt."

"Not always, George."

"It may be done with months of agony;—but there was no such agony with you."

"Who can tell?"

"But you will tell me the cure was made. I thought so, and therefore thought that I should find you changed. I thought that you, who had been all fire, would now have turned yourself into soft-flowing milk and honey, and have become fit for the life in store for you. With such a one I might have travelled from Moscow to Malta without danger. The woman fit to be John Grey's wife would certainly do me no harm,—could not touch my happiness. I might have loved her once,—might still love the memory of what she had been; but her, in her new form, after her new birth,—such a one as that, Alice, could be nothing to me. Don't mistake me. I have enough of wisdom in me to know how much better, ay, and happier a woman she might be. It was not that I thought you had descended in the scale; but I gave you credit for virtues which you have not acquired. Alice, that wholesome diet of which I spoke is not your diet. You would starve on it, and perish."

He had spoken with great energy, but still in a low voice, having turned full round upon the table, with both his arms upon it, and his face stretched out far over towards her. She was looking full at him; and, as I have said before, that scar and his gloomy eyes and thick eyebrows seemed to make up the whole of his face. But the scar had never been ugly to her. She knew the story, and when he was her lover she had taken pride in the mark of the wound. She looked at him, but though he paused she did not speak. The music of the river was still in her ears, and there came upon her a struggle as though she were striving to understand its song. Were the waters also telling her of the mistake she had made in accepting Mr. Grey as her husband? What her cousin was now telling her,—was it not a repetition of words which she had spoken to herself hundreds of times during the last two months? Was she not telling herself daily,—hourly,—always,—in every thought of her life, that in accepting Mr. Grey she had assumed herself to be mistress of virtues which she did not possess? Had she not, in truth, rioted upon brandy, till the innocence of milk was unfitted for her? This man now came and rudely told her all this,—but did he not tell her the truth? She sat silent and convicted; only gazing into his face when his speech was done.

"I have learned this since we have been again together, Alice; and finding you, not the angel I had supposed, finding you to be the same woman I had once loved,—the safety that I anticipated has not fallen to my lot. That's all. Here's Kate, and now we'll go for our walk."

CHAPTER VI
THE BRIDGE OVER THE RHINE

"George," said Kate, speaking before she quite got up to them, "will you tell me whether you have been preparing all your things for an open sale by auction?" Then she stole a look at Alice, and having learned from that glance that something had occurred which prevented Alice from joining her in her raillery, she went on with it herself rapidly, as though to cover Alice's confusion, and give her time to rally before they should all move. "Would you believe it? he had three razors laid out on his table—"

"A man must shave,—even at Basle."

"But not with three razors at once; and three hair-brushes, and half a dozen toothbrushes, and a small collection of combs, and four or five little glass bottles, looking as though they contained poison,—all with silver tops. I can only suppose you desired to startle the weak mind of the chambermaid. I have put them all up; but remember this, if they are taken out again you are responsible. And I will not put up your boots, George. What can you have wanted with three pairs of boots at Basle?"

"When you have completed the list of my wardrobe we'll go out upon the bridge. That is, if Alice likes it."

"Oh, yes; I shall like it."

"Come along then," said Kate. And so they moved away. When they got upon the bridge Alice and Kate were together, while George strolled behind them, close to them, but not taking any part in their conversation,—as though he had merely gone with them as an escort. Kate seemed to be perfectly content with this arrangement, chattering to Alice, so that she might show that there was nothing serious on the minds of any of them. It need hardly be said that Alice at this time made no appeal to George to join them. He followed them at their heels, with his hands behind his back, looking down upon the pavement and simply waiting upon their pleasure.

"Do you know," said Kate, "I have a very great mind to run away."

"Where do you want to run to?"

"Well;—that wouldn't much signify. Perhaps I'd go to the little inn at Handek. It's a lonely place, where nobody would hear of me,—and I should have the waterfall. I'm afraid they'd want to have their bill paid. That would be the worst of it."

"But why run away just now?"

"I won't, because you wouldn't like going home with George alone,—and I suppose he'd be bound to look after me, as he's doing now. I wonder what he thinks of having to walk over the bridge after us girls. I suppose he'd be in that place down there drinking beer, if we weren't here."

"If he wanted to go, I dare say he would, in spite of us."

"That's ungrateful of you, for I'm sure we've never been kept in a moment by his failing us. But as I was saying, I do dread going home. You are going to John Grey, which may be pleasant enough; but I'm going—to Aunt Greenow."

"It's your own choice."

"No, it's not. I haven't any choice in the matter. Of course I might refuse to speak to Aunt Greenow, and nobody could make me;—but practically I haven't any choice in the matter. Fancy a month at Yarmouth with no companion but such a woman as that!"

"I shouldn't mind it. Aunt Greenow always seems to me to be a very good sort of woman."

"She may be a good woman, but I must say I think she's of a bad sort. You've never heard her talk about her husband?"

"No, never; I think she did cry a little the first day she came to Queen Anne Street, but that wasn't unnatural."

"He was thirty years older than herself."

"But still he was her husband. And even if her tears are assumed, what of that? What's a woman to do? Of course she was wrong to marry him. She was thirty-five, and had nothing, while he was sixty-five, and was very rich. According to all accounts she made him a very good wife, and now that she's got all his money, you wouldn't have her go about laughing within three months of his death."

"No; I wouldn't have her laugh; but neither would I have her cry. And she's quite right to wear weeds; but she needn't be so very outrageous in the depth of her hems, or so very careful that her caps are becoming. Her eyes will be worn out by their double service. They are always red with weeping, and yet she is ready every minute with a full battery of execution for any man that she sees."

"Then why have you consented to go to Yarmouth with her?"

"Just because she's got forty thousand pounds. If Mr. Greenow had left her with a bare maintenance I don't suppose I should ever have held out my hand to her."

"Then you're as bad as she is."

"Quite as bad;—and that's what makes me want to run away. But it isn't my own fault altogether. It's the fault of the world at large. Does anybody ever drop their rich relatives? When she proposed to take me to Yarmouth, wasn't it natural that the squire should ask me to go? When I told George, wasn't it natural that he should say, 'Oh, go by all means. She's got forty thousand pounds!' One can't pretend to be wiser or better than one's relatives. And after all what can I expect from her money?"

"Nothing, I should say."

"Not a halfpenny. I'm nearly thirty and she's only forty, and of course she'll marry again. I will say of myself, too, that no person living cares less for money."

"I should think no one."

"Yet one sticks to one's rich relatives. It's the way of the world." Then she paused a moment. "But shall I tell you, Alice, why I do stick to her? Perhaps you'll think the object as mean as though I wanted her money myself."

"Why is it?"

"Because it is on the cards that she may help George in his career. I do not want money, but he may. And for such purposes as his, I think it fair that all the family should contribute. I feel sure that he would make a name for himself in Parliament; and if I had my way I would spend every shilling of Vavasor money in putting him there. When I told the squire so I thought he would have eaten me. I really did think he would have turned me out of the house."

"And serve you right too after what had happened."

"I didn't care. Let him turn me out. I was determined he should know what I thought. He swore at me; and then he was so unhappy at what he had done that he came and kissed me that night in my bedroom, and gave me a ten-pound note. What do you think I did with it? I sent it as a contribution to the next election and George has it now locked up in a box. Don't you tell him that I told you."

Then they stopped and leaned for a while over the parapet of the bridge. "Come here, George," said Kate; and she made room for him between herself and Alice. "Wouldn't you like to be swimming down there as those boys were doing when we went out into the balcony? The water looks so enticing."

"I can't say I should;—unless it might be a pleasant way of swimming into the next world."

"I should so like to feel myself going with the stream," said Kate; "particularly by this light. I can't fancy in the least that I should be drowned."

"I can't fancy anything else," said Alice.

"It would be so pleasant to feel the water gliding along one's limbs, and to be carried away headlong,—knowing that you were on the direct road to Rotterdam."

"And so arrive there without your clothes," said George.

"They would be brought after in a boat. Didn't you see that those boys had a boat with them? But if I lived here, I'd never do it except by moonlight. The water looks so clear and bright now, and the rushing sound of it is so soft! The sea at Yarmouth won't be anything like that I suppose."

Neither of them any longer answered her, and yet she went on talking about the river, and their aunt, and her prospects at Yarmouth. Neither of them answered her, and yet it seemed that they had not a word to say to each other. But still they stood there looking down upon the river, and every now and then Kate's voice was to be heard, preventing the feeling which might otherwise have arisen that their hearts were too full for speech.

At last Alice seemed to shiver. There was a slight trembling in her arms, which George felt rather than saw. "You are cold," he said.

"No indeed."

"If you are let us go in. I thought you shivered with the night air."

"It wasn't that. I was thinking of something. Don't you ever think of things that make you shiver?"

"Indeed I do, very often;—so often that I have to do my shiverings inwardly. Otherwise people would think I had the palsy."

"I don't mean things of moment," said Alice. "Little bits of things make me do it;—perhaps a word that I said and ought not to have said ten years ago;—the most ordinary little mistakes, even my own past thoughts to myself about the merest trifles. They are always making me shiver."

"It's not because you have committed any murder then."

"No; but it's my conscience all the same, I suppose."

"Ah! I'm not so good as you. I doubt it's not my conscience at all. When I think of a chance I've let go by, as I have thousands, then it is that I shiver. But, as I tell you, I shiver inwardly. I've been in one long shiver ever since we came out because of one chance that I let go by. Come, we'll go in. We've to be up at five o'clock, and now it's eleven. I'll do the rest of my shivering in bed."

"Are you tired of being out?" said Kate, when the other two began to move.

"Not tired of being out, but George reminds me that we have to be up at five."

"I wish George would hold his tongue. We can't come to the bridge at Basle every night in our lives. If one found oneself at the top of Sinai I'm afraid the first feeling would be one of fear lest one wouldn't be down in time to dress for dinner. Are you aware, George, that the king of rivers is running beneath your feet, and that the moon is shining with a brilliance you never see at home?"

"I'll stay here all night if you'll put off going to-morrow," said George.

"Our money wouldn't hold out," said Kate.

"Don't talk about Sinai any more after that," said he, "but let's go in to bed."

They walked across the bridge back to the hotel in the same manner as before, the two girls going together with the young man after them, and so they went up the front steps of the hotel, through the hall, and on to the stairs. Here George handed Alice her candle, and as he did so he whispered a few words to her. "My shivering fit has to come yet," said he, "and will last me the whole night." She would have given much to be able to answer him lightly, as though what he had said had meant nothing;—but she couldn't do it; the light speech would not come to her. She was conscious of all this, and went away to her own room without answering him at all. Here she sat down at the window looking out upon the river till Kate should join her. Their rooms opened through from one to the other, and she would not begin her packing till her cousin should come.

But Kate had gone with her brother, promising, as she did so, that she would be back in half a minute. That half minute was protracted beyond half an hour. "If you'll take my advice," said Kate, at last, standing up with her candle in her hand, "you'll ask her in plain words to give you another chance. Do it to-morrow at Strasbourg; you'll never have a better opportunity."

"And bid her throw John Grey over!"

"Don't say anything about John Grey; leave her to settle that matter with herself. Believe me that she has quite courage enough to dispose of John Grey, if she has courage enough to accept your offer."

"Kate, you women never understand each other. If I were to do that, all her most powerful feelings would be arrayed in arms against me. I must leave her to find out first that she wishes to be rid of her engagement."

"She has found that out long ago. Do you think I don't know what she wishes? But if you can't bring yourself to speak to her, she'll marry him in spite of her wishes."

"Bring myself! I've never been very slow in bringing myself to speak to any one when there was need. It isn't very pleasant sometimes, but I do it, if I find occasion."

"But surely it must be pleasant with her. You must be glad to find that she still loves you. You still love her, I suppose?"

"Upon my word I don't know."

"Don't provoke me, George. I'm moving heaven and earth to bring you two together; but if I didn't think you loved her, I'd go to her at once and bid her never see you again."

"Upon my word, Kate, I sometimes think it would be better if you'd leave heaven and earth alone."

"Then I will. But of all human beings, surely you're the most ungrateful."

"Why shouldn't she marry John Grey if she likes him?"

"But she doesn't like him. And I hate him. I hate the sound of his voice, and the turn of his eye, and that slow, steady movement of his,—as though he was always bethinking himself that he wouldn't wear out his clothes."

"I don't see that your hating him ought to have anything to do with it."

"If you're going to preach morals, I'll leave you. It's the darling wish of my heart that she should be your wife. If you ever loved anybody,—and I sometimes doubt whether you ever did,—but if you did, you loved her."

"Did and do are different things."

"Very well, George; then I have done. It has been the same in every twist and turn of my life. In everything that I have striven to do for you, you have thrown yourself over, in order that I might be thrown over too. But I believe you say this merely to vex me."

"Upon my word, Kate, I think you'd better go to bed."

"But not till I've told her everything. I won't leave her to be deceived and ill-used again."

"Who is ill-using her now? Is it not the worst of ill-usage, trying to separate her from that man?"

"No;—if I thought so, I would have no hand in doing it. She would be miserable with him, and make him miserable as well. She does not really love him. He loves her, but I've nothing to do with that. It's nothing to me if he breaks his heart."

"I shall break mine if you don't let me go to bed."

With that she went away and hurried along the corridor, till she came to her cousin's room. She found Alice still seated at the window, or rather kneeling on the chair, with her head out through the lattice. "Why, you lazy creature," said Kate; "I declare you haven't touched a thing."

"You said we'd do it together."

"But he has kept me. Oh, what a man he is! If he ever does get married, what will his wife do with him?"

"I don't think he ever will," said Alice.

"Don't you? I dare say you understand him better than I do. Sometimes I think that the only thing wanting to make him thoroughly good, is a wife. But it isn't every woman that would do for him. And the woman who marries him should have high courage. There are moments with him when he is very wild; but he never is cruel and never hard. Is Mr.. Grey ever hard?"

"Never; nor yet wild."

"Oh, certainly not that. I'm quite sure he's never wild."

"When you say that, Kate, I know that you mean to abuse him."

"No; upon my word. What's the good of abusing him to you? I like a man to be wild,—wild in my sense. You knew that before."

"I wonder whether you'd like a wild man for yourself?"

"Ah! that's a question I've never asked myself. I've been often curious to consider what sort of husband would suit you, but I've had very few thoughts about a husband for myself. The truth is, I'm married to George. Ever since—"

"Ever since what?"

"Since you and he were parted, I've had nothing to do in life but to stick to him. And I shall do so to the end,—unless one thing should happen."

"And what's that?"

"Unless you should become his wife after all. He will never marry anybody else."

"Kate, you shouldn't allude to such a thing now. You know that it's impossible."

"Well, perhaps so. As far as I'm concerned, it is all the better for me. If George ever married, I should have nothing to do in the world;—literally nothing—nothing—nothing—nothing!"

"Kate, don't talk in that way," and Alice came up to her and embraced her.

"Go away," said she. "Go, Alice; you and I must part. I cannot bear it any longer. You must know it all. When you are married to John Grey, our friendship must be over. If you became George's wife I should become nobody. I've nothing else in the world. You and he would be so all-sufficient for each other, that I should drop away from you like an old garment. But I'd give up all, everything, every hope I have, to see you become George's wife. I know myself not to be good. I know myself to be very bad, and yet I care nothing for myself. Don't Alice, don't; I don't want your caresses. Caress him, and I'll kneel at your feet and cover them with kisses." She had now thrown herself upon a sofa, and had turned her face away to the wall.

"Kate, you shouldn't speak in that way."

"Of course I shouldn't,—but I do."

"You, who know everything, must know that I cannot marry your brother,—even if he wished it."

"He does wish it."

"Not though I were under no other engagement."

"And why not?" said Kate, again starting up. "What is there to separate you from George now, but that unfortunate affair, that will end in the misery of you all. Do you think I can't see? Don't I know which of the two men you like best?"

"You are making me sorry, Kate, that I have ventured to come here in your brother's company. It is not only unkind of you to talk to me in this way, but worse than that—it is indelicate."

"Oh, indelicate! How I do hate that word. If any word in the language reminds me of a whited sepulchre it is that;—all clean and polished outside with filth and rottenness within. Are your thoughts delicate? that's the thing. You are engaged to marry John Grey. That may be delicate enough if you love him truly, and feel yourself fitted to be his wife; but it's about the most indelicate thing you can do, if you love any one better than him. Delicacy with many women is like their cleanliness. Nothing can be nicer than the whole outside get-up, but you wouldn't wish to answer for anything beneath."

"If you think ill of me like that—"

"No; I don't think ill of you. How can I think ill of you when I know that all your difficulties have come from him? It hasn't been your fault; it has been his throughout. It is he who has driven you to sacrifice yourself on this altar. If we can, both of us, manage to lay aside all delicacy and pretence, and dare to speak the truth, we shall acknowledge that it is so. Had Mr. Grey come to you while things were smooth between you and George, would you have thought it possible that he could be George's rival in your estimation? It is Hyperion to Satyr."

"And which is the Satyr?"

"I'll leave your heart to tell you. You know what is the darling wish of my heart. But, Alice, if I thought that Mr. Grey was to you Hyperion,—if I thought that you could marry him with that sort of worshipping, idolatrous love which makes a girl proud as well as happy in her marriage, I wouldn't raise a little finger to prevent it."

To this Alice made no answer, and then Kate allowed the matter to drop. Alice made no answer, though she felt that she was allowing judgement to go against her by default in not doing so. She had intended to fight bravely, and to have maintained the excellence of her present position as the affianced bride of Mr. Grey, but she felt that she had failed. She felt that she had, in some sort, acknowledged that the match was one to be deplored;—that her words in her own defence would by no means have satisfied Mr. Grey, if Mr.. Grey could have heard them;—that they would have induced him to offer her back her troth rather than have made him happy as a lover. But she had nothing further to say. She could do something. She would hurry home and bid him name the earliest day he pleased. After that her cousin would cease to disturb her in her career.

It was nearly one o'clock before the two girls began to prepare for their morning start, and Alice, when they had finished their packing, seemed to be worn out with fatigue. "If you are tired, dear, we'll put it off," said Kate. "Not for worlds," said Alice. "For half a word we'll do it," continued Kate. "I'll slip out to George and tell him, and there's nothing he'd like so much." But Alice would not consent.

About two they got into bed, and punctually at six they were at the railway station. "Don't speak to me," said George, when he met them at their door in the passage. "I shall only yawn in your face." However, they were in time,—which means abroad that they were at the station half an hour before their train started,—and they went on upon their journey to Strasbourg.

There is nothing further to be told of their tour. They were but two days and nights on the road from Basle to London; and during those two days and nights neither George nor Kate spoke a word to Alice of her marriage, nor was any allusion made to the balcony at the inn, or to the bridge over the river.

CHAPTER VII
AUNT GREENOW

Kate Vavasor remained only three days in London before she started for Yarmouth; and during those three days she was not much with her cousin. "I'm my aunt's, body and soul, for the next six weeks," she said to Alice, when she did come to Queen Anne Street on the morning after her arrival. "And she is exigeant in a manner I can't at all explain to you. You mustn't be surprised if I don't even write a line. I've escaped by stealth now. She went up-stairs to try on some new weeds for the seaside, and then I bolted." She did not say a word about George; nor during those three days, nor for some days afterwards, did George show himself. As it turned out afterwards, he had gone off to Scotland, and had remained a week among the grouse. Thus, at least, he had accounted for himself and his movements; but all George Vavasor's friends knew that his goings out and comings in were seldom accounted for openly like those of other men.

It will perhaps be as well to say a few words about Mrs. Greenow before we go with her to Yarmouth. Mrs. Greenow was the only daughter and the youngest child of the old squire at Vavasor Hall. She was just ten years younger than her brother John, and I am inclined to think that she was almost justified in her repeated assertion that the difference was much greater than ten years, by the freshness of her colour, and by the general juvenility of her appearance. She certainly did not look forty, and who can expect a woman to proclaim herself to be older than her looks? In early life she had been taken from her father's house, and had lived with relatives in one of the large towns in the north of England. It is certain she had not been quite successful as a girl. Though she had enjoyed the name of being a beauty, she had not the usual success which comes from such repute. At thirty-four she was still unmarried. She had, moreover, acquired the character of being a flirt; and I fear that the stories which were told of her, though doubtless more than half false, had in them sufficient of truth to justify the character. Now this was very sad, seeing that Arabella Vavasor had no fortune, and that she had offended her father and brothers by declining to comply with their advice at certain periods of her career. There was, indeed, considerable trouble in the minds of the various male Vavasors with reference to Arabella, when tidings suddenly reached the Hall that she was going to be married to an old man.

She was married to the old man; and the marriage fortunately turned out satisfactorily, at any rate for the old man and for her family. The Vavasors were relieved from all further trouble, and were as much surprised as gratified when they heard that she did her duty well in her new position. Arabella had long been a thorn in their side, never having really done anything which they could pronounce to be absolutely wrong, but always giving them cause for fear. Now they feared no longer. Her husband was a retired merchant, very rich, not very strong in health, and devoted to his bride. Rumours soon made their way to Vavasor Hall, and to Queen Anne Street, that Mrs. Greenow was quite a pattern wife, and that Mr. Greenow considered himself to be the happiest old man in Lancashire. And now in her prosperity she quite forgave the former slights which had been put upon her by her relatives. She wrote to her dear niece Alice, and to her dearest niece Kate, and sent little presents to her father. On one occasion she took her husband to Vavasor Hall, and there was a regular renewal of all the old family feelings. Arabella's husband was an old man, and was very old for his age; but the whole thing was quite respectable, and there was, at any rate, no doubt about the money. Then Mr. Greenow died; and the widow, having proved the will, came up to London and claimed the commiseration of her nieces.

"Why not go to Yarmouth with her for a month?" George had said to Kate. "Of course it will be a bore. But an aunt with forty thousand pounds has a right to claim attention." Kate acknowledged the truth of the argument and agreed to go to Yarmouth for a month. "Your aunt Arabella has shown herself to be a very sensible woman," the old squire had written; "much more sensible than anybody thought her before her marriage. Of course you should go with her if she asks you." What aunt, uncle, or cousin, in the uncontrolled possession of forty thousand pounds was ever unpopular in the family?

Yarmouth is not a very prepossessing place to the eye. To my eye, at any rate, it is not so. There is an old town with which summer visitors have little or nothing to do; and there are the new houses down by the sea-side, to which, at any rate, belongs the full advantage of sea air. A kind of esplanade runs for nearly a mile along the sands, and there are built, or in the course of building, rows of houses appropriated to summer visitors all looking out upon the sea. There is no beauty unless the yellow sandy sea can be called beautiful. The coast is low and straight, and the east wind blows full upon it. But the place is healthy; and Mrs. Greenow was probably right in thinking that she might there revive some portion of the health which she had lost in watching beside the couch of her departing lord.

"Omnibus;—no, indeed. Jeannette, get me a fly." These were the first words Mrs. Greenow spoke as she put her foot upon the platform at the Yarmouth station. Her maid's name was Jenny; but Kate had already found, somewhat to her dismay, that orders had been issued before they left London that the girl was henceforth to be called Jeannette. Kate had also already found that her aunt could be imperious; but this taste for masterdom had not shown itself so plainly in London as it did from the moment that the train had left the station at Shoreditch. In London Mrs. Greenow had been among Londoners, and her career had hitherto been provincial. Her spirit, no doubt, had been somewhat cowed by the novelty of her position. But when she felt herself to be once beyond the stones as the saying used to be, she was herself again; and at Ipswich she had ordered Jeannette to get her a glass of sherry with an air which had created a good deal of attention among the guards and porters.

The fly was procured; and with considerable exertion all Mrs. Greenow's boxes, together with the more moderate belongings of her niece and maid, were stowed on the top of it, round upon the driver's body on the coach box, on the maid's lap, and I fear in Kate's also, and upon the vacant seat.

"The large house in Montpelier Parade," said Mrs. Greenow.

"They is all large, ma'am," said the driver.

"The largest," said Mrs. Greenow.

"They're much of a muchness," said the driver.

"Then Mrs. Jones's," said Mrs. Greenow. "But I was particularly told it was the largest in the row."

"I know Mrs. Jones's well," said the driver, and away they went.

Mrs. Jones's house was handsome and comfortable; but I fear Mrs. Greenow's satisfaction in this respect was impaired by her disappointment in finding that it was not perceptibly bigger than those to the right and left of her. Her ambition in this and in other similar matters would have amused Kate greatly had she been a bystander, and not one of her aunt's party. Mrs. Greenow was good-natured, liberal, and not by nature selfish; but she was determined not to waste the good things which fortune had given, and desired that all the world should see that she had forty thousand pounds of her own. And in doing this she was repressed by no feeling of false shame. She never hesitated in her demands through bashfulness. She called aloud for such comfort and grandeur as Yarmouth could afford her, and was well pleased that all around should hear her calling. Joined to all this was her uncontrolled grief for her husband's death.

"Dear Greenow! sweet lamb! Oh, Kate, if you'd only known that man!" When she said this she was sitting in the best of Mrs. Jones's sitting-rooms, waiting to have dinner announced. She had taken a drawing-room and dining-room, "because," as she had said, "she didn't see why people should be stuffy when they went to the seaside;—not if they had means to make themselves comfortable."

"Oh, Kate, I do wish you'd known him!"

"I wish I had," said Kate,—very untruly. "I was unfortunately away when he went to Vavasor Hall."

"Ah, yes; but it was at home, in the domestic circle, that Greenow should have been seen to be appreciated. I was a happy woman, Kate, while that lasted." And Kate was surprised to see that real tears—one or two on each side—were making their way down her aunt's cheeks. But they were soon checked with a handkerchief of the broadest hem and of the finest cambric.

"Dinner, ma'am," said Jeannette, opening the door.

"Jeannette, I told you always to say that dinner was served."

"Dinner's served then," said Jeannette in a tone of anger.

"Come, Kate," said her aunt. "I've but little appetite myself, but there's no reason you shouldn't eat your dinner. I specially wrote to Mrs. Jones to have some sweetbread. I do hope she's got a decent cook. It's very little I eat myself, but I do like to see things nice."

The next day was Sunday; and it was beautiful to see how Mrs. Greenow went to church in all the glory of widowhood. There had been a great unpacking after that banquet on the sweetbread, and all her funereal millinery had been displayed before Kate's wondering eyes. The charm of the woman was in this,—that she was not in the least ashamed of anything that she did. She turned over all her wardrobe of mourning, showing the richness of each article, the stiffness of the crape, the fineness of the cambric, the breadth of the frills,—telling the price of each to a shilling, while she explained how the whole had been amassed without any consideration of expense. This she did with all the pride of a young bride when she shows the glories of her trousseau to the friend of her bosom. Jeannette stood by the while, removing one thing and exhibiting another. Now and again through the performance, Mrs. Greenow would rest a while from her employment, and address the shade of the departed one in terms of most endearing affection. In the midst of this Mrs. Jones came in; but the widow was not a whit abashed by the presence of the stranger. "Peace be to his manes!" she said at last, as she carefully folded up a huge black crape mantilla. She made, however, but one syllable of the classical word, and Mrs. Jones thought that her lodger had addressed herself to the mortal "remains" of her deceased lord.

"Peace be to his manes.

"He is left her uncommon well off, I suppose," said Mrs. Jones to Jeannette.

"You may say that, ma'am. It's more nor a hundred thousand of pounds!"

"No!"

"Pounds of sterling, ma'am! Indeed it is;—to my knowledge."

"Why don't she have a carriage?"

"So she do;—but a lady can't bring her carriage down to the sea when she's only just buried her husband as one may say. What'd folks say if they saw her in her own carriage? But it ain't because she can't afford it, Mrs. Jones. And now we're talking of it you must order a fly for church to-morrow, that'll look private, you know. She said I was to get a man that had a livery coat and gloves."

The man with the coat and gloves was procured; and Mrs. Greenow's entry into church made quite a sensation. There was a thoughtfulness about her which alone showed that she was a woman of no ordinary power. She foresaw all necessities, and made provision for all emergencies. Another would not have secured an eligible sitting, and been at home in Yarmouth church, till half the period of her sojourn there was over. But Mrs. Greenow had done it all. She walked up the middle aisle with as much self-possession as though the chancel had belonged to her family for years; and the respectable pew-opener absolutely deserted two or three old ladies whom she was attending, to show Mrs. Greenow into her seat. When seated, she was the cynosure of all eyes. Kate Vavasor became immediately aware that a great sensation had been occasioned by their entrance, and equally aware that none of it was due to her. I regret to say that this feeling continued to show itself throughout the whole service. How many ladies of forty go to church without attracting the least attention! But it is hardly too much to say that every person in that church had looked at Mrs. Greenow. I doubt if there was present there a single married lady who, on leaving the building, did not speak to her husband of the widow. There had prevailed during the whole two hours a general though unexpressed conviction that something worthy of remark had happened that morning. It had an effect even upon the curate's reading; and the incumbent, while preaching his sermon, could not keep his eyes off that wonderful bonnet and veil.

On the next morning, before eleven, Mrs. Greenow's name was put down at the Assembly Room. "I need hardly say that in my present condition I care nothing for these things. Of course I would sooner be alone. But, my dear Kate, I know what I owe to you."

Kate, with less intelligence than might have been expected from one so clever, began to assure her aunt that she required no society; and that, coming thus with her to the seaside in the early days of her widowhood, she had been well aware that they would live retired. But Mrs. Greenow soon put her down, and did so without the slightest feeling of shame or annoyance on her own part. "My dear," she said, "in this matter you must let me do what I know to be right. I should consider myself to be very selfish if I allowed my grief to interfere with your amusements."

"But, aunt, I don't care for such amusements."

"That's nonsense, my dear. You ought to care for them. How are you to settle yourself in life if you don't care for them?"

"My dear aunt, I am settled."

"Settled!" said Mrs. Greenow, astounded, as though there must have been some hidden marriage of which she had not heard. "But that's nonsense. Of course you're not settled; and how are you to be, if I allow you to shut yourself up in such a place as this,—just where a girl has a chance?"

It was in vain that Kate tried to stop her. It was not easy to stop Mrs. Greenow when she was supported by the full assurance of being mistress of the place and of the occasion. "No, my dear; I know very well what I owe to you, and I shall do my duty. As I said before, society can have no charms now for such a one as I am. All that social intercourse could ever do for me lies buried in my darling's grave. My heart is desolate, and must remain so. But I'm not going to immolate you on the altars of my grief. I shall force myself to go out for your sake, Kate."

"But, dear aunt, the world will think it so odd, just at present."

"I don't care twopence for the world. What can the world do to me? I'm not dependent on the world,—thanks to the care of that sainted lamb. I can hold my own; and as long as I can do that the world won't hurt me. No, Kate, if I think a thing's right I shall do it. I mean to make the place pleasant for you if I can, and the world may object if it likes."

Mrs. Greenow was probably right in her appreciation of the value of her independence. Remarks may perhaps have been made by the world of Yarmouth as to her early return to society. People, no doubt, did remind each other that old Greenow was hardly yet four months buried. Mrs. Jones and Jeannette probably had their little jokes down-stairs. But this did not hurt Mrs. Greenow. What was said, was not said in her hearing, Mrs. Jones's bills were paid every Saturday with admirable punctuality; and as long as this was done everybody about the house treated the lady with that deference which was due to the respectability of her possessions. When a recently bereaved widow attempts to enjoy her freedom without money, then it behoves the world to speak aloud;—and the world does its duty.

Numerous people came to call at Montpelier Parade, and Kate was astonished to find that her aunt had so many friends. She was indeed so bewildered by these strangers that she could hardly ascertain whom her aunt had really known before, and whom she now saw for the first time. Somebody had known somebody who had known somebody else, and that was allowed to be a sufficient introduction,—always presuming that the existing somebody was backed by some known advantages of money or position. Mrs. Greenow could smile from beneath her widow's cap in a most bewitching way. "Upon my word then she is really handsome," Kate wrote one day to Alice. But she could also frown, and knew well how to put aside, or, if need be, to reprobate any attempt at familiarity from those whose worldly circumstances were supposed to be disadvantageous.

"My dear aunt," said Kate one morning after their walk upon the pier, "how you did snub that Captain Bellfield!"

"Captain Bellfield, indeed! I don't believe he's a captain at all. At any rate he has sold out, and the tradesmen have had a scramble for the money. He was only a lieutenant when the 97th were in Manchester, and I'm sure he's never had a shilling to purchase since that."

"But everybody here seems to know him."

"Perhaps they do not know so much of him as I do. The idea of his having the impudence to tell me I was looking very well! Nothing can be so mean as men who go about in that way when they haven't money enough in their pockets to pay their washerwomen."

"But how do you know, aunt, that Captain Bellfield hasn't paid his washerwoman?"

"I know more than you think, my dear. It's my business. How could I tell whose attentions you should receive and whose you shouldn't, if I didn't inquire into these things?"

It was in vain that Kate rebelled, or attempted to rebel against this more than maternal care. She told her aunt that she was now nearly thirty, and that she had managed her own affairs, at any rate with safety, for the last ten years;—but it was to no purpose. Kate would get angry; but Mrs. Greenow never became angry. Kate would be quite in earnest; but Mrs. Greenow would push aside all that her niece said as though it were worth nothing. Kate was an unmarried woman with a very small fortune, and therefore, of course, was desirous of being married with as little delay as possible. It was natural that she should deny that it was so, especially at this early date in their mutual acquaintance. When the niece came to know her aunt more intimately, there might be confidence between them, and then they would do better. But Mrs. Greenow would spare neither herself nor her purse on Kate's behalf, and she would be a dragon of watchfulness in protecting her from the evil desires of such useless men as Captain Bellfield.

"I declare, Kate, I don't understand you," she said one morning to her niece as they sat together over a late breakfast. They had fallen into luxurious habits, and I am afraid it was past eleven o'clock, although the breakfast things were still on the table. Kate would usually bathe before breakfast, but Mrs. Greenow was never out of her room till half-past ten.

"I like the morning for contemplation," she once said. "When a woman has gone through all that I have suffered she has a great deal to think of." "And it is so much more comfortable to be a-thinking when one's in bed," said Jeannette, who was present at the time. "Child, hold your tongue," said the widow. "Yes, ma'am," said Jeannette. But we'll return to the scene at the breakfast-table.

"What don't you understand, aunt?"

"You only danced twice last night, and once you stood up with Captain Bellfield."

"On purpose to ask after that poor woman who washes his clothes without getting paid for it."

"Nonsense, Kate; you didn't ask him anything of the kind, I'm sure. It's very provoking. It is indeed."

"But what harm can Captain Bellfield do me?"

"What good can he do you? That's the question. You see, my dear, years will go by. I don't mean to say you ain't quite as young as ever you were, and nothing can be nicer and fresher than you are;—especially since you took to bathing."

"Oh, aunt, don't!"

"My dear, the truth must be spoken. I declare I don't think I ever saw a young woman so improvident as you are. When are you to begin to think about getting married if you don't do it now?"

"I shall never begin to think about it, till I buy my wedding clothes."

"That's nonsense,—sheer nonsense. How are you to get wedding clothes if you have never thought about getting a husband? Didn't I see Mr.. Cheesacre ask you for a dance last night?"

"Yes, he did; while you were talking to Captain Bellfield yourself, aunt."

"Captain Bellfield can't hurt me, my dear. And why didn't you dance with Mr. Cheesacre?"

"He's a fat Norfolk farmer, with not an idea beyond the virtues of stall-feeding."

"My dear, every acre of it is his own land,—every acre! And he bought another farm for thirteen thousand pounds only last autumn. They're better than the squires,—some of those gentlemen farmers; they are indeed. And of all men in the world they're the easiest managed."

"That's a recommendation, no doubt."

"Of course it is;—a great recommendation."

Mrs. Greenow had no idea of joking when her mind was intent on serious things. "He's to take us to the picnic to-morrow, and I do hope you'll manage to let him sit beside you. It'll be the place of honour, because he gives all the wine. He's picked up with that man Bellfield, and he's to be there; but if you allow your name to be once mixed up with his, it will be all over with you as far as Yarmouth is concerned."

"I don't at all want to be mixed up with Captain Bellfield, as you call it," said Kate. Then she subsided into her novel, while Mrs. Greenow busied herself about the good things for the picnic. In truth, the aunt did not understand the niece. Whatsoever might be the faults of Kate Vavasor, an unmaidenly desire of catching a husband for herself was certainly not one of them.

CHAPTER VIII
MR. CHEESACRE

Yarmouth is not a happy place for a picnic. A picnic should be held among green things. Green turf is absolutely an essential. There should be trees, broken ground, small paths, thickets, and hidden recesses. There should, if possible, be rocks, old timber, moss, and brambles. There should certainly be hills and dales,—on a small scale; and above all, there should be running water. There should be no expanse. Jones should not be able to see all Greene's movements, nor should Augusta always have her eye upon her sister Jane. But the spot chosen for Mr. Cheesacre's picnic at Yarmouth had none of the virtues above described. It was on the seashore. Nothing was visible from the site but sand and sea. There were no trees there and nothing green;—neither was there any running water. But there was a long, dry, flat strand; there was an old boat half turned over, under which it was proposed to dine; and in addition to this, benches, boards, and some amount of canvas for shelter were provided by the liberality of Mr. Cheesacre. Therefore it was called Mr. Cheesacre's picnic.

But it was to be a marine picnic, and therefore the essential attributes of other picnics were not required. The idea had come from some boating expeditions, in which mackerel had been caught, and during which food had been eaten, not altogether comfortably, in the boats. Then a thought had suggested itself to Captain Bellfield that they might land and eat their food, and his friend Mr. Cheesacre had promised his substantial aid. A lady had surmised that Ormesby sands would be the very place for dancing in the cool of the evening. They might "Dance on the sand," she said, "and yet no footing seen." And so the thing had progressed, and the picnic been inaugurated.

It was Mr. Cheesacre's picnic undoubtedly. Mr. Cheesacre was to supply the boats, the wine, the cigars, the music, and the carpenter's work necessary for the turning of the old boat into a banqueting saloon. But Mrs. Greenow had promised to provide the eatables, and enjoyed as much of the *éclat* as the master of the festival. She had known Mr. Cheesacre now for ten days and was quite intimate with him. He was a stout, florid man, of about forty-five, a bachelor, apparently much attached to ladies' society, bearing no sign of age except that he was rather bald, and that grey hairs had mixed themselves with his whiskers, very fond of his farming, and yet somewhat ashamed of it when he found himself in what he considered to be polite circles. And he was, moreover, a little inclined to seek the honour which comes from a well-filled and liberally-opened purse. He liked to give a man a dinner and then to boast of the dinner he had given. He was very proud when he could talk of having mounted, for a day's hunting, any man who might be supposed to be of higher rank than himself. "I had Grimsby with me the other day,—the son of old Grimsby of Hatherwick, you know. Blessed if he didn't stake my bay mare. But what matters? I mounted him again the next day just the same." Some people thought he was soft, for it was very well known throughout Norfolk that young Grimsby would take a mount wherever he could get it. In these days Mrs. Greenow had become intimate with Mr. Cheesacre, and had already learned that he was the undoubted owner of his own acres.

"It wouldn't do for me," she had said to him, "to be putting myself forward, as if I were giving a party myself, or anything of that sort;—would it now?"

"Well, perhaps not. But you might come with us."

"So I will, Mr. Cheesacre, for that dear girl's sake. I should never forgive myself if I debarred her from all the pleasures of youth, because of my sorrows. I need hardly say that at such a time as this nothing of that sort can give me any pleasure."

"I suppose not," said Mr. Cheesacre, with solemn look.

"Quite out of the question." And Mrs. Greenow wiped away her tears. "For though as regards age I might dance on the sands as merrily as the best of them—"

"That I'm sure you could, Mrs. Greenow."

"How's a woman to enjoy herself if her heart lies buried?"

"But it won't be so always, Mrs. Greenow."

Mrs. Greenow shook her head to show that she hardly knew how to answer such a question. Probably it would be so always;—but she did not wish to put a damper on the present occasion by making so sad a declaration. "But as I was saying," continued she—"if you and I do it between us won't that be the surest way of having it come off nicely?"

Mr. Cheesacre thought that it would be the best way.

"Exactly so;—I'll do the meat and pastry and fruit, and you shall do the boats and the wine."

"And the music," said Cheesacre, "and the expenses at the place." He did not choose that any part of his outlay should go unnoticed.

"I'll go halves in all that if you like," said Mrs. Greenow. But Mr.. Cheesacre had declined this. He did not begrudge the expense, but only wished that it should be recognised.

"And, Mr. Cheesacre," continued Mrs. Greenow. "I did mean to send the music; I did, indeed."

"I couldn't hear of it, Mrs. Greenow."

"But I mention it now, because I was thinking of getting Blowehard to come. That other man, Flutey, wouldn't do at all out in the open air."

"It shall be Blowehard," said Mr. Cheesacre; and it was Blowehard. Mrs. Greenow liked to have her own way in these little things, though her heart did lie buried.

On the morning of the picnic Mr. Cheesacre came down to Montpelier Parade with Captain Bellfield, whose linen on that occasion certainly gave no outward sign of any quarrel between him and his washerwoman. He was got up wonderfully, and was prepared at all points for the day's work. He had on a pseudo-sailor's jacket, very liberally ornamented with brass buttons, which displayed with great judgement the exquisite shapes of his pseudo-sailor's duck trousers. Beneath them there was a pair of very shiny patent-leather shoes, well adapted for dancing on the sand, presuming him to be anxious of doing so, as Venus offered to do, without leaving any footmarks. His waistcoat was of a delicate white fabric, ornamented with very many gilt buttons. He had bejewelled studs in his shirt, and yellow kid gloves on his hands; having, of course, another pair in his pocket for the necessities of the evening. His array was quite perfect, and had stricken dismay into the heart of his friend Cheesacre, when he joined that gentleman. He was a well-made man, nearly six feet high, with dark hair, dark whiskers, and dark moustache, nearly black, but of that suspicious hue which to the observant beholder seems always to tell a tale of the hairdresser's shop. He was handsome, too, with well-arranged features,—but carrying, perhaps, in his nose some first symptoms of the effects of midnight amusements. Upon the whole, however, he was a nice man to look at—for those who like to look on nice men of that kind.

Cheesacre, too, had adopted something of a sailor's garb. He had on a jacket of a rougher sort, coming down much lower than that of the captain, being much looser, and perhaps somewhat more like a garment which a possible seaman might possibly wear. But he was disgusted with himself the moment that he saw Bellfield. His heart had been faint, and he had not dared to ornament himself boldly as his friend had done. "I say, Guss, you are a swell," he exclaimed. It may be explained that Captain Bellfield had been christened Gustavus.

"I don't know much about that," said the captain; "my fellow sent me this toggery, and said that it was the sort of thing. I'll change with you if you like it." But Cheesacre could not have worn that jacket, and he walked on, hating himself.

It will be remembered that Mrs. Greenow had spoken with considerable severity of Captain Bellfield's pretensions when discussing his character with her niece; but, nevertheless, on the present occasion she received him with most gracious smiles. It may be that her estimate of his character had been altered, or that she was making sacrifice of her own feelings in consideration of Mr. Cheesacre, who was known to be the captain's intimate friend. But she had smiles for both of them. She had a wondrous power of smiling; and could, upon occasion, give signs of peculiar favour to half a dozen different gentlemen in as many minutes. They found her in the midst of hampers which were not yet wholly packed, while Mrs. Jones, Jeannette, and the cook of the household moved around her, on the outside of the circle, ministering to her wants. She had in her hand an outspread clean napkin, and she wore fastened round her dress a huge coarse apron, that she might thus be protected from some possible ebullition of gravy, or escape of salad mixture, or cream; but in other respects she was clothed in the fullest honours of widowhood. She had not mitigated her weeds by half an inch. She had scorned to make any compromise between the world of pleasure and the world of woe. There she was, a widow, declared by herself to be of four months' standing, with a buried heart, making ready a dainty banquet with skill and liberality. She was ready on the instant to sit down upon the baskets in which the grouse pie had been just carefully inhumed, and talked about her sainted lamb with a deluge of tears. If anybody didn't like it, that person—might do the other thing. Mr. Cheesacre and Captain Bellfield thought that they did like it.

"Oh, Mr. Cheesacre, if you haven't caught me before I've half done! Captain Bellfield, I hope you think my apron becoming."

"Everything that you wear, Mrs. Greenow, is always becoming."

"Don't talk in that way when you know—; but never mind—we will think of nothing sad to-day if we can help it. Will we, Mr.. Cheesacre?"

"Oh dear no; I should think not;—unless it should come on to rain."

"It won't rain—we won't think of such a thing. But, by the by, Captain Bellfield, I and my niece do mean to send out a few things, just in a bag you know, so that we may tidy ourselves up a little after the sea. I don't want it mentioned, because if it gets about among the other ladies, they'd think we wanted to make a dressing of it;—and there wouldn't be room for them all; would there?"

"No; there wouldn't," said Mr. Cheesacre, who had been out on the previous evening, inspecting, and perhaps limiting, the carpenters in their work.

"That's just it," said Mrs. Greenow. "But there won't be any harm, will there, Mr. Cheesacre, in Jeanette's going out with our things? She'll ride in the cart, you know, with the eatables. I know Jeannette's a friend of yours."

"We shall be delighted to have Jeanette," said Mr. Cheesacre.

"Thank ye, sir," said Jeannette, with a curtsey.

"Jeannette, don't you let Mr. Cheesacre turn your head; and mind you behave yourself and be useful. Well; let me see;—what else is there? Mrs. Jones, you might as well give me that ham now. Captain Bellfield, hand it over. Don't you put it into the basket, because you'd turn it the wrong side down. There now, if you haven't nearly made me upset the apricot pie." Then, in the transfer of the dishes between the captain and the widow, there occurred some little innocent by-play, which seemed to give offence to Mr. Cheesacre; so that that gentleman turned his back upon the hampers and took a step away towards the door.

Mrs. Greenow saw the thing at a glance, and immediately applied herself to cure the wound. "What do you think, Mr. Cheesacre," said she, "Kate wouldn't come down because she didn't choose that you should see her with an apron on over her frock!"

"I'm sure I don't know why Miss Vavasor should care about my seeing her."

"Nor I either. That's just what I said. Do step up into the drawing-room; you'll find her there, and you can make her answer for herself."

"She wouldn't come down for me," said Mr. Cheesacre. But he didn't stir. Perhaps he wasn't willing to leave his friend with the widow.

At length the last of the dishes was packed and Mrs. Greenow went up-stairs with the two gentlemen. There they found Kate and two or three other ladies who had promised to embark under the protection of Mrs. Greenow's wings. There were the two Miss Fairstairs, whom Mrs. Greenow had especially patronized, and who repaid that lady for her kindness by an amount of outspoken eulogy which startled Kate by its audacity.

"Your dear aunt!" Fanny Fairstairs had said on coming into the room. "I don't think I ever came across a woman with such genuine milk of human kindness!"

"Nor with so much true wit," said her sister Charlotte,—who had been called Charlie on the sands of Yarmouth for the last twelve years.

When the widow came into the room, they flew at her and devoured her with kisses, and swore that they had never seen her looking so well. But as the bright new gloves which both the girls wore had been presents from Mrs. Greenow, they certainly did owe her some affection. There are not many ladies who would venture to bestow such gifts upon their friends after so very short an acquaintance; but Mrs. Greenow had a power that was quite her own in such matters. She was already on a very confidential footing with the Miss Fairstairs, and had given them much useful advice as to their future prospects.

And then was there a Mrs. Green, whose husband was first-lieutenant on board a man-of-war on the West Indian Station. Mrs. Green was a quiet, ladylike little woman, rather pretty, very silent, and, as one would have thought, hardly adapted for the special intimacy of Mrs. Greenow. But Mrs. Greenow had found out that she was alone, not very rich, and in want of the solace of society. Therefore she had, from sheer good-nature, forced herself upon Mrs. Green, and Mrs. Green, with much trepidation, had consented to be taken to the picnic. "I know your husband would like it," Mrs. Greenow had said, "and I hope I may live to tell him that I made you go."

There came in also a brother of the Fairstairs girls, Joe Fairstairs, a lanky, useless, idle young man, younger than them, who was supposed to earn his bread in an attorney's office at Norwich, or rather to be preparing to earn it at some future time, and who was a heavy burden upon all his friends. "We told Joe to come to the house," said Fanny to the widow, apologetically, "because we thought he might be useful in carrying down the cloaks." Mrs. Greenow smiled graciously upon Joe, and assured him that she was charmed to see him, without any reference to such services as those mentioned.

And then they started. When they got to the door both Cheesacre and the captain made an attempt to get possession of the widow's arm. But she had it all arranged. Captain Bellfield found himself constrained to attend to Mrs. Green, while Mr. Cheesacre walked down to the beach beside Kate Vavasor. "I'll take your arm, Mr. Joe," said the widow, "and the girls shall come with us." But when they got to the boats, round which the other comers to the picnic were already assembled, Mr. Cheesacre,—although both the boats were for the day his own,—found himself separated from the widow. He got into that which contained Kate Vavasor, and was shoved off from the beach while he saw Captain Bellfield arranging Mrs. Greenow's drapery. He had declared to himself that it should be otherwise; and that as he had to pay the piper, the piper should play as he liked it. But Mrs. Greenow with a word or two had settled it all, and Mr. Cheesacre had found himself to be powerless. "How absurd Bellfield looks in that jacket, doesn't he?" he said to Kate, as he took his seat in the boat.

"Do you think so? I thought it was so very pretty and becoming for the occasion."

Mr. Cheesacre hated Captain Bellfield, and regretted more than ever that he had not done something for his own personal adornment. He could not endure to think that his friend, who paid for nothing, should carry away the honours of the morning and defraud him of the delights which should justly belong to him, "It may be becoming," said Cheesacre; "but don't you think it's awfully extravagant?"

"As to that I can't tell. You see I don't at all know what is the price of a jacket covered all over with little brass buttons."

"And the waistcoat, Miss Vavasor!" said Cheesacre, almost solemnly.

"The waistcoat I should think must have been expensive."

"Oh, dreadful! and he's got nothing, Miss Vavasor; literally nothing. Do you know,"—and he reduced his voice to a whisper as he made this communication,—"I lent him twenty pounds the day before yesterday; I did indeed. You won't mention it again, of course. I tell you, because, as you are seeing a good deal of him just now, I think it right that you should know on what sort of a footing he stands." It's all fair, they say, in love and war, and this small breach of confidence was, we must presume, a love stratagem on the part of Mr. Cheesacre. He was at this time smitten with the charms both of the widow and of the niece, and he constantly found that the captain was interfering with him on whichever side he turned himself. On the present occasion he had desired to take the widow for his share, and was, upon the whole, inclined to think that the widow was the more worthy of his attentions. He had made certain little inquiries within the last day or two, the answers to which had been satisfactory. These he had by no means communicated to his friend, to whom, indeed, he had expressed an opinion that Mrs. Greenow was after all only a flash in the pan. "She does very well pour passer le temps," the captain had answered. Mr. Cheesacre had not quite understood the exact gist of the captain's meaning, but had felt certain that his friend was playing him false.

"I don't want it to be mentioned again, Miss Vavasor," he continued.

"Such things should not be mentioned at all," Kate replied, having been angered at the insinuation that the nature of Captain Bellfield's footing could be a matter of any moment to her.

"No, they shouldn't; and therefore I know that I'm quite safe with you, Miss Vavasor. He's a very pleasant fellow, very; and has seen the world,— uncommon; but he's better for eating and drinking with than he is for buying and selling with, as we say in Norfolk. Do you like Norfolk, Miss Vavasor?"

"I never was in it before, and now I've only seen Yarmouth."

"A nice place, Yarmouth, very; but you should come up and see our lands. I suppose you don't know that we feed one-third of England during the winter months."

"Dear me!"

"We do, though; nobody knows what a county Norfolk is. Taking it altogether, including the game you know, and Lord Nelson, and its watering-places and the rest of it, I don't think there's a county in England to beat it. Fancy feeding one-third of all England and Wales!"

"With bread and cheese, do you mean, and those sort of things?"

"Beef!" said Mr. Cheesacre, and in his patriotic energy he repeated the word aloud. "Beef! Yes indeed; but if you were to tell them that in London they wouldn't believe you. Ah! you should certainly come down and see our lands. The 7.45 a.m. train would take you through Norwich to my door, as one may say, and you would be back by the 6.22 p.m." In this way he brought himself back again into good-humour, feeling, that in the absence of the widow, he could not do better than make progress with the niece.

In the mean time Mrs. Greenow and the captain were getting on very comfortably in the other boat. "Take an oar, Captain," one of the men had said to him as soon as he had placed the ladies. "Not to-day, Jack," he had answered. "I'll content myself with being bo'san this morning." "The best thing as the bo'san does is to pipe all hands to grog," said the man. "I won't be behind in that either," said the captain; and so they all went on swimmingly.

"What a fine generous fellow your friend, Mr. Cheesacre, is!" said the widow.

"Yes, he is; he's a capital fellow in his way. Some of these Norfolk farmers are no end of good fellows."

"And I suppose he's something more than a common farmer. He's visited by the people about where he lives, isn't he?"

"Oh, yes, in a sort of a way. The county people, you know, keep themselves very much to themselves."

"That's of course. But his house;—he has a good sort of place, hasn't he?"

"Yes, yes;—a very good house;—a little too near to the horse-pond for my taste. But when a man gets his money out of the till, he mustn't be ashamed of the counter;—must he, Mrs. Greenow?"

"But he could live like a gentleman if he let his own land, couldn't he?"

"That depends upon how a gentleman wishes to live." Here the privacy of their conversation was interrupted by an exclamation from a young lady to the effect that Charlie Fairstairs was becoming sick. This Charlie stoutly denied, and proved the truth of her assertion by her behaviour. Soon after this they completed their marine adventures, and prepared to land close to the spot at which the banquet was prepared.

CHAPTER IX
THE RIVALS

There had been a pretence of fishing, but no fish had been caught. It was soon found that such an amusement would interfere with the ladies' dresses, and the affairs had become too serious to allow of any trivial interruption. "I really think, Mr. Cheesacre," an anxious mother had said, "that you'd better give it up. The water off the nasty cord has got all over Maria's dress, already." Maria made a faint protest that it did not signify in the least; but the fishing was given up,—not without an inward feeling on the part of Mr. Cheesacre that if Maria chose to come out with him in his boat, having been invited especially to fish, she ought to have put up with the natural results. "There are people who like to take everything and never like to give anything," he said to Kate afterwards, as he was walking up with her to the picnic dinner. But he was unreasonable and unjust. The girls had graced his party with their best hats and freshest muslins, not that they might see him catch a mackerel, but that they might flirt and dance to the best advantage. "You can't suppose that any girl will like to be drenched with sea-water when she has taken so much trouble with her starch," said Kate. "Then she shouldn't come fishing," said Mr. Cheesacre. "I hate such airs."

But when they arrived at the old boat, Mrs. Greenow shone forth pre-eminently as the mistress of the occasion, altogether overshadowing Mr. Cheesacre by the extent of her authority. There was a little contest for supremacy between them, invisible to the eyes of the multitude; but Mr. Cheesacre in such a matter had not a chance against Mrs. Greenow. I am disposed to think that she would have reigned even though she had not contributed to the eatables; but with that point in her favour, she was able to make herself supreme. Jeannette, too, was her servant, which was a great thing. Mr. Cheesacre soon gave way; and though he bustled about and was conspicuous, he bustled about in obedience to orders received, and became a head servant. Captain Bellfield also made himself useful, but he drove Mr. Cheesacre into paroxysms of suppressed anger by giving directions, and by having those directions obeyed. A man to whom he had lent twenty pounds the day before yesterday, and who had not contributed so much as a bottle of champagne!

"We're to dine at four, and now it's half-past three," said Mrs. Greenow, addressing herself to the multitude.

"And to begin to dance at six," said an eager young lady.

"Maria, hold your tongue," said the young lady's mother.

"Yes, we'll dine at four," said Mr. Cheesacre. "And as for the music, I've ordered it to be here punctual at half-past five. We're to have three horns, cymbals, triangle, and a drum."

"How very nice; isn't it, Mrs. Greenow?" said Charlie Fairstairs.

"And now suppose we begin to unpack," said Captain Bellfield. "Half the fun is in arranging the things."

"Oh, dear, yes; more than half," said Fanny Fairstairs.

"Bellfield, don't mind about the hampers," said Cheesacre. "Wine is a ticklish thing to handle, and there's my man there to manage it."

"It's odd if I don't know more about wine than the boots from the hotel," said Bellfield. This allusion to the boots almost cowed Mr. Cheesacre, and made him turn away, leaving Bellfield with the widow.

There was a great unpacking, during which Captain Bellfield and Mrs. Greenow constantly had their heads in the same hamper. I by no means intend to insinuate that there was anything wrong in this. People engaged together in unpacking pies and cold chickens must have their heads in the same hamper. But a great intimacy was thereby produced, and the widow seemed to have laid aside altogether that prejudice of hers with reference to the washerwoman. There was a long table placed on the sand, sheltered by the upturned boat from the land side, but open towards the sea, and over this, supported on poles, there was an awning. Upon the whole the arrangement was not an uncomfortable one for people who had selected so very uncomfortable a dining-room as the sand of the sea-shore. Much was certainly due to Mr. Cheesacre for the expenditure he had incurred, — and something perhaps to Captain Bellfield for his ingenuity in having suggested it.

Now came the placing of the guests for dinner, and Mr. Cheesacre made another great effort. "I'll tell you what," he said, aloud, "Bellfield and I will take the two ends of the table, and Mrs. Greenow shall sit at my right hand." This was not only boldly done, but there was a propriety in it which at first sight seemed to be irresistible. Much as he had hated and did hate the captain, he had skilfully made the proposition in such a way as to flatter him, and it seemed for a few moments as though he were going to have it all his own way. But Captain Bellfield was not a man to submit to defeat in such a matter as this without an effort. "I don't think that will do," said he. "Mrs. Greenow gives the dinner, and Cheesacre gives the wine. We must have them at the two ends of the table. I am sure Mrs. Greenow won't refuse to allow me to hand her to the place which belongs to her. I will sit at her right hand and be her minister." Mrs. Greenow did not refuse,—and so the matter was adjusted.

Mr. Cheesacre took his seat in despair. It was nothing to him that he had Kate Vavasor at his left hand. He liked talking to Kate very well, but he could not enjoy that pleasure while Captain Bellfield was in the very act of making progress with the widow. "One would think that he had given it himself; wouldn't you?" he said to Maria's mother, who sat at his right hand.

The lady did not in the least understand him. "Given what?" said she.

"Why, the music and the wine and all the rest of it. There are some people full of that kind of impudence. How they manage to carry it on without ever paying a shilling, I never could tell. I know I have to pay my way, and something over and beyond generally."

Maria's mother said, "Yes, indeed." She had other daughters there besides Maria, and was looking down the table to see whether they were judiciously placed. Her beauty, her youngest one, Ophelia, was sitting next to that ne'er-do-well Joe Fairstairs, and this made her unhappy. "Ophelia, my dear, you are dreadfully in the draught; there's a seat up here, just opposite, where you'll be more comfortable."

"There's no draught here, mamma," said Ophelia, without the slightest sign of moving. Perhaps Ophelia liked the society of that lanky, idle, useless young man.

The mirth of the table certainly came from Mrs. Greenow's end. The widow had hardly taken her place before she got up again and changed with the captain. It was found that the captain could better carve the great grouse pie from the end than from the side. Cheesacre, when he saw this, absolutely threw down his knife and fork violently upon the table. "Is anything the matter?" said Maria's mother.

"Matter!" said he. Then he shook his head in grief of heart and vexation of spirit, and resumed his knife and fork. Kate watched it all, and was greatly amused. "I never saw a man so nearly broken-hearted," she said, in her letter to Alice the next day. "Eleven, thirteen, eighteen, twenty-one," said Cheesacre to himself, reckoning up in his misery the number of pounds sterling which he would have to pay for being ill-treated in this way.

"Ladies and gentlemen," said Captain Bellfield, as soon as the eating was over, "if I may be permitted to get upon my legs for two minutes, I am going to propose a toast to you." The real patron of the feast had actually not yet swallowed his last bit of cheese. The thing was indecent in the violence of its injustice.

Captain Bellfield proposes a toast.

"If you please, Captain Bellfield," said the patron, indifferent to the cheese in his throat, "I'll propose the toast."

"Nothing on earth could be better, my dear fellow," said the captain, "and I'm sure I should be the last man in the world to take the job out of the hands of one who would do it so much better than I can; but as it's your health that we're going to drink, I really don't see how you are to do it."

Cheesacre grunted and sat down. He certainly could not propose his own health, nor did he complain of the honour that was to be done him. It was very proper that his health should be drunk, and he had now to think of the words in which he would return thanks. But the extent of his horror may be imagined when Bellfield got up and made a most brilliant speech in praise of Mrs. Greenow. For full five minutes he went on without mentioning the name of Cheesacre. Yarmouth, he said, had never in his days been so blessed as it had been this year by the presence of the lady who was now with them.

She had come among them, he declared, forgetful of herself and of her great sorrows, with the sole desire of adding something to the happiness of others. Then Mrs. Greenow had taken out her pocket-handkerchief, sweeping back the broad ribbons of her cap over her shoulders. Altogether the scene was very affecting, and Cheesacre was driven to madness. They were the very words that he had intended to speak himself.

"I hate all this kind of thing," he said to Kate. "It's so fulsome."

"After-dinner speeches never mean anything," said Kate.

At last, when Bellfield had come to an end of praising Mrs. Greenow, he told the guests that he wished to join his friend Mr. Cheesacre in the toast, the more so as it could hardly be hoped that Mrs. Greenow would herself rise to return thanks. There was no better fellow than his friend Cheesacre, whom he had known for he would not say how many years. He was quite sure they would all have the most sincere pleasure in joining the health of Mr. Cheesacre with that of Mrs. Greenow. Then there was a clattering of glasses and a murmuring of healths, and Mr. Cheesacre slowly got upon his legs.

"I'm very much obliged to this company," said he, "and to my friend Bellfield, who really is,—but perhaps that doesn't signify now. I've had the greatest pleasure in getting up this little thing, and I'd made up my mind to propose Mrs. Greenow's health; but, h'm, ha, no doubt it has been in better hands. Perhaps, considering all things, Bellfield might have waited."

"With such a subject on my hands, I couldn't wait a moment."

"I didn't interrupt you, Captain Bellfield, and perhaps you'll let me go on without interrupting me. We've all drunk Mrs. Greenow's health, and I'm sure she's very much obliged. So am I for the honour you've done me. I have taken some trouble in getting up this little thing, and I hope you like it. I think somebody said something about liberality. I beg to assure you that I don't think of that for a moment. Somebody must pay for these sort of things, and I'm always very glad to take my turn. I dare say Bellfield will give us the next picnic, and if he'll appoint a day before the end of the month, I shall be happy to be one of the party." Then he sat down with some inward satisfaction, fully convinced that he had given his enemy a fatal blow.

"Nothing on earth would give me so much pleasure," said Bellfield. After that he turned again to Mrs. Greenow and went on with his private conversation.

There was no more speaking, nor was there much time for other after-dinner ceremonies. The three horns, the cymbals, the triangle, and the drum were soon heard tuning-up behind the banqueting-hall, and the ladies went to the further end of the old boat to make their preparations for the dance. Then it was that the thoughtful care of Mrs. Greenow, in having sent Jeannette with brushes, combs, clean handkerchiefs, and other little knick-knackeries, became so apparent. It was said that the widow herself actually changed her cap,—which was considered by some to be very unfair, as there had been an understanding that there should be no dressing. On such occasions ladies are generally willing to forego the advantage of dressing on the condition that other ladies shall forego the same advantage; but when this compact is broken by any special lady, the treason is thought to be very treacherous. It is as though a fencer should remove the button from the end of his foil. But Mrs. Greenow was so good-natured in tendering the services of Jeannette to all the young ladies, and was so willing to share with others those good things of the toilet which her care had provided, that her cap was forgiven her by the most of those present.

When ladies have made up their minds to dance they will dance let the circumstances of the moment be ever so antagonistic to that exercise. A ploughed field in February would not be too wet, nor the side of a house too uneven. In honest truth the sands of the seashore are not adapted for the exercise. It was all very well for Venus to make the promise, but when making it she knew that Adonis would not keep her to her word. Let any lightest-limbed nymph try it, and she will find that she leaves most palpable footing. The sands in question were doubtless compact, firm, and sufficiently moist to make walking on them comfortable; but they ruffled themselves most uncomfortably under the unwonted pressure to which they were subjected. Nevertheless our friends did dance on the sands; finding, however, that quadrilles and Sir Roger de Coverley suited them better than polkas and waltzes.

"No, my friend, no," Mrs. Greenow said to Mr. Cheesacre when that gentleman endeavoured to persuade her to stand up; "Kate will be delighted I am sure to join you,—but as for me, you must excuse me."

But Mr. Cheesacre was not inclined at that moment to ask Kate Vavasor to dance with him. He was possessed by an undefined idea that Kate had snubbed him, and as Kate's fortune was, as he said, literally nothing, he was not at all disposed to court her favour at the expense of such suffering to himself.

"I'm not quite sure that I'll dance myself," said he, seating himself in a corner of the tent by Mrs. Greenow's side. Captain Bellfield at that moment was seen leading Miss Vavasor away to a new place on the sands, whither he was followed by a score of dancers; and Mr. Cheesacre saw that now at last he might reap the reward for which he had laboured. He was alone with the widow, and having been made bold by wine, had an opportunity of fighting his battle, than which none better could ever be found. He was himself by no means a poor man, and he despised poverty in others. It was well that there should be poor gentry, in order that they might act as satellites to those who, like himself, had money. As to Mrs. Greenow's money, there was no doubt. He knew it all to a fraction. She had spread for herself, or some one else had spread for her, a report that her wealth was almost unlimited; but the forty thousand pounds was a fact, and any such innocent fault as that little fiction might well be forgiven to a woman endorsed with such substantial virtues. And she was handsome too. Mr. Cheesacre, as he regarded her matured charms, sometimes felt that he should have been smitten even without the forty thousand pounds. "By George! there's flesh and blood," he had once said to his friend Bellfield before he had begun to suspect that man's treachery. His admiration must then have been sincere, for at that time the forty thousand pounds was not an ascertained fact. Looking at the matter in all its bearings Mr. Cheesacre thought that he couldn't do better. His wooing should be fair, honest, and above board. He was a thriving man, and what might not they two do in Norfolk if they put their wealth together?

"Oh, Mr. Cheesacre, you should join them," said Mrs. Greenow; "they'll not half enjoy themselves without you. Kate will think that you mean to neglect her."

"I shan't dance, Mrs. Greenow, unless you like to stand up for a set."

"No, my friend, no; I shall not do that. I fear you forget how recent has been my bereavement. Your asking me is the bitterest reproach to me for having ventured to join your festive board."

"Upon my honour I didn't mean it, Mrs. Greenow. I didn't mean it, indeed."

"I do not suspect you. It would have been unmanly."

"And nobody can say that of me. There isn't a man or woman in Norfolk that wouldn't say I was manly."

"I'm quite sure of that."

"I have my faults, I'm aware."

"And what are your faults, Mr. Cheesacre?"

"Well; perhaps I'm extravagant. But it's only in these kind of things you know, when I spend a little money for the sake of making my friends happy. When I'm about, on the lands at home, I ain't extravagant, I can tell you."

"Extravagance is a great vice."

"Oh, I ain't extravagant in that sense;—not a bit in the world. But when a man's enamoured, and perhaps looking out for a wife, he does like to be a little free, you know."

"And are you looking out for a wife, Mr. Cheesacre?"

"If I told you I suppose you'd only laugh at me."

"No; indeed I would not. I am not given to joking when any one that I regard speaks to me seriously."

"Ain't you though? I'm so glad of that. When one has really got a serious thing to say, one doesn't like to have fun poked at one."

"And, besides, how could I laugh at marriages, seeing how happy I have been in that condition?—so—very—happy," and Mrs. Greenow put up her handkerchief to her eyes.

"So happy that you'll try it again some day; won't you?"

"Never, Mr. Cheesacre; never. Is that the way you talk of serious things without joking? Anything like love—love of that sort—is over for me. It lies buried under the sod with my poor dear departed saint."

"But, Mrs. Greenow,"—and Cheesacre, as he prepared to argue the question with her, got nearer to her in the corner behind the table,—"But, Mrs. Greenow, care killed a cat, you know."

"And sometimes I think that care will kill me."

"No, by George; not if I can prevent it."

"You're very kind, Mr. Cheesacre; but there's no preventing such care as mine."

"Isn't there though? I'll tell you what, Mrs. Greenow; I'm in earnest, I am indeed. If you'll inquire, you'll find there isn't a fellow in Norfolk pays his way better than I do, or is better able to do it. I don't pay a sixpence of rent, and I sit upon seven hundred acres of as good land as there is in the county. There's not an acre that won't do me a bullock and a half. Just put that and that together, and see what it comes to. And, mind you, some of these fellows that farm their own land are worse off than if they'd rent to pay. They've borrowed so much to carry on with, that the interest is more than rent. I don't owe a sixpence to ere a man or ere a company in the world. I can walk into every bank in Norwich without seeing my master. There ain't any of my paper flying about, Mrs. Greenow. I'm Samuel Cheesacre of Oileymead, and it's all my own." Mr. Cheesacre, as he thus spoke of his good fortunes and firm standing in the world, became impetuous in the energy of the moment, and brought down his fist powerfully on the slight table before them. The whole fabric rattled, and the boat resounded, but the noise he had made seemed to assist him. "It's all my own, Mrs. Greenow, and the half of it shall be yours if you'll please to take it;" then he stretched out his hand to her, not as though he intended to grasp hers in a grasp of love, but as if he expected some hand-pledge from her as a token that she accepted the bargain.

"If you'd known Greenow, Mr. Cheesacre—"

"I've no doubt he was a very good sort of man."

"If you'd known him, you would not have addressed me in this way."

"What difference would that make? My idea is that care killed a cat, as I said before. I never knew what was the good of being unhappy. If I find early mangels don't do on a bit of land, then I sow late turnips; and never cry after spilt milk. Greenow was the early mangels; I'll be the late turnips. Come then, say the word. There ain't a bedroom in my house,—not one of the front ones,—that isn't mahogany furnished!"

"What's furniture to me?" said Mrs. Greenow, with her handkerchief to her eyes.

Just at this moment Maria's mother stepped in under the canvas. It was most inopportune. Mr. Cheesacre felt that he was progressing well, and was conscious that he had got safely over those fences in the race which his bashfulness would naturally make difficult to him. He knew that he had done this under the influence of the champagne, and was aware that it might not be easy to procure again a combination of circumstances that would be so beneficial to him. But now he was interrupted just as he was expecting success. He was interrupted, and felt himself to be looking like a guilty creature under the eye of the strange lady. He had not a word to say; but drawing himself suddenly a foot and half away from the widow's side, sat there confessing his guilt in his face.

Mrs. Greenow felt no guilt, and was afraid of no strange eyes. "Mr. Cheesacre and I are talking about farming," she said.

"Oh; farming!" answered Maria's mother.

"Mr. Cheesacre thinks that turnips are better than early mangels," said Mrs. Greenow.

"Yes, I do," said Cheesacre,

"I prefer the early mangels," said Mrs. Greenow. "I don't think nature ever intended those late crops. What do you say, Mrs. Walker?"

"I daresay Mr. Cheesacre understands what he's about when he's at home," said the lady.

"I know what a bit of land can do as well as any man in Norfolk," said the gentleman.

"It may be very well in Norfolk," said Mrs. Greenow, rising from her seat; "but the practice isn't thought much of in the other counties with which I am better acquainted."

"I'd just come in to say that I thought we might be getting to the boats," said Mrs. Walker. "My Ophelia is so delicate." At this moment the delicate Ophelia was to be seen, under the influence of the music, taking a distant range upon the sands with Joe Fairstairs' arm round her waist. The attitude was justified by the tune that was in progress, and there is no reason why a galop on the sands should have any special termination in distance, as it must have in a room. But, under such circumstances, Mrs. Walker's solicitude was not unreasonable.

The erratic steps of the distant dancers were recalled and preparations were made for the return journey. Others had strayed besides the delicate Ophelia and the idle Joe, and some little time was taken up in collecting the party. The boats had to be drawn down, and the boatmen fetched from their cans and tobacco-pipes. "I hope they're sober," said Mrs. Walker, with a look of great dismay.

"Sober as judges," said Bellfield, who had himself been looking after the remains of Mr. Cheesacre's hampers, while that gentleman had been so much better engaged in the tent.

"Because," continued Mrs. Walker, "I know that they play all manner of tricks when they're—in liquor. They'd think nothing of taking us out to sea, Mrs. Greenow."

"Oh, I do wish they would," said Ophelia.

"Ophelia, mind you come in the boat with me," said her mother, and she looked very savage when she gave the order. It was Mrs. Walker's intention that that boat should not carry Joe Fairstairs. But Joe and her daughter together were too clever for her. When the boats went off she found herself to be in that one over which Mr. Cheesacre presided, while the sinning

Ophelia with her good-for-nothing admirer were under the more mirthful protection of Captain Bellfield.

"Mamma will be so angry," said Ophelia, "and it was all your fault. I did mean to go into the other boat. Don't, Mr. Fairstairs." Then they got settled down in their seats, to the satisfaction, let us hope, of them both.

Mr. Cheesacre had vainly endeavoured to arrange that Mrs. Greenow should return with him. But not only was Captain Bellfield opposed to such a change in their positions, but so also was Mrs. Greenow. "I think we'd better go back as we came," she said, giving her hand to the Captain.

"Oh, certainly," said Captain Bellfield. "Why should there be any change? Cheesacre, old fellow, mind you look after Mrs. Walker. Come along, my hearty." It really almost appeared that Captain Bellfield was addressing Mrs. Greenow as "his hearty," but it must be presumed that the term of genial endearment was intended for the whole boat's load. Mrs. Greenow took her place on the comfortable broad bench in the stern, and Bellfield seated himself beside her, with the tiller in his hand.

"If you're going to steer, Captain Bellfield, I beg that you'll be careful."

"Careful,—and with you on board!" said the Captain. "Don't you know that I would sooner perish beneath the waves than that a drop of water should touch you roughly?"

"But you see, we might perish beneath the waves together."

"Together! What a sweet word that is;—perish together! If it were not that there might be something better even than that, I would wish to perish in such company."

"But I should not wish anything of the kind, Captain Bellfield, and therefore pray be careful."

There was no perishing by water on that occasion. Mr. Cheesacre's boat reached the pier at Yarmouth first, and gave up its load without accident. Very shortly afterwards Captain Bellfield's crew reached the same place in the same state of preservation. "There," said he, as he handed out Mrs. Greenow. "I have brought you to no harm, at any rate as yet."

"And, as I hope, will not do so hereafter."

"May the heavens forbid it, Mrs. Greenow! Whatever may be our lots hereafter,—yours I mean and mine,—I trust that yours may be free from all disaster. Oh, that I might venture to hope that, at some future day, the privilege might be mine of protecting you from all danger!"

"I can protect myself very well, I can assure you. Good night, Captain Bellfield. We won't take you and Mr. Cheesacre out of your way;—will we, Kate? We have had a most pleasant day."

They were now upon the esplanade, and Mrs. Greenow's house was to the right, whereas the lodgings of both the gentlemen were to the left. Each of them fought hard for the privilege of accompanying the widow to her door; but Mrs. Greenow was self-willed, and upon this occasion would have neither of them. "Mr. Joe Fairstairs must pass the house," said she, "and he will see us home. Mr. Cheesacre, good night. Indeed you shall not;—not a step." There was that in her voice which induced Mr. Cheesacre to obey her, and which made Captain Bellfield aware that he would only injure his cause if he endeavoured to make further progress in it on the present occasion.

"Well, Kate, what do you think of the day?" the aunt said when she was alone with her niece.

"I never think much about such days, aunt. It was all very well, but I fear I have not the temperament fitted for enjoying the fun. I envied Ophelia Walker because she made herself thoroughly happy."

"I do like to see girls enjoy themselves," said Mrs. Greenow, "I do, indeed;—and young men too. It seems so natural; why shouldn't young people flirt?"

"Or old people either for the matter of that?"

"Or old people either,—if they don't do any harm to anybody. I'll tell you what it is, Kate; people have become so very virtuous, that they're driven into all manner of abominable resources for amusement and occupation. If I had sons and daughters I should think a little flirting the very best thing for them as a safety valve. When people get to be old, there's a difficulty. They want to flirt with the young people and the young people don't want them. If the old people would be content to flirt together, I don't see why they should ever give it up;—till they're obliged to give up every thing, and go away."

That was Mrs. Greenow's doctrine on the subject of flirtation.

CHAPTER X
NETHERCOATS

We will leave Mrs. Greenow with her niece and two sisters at Yarmouth, and returning by stages to London, will call upon Mr. Grey at his place in Cambridgeshire as we pass by. I believe it is conceded by all the other counties, that Cambridgeshire possesses fewer rural beauties than any other county in England. It is very flat; it is not well timbered; the rivers are merely dikes; and in a very large portion of the county the farms and fields are divided simply by ditches—not by hedgerows. Such arrangements are, no doubt, well adapted for agricultural purposes, but are not conducive to rural beauty. Mr. Grey's residence was situated in a part of Cambridgeshire in which the above-named characteristics are very much marked. It was in the Isle of Ely, some few miles distant from the Cathedral town, on the side of a long straight road, which ran through the fields for miles without even a bush to cheer it. The name of his place was Nethercoats, and here he lived generally throughout the year, and here he intended to live throughout his life.

His father had held a prebendal stall at Ely in times when prebendal stalls were worth more than they are at present, and having also been possessed of a living in the neighbourhood, had amassed a considerable sum of money. With this he had during his life purchased the property of Nethercoats, and had built on it the house in which his son now lived. He had married late in life, and had lost his wife soon after the birth of an only child. The house had been built in his own parish, and his wife had lived there for a few months and had died there. But after that event the old clergyman had gone back to his residence in the Close at Ely, and there John Grey had had the home of his youth. He had been brought up under his father's eye, having been sent to no public school. But he had gone to Cambridge, had taken college honours, and had then, his father dying exactly at this time, declined to accept a fellowship. His father had left to him an income of some fifteen hundred a year, and with this he sat himself down, near to his college friends, near also to the old cathedral which he loved, in the house which his father had built.

But though Nethercoats possessed no beauty of scenery, though the country around it was in truth as uninteresting as any country could be, it had many delights of its own. The house itself was as excellent a residence for a country gentleman of small means as taste and skill together could construct. I doubt whether prettier rooms were ever seen than the drawing-room, the library, and the dining-room at Nethercoats. They were all on the ground-floor, and all opened out on to the garden and lawn. The library, which was the largest of the three, was a handsome chamber, and so filled as to make it well known in the University as one of the best private collections in that part of England. But perhaps the gardens of Nethercoats constituted its greatest glory. They were spacious and excellently kept up, and had been originally laid out with that knowledge of gardening without which no garden, merely as a garden, can be effective. And such, of necessity, was the garden of Nethercoats. Fine single forest trees there were none there, nor was it possible that there should have been any such. Nor could there be a clear rippling stream with steep green banks, and broken rocks lying about its bed. Such beauties are beauties of landscape, and do not of their nature belong to a garden. But the shrubs of Nethercoats were of the rarest kind, and had been long enough in their present places to have reached the period of their beauty. Nothing had been spared that a garden could want. The fruit-trees were perfect in their kind, and the glass-houses were so good and so extensive that John Grey in his prudence was some times tempted to think that he had too much of them.

It must be understood that there were no grounds, according to the meaning usually given to that word, belonging to the house at Nethercoats. Between the garden and the public road there was a paddock belonging to the house, along the side of which, but divided from it by a hedge and shrubbery, ran the private carriageway up to the house. This swept through the small front flower-garden, dividing it equally; but the lawns and indeed the whole of that which made the beauty of the place lay on the back of the house, on which side opened the windows from the three sitting-rooms. Down on the public road there stood a lodge at which lived one of the gardeners. There was another field of some six or seven acres, to which there was a gate from the corner of the front paddock, and which went round two sides of the garden. This was Nethercoats, and the whole estate covered about twelve acres.

It was not a place for much bachelor enjoyment of that sort generally popular with bachelors; nevertheless Mr. Grey had been constant in his residence there for the seven years which had now elapsed since he had left his college. His easy access to Cambridge had probably done much to mitigate what might otherwise have been the too great tedium of his life; and he had, prompted thereto by early associations, found most of his society in the Close of Ely Cathedral. But, with all the delight he could derive from these two sources, there had still been many solitary hours in his life, and he had gradually learned to feel that he of all men wanted a companion in his home.

His visits to London had generally been short and far between, occasioned probably by some need in the library, or by the necessity of some slight literary transaction with the editor or publisher of a periodical. In one of these visits he had met Alice Vavasor, and had remained in Town,—I will not say till Alice had promised to share his home in Cambridgeshire, but so long that he had resolved before he went that he would ask her to do so. He had asked her, and we know that he had been successful. He had obtained her promise, and from that moment all his life had been changed for him. Hitherto at Nethercoats his little smoking-room, his books, and his plants had been everything to him. Now he began to surround himself with an infinity of feminine belongings, and to promise himself an infinity of feminine blessings, wondering much that he should have been content to pass so long a portion of his life in the dull seclusion which he had endured. He was not by nature an impatient man; but now he became impatient, longing for the fruition of his new idea of happiness,—longing to have that as his own which he certainly loved beyond all else in the world, and which, perhaps, was all he had ever loved with the perfect love of equality. But though impatient, and fully aware of his own impatience, he acknowledged to himself that Alice could not be expected to share it. He could plan nothing now,—could have no pleasure in life that she was not expected to share. But as yet it could not be so with her. She had her house in London, her town society, and her father. And, inasmuch as the change for her would be much greater than it would be for him, it was natural that she should require some small delay. He had not pressed her. At least he had not pressed her with that eager pressure which a girl must resist with something of the opposition of a contest, if she resist it at all. But in truth his impatience was now waxing strong, and during the absence in Switzerland of which we have spoken, he resolved that a marriage very late in the autumn,—that a marriage even in winter, would be better than a marriage postponed till the following year. It was not yet late in August when the party returned from their tour. Would not a further delay of two months suffice for his bride?

Alice had written to him occasionally from Switzerland, and her first two letters had been very charming. They had referred almost exclusively to the tour, and had been made pleasant with some slightly coloured account of George Vavasor's idleness, and of Kate's obedience to her brother's behests. Alice had never written much of love in her love-letters, and Grey was well enough contented with her style, though it was not impassioned. As for doubting her love, it was not in the heart of the man to do so after it had been once assured to him by her word. He could not so slightly respect himself or her as to leave room for such a doubt in his bosom. He was a man who could never have suggested to himself that a woman loved him till the fact was there before him; but who having ascertained, as he might think, the fact, could never suggest to himself that her love would fail him. Her first two letters from Switzerland had been very pleasant; but after that there had seemed to have crept over her a melancholy which she unconsciously transferred to her words, and which he could not but taste in them,—at first unconsciously, also, but soon with so plain a flavour that he recognised it, and made it a matter of mental inquiry. During the three or four last days of the journey, while they were at Basle and on their way home, she had not written. But she did write on the day after her arrival, having then received from Mr. Grey a letter, in which he told her how very much she would add to his happiness if she would now agree that their marriage should not be postponed beyond the end of October. This letter she found in her room on her return, and this she answered at once. And she answered it in such words that Mr. Grey resolved that he would at once go to her in London. I will give her letter at length, as I shall then be best able to proceed with my story quickly.

Queen Anne Street,
— August, 186—.

Dearest John,—
We reached home yesterday tired enough, as we came through from Paris without stopping. I may indeed say that we came through from Strasbourg, as we only slept in Paris. I don't like Strasbourg. A steeple, after all, is not everything, and putting the steeple aside, I don't think the style is good. But the hotel was uncomfortable, which goes for so much;—and then we were saturated with beauty of a better kind.

I got your letter directly I came in last night, and I suppose I had better dash at it at once. I would so willingly delay doing so, saying nice little things the while, did I not know that this would be mere cowardice. Whatever happens I won't be a coward, and therefore I will tell you at once that I cannot let you hope that we should be married this year. Of course you will ask me why, as you have a right to do, and of course I am bound to answer. I do not know that I can give any answer with which you will not have a right to complain. If it be so, I can only ask your pardon for the injury I am doing you.

Marriage is a great change in life,—much greater to me than to you, who will remain in your old house, will keep your old pursuits, will still be your own master, and will change in nothing,—except in this, that you will have a companion who probably may not be all that you expect. But I must change everything. It will be to me as though I were passing through a grave to a new world. I shall see nothing that I have been accustomed to see, and must abandon all the ways of life that I have hitherto adopted. Of course I should have thought of this before I accepted you; and I did think of it. I made up my mind that, as I truly loved you, I would risk the change;—that I would risk it for your sake and for mine, hoping that I might add something to your happiness, and that I might secure my own. Dear John, do not suppose that I despair that it may be so; but, indeed, you must not hurry me. I must tune myself to the change that I have to make. What if I should wake some morning after six months living with you, and tell you that the quiet of your home was making me mad?

You must not ask me again till the winter shall have passed away. If in the meantime I shall find that I have been wrong, I will humbly confess that I have wronged you, and ask you to forgive me. And I will freely admit this. If the delay which I now purpose is so contrary to your own plans as to make your marriage, under such circumstances, not that which you had expected, I know that you are free to tell me so, and to say that our engagement shall be over. I am well aware that I can have no right to bind you to a marriage at one period which you had only contemplated as to take place at another period. I think I may promise that I will obey any wish you may express in anything,— except in that one thing which you urged in your last letter.

Kate is going down to Yarmouth with Mrs. Greenow, and I shall see no more of her probably till next year, as she will be due in Westmoreland after that. George left me at the door when he brought me home, and declared that he intended to vanish out of London. Whether in town or out, he is never to be seen at this period of the year. Papa offers to go to Ramsgate for a fortnight, but he looks so wretched when he makes the offer, that I shall not have the heart to hold him to it. Lady Macleod very much wants me to go to

Cheltenham. I very much want not to go, simply because I can never agree with her about anything; but it will probably end in my going there for a week or two. Over and beyond that, I have no prospects before Christmas which are not purely domestic. There is a project that we shall all eat our Christmas dinner at Vavasor Hall,—of course not including George,—but this project is quite in the clouds, and, as far as I am concerned, will remain there.

Dear John, let me hear that this letter does not make you unhappy.

Most affectionately yours,
Alice Vavasor.

At Nethercoats, the post was brought in at breakfast-time, and Mr. Grey was sitting with his tea and eggs before him, when he read Alice's letter. He read it twice before he began to think what he would do in regard to it, and then referred to one or two others which he had received from Switzerland,—reading them also very carefully. After that, he took up the slouch hat which he had been wearing in the garden before he was called to his breakfast, and, with the letters in his hand, sauntered down among the shrubs and lawns.

He knew, he thought he knew, that there was more in Alice's mind than a mere wish for delay. There was more in it than that hesitation to take at once a step which she really desired to take, if not now, then after some short interval. He felt that she was unhappy, and unhappy because she distrusted the results of her marriage; but it never for a moment occurred to him that, therefore, the engagement between them should be broken. In the first place he loved her too well to allow of his admitting such an idea without terrible sorrow to himself. He was a constant, firm man, somewhat reserved, and unwilling to make new acquaintances, and, therefore, specially unwilling to break away from those which he had made. Undoubtedly, had he satisfied himself that Alice's happiness demanded such a sacrifice of himself, he would have made it, and made it without a word of complaint. The blow would not have prostrated him, but the bruise would have remained on his heart, indelible, not to be healed but by death. He would have submitted, and no man would have seen that he had been injured. But it did not once occur to him that such a proceeding on his part would be beneficial to Alice. Without being aware of it, he reckoned himself to be the nobler creature of the two, and now thought of her as of one wounded, and wanting a cure. Some weakness had fallen on her, and strength must be given to her from another. He did not in the least doubt her love, but he knew that she had been associated, for a few weeks past, with two persons whose daily conversation would be prone to weaken the tone of her mind. He no more thought of giving her up than a man thinks of having his leg cut off because he has sprained his sinews. He would go up to town and see her, and would not even yet abandon all hope that she might be found sitting at his board when Christmas should come. By that day's post he wrote a short note to her.

"Dearest Alice," he said, "I have resolved to go to London at once. I will be with you in the evening at eight, the day after to-morrow."

"Yours, J. G."

There was no more in the letter than that.

"And now," she said, when she received it, "I must dare to tell him the whole truth."

CHAPTER XI
JOHN GREY GOES TO LONDON

And what was the whole truth? Alice Vavasor, when she declared to herself that she must tell her lover the whole truth, was expressing to herself her intention of putting an end to her engagement with Mr. Grey. She was acknowledging that that which had to be told was not compatible with the love and perfect faith which she owed to the man who was her affianced husband. And yet, why should it be so? She did not intend to tell him that she had been false in her love to him. It was not that her heart had again veered itself round and given itself to that wild cousin of hers. Though she might feel herself constrained to part from John Grey, George Vavasor could never be her husband. Of that she assured herself fifty times during the two days' grace which had been allowed her. Nay, she went farther than that with herself, and pronounced a verdict against any marriage as possible to her if she now decided against this marriage which had for some months past been regarded as fixed by herself and all her friends.

People often say that marriage is an important thing, and should be much thought of in advance, and marrying people are cautioned that there are many who marry in haste and repent at leisure. I am not sure, however, that marriage may not be pondered over too much; nor do I feel certain that the leisurely repentance does not as often follow the leisurely marriages as it does the rapid ones. That some repent no one can doubt; but I am inclined to believe that most men and women take their lots as they find them, marrying as the birds do by force of nature, and going on with their mates with a general, though not perhaps an undisturbed satisfaction, feeling inwardly assured that Providence, if it have not done the very best for them, has done for them as well as they could do for themselves with all the thought in the world. I do not know that a woman can assure to herself, by her own prudence and taste, a good husband any more than she can add two cubits to her stature; but husbands have been made to be decently good, —and wives too, for the most part, in our country, —so that the thing does not require quite so much thinking as some people say.

That Alice Vavasor had thought too much about it, I feel quite sure. She had gone on thinking of it till she had filled herself with a cloud of doubts which even the sunshine of love was unable to drive from her heavens. That a girl should really love the man she intends to marry,—that, at any rate, may be admitted. But love generally comes easily enough. With all her doubts Alice never doubted her love for Mr. Grey. Nor did she doubt his character, nor his temper, nor his means. But she had gone on thinking of the matter till her mind had become filled with some undefined idea of the importance to her of her own life. What should a woman do with her life? There had arisen round her a flock of learned ladies asking that question, to whom it seems that the proper answer has never yet occurred. Fall in love, marry the man, have two children, and live happy ever afterwards. I maintain that answer has as much wisdom in it as any other that can be given;—or perhaps more. The advice contained in it cannot, perhaps, always be followed to the letter; but neither can the advice of the other kind, which is given by the flock of learned ladies who ask the question.

A woman's life is important to her,—as is that of a man to him,—not chiefly in regard to that which she shall do with it. The chief thing for her to look to is the manner in which that something shall be done. It is of moment to a young man when entering life to decide whether he shall make hats or shoes; but not of half the moment that will be that other decision, whether he shall make good shoes or bad. And so with a woman;—if she shall have recognised the necessity of truth and honesty for the purposes of her life, I do not know that she need ask herself many questions as to what she will do with it.

Alice Vavasor was ever asking herself that question, and had by degrees filled herself with a vague idea that there was a something to be done; a something over and beyond, or perhaps altogether beside that marrying and having two children;—if she only knew what it was. She had filled herself, or had been filled by her cousins, with an undefined ambition that made her restless without giving her any real food for her mind. When she told herself that she would have no scope for action in that life in Cambridgeshire which Mr. Grey was preparing for her, she did not herself know what she meant by action. Had any one accused her of being afraid to separate herself from London society, she would have declared that she went very little into society and disliked that little. Had it been whispered to her that she loved the neighbourhood of the shops, she would have scorned the whisperer. Had it been suggested that the continued rattle of the big city was necessary to her happiness, she would have declared that she and her father had picked out for their residence the quietest street in London because she could not bear noise;—and yet she told herself that she feared to be taken into the desolate calmness of Cambridgeshire.

When she did contrive to find any answer to that question as to what she should do with her life, — or rather what she would wish to do with it if she were a free agent, it was generally of a political nature. She was not so far advanced as to think that women should be lawyers and doctors, or to wish that she might have the privilege of the franchise for herself; but she had undoubtedly a hankering after some second-hand political manœuvering. She would have liked, I think, to have been the wife of the leader of a Radical opposition, in the time when such men were put into prison, and to have kept up for him his seditious correspondence while he lay in the Tower. She would have carried the answers to him inside her stays, — and have made long journeys down into northern parts without any money, if the cause required it. She would have liked to have around her ardent spirits, male or female, who would have talked of "the cause," and have kept alive in her some flame of political fire. As it was, she had no cause. Her father's political views were very mild. Lady Macleod's were deadly conservative. Kate Vavasor was an aspiring Radical just now, because her brother was in the same line; but during the year of the love-passages between George and Alice, George Vavasor's politics had been as conservative as you please. He did not become a Radical till he had quarrelled with his grandfather. Now, indeed, he was possessed of very advanced views, — views with which Alice felt that she could sympathize. But what would be the use of sympathizing down in Cambridgeshire? John Grey had, so to speak, no politics. He had decided views as to the treatment which the Roman Senate received from Augustus, and had even discussed with Alice the conduct of the Girondists at the time of Robespierre's triumph; but for Manchester and its cares he had no apparent solicitude, and had declared to Alice that he would not accept a seat in the British House of Commons if it were offered to him free of expense. What political enthusiasm could she indulge with such a companion down in Cambridgeshire?

She thought too much of all this, — and was, if I may say, over-prudent in calculating the chances of her happiness and of his. For, to give her credit for what was her due, she was quite as anxious on the latter head as on the former. "I don't care for the Roman Senate," she would say to herself. "I don't care much for the Girondists. How am I to talk to him day after day, night after night, when we shall be alone together?"

No doubt her tour in Switzerland with her cousin had had some effect in making such thoughts stronger now than they had ever been. She had not again learned to love her cousin. She was as firmly sure as ever that she could never love him more. He had insulted her love; and though she had forgiven him and again enrolled him among her dearest friends, she could never again feel for him that passion which a woman means when she acknowledges that she is in love. That, as regarded her and George Vavasor, was over. But, nevertheless, there had been a something of romance during those days in Switzerland which she feared she would regret when she found herself settled at Nethercoats. She envied Kate. Kate could, as his sister, attach herself on to George's political career, and obtain from it all that excitement of life which Alice desired for herself. Alice could not love her cousin and marry him; but she felt that if she could do so without impropriety she would like to stick close to him like another sister, to spend her money in aiding his career in Parliament as Kate would do, and trust herself and her career into the boat which he was to command. She did not love her cousin; but she still believed in him,—with a faith which he certainly did not deserve.

As the two days passed over her, her mind grew more and more fixed as to its purpose. She would tell Mr. Grey that she was not fit to be his wife— and she would beg him to pardon her and to leave her. It never occurred to her that perhaps he might refuse to let her go. She felt quite sure that she would be free as soon as she had spoken the word which she intended to speak. If she could speak it with decision she would be free, and to attain that decision she would school herself with her utmost strength. At one moment she thought of telling all to her father and of begging him to break the matter to Mr. Grey; but she knew that her father would not understand her, and that he would be very hostile to her,—saying hard, uncomfortable words, which would probably be spared if the thing were done before he was informed. Nor would she write to Kate, whose letters to her at this time were full of wit at the expense of Mrs. Greenow. She would tell Kate as soon as the thing was done, but not before. That Kate would sympathize with her, she was quite certain.

So the two days passed by and the time came at which John Grey was to be there. As the minute hand on the drawing-room clock came round to the full hour, she felt that her heart was beating with a violence which she could not repress. The thing seemed to her to assume bigger dimensions than it had hitherto done. She began to be aware that she was about to be guilty of a great iniquity, when it was too late for her to change her mind. She could not bring herself to resolve that she would, on the moment, change her mind. She believed that she could never pardon herself such weakness. But yet she felt herself to be aware that her purpose was wicked. When the knock at the door was at last heard she trembled and feared that she would almost be unable to speak to him. Might it be possible that there should yet be a reprieve for her? No; it was his step on the stairs, and there he was in the room with her.

"My dearest," he said, coming to her. His smile was sweet and loving as it ever was, and his voice had its usual manly, genial, loving tone. As he walked across the room Alice felt that he was a man of whom a wife might be very proud. He was tall and very handsome, with brown hair, with bright blue eyes, and a mouth like a god. It was the beauty of his mouth, — beauty which comprised firmness within itself, that made Alice afraid of him. He was still dressed in his morning clothes; but he was a man who always seemed to be well dressed. "My dearest," he said, advancing across the room, and before she knew how to stop herself or him, he had taken her in his arms and kissed her.

He did not immediately begin about the letter, but placed her upon the sofa, seating himself by her side, and looked into her face with loving eyes, — not as though to scrutinize what might be amiss there, but as though determined to enjoy to the full his privilege as a lover. There was no reproach at any rate in his countenance; — none as yet; nor did it seem that he thought that he had any cause for fear. They sat in this way for a moment or two in silence, and during those moments Alice was summoning up her courage to speak. The palpitation at her heart was already gone, and she was determined that she would speak.

"Though I am very glad to see you," she said, at last, "I am sorry that my letter should have given you the trouble of this journey "

"Trouble!" he said. "Nay, you ought to know that it is no trouble. I have not enough to do down at Nethercoats to make the running up to you at any time an unpleasant excitement. So your Swiss journey went off pleasantly?"

"Yes; it went off very pleasantly." This she said in that tone of voice which clearly implies that the speaker is not thinking of the words spoken.

"And Kate has now left you?"

"Yes; she is with her aunt, at the seaside."

"So I understand; — and your cousin George?"

"I never know much of George's movements. He may be in Town, but I have not seen him since I came back."

"Ah! that is the way with friends living in London. Unless circumstances bring them together, they are in fact further apart than if they lived fifty miles asunder in the country. And he managed to get through all the trouble without losing your luggage for you very often?"

"If you were to say that we did not lose his, that would be nearer the mark. But, John, you have come up to London in this sudden way to speak to me about my letter to you. Is it not so?"

"Certainly it is so. Certainly I have."

"I have thought much, since, of what I then wrote, very much,—very much, indeed; and I have learned to feel sure that we had better—"

"Stop, Alice; stop a moment, love. Do not speak hurriedly. Shall I tell you what I learned from your letter?"

"Yes; tell me, if you think it better that you should do so."

"Perhaps it may be better. I learned, love, that something had been said or done during your journey,—or perhaps only something thought, that had made you melancholy, and filled your mind for a while with those unsubstantial and indefinable regrets for the past which we are all apt to feel at certain moments of our life. There are few of us who do not encounter, now and again, some of that irrational spirit of sadness which, when over-indulged, drives men to madness and self-destruction. I used to know well what it was before I knew you; but since I have had the hope of having you in my house, I have banished it utterly. In that I think I have been stronger than you. Do not speak under the influence of that spirit till you have thought whether you, too, cannot banish it."

"I have tried, and it will not be banished."

"Try again, Alice. It is a damned spirit, and belongs neither to heaven nor to earth. Do not say to me the words that you were about to say till you have wrestled with it manfully. I think I know what those words were to be. If you love me, those words should not be spoken. If you do not—"

"If I do not love you, I love no one upon earth."

"I believe it. I believe it as I believe in my own love for you. I trust your love implicitly, Alice. I know that you love me. I think I can read your mind. Tell me that I may return to Cambridgeshire, and again plead my cause for an early marriage from thence. I will not take such speech from you to mean more than it says!"

She sat quiet, looking at him—looking full into his face. She had in nowise changed her mind, but after such words from him, she did not know how to declare to him her resolution. There was something in his manner that awed her,—and something also that softened her.

"Tell me," said he, "that I may see you again to-morrow morning in our usual quiet, loving way, and that I may return home to-morrow evening. Pronounce a yea to that speech from me, and I will ask for nothing further."

"No; I cannot do so," she said. And the tone of her voice, as she spoke, was different to any tone that he had heard before from her mouth.

"Is that melancholy fiend too strong for you?" He smiled as he said this, and as he smiled, he took her hand. She did not attempt to withdraw it, but sat by him in a strange calmness, looking straight before her into the middle of the room. "You have not struggled with it. You know, as I do, that it is a bad fiend and a wicked one,—a fiend that is prompting you to the worst cruelty in the world. Alice! Alice! Alice! Try to think of all this as though some other person were concerned. If it were your friend, what advice would you give her?"

"If it were your friend, what advice would you give her?

"I would bid her tell the man who had loved her,—that is, if he were noble, good, and great,—that she found herself to be unfit to be his wife;

and then I would bid her ask his pardon humbly on her knees." As she said this, she sank before him on to the floor, and looked up into his face with an expression of sad contrition which almost drew him from his purposed firmness.

He had purposed to be firm,—to yield to her in nothing, resolving to treat all that she might say as the hallucination of a sickened imagination,— as the effect of absolute want of health, for which some change in her mode of life would be the best cure. She might bid him begone in what language she would. He knew well that such was her intention. But he would not allow a word coming from her in such a way to disturb arrangements made for the happiness of their joint lives. As a loving husband would treat a wife, who, in some exceptional moment of a melancholy malady, should declare herself unable to remain longer in her home, so would he treat her. As for accepting what she might say as his dismissal, he would as soon think of taking the fruit-trees from the southern wall because the sun sometimes shines from the north. He could not treat either his interests or hers so lightly as that.

"But what if he granted no such pardon, Alice? I will grant none such. You are my wife, my own, my dearest, my chosen one. You are all that I value in the world, my treasure and my comfort, my earthly happiness and my gleam of something better that is to come hereafter. Do you think that I shall let you go from me in that way? No, love. If you are ill I will wait till your illness is gone by; and, if you will let me, I will be your nurse."

"I am not ill."

"Not ill with any defined sickness. You do not shake with ague, nor does your head rack you with aching; but yet you may be ill. Think of what has passed between us. Must you not be ill when you seek to put an end to all that without any cause assigned."

"You will not hear my reasons,"—she was still kneeling before him and looking up into his face.

"I will hear them if you will tell me that they refer to any supposed faults of my own."

"No, no, no!"

"Then I will not hear them. It is for me to find out your faults, and when I have found out any that require complaint, I will come and make it. Dear

Alice, I wish you knew how I long for you." Then he put his hand upon her hair, as though he would caress her.

But this she would not suffer, so she rose slowly, and stood with her hand upon the table in the middle of the room. "Mr. Grey—" she said.

"If you will call me so, I shall think it only a part of your malady."

"Mr. Grey," she continued, "I can only hope that you will take me at my word."

"Oh, but I will not; certainly I will not, if that would be adverse to my own interests."

"I am thinking of your interests; I am, indeed;—at any rate as much as of my own. I feel quite sure that I should not make you happy as your wife,—quite sure; and feeling that, I think that I am right, even after all that has passed, to ask your forgiveness, and to beg that our engagement may be over."

"No, Alice, no; never with my consent. I cannot tell you with what contentment I would marry you to-morrow,—to-morrow, or next month, or the month after. But if it cannot be so, then I will wait. Nothing but your marriage with some one else would convince me."

"I cannot convince you in that way," she said, smiling.

"You will convince me in no other. You have not spoken to your father of this as yet?"

"Not as yet."

"Do not do so, at any rate for the present. You will own that it might be possible that you would have to unsay what you had said."

"No; it is not possible."

"Give yourself and me the chance. It can do no harm. And, Alice, I ask you now for no reasons. I will not ask your reasons, or even listen to them, because I do not believe that they will long have effect even on yourself. Do you still think of going to Cheltenham?"

"I have decided nothing as yet."

"If I were you, I would go. I think a change of air would be good for you."

"Yes; you treat me as though I were partly silly, and partly insane; but it is not so. The change you speak of should be in my nature, and in yours."

He shook his head and still smiled. There was something in the imperturbed security of his manner which almost made her angry with him. It seemed as though he assumed so great a superiority that he felt himself able to treat any resolve of hers as the petulance of a child. And though he spoke in strong language of his love, and of his longing that she should come to him, yet he was so well able to command his feelings, that he showed no sign of grief at the communication she had made to him. She did not doubt his love, but she believed him to be so much the master of his love, — as he was the master of everything else, that her separation from him would cause him no uncontrollable grief. In that she utterly failed to understand his character. Had she known him better, she might have been sure that such a separation now would with him have carried its mark to the grave. Should he submit to her decision, he would go home and settle himself to his books the next day; but on no following day would he be again capable of walking forth among his flowers with an easy heart. He was a strong, constant man, perhaps over-conscious of his own strength; but then his strength was great. "He is perfect!" Alice had said to herself often. "Oh that he were less perfect!"

He did not stay with her long after the last word that has been recorded. "Perhaps," he said, as for a moment he held her hand at parting, "I had better not come to-morrow."

"No, no; it is better not."

"I advise you not to tell your father of this, and doubtless you will think of it before you do so. But if you do tell him, let me know that you have done so."

"Why that?"

"Because in such case I also must see him. God bless you, Alice! God bless you, dearest, dearest Alice!" Then he went, and she sat there on the sofa without moving, till she heard her father's feet as he came up the stairs.

"What, Alice, are you not in bed yet?"

"Not yet, papa."

"And so John Grey has been here. He has left his stick in the hall. I should know it among a thousand."

"Yes; he has been here."

"Is anything the matter, Alice?"

"No, papa, nothing is the matter."

"He has not made himself disagreeable, has he?"

"Not in the least. He never does anything wrong. He may defy man or woman to find fault with him."

"So that is it, is it? He is just a shade too good. Well, I have always thought that myself. But it's a fault on the right side."

"It's no fault, Papa. If there be any fault, it is not with him. But I am yawning and tired, and I will go to bed."

"Is he to be here to-morrow?"

"No; he returns to Nethercoats early. Good night, papa."

Mr. Vavasor, as he went up to his bedroom, felt sure that there had been something wrong between his daughter and her lover. "I don't know how she'll ever put up with him," he said to himself, "he is so terribly conceited. I shall never forget how he went on about Charles Kemble, and what a fool he made of himself."

Alice, before she went to bed, sat down and wrote a letter to her cousin Kate.

CHAPTER XII
MR. GEORGE VAVASOR AT HOME

It cannot perhaps fairly be said that George Vavasor was an unhospitable man, seeing that it was his custom to entertain his friends occasionally at Greenwich, Richmond, or such places; and he would now and again have a friend to dine with him at his club. But he never gave breakfasts, dinners, or suppers under his own roof. During a short period of his wine-selling career, at which time he had occupied handsome rooms over his place of business in New Burlington Street, he had presided at certain feasts given to customers or expectant customers by the firm; but he had not found this employment to his taste, and had soon relinquished it to one of the other partners. Since that he had lived in lodgings in Cecil Street,—down at the bottom of that retired nook, near to the river and away from the Strand. Here he had simply two rooms on the first floor, and hither his friends came to him very rarely. They came very rarely on any account. A stray man might now and then pass an hour with him here; but on such occasions the chances were that the visit had some reference, near or distant, to affairs of business. Eating or drinking there was never any to be found here by the most intimate of his allies. His lodgings were his private retreat, and they were so private that but few of his friends knew where he lived.

And had it been possible he would have wished that no one should have known his whereabouts. I am not aware that he had any special reason for this peculiarity, or that there was anything about his mode of life that required hiding; but he was a man who had always lived as though secrecy in certain matters might at any time become useful to him. He had a mode of dressing himself when he went out at night that made it almost impossible that any one should recognise him. The people at his lodgings did not even know that he had relatives, and his nearest relatives hardly knew that he had lodgings. Even Kate had never been at the rooms in Cecil Street, and addressed all her letters to his place of business or his club. He was a man who would bear no inquiry into himself. If he had been out of view for a month, and his friends asked him where he had been, he always answered the question falsely, or left it unanswered. There are many men of whom everybody knows all about all their belongings;—as to whom everybody knows where they live, whither they go, what is their means, and how they spend it. But there are others of whom no man knows anything, and George Vavasor was such a one. For myself I like the open babbler the best. Babbling may be a weakness, but to my thinking mystery is a vice.

Vavasor also maintained another little establishment, down in Oxfordshire; but the two establishments did not even know of each other's existence. There was a third, too, very closely hidden from the world's eye, which shall be nameless; but of the establishment in Oxfordshire he did sometimes speak, in very humble words, among his friends. When he found himself among hunting men, he would speak of his two nags at Roebury, saying that he had never yet been able to mount a regular hunting stable, and that he supposed he never would; but that there were at Roebury two indifferent beasts of his if any one chose to buy them. And men very often did buy Vavasor's horses. When he was on them they always went well and sold themselves readily. And though he thus spoke of two, and perhaps did not keep more during the summer, he always seemed to have horses enough when he was down in the country. No one even knew George Vavasor not to hunt because he was short of stuff. And here, at Roebury, he kept a trusty servant, an ancient groom with two little bushy grey eyes which looked as though they could see through a stable door. Many were the long whisperings which George and Bat Smithers carried on at the stable door, in the very back depth of the yard attached to the hunting inn at Roebury. Bat regarded his master as a man wholly devoted to horses, but often wondered why he was not more regular in his sojournings in Oxfordshire. Of any other portion of his master's life Bat knew nothing. Bat could give the address of his master's club in London, but he could give no other address.

But though Vavasor's private lodgings were so very private, he had, nevertheless, taken some trouble in adorning them. The furniture in the sitting-room was very neat, and the book-shelves were filled with volumes that shone with gilding on their backs. The inkstand, the paper-weight, the envelope case on his writing-table were all handsome. He had a single good portrait of a woman's head hanging on one of his walls. He had a special place adapted for his pistols, others for his foils, and again another for his whips. The room was as pretty a bachelor's room as you would wish to enter, but you might see, by the position of the single easy-chair that was brought forward, that it was seldom appropriated to the comfort of more than one person. Here he sat lounging over his breakfast, late on a Sunday morning in September, when all the world was out of town. He was reading a letter which had just been brought down to him from his club. Though the writer of it was his sister Kate, she had not been privileged to address it to his private lodgings. He read it very quickly, running rapidly over its contents, and then threw it aside from him as though it were of no moment, keeping, however, an enclosure in his hand. And yet the letter was of much moment, and made him think deeply. "If I did it at all," said he, "it would be more with the object of cutting him out than with any other."

The reader will hardly require to be told that the him in question was John Grey, and that Kate's letter was one instigating her brother to renew his love affair with Alice. And Vavasor was in truth well inclined to renew it, and would have begun the renewing it at once, had he not doubted his power with his cousin. Indeed it has been seen that he had already attempted some commencement of such renewal at Basle. He had told Kate more than once that Alice's fortune was not much, and that her beauty was past its prime; and he would no doubt repeat the same objections to his sister with some pretence of disinclination. It was not his custom to show his hand to the players at any game that he played. But he was, in truth, very anxious to obtain from Alice a second promise of her hand. How soon after that he might marry her, would be another question.

Perhaps it was not Alice's beauty that he coveted, nor yet her money exclusively. Nevertheless he thought her very beautiful, and was fully aware that her money would be of great service to him. But I believe that he was true in that word that he spoke to himself, and that his chief attraction was the delight which he would have in robbing Mr. Grey of his wife. Alice had once been his love, had clung to his side, had whispered love to him, and he had enough of the weakness of humanity in him to feel the soreness arising from her affection for another. When she broke away from him he had acknowledged that he had been wrong, and when, since her engagement with Mr. Grey, he had congratulated her, he had told her in his quiet, half-whispered, impressive words how right she was; but not the less, therefore, did he feel himself hurt that John Grey should be her lover. And when he had met this man he had spoken well of him to his sister, saying that he was a gentleman, a scholar, and a man of parts; but not the less had he hated him from the first moment of his seeing him. Such hatred under such circumstances was almost pardonable. But George Vavasor, when he hated, was apt to follow up his hatred with injury. He could not violently dislike a man and yet not wish to do him any harm. At present, as he sat lounging in his chair, he thought that he would like to marry his cousin Alice; but he was quite sure that he would like to be the means of putting a stop to the proposed marriage between Alice and John Grey.

Kate had been very false to her friend, and had sent up to her brother the very letter which Alice had written to her after that meeting in Queen Anne Street which was described in the last chapter,—or rather a portion of it, for with the reserve common to women she had kept back the other half. Alice had declared to herself that she would be sure of her cousin's sympathy, and had written out all her heart on the matter, as was her wont when writing to Kate. "But you must understand," she wrote, "that all that I said to him went with him for nothing. I had determined to make him know that everything between us must be over, but I failed. I found that I had no words at command, but that he was able to talk to me as though I were a child. He told me that I was sick and full of phantasies, and bade me change the air. As he spoke in this way, I could not help feeling how right he was to use me so; but I felt also that he, in his mighty superiority, could never be a fitting husband for a creature so inferior to him as I am. Though I altogether failed to make him understand that it was so, every moment that we were together made me more fixed in my resolution."

This letter from Alice to Kate, Vavasor read over and over again, though Kate's letter to himself, which was the longer one, he had thrown aside after the first glance. There was nothing that he could learn from that. He was as good a judge of the manner in which he would play his own game as Kate could be; but in this matter he was to learn how he would play his game from a knowledge of the other girl's mind. "She'll never marry him, at any rate," he said to himself, "and she is right. He'd make an upper servant of her; very respectable, no doubt, but still only an upper servant. Now with me;—well, I hardly know what I should make of her. I cannot think of myself as a man married." Then he threw her letter after Kate's, and betook himself to his newspaper and his cigar.

It was two hours after this, and he still wore his dressing-gown, and he was still lounging in his easy-chair, when the waiting-maid at the lodgings brought him up word that a gentleman wished to see him. Vavasor kept no servant of his own except that confidential groom down at Bicester. It was a rule with him that people could be better served and cheaper served by other people's servants than by their own. Even in the stables at Bicester the innkeeper had to find what assistance was wanted, and charge for it in the bill. And George Vavasor was no Sybarite. He did not deem it impracticable to put on his own trousers without having a man standing at his foot to hold up the leg of the garment. A valet about a man knows a great deal of a man's ways, and therefore George had no valet.

"A gentleman!" said he to the girl. "Does the gentleman look like a public-house keeper?"

"Well, I think he do," said the girl.

"Then show him up," said George.

And the gentleman was a public-house keeper. Vavasor was pretty sure of his visitor before he desired the servant to give him entrance. It was Mr. Grimes from the "Handsome Man" public-house and tavern, in the Brompton Road, and he had come by appointment to have a little conversation with Mr. Vavasor on matters political. Mr. Grimes was a man who knew that business was business, and as such had some considerable weight in his own neighbourhood. With him politics was business, as well as beer, and omnibus-horses, and foreign wines;—in the fabrication of which latter article Mr. Grimes was supposed to have an extended experience. To such as him, when intent on business, Mr. Vavasor was not averse to make known the secrets of his lodging-house; and now, when the idle of London world was either at morning church or still in bed, Mr. Grimes had come out by appointment to do a little political business with the lately-rejected member for the Chelsea Districts.

Vavasor had been, as I have said, lately rejected, and the new member who had beaten him at the hustings had sat now for one session in parliament. Under his present reign he was destined to the honour of one other session, and then the period of his existing glory,—for which he was said to have paid nearly six thousand pounds,—would be over. But he might be elected again, perhaps for a full period of six sessions; and it might be hoped that this second election would be conducted on more economical principles. To this, the economical view of the matter, Mr. Grimes was very much opposed, and was now waiting upon George Vavasor in Cecil Street, chiefly with the object of opposing the new member's wishes on this head. No doubt Mr. Grimes was personally an advocate for the return of Mr. Vavasor, and would do all in his power to prevent the re-election of the young Lord Kilfenora, whose father, the Marquis of Bunratty, had scattered that six thousand pounds among the electors and non-electors of Chelsea; but his main object was that money should be spent. "'Tain't altogether for myself," he said to a confidential friend in the same way of business; "I don't get so much on it. Perhaps sometimes not none. May be I've a bill agin some of those gents not paid this werry moment. But it's the game I looks to. If the game dies away, it'll never be got up again;—never. Who'll care about elections then? Anybody'd go and get hisself elected if we was to let the game go by!" And so, that the game might not go by, Mr. Grimes was now present in Mr. George Vavasor's rooms.

"Well Mr. Grimes," said George, "how are you this morning? Sit down, Mr. Grimes. If every man were as punctual as you are, the world would go like clock-work; wouldn't it?"

"Business is business, Mr. Vavasor," said the publican, after having made his salute, and having taken his chair with some little show of mock modesty. "That's my maxim. If I didn't stick to that, nothing wouldn't ever stick to me; and nothing doesn't much as it is. Times is very bad, Mr. Vavasor."

"Of course they are. They're always bad. What was the Devil made for, except that they should be bad? But I should have thought you publicans were the last men who ought to complain."

"Lord love you, Mr. Vavasor; why, I suppose of all the men as is put upon, we're put upon the worst. What's the good of drawing of beer, if the more you draw the more you don't make. Yesterday as ever was was Saturday, and we drawed three pound ten and nine. What'll that come to, Mr. Vavasor, when you reckons it up with the brewer? Why, it's a next to nothing. You knows that well enough."

"Upon my word I don't. But I know you don't sell a pint of beer without getting a profit out of it."

"Lord love you, Mr. Vavasor. If I hadn't nothink to look to but beer I couldn't keep a house over my head; no I couldn't. That house of mine belongs to Meux's people; and very good people they are too;—have made a sight of money; haven't they, Mr. Vavasor? I has to get my beer from them in course. Why not, when it's their house? But if I sells their stuff as I gets it, there ain't a halfpenny coming to me out of a gallon. Look at that, now."

"But then you don't sell it as you get it. You stretch it."

"That's in course. I'm not going to tell you a lie, Mr. Vavasor. You know what's what as well as I do, and a sight better, I expect. There's a dozen different ways of handling beer, Mr. Vavasor. But what's the use of that, when they can take four or five pounds a day over the counter for their rot-gut stuff at the 'Cadogan Arms,' and I can't do no better nor yet perhaps so well, for a real honest glass of beer. Stretch it! It's my belief the more you poison their liquor, the more the people likes it!"

Mr. Grimes was a stout man, not very tall, with a mottled red face, and large protruding eyes. As regards his own person, Mr. Grimes might have been taken as a fair sample of the English innkeeper, as described for many years past. But in his outer garments he was very unlike that description. He wore a black, swallow-tailed coat, made, however, to set very loose upon his back, a black waistcoat, and black pantaloons. He carried, moreover, in his hands a black chimney-pot hat. Not only have the top-boots and breeches vanished from the costume of innkeepers, but also the long, particoloured waistcoat, and the birds'-eye fogle round their necks. They get themselves up to look like Dissenting ministers or undertakers, except that there is still a something about their rosy gills which tells a tale of the spigot and corkscrew.

Mr. Grimes had only just finished the tale of his own hard ways as a publican, when the door-bell was again rung. "There's Scruby," said George Vavasor, "and now we can go to business."

CHAPTER XIII
MR. GRIMES GETS HIS ODD MONEY

The handmaiden at George Vavasor's lodgings announced "another gent," and then Mr. Scruby entered the room in which were seated George, and Mr. Grimes the publican from the "Handsome Man" on the Brompton Road. Mr. Scruby was an attorney from Great Marlborough Street, supposed to be very knowing in the ways of metropolitan elections; and he had now stepped round, as he called it, with the object of saying a few words to Mr. Grimes, partly on the subject of the forthcoming contest at Chelsea, and partly on that of the contest last past. These words were to be said in the presence of Mr. Vavasor, the person interested. That some other words had been spoken between Mr. Scruby and Mr. Grimes on the same subjects behind Mr. Vavasor's back I think very probable. But even though this might have been so I am not prepared to say that Mr. Vavasor had been deceived by their combinations.

The two men were very civil to each other in their salutations, the attorney assuming an air of patronizing condescension, always calling the other Grimes; whereas Mr. Scruby was treated with considerable deference by the publican, and was always called Mr. Scruby. "Business is business," said the publican as soon as these salutations were over; "isn't it now, Mr. Scruby?"

"And I suppose Grimes thinks Sunday morning a particularly good time for business," said the attorney, laughing.

"It's quiet, you know," said Grimes. "But it warn't me as named Sunday morning. It was Mr. Vavasor here. But it is quiet; ain't it, Mr. Scruby?"

Mr. Scruby acknowledged that it was quiet, especially looking out over the river, and then they proceeded to business. "We must pull the governor through better next time than we did last," said the attorney.

"Of course we must, Mr. Scruby; but, Lord love you, Mr. Vavasor, whose fault was it? What notice did I get,—just tell me that? Why, Travers's name was up on the liberal interest ever so long before the governor had ever thought about it."

"Nobody is blaming you, Mr. Grimes," said George.

"And nobody can't, Mr. Vavasor. I done my work true as steel, and there ain't another man about the place as could have done half as much. You ask Mr. Scruby else. Mr. Scruby knows, if ere a man in London does. I tell you what it is, Mr. Vavasor, them Chelsea fellows, who lives mostly down by the river, ain't like your Maryboners or Finsburyites. It wants something of a man to manage them. Don't it Mr. Scruby?"

"It wants something of a man to manage any of them as far as my experience goes," said Mr. Scruby.

"Of course it do; and there ain't one in London knows so much about it as you do, Mr. Scruby. I will say that for you. But the long and the short of it is this;—business is business, and money is money."

"Money is money, certainly," said Mr. Scruby. "There's no doubt in the world about that, Grimes;—and a deal of it you had out of the last election."

"No, I hadn't; begging your pardon, Mr. Scruby, for making so free. What I had to my own cheek wasn't nothing to speak of. I wasn't paid for my time; that's what I wasn't. You look how a publican's business gets cut up at them elections;—and then the state of the house afterwards! What would the governor say to me if I was to put down painting inside and out in my little bill?"

"It doesn't seem to make much difference how you put it down," said Vavasor. "The total is what I look at."

"Just so, Mr. Vavasor; just so. The total is what I looks at too. And I has to look at it a deuced long time before I gets it. I ain't a got it yet; have I, Mr. Vavasor?"

"Well; if you ask me I should say you had," said George. "I know I paid Mr. Scruby three hundred pounds on your account."

"And I got every shilling of it, Mr. Vavasor. I'm not a going to deny the money, Mr. Vavasor. You'll never find me doing that. I'm as round as your hat, and as square as your elbow,—I am. Mr. Scruby knows me; don't you, Mr. Scruby?"

"Perhaps I know you too well, Grimes."

"No you don't, Mr. Scruby; not a bit too well. Nor I don't know you too well, either. I respect you, Mr. Scruby, because you're a man as understands your business. But as I was saying, what's three hundred pounds when a man's bill is three hundred and ninety-two thirteen and fourpence?"

"I thought that was all settled, Mr. Scruby," said Vavasor.

"Why you see, Mr. Vavasor, it's very hard to settle these things. If you ask me whether Mr. Grimes here can sue you for the balance, I tell you very plainly that he can't. We were a little short of money when we came to a settlement, as is generally the case at such times, and so we took Mr. Grimes' receipt for three hundred pounds."

"Of course you did, Mr. Scruby."

"Not on account, but in full of all demands."

"Now Mr. Scruby!" and the publican as he made this appeal looked at the attorney with an expression of countenance which was absolutely eloquent. "Are you going to put me off with such an excuse as that?" so the look spoke plainly enough. "Are you going to bring up my own signature against me, when you know very well that I shouldn't have got a shilling at all for the next twelve months if I hadn't given it? Oh Mr. Scruby!" That's what Mr. Grimes' look said, and both Mr. Scruby and Mr. Vavasor understood it perfectly.

"In full of all demands," said Mr. Scruby, with a slight tone of triumph in his voice, as though to show that Grimes' appeal had no effect at all upon his conscience. "If you were to go into a court of law, Grimes, you wouldn't have a leg to stand upon."

"A court of law? Who's a going to law with the governor, I should like to know? not I; not if he didn't pay me them ninety-two pounds thirteen and fourpence for the next five years."

"Five years or fifteen would make no difference," said Scruby. "You couldn't do it."

"And I ain't a going to try. That's not the ticket I've come here about, Mr. Vavasor, this blessed Sunday morning. Going to law, indeed! But Mr. Scruby, I've got a family."

"Not in the vale of Taunton, I hope," said George.

"They is at the 'Handsome Man' in the Brompton Road, Mr. Vavasor; and I always feels that I owes my first duty to them. If a man don't work for his family, what do he work for?"

"Come, come, Grimes," said Mr. Scruby. "What is it you're at? Out with it, and don't keep us here all day."

"What is it I'm at, Mr. Scruby? As if you didn't know very well what I'm at. There's my house;—in all them Chelsea districts it's the most convenientest of any public as is open for all manner of election purposes. That's given up to it."

"And what next?" said Scruby.

"The next is, I myself. There isn't one of the lot of 'em can work them Chelsea fellows down along the river unless it is me. Mr. Scruby knows that. Why I've been a getting of them up with a view to this very job ever since;— why ever since they was a talking of the Chelsea districts. When Lord Robert was a coming in for the county on the religious dodge, he couldn't have worked them fellows anyhow, only for me. Mr. Scruby knows that."

"Let's take it all for granted, Mr. Grimes," said Vavasor. "What comes next?"

"Well;—them Bunratty people; it is they as has come next. They know which side their bread is likely to be buttered; they do. They're a bidding for the 'Handsome Man' already; they are."

"And you'd let your house to the Tory party, Grimes!" said Mr. Scruby, in a tone in which disgust and anger were blended.

"Who said anything of my letting my house to the Tory party, Mr. Scruby? I'm as round as your hat, Mr. Scruby, and as square as your elbow; I am. But suppose as all the liberal gents as employs you, Mr. Scruby, was to turn again you and not pay you your little bills, wouldn't you have your eyes open for customers of another kind? Come now, Mr. Scruby?"

"I'm as round as your hat, and as square as your elbow; I

"You won't make much of that game, Grimes."

"Perhaps not; perhaps not. There's a risk in all these things; isn't there, Mr. Vavasor? I should like to see you a Parliament gent; I should indeed. You'd be a credit to the districts; I really think you would."

"I'm much obliged by your good opinion, Mr. Grimes," said George.

"When I sees a gent coming forward I knows whether he's fit for Parliament, or whether he ain't. I says you are fit. But Lord love you, Mr. Vavasor; it's a thing a gentleman always has to pay for."

"That's true enough; a deal more than it's worth, generally."

"A thing's worth what it fetches. I'm worth what I'll fetch; that's the long and the short of it. I want to have my balance, that's the truth. It's the odd money in a man's bill as always carries the profit. You ask Mr. Scruby else;—only with a lawyer it's all profit I believe."

"That's what you know about it," said Scruby.

"If you cut off a man's odd money," continued the publican, "you break his heart. He'd almost sooner have that and leave the other standing. He'd call the hundreds capital, and if he lost them at last, why he'd put it down as being in the way of trade. But the odd money;—he looks at that, Mr. Vavasor, as in a manner the very sweat of his brow, the work of his own hand; that's what goes to his family, and keeps the pot a boiling down-stairs. Never stop a man's odd money, Mr. Vavasor; that is, unless he comes it very strong indeed."

"And what is it you want now?" said Scruby.

"I wants ninety-two pounds thirteen and fourpence, Mr. Scruby, and then we'll go to work for the new fight with contented hearts. If we're to begin at all, it's quite time; it is indeed, Mr. Vavasor."

"And what you mean us to understand is, that you won't begin at all without your money," said the lawyer.

"That's about it, Mr. Scruby."

"Take a fifty-pound note, Grimes," said the lawyer.

"Fifty-pound notes are not so ready," said George.

"Oh, he'll be only too happy to have your acceptance; won't you, Grimes."

"Not for fifty pounds, Mr. Scruby. It's the odd money that I wants. I don't mind the thirteen and four, because that's neither here nor there among friends, but if I didn't get all them ninety-two pounds I should be a broken-hearted man; I should indeed, Mr. Vavasor. I couldn't go about your work for next year so as to do you justice among the electors. I couldn't indeed."

"You'd better give him a bill for ninety pounds at three months, Mr. Vavasor. I have no doubt he has got a stamp in his pocket."

"That I have, Mr. Scruby; there ain't no mistake about that. A bill stamp is a thing that often turns up convenient with gents as mean business like Mr. Vavasor and you. But you must make it ninety-two; you must indeed, Mr. Vavasor. And do make it two months if you can, Mr. Vavasor; they do charge so unconscionable on ninety days at them branch banks; they do indeed."

George Vavasor and Mr. Scruby, between them, yielded at last, so far as to allow the bill to be drawn for ninety-two pounds, but they were stanch as to the time. "If it must be, it must," said the publican, with a deep sigh, as he folded up the paper and put it into the pocket of a huge case which he carried. "And now, gents, I'll tell you what it is. We'll make safe work of this here next election. We know what's to be our little game in time, and if we don't go in and win, my name ain't Jacob Grimes, and I ain't the landlord of the 'Handsome Man.' As you gents has perhaps got something to say among yourselves, I'll make so bold as to wish you good morning." So, with that, Mr. Grimes lifted his hat from the floor, and bowed himself out of the room.

"You couldn't have done it cheaper; you couldn't, indeed," said the lawyer, as soon as the sound of the closing front door had been heard.

"Perhaps not; but what a thief the man is! I remember your telling me that the bill was about the most preposterous you had ever seen."

"So it was, and if we hadn't wanted him again of course we shouldn't have paid him. But we'll have it all off his next account, Mr. Vavasor,— every shilling of it. It's only lent; that's all;—it's only lent."

"But one doesn't want to lend such a man money, if one could help it."

"That's true. If you look at it in that light, it's quite true. But you see we cannot do without him. If he hadn't got your bill, he'd have gone over to the other fellows before the week was over; and the worst of it would have been that he knows our hand. Looking at it all round you've got him cheap, Mr. Vavasor;—you have, indeed."

"Looking at it all round is just what I don't like, Mr. Scruby, But if a man will have a whistle, he must pay for it."

"You can't do it cheap for any of these metropolitan seats; you can't, indeed, Mr. Vavasor. That is, a new man can't. When you've been in four or five times, like old Duncombe, why then, of course, you may snap your fingers at such men as Grimes. But the Chelsea districts ain't dear. I don't call them by any means dear. Now Marylebone is dear,—and so is Southwark. It's dear, and nasty; that's what the borough is. Only that I never tell tales, I could tell you a tale, Mr. Vavasor, that'd make your hair stand on end; I could indeed."

"Ah! the game is hardly worth the candle, I believe."

"That depends on what way you choose to look at it. A seat in Parliament is a great thing to a man who wants to make his way;—a very great thing;—specially when a man's young, like you, Mr. Vavasor."

"Young!" said George. "Sometimes it seems to me as though I've been living for a hundred years. But I won't trouble you with that, Mr. Scruby, and I believe I needn't keep you any longer." With that, he got up and bowed the attorney out of the room, with just a little more ceremony than he had shown to the publican.

"Young!" said Vavasor to himself, when he was left alone. "There's my uncle, or the old squire,—they're both younger men than I am. One cares for his dinner, and the other for his bullocks and his trees. But what is there that I care for, unless it is not getting among the sheriff's officers for debt?" Then he took out a little memorandum-book from his breast-pocket, and having made in it an entry as to the amount and date of that bill which he had just accepted on the publican's behalf, he conned over the particulars of its pages. "Very blue; very blue, indeed," he said to himself when he had completed the study. "But nobody shall say I hadn't the courage to play the game out, and that old fellow must die some day, one supposes. If I were not a fool, I should make it up with him before he went; but I am a fool, and shall remain so to the last." Soon after that he dressed himself slowly, reading a little every now and then as he did so. When his toilet was completed, and his Sunday newspapers sufficiently perused, he took up his hat and umbrella and sauntered out.

CHAPTER XIV
ALICE VAVASOR BECOMES TROUBLED

Kate Vavasor had sent to her brother only the first half of her cousin's letter, that half in which Alice had attempted to describe what had taken place between her and Mr. Grey. In doing this, Kate had been a wicked traitor,—a traitor to that feminine faith against which treason on the part of one woman is always unpardonable in the eyes of other women. But her treason would have been of a deeper die had she sent the latter portion, for in that Alice had spoken of George Vavasor himself. But even of this treason, Kate would, I think, have been guilty, had the words which Alice wrote been of a nature to serve her own purpose if read by her brother. But they had not been of this nature. They had spoken of George as a man with whom any closer connection than that which existed at present was impossible, and had been written with the view of begging Kate to desist from making futile attempts in that direction. "I feel myself driven," Alice had said, "to write all this, as otherwise,—if I were simply to tell you that I have resolved to part from Mr. Grey,—you would think that the other thing might follow. The other thing cannot follow. I should think myself untrue in my friendship to you if I did not tell you about Mr. Grey; and you will be untrue in your friendship to me if you take advantage of my confidence by saying more about your brother." This part of Alice's letter Kate had not sent to George Vavasor;—"But the other thing shall follow," Kate had said, as she read the words for the second time, and then put the papers into her desk. "It shall follow."

To give Kate Vavasor her due, she was, at any rate, unselfish in her intrigues. She was obstinately persistent, and she was moreover unscrupulous, but she was not selfish. Many years ago she had made up her mind that George and Alice should be man and wife, feeling that such a marriage would be good at any rate for her brother. It had been almost brought about, and had then been hindered altogether through a fault on her brother's part. But she had forgiven him this sin as she had forgiven many others, and she was now at work in his behalf again, determined that they two should be married, even though neither of them might be now anxious that it should be so. The intrigue itself was dear to her, and success in it was necessary to her self-respect.

She answered Alice's letter with a pleasant, gossiping epistle, which shall be recorded, as it will tell us something of Mrs. Greenow's proceedings at Yarmouth. Kate had promised to stay at Yarmouth for a month, but she had already been there six weeks, and was still under her aunt's wing.

Yarmouth, October, 186—.

Dearest Alice,

Of course I am delighted. It is no good saying that I am not. I know how difficult it is to deal with you, and therefore I sit down to answer your letter with fear and trembling, lest I should say a word too much, and thereby drive you back, or not say quite enough and thereby fail to encourage you on. Of course I am glad. I have long thought that Mr. Grey could not make you happy, and as I have thought so, how can I not be glad? It is no use saying that he is good and noble, and all that sort of thing. I have never denied it. But he was not suited to you, and his life would have made you wretched. Ergo, I rejoice. And as you are the dearest friend I have, of course I rejoice mightily.

I can understand accurately the sort of way in which the interview went. Of course he had the best of it. I can see him so plainly as he stood up in unruffled self-possession, ignoring all that you said, suggesting that you were feverish or perhaps bilious, waving his hand over you a little, as though that might possibly do you some small good, and then taking his leave with an assurance that it would be all right as soon as the wind changed. I suppose it's very noble in him, not taking you at your word, and giving you, as it were, another chance; but there is a kind of nobility which is almost too great for this world. I think very well of you, my dear, as women go, but I do not think well enough of you to believe that you are fit to be Mr. John Grey's wife.

Of course I'm very glad. You have known my mind from the first to the last, and, therefore, what would be the good of my mincing matters? No woman wishes her dearest friend to marry a man to whom she herself is antipathetic.

You would have been as much lost to me, had you become Mrs. Grey of Nethercoats, Cambridgeshire, as though you had gone to heaven. I don't say but what Nethercoats may be a kind of heaven,—but then one doesn't wish one's friend that distant sort of happiness. A flat Eden I can fancy it, hemmed in by broad dykes, in which cream and eggs are very plentiful, where an Adam and an Eve might drink the choicest tea out of the finest china, with toast buttered to perfection, from year's end to year's end; into which no money troubles would ever find their way, nor yet any naughty novels. But such an Eden is not tempting to me, nor, as I think, to you. I can fancy you stretching your poor neck over the dyke, longing to fly away that you might cease to be at rest, but knowing that the matrimonial dragon was too strong for any such flight. If ever bird banged his wings to pieces against gilded bars, you would have banged yours to pieces in that cage.

You say that you have failed to make him understand that the matter is settled. I need not say that of course it is settled, and that he must be made to understand it. You owe it to him now to put him out of all doubt. He is, I suppose, accessible to the words of a mortal, god though he be. But I do not fear about this, for, after all, you have as much firmness about you as most people;—perhaps as much as he has at bottom, though you may not have so many occasions to show it.

As to that other matter I can only say that you shall be obliged, as far as it is in my power to obey you. For what may come out from me by word of mouth when we are together, I will not answer with certainty. But my pen is under better control, and it shall not write the offending name.

And now I must tell you a little about myself;—or rather, I am inclined to spin a yarn, and tell you a great deal. I have got such a lover! But I did describe him before. Of course it's Mr. Cheesacre. If I were to say he hasn't declared himself, I should hardly give you a fair idea of my success. And yet he has not declared himself,—and, which is worse, is very anxious to marry a rival. But it's a strong point in my favour that my rival wants him to take me, and that he will assuredly be driven to make me an offer sooner or later, in obedience to her orders. My aunt is my rival, and I do not feel the least doubt as to his having offered to her half a dozen times. But then she has another lover, Captain Bellfield, and I see that she prefers him. He is a penniless scamp and looks as though he drank. He paints his whiskers too, which I don't like; and, being forty, tries to look like twenty-five. Otherwise he is agreeable enough, and I rather approve of my aunt's taste in preferring him. But my lover has solid attractions, and allures me on by a description of the fat cattle which he sends to market. He is a man of substance, and should I ever become Mrs. Cheesacre, I have reason to think that I shall not be left in want. We went up to his place on a visit the other day. Oileymead is the name of my future home;—not so pretty as Nethercoats, is it? And we had such a time there! We reached the place at ten and left it at four, and he managed to give us three meals. I'm sure we had before our eyes at different times every bit of china, delf, glass, and plate in the establishment. He made us go into the cellar, and told us how much wine he had got there, and how much beer. "It's all paid for, Mrs. Greenow, every bottle of it," he said, turning round to my aunt, with a pathetic earnestness, for which I had hardly given him credit. "Everything in this house is my own; it's all paid for. I don't call anything a man's own till it's paid for. Now that jacket that Bellfield swells about with on the sands at Yarmouth,—that's not his own,—and it's not like to be either." And then he winked his eye as though bidding my aunt to think of that before she encouraged such a lover as Bellfield. He took us into every bedroom, and disclosed to us all the glories of his upper chambers. It would have done you good to see him lifting the counterpanes, and bidding my aunt feel the texture of the blankets! And then to see her turn round to me and say:—"Kate, it's simply the best-furnished house I ever went over in my life!"—"It does seem very comfortable," said I. "Comfortable!" said he. "Yes, I don't think there's anybody can say that Oileymead isn't comfortable." I did so think of you and Nethercoats. The attractions are the same;—only in the one place you would have a god for your keeper, and in the other a brute. For myself, if ever I'm to have a keeper at all, I shall prefer a man. But when we got to the farmyard his eloquence reached the highest pitch. "Mrs. Greenow," said he, "look at that," and he pointed to heaps of manure raised like the streets of a little city. "Look at that!" "There's a great deal," said my aunt. "I believe you," said he. "I've more muck upon this place here than any farmer in Norfolk, gentle or simple; I don't care who the other is." Only fancy, Alice; it may all be mine; the blankets, the wine, the muck, and the rest of it. So my aunt assured me when we got home that evening. When I remarked that the wealth had been exhibited to her and not to me, she did not affect to deny it, but treated that as a matter of no moment. "He wants a wife, my dear," she said, "and you may pick him up to-morrow by putting out your hand." When I remarked that his mind seemed to be intent on low things, and specially named the muck, she only laughed at me. "Money's never dirty," she said, "nor yet what makes money." She talks of taking lodgings in Norwich for the winter, saying that in her widowed state she will be as well there as anywhere else, and she wants me to stay with her up to Christmas. Indeed she first proposed the Norwich plan on the ground that it might be useful to me,—with a view to Mr. Cheesacre, of course; but I fancy that she is unwilling to tear herself away from Captain Bellfield. At any rate to Norwich she will go, and I have promised not to leave her before the second week in November. With all her absurdities I like her. Her faults are terrible faults, but she has not the fault of hiding them by falsehood. She is never stupid, and she is very good-natured. She would have allowed me to equip myself from head to foot at her expense, if I would have accepted her liberality, and absolutely offered to give me my trousseau if I would marry Mr. Cheesacre.

I live in the hope that you will come down to the old place at Christmas. I won't offend you more than I can help. At any rate he won't be there. And if I don't see you there, where am I to see you? If I were you I would certainly not go to Cheltenham. You are never happy there.

Do you ever dream of the river at Basle? I do;—so often.

Most affectionately yours,

Kate Vavasor.

"Mrs. Greenow, look at that."

Alice had almost lost the sensation created by the former portion of
Kate's letter by the fun of the latter, before she had quite made that sensation
her own. The picture of the Cambridgeshire Eden would have displeased her
had she dwelt upon it, and the allusion to the cream and toast would have had
the very opposite effect to that which Kate had intended. Perhaps Kate had
felt this, and had therefore merged it all in her stories about Mr. Cheesacre.
"I will go to Cheltenham," she said to herself. "He has recommended it. I
shall never be his wife;—but, till we have parted altogether, I will show
him that I think well of his advice." That same afternoon she told her father
that she would go to Lady Macleod's at Cheltenham before the end of the
month. She was, in truth, prompted to this by a resolution, of which she
was herself hardly conscious, that she would not at this period of her life
be in any way guided by her cousin. Having made up her mind about Mr.
Grey, it was right that she should let her cousin know her purpose; but she
would never be driven to confess to herself that Kate had influenced her in
the matter. She would go to Cheltenham. Lady Macleod would no doubt

vex her by hourly solicitations that the match might be renewed; but, if she knew herself, she had strength to withstand Lady Macleod.

She received one letter from Mr. Grey before the time came for her departure, and she answered it, telling him of her intention;—telling him also that she now felt herself bound to explain to her father her present position. "I tell you this," she said, "in consequence of what you said to me on the matter. My father will know it to-morrow, and on the following morning I shall start for Cheltenham. I have heard from Lady Macleod and she expects me."

On the following morning she did tell her father, standing by him as he sat at his breakfast. "What!" said he, putting down his tea-cup and looking up into her face; "What! not marry John Grey!"

"No, papa; I know how strange you must think it."

"And you say that there has been no quarrel."

"No;—there has been no quarrel. By degrees I have learned to feel that I should not make him happy as his wife."

"It's d——d nonsense," said Mr. Vavasor. Now such an expression as this from him, addressed to his daughter, showed that he was very deeply moved.

"Oh, papa! don't talk to me in that way."

"But it is. I never heard such trash in my life. If he comes to me I shall tell him so. Not make him happy! Why can't you make him happy?"

"We are not suited to each other."

"But what's the matter with him? He's a gentleman."

"Yes; he's a gentleman."

"And a man of honour, and with good means, and with all that knowledge and reading which you profess to like. Look here, Alice; I am not going to interfere, nor shall I attempt to make you marry anyone. You are your own mistress as far as that is concerned. But I do hope, for your sake and for mine,—I do hope that there is nothing again between you and your cousin."

"There is nothing, papa."

"I did not like your going abroad with him, though I didn't choose to interrupt your plan by saying so. But if there were anything of that kind going on, I should be bound to tell you that your cousin's position at present is not a good one. Men do not speak well of him."

"There is nothing between us, papa; but if there were, men speaking ill of him would not deter me."

"And men speaking well of Mr. Grey will not do the other thing. I know very well that women can be obstinate."

"I haven't come to this resolution without thinking much about it, papa."

"I suppose not. Well;—I can't say anything more. You are your own mistress, and your fortune is in your own keeping. I can't make you marry John Grey. I think you very foolish, and if he comes to me I shall tell him so. You are going down to Cheltenham, are you?"

"Yes, papa; I have promised Lady Macleod."

"Very well. I'd sooner it should be you than me; that's all I can say." Then he took up his newspaper, thereby showing that he had nothing further to say on the matter, and Alice left him alone.

The whole thing was so vexatious that even Mr. Vavasor was disturbed by it. As it was not term time he had no signing to do in Chancery Lane, and could not, therefore, bury his unhappiness in his daily labour,—or rather in his labour that was by no means daily. So he sat at home till four o'clock, expressing to himself in various phrases his wonder that "any man alive should ever rear a daughter." And when he got to his club the waiters found him quite unmanageable about his dinner, which he ate alone, rejecting all proposition of companionship. But later in the evening he regained his composure over a glass of whiskey-toddy and a cigar. "She's got her own money," he said to himself, "and what does it matter? I don't suppose she'll marry her cousin. I don't think she's fool enough for that. And after all she'll probably make it up again with John Grey." And in this way he determined that he might let this annoyance run off him, and that he need not as a father take the trouble of any interference.

But while he was at his club there came a visitor to Queen Anne Street, and that visitor was the dangerous cousin of whom, according to his uncle's testimony, men at present did not speak well. Alice had not seen him since they had parted on the day of their arrival in London,—nor, indeed, had heard of his whereabouts. In the consternation of her mind at this step which she was taking,—a step which she had taught herself to regard as essentially her duty before it was taken, but which seemed to herself to be false and treacherous the moment she had taken it,—she had become aware that she had been wrong to travel with her cousin. She felt sure,—she thought that she was sure,—that her doing so had in nowise affected her dealings with Mr. Grey. She was very certain,—she thought that she was certain,—that she would have rejected him just the same had she never gone to Switzerland. But every one would say of her that her journey to Switzerland with such companions had produced that result. It had been unlucky and she was sorry for it, and she now wished to avoid all communication with her cousin till this affair should be altogether over. She was especially unwilling to see him; but she had not felt it necessary to give any special injunctions as to his admittance; and now, before she had time to think of it,—on the eve of her departure for Cheltenham,—he was in the room with her, just as the dusk of the October evening was coming on. She was sitting away from the fire, almost behind the window-curtains, thinking of John Grey and very unhappy in her thoughts, when George Vavasor was announced. It will of course be understood that Vavasor had at this time received his sister's letter. He had received it, and had had time to consider the matter since the Sunday morning on which we saw him in his own rooms in Cecil Street. "She can turn it all into capital to-morrow, if she pleases," he had said to himself when thinking of her income. But he had also reminded himself that her grandfather would probably enable him to settle an income out of the property upon Alice, in the event of their being married. And then he had also felt that he could have no greater triumph than "walking atop of John Grey," as he called it. His return for the Chelsea Districts would hardly be sweeter to him than that.

"You must have thought I had vanished out of the world," said George, coming up to her with his extended hand.

Alice was confused, and hardly knew how to address him. "Somebody told me that you were shooting," she said after a pause.

"So I was, but my shooting is not like the shooting of your great Nimrods,—men who are hunters upon the earth. Two days among the grouse and two more among the partridges are about the extent of it. Capel Court is the preserve in which I am usually to be found."

Alice knew nothing of Capel Court, and said, "Oh, indeed."

"Have you heard from Kate?" George asked.

"Yes, once or twice; she is still at Yarmouth with Aunt Greenow."

"And is going to Norwich, as she says. Kate seems to have made a league with Aunt Greenow. I, who don't pretend to be very disinterested in money matters, think that she is quite right. No doubt Aunt Greenow may marry again, but friends with forty thousand pounds are always agreeable."

"I don't believe that Kate thinks much of that," said Alice.

"Not so much as she ought, I dare say. Poor Kate is not a rich woman, or, I fear, likely to become one. She doesn't seem to dream of getting married, and her own fortune is less than a hundred a year."

"Girls who never dream of getting married are just those who make the best marriages at last," said Alice.

"Perhaps so, but I wish I was easier about Kate. She is the best sister a man ever had."

"Indeed she is."

"And I have done nothing for her as yet. I did think, while I was in that wine business, that I could have done anything I pleased for her. But my grandfather's obstinacy put me out of that; and now I'm beginning the world again,—that is, comparatively. I wonder whether you think I'm wrong in trying to get into Parliament?"

"No; quite right. I admire you for it. It is just what I would do in your place. You are unmarried, and have a right to run the risk."

"I am so glad to hear you speak like that," said he. He had now managed to take up that friendly, confidential, almost affectionate tone of talking which he had so often used when abroad with her, and which he had failed to assume when first entering the room.

"I have always thought so."

"But you have never said it."

"Haven't I? I thought I had."

"Not heartily like that. I know that people abuse me;—my own people, my grandfather, and probably your father,—saying that I am reckless and the rest of it. I do risk everything for my object; but I do not know that any one can blame me,—unless it be Kate. To whom else do I owe anything?"

"Kate does not blame you."

"No; she sympathizes with me; she, and she only, unless it be you." Then he paused for an answer, but she made him none. "She is brave enough to give me her hearty sympathy. But perhaps for that very reason I ought to be the more chary in endangering the only support that she is like to have. What is ninety pounds a year for the maintenance of a single lady?"

"I hope that Kate will always live with me," said Alice; "that is, as soon as she has lost her home at Vavasor Hall."

He had been very crafty and had laid a trap for her. He had laid a trap for her, and she had fallen into it. She had determined not to be induced to talk of herself; but he had brought the thing round so cunningly that the words were out of her mouth before she remembered whither they would lead her. She did remember this as she was speaking them, but then it was too late.

"What;—at Nethercoats?" said he. "Neither she nor I doubt your love, but few men would like such an intruder as that into their household, and of all men Mr. Grey, whose nature is retiring, would like it the least."

"I was not thinking of Nethercoats," said Alice.

"Ah, no; that is it, you see. Kate says so often to me that when you are married she will be alone in the world."

"I don't think she will ever find that I shall separate myself from her."

"No; not by any will of your own. Poor Kate! You cannot be surprised that she should think of your marriage with dread. How much of her life has been made up of her companionship with you;—and all the best of it too! You ought not to be angry with her for regarding your withdrawal into Cambridgeshire with dismay."

Alice could not act the lie which now seemed to be incumbent on her. She could not let him talk of Nethercoats as though it were to be her future home. She made the struggle, and she found that she could not do it. She was unable to find the words which should tell no lie to the ear, and which should yet deceive him. "Kate may still live with me," she said slowly. "Everything is over between me and Mr. Grey."

"Alice!—is that true?"

"Yes, George; it is true. If you will allow me to say so, I would rather not talk about it;—not just at present."

"And does Kate know it?"

"Yes, Kate knows it."

"And my uncle?"

"Yes, papa knows it also."

"Alice, how can I help speaking of it? How can I not tell you that I am rejoiced that you are saved from a thraldom which I have long felt sure would break your heart?"

"Pray do not talk of it further."

"Well; if I am forbidden I shall of course obey. But I own it is hard to me. How can I not congratulate you?" To this she answered nothing, but beat with her foot upon the floor as though she were impatient of his words. "Yes, Alice, I understand. You are angry with me," he continued. "And yet you have no right to be surprised that when you tell me this I should think of all that passed between us in Switzerland. Surely the cousin who was with you then has a right to say what he thinks of this change in your life; at any rate he may do so, if as in this case he approves altogether of what you are doing."

"I am glad of your approval, George; but pray let that be an end to it."

After that the two sat silent for a minute or two. She was waiting for him to go, but she could not bid him leave the house. She was angry with herself, in that she had allowed herself to tell him of her altered plans, and she was angry with him because he would not understand that she ought to be spared all conversation on the subject. So she sat looking through the window at the row of gaslights as they were being lit, and he remained in his chair with his elbow on the table and his head resting on his hand.

"Do you remember asking me whether I ever shivered," he said at last; "—whether I ever thought of things that made me shiver? Don't you remember; on the bridge at Basle?"

"Yes; I remember."

"Well, Alice;—one cause for my shivering is over. I won't say more than that now. Shall you remain long at Cheltenham?"

"Just a month."

"And then you come back here?"

"I suppose so. Papa and I will probably go down to Vavasor Hall before Christmas. How much before I cannot say."

"I shall see you at any rate after your return from Cheltenham? Of course Kate will know, and she will tell me."

"Yes; Kate will know. I suppose she will stay here when she comes up from Norfolk. Good-bye."

"Good-bye, Alice. I shall have fewer fits of that inward shivering that you spoke of,—many less, on account of what I have now heard. God bless you, Alice; good-bye."

"Good-bye, George."

As he went he took her hand and pressed it closely between his own. In those days when they were lovers,—engaged lovers, a close, long-continued pressure of her hand had been his most eloquent speech of love. He had not been given to many kisses,—not even to many words of love. But he would take her hand and hold it, even as he looked away from her, and she remembered well the touch of his palm. It was ever cool,—cool, and with a surface smooth as a woman's,—a small hand that had a firm grip. There had been days when she had loved to feel that her own was within it, when she trusted in it, and intended that it should be her staff through life. Now she distrusted it; and as the thoughts of the old days came upon her, and the remembrance of that touch was recalled, she drew her hand away rapidly. Not for that had she driven from her as honest a man as had ever wished to mate with a woman. He, George Vavasor, had never so held her hand since the day when they had parted, and now on this first occasion of her freedom she felt it again. What did he think of her? Did he suppose that she could transfer her love in that way, as a flower may be taken from one buttonhole and placed in another? He read it all, and knew that he was hurrying on too quickly. "I can understand well," he said in a whisper, "what your present feelings are; but I do not think you will be really angry with me because I have been unable to repress my joy at what I cannot but regard as your release from a great misfortune." Then he went.

"My release!" she said, seating herself on the chair from which he had risen. "My release from a misfortune! No;—but my fall from heaven! Oh, what a man he is! That he should have loved me, and that I should have driven him away from me!" Her thoughts travelled off to the sweetness of that home at Nethercoats, to the excellence of that master who might have been hers; and then in an agony of despair she told herself that she had been an idiot and a fool, as well as a traitor. What had she wanted in life that she should have thus quarrelled with as happy a lot as ever had been offered to a woman? Had she not been mad, when she sent from her side the only man that she loved,—the only man that she had ever truly respected? For hours she sat there, all alone, putting out the candles which the servant had lighted for her, and leaving untasted the tea that was brought to her.

Poor Alice! I hope that she may be forgiven. It was her special fault, that when at Rome she longed for Tibur, and when at Tibur she regretted Rome. Not that her cousin George is to be taken as representing the joys of the great capital, though Mr. Grey may be presumed to form no inconsiderable part of the promised delights of the country. Now that she had sacrificed her Tibur, because it had seemed to her that the sunny quiet of its pastures lacked the excitement necessary for the happiness of life, she was again prepared to quarrel with the heartlessness of Rome, and already was again sighing for the tranquillity of the country.

Sitting there, full of these regrets, she declared to herself that she would wait for her father's return, and then, throwing herself upon his love and upon his mercy, would beg him to go to Mr. Grey and ask for pardon for her. "I should be very humble to him," she said; "but he is so good, that I may dare to be humble before him." So she waited for her father. She waited till twelve, till one, till two;—but still he did not come. Later than that she did not dare to wait for him. She feared to trust him on such business returning so late as that,—after so many cigars; after, perhaps, some superfluous beakers of club nectar. His temper at such a moment would not be fit for such work as hers. But if he was late in coming home, who had sent him away from his home in unhappiness? Between two and three she went to bed, and on the following morning she left Queen Anne Street for the Great Western Station before her father was up.

CHAPTER XV
PARAMOUNT CRESCENT

Lady Macleod lived at No. 3, Paramount Crescent, in Cheltenham, where she occupied a very handsome first-floor drawing-room, with a bedroom behind it, looking over a stable-yard, and a small room which would have been the dressing-room had the late Sir Archibald been alive, but which was at present called the dining-room: and in it Lady Macleod did dine whenever her larger room was to be used for any purposes of evening company. The vicinity of the stable-yard was not regarded by the tenant as among the attractions of the house; but it had the effect of lowering the rent, and Lady Macleod was a woman who regarded such matters. Her income, though small, would have sufficed to enable her to live removed from such discomforts; but she was one of those women who regard it as a duty to leave something behind them,—even though it be left to those who do not at all want it; and Lady Macleod was a woman who wilfully neglected no duty. So she pinched herself, and inhaled the effluvia of the stables, and squabbled with the cabmen, in order that she might bequeath a thousand pounds or two to some Lady Midlothian, who cared, perhaps, little for her, and would hardly thank her memory for the money.

Had Alice consented to live with her, she would have merged that duty of leaving money behind her in that other duty of finding a home for her adopted niece. But Alice had gone away, and therefore the money was due to Lady Midlothian rather than to her. The saving, however, was postponed whenever Alice would consent to visit Cheltenham; and a bedroom was secured for her which did not look out over the stables. Accommodation was also found for her maid much better than that provided for Lady Macleod's own maid. She was a hospitable, good old woman, painfully struggling to do the best she could in the world. It was a pity that she was such a bore, a pity that she was so hard to cabmen and others, a pity that she suspected all tradesmen, servants, and people generally of a rank of life inferior to her own, a pity that she was disposed to condemn for ever and ever so many of her own rank because they played cards on week days, and did not go to church on Sundays,—and a pity, as I think above all, that while she was so suspicious of the poor she was so lenient to the vices of earls, earl's sons, and such like.

Alice, having fully considered the matter, had thought it most prudent to tell Lady Macleod by letter what she had done in regard to Mr. Grey. There had been many objections to the writing of such a letter, but there appeared to be stronger objection to that telling it face to face which would have been forced upon her had she not written. There would in such case have arisen on Lady Macleod's countenance a sternness of rebuke which Alice did not choose to encounter. The same sternness of rebuke would come upon the countenance on receipt of the written information; but it would come in its most aggravated form on the immediate receipt of the letter, and some of its bitterness would have passed away before Alice's arrival. I think that Alice was right. It is better for both parties that any great offence should be confessed by letter.

But Alice trembled as the cab drew up at No. 3, Paramount Crescent. She met her aunt, as was usual, just inside the drawing-room door, and she saw at once that if any bitterness had passed away from that face, the original bitterness must indeed have been bitter. She had so timed her letter that Lady Macleod should have no opportunity of answering it. The answer was written there in the mingled anger and sorrow of those austere features.

"Alice!" she said, as she took her niece in her arms and kissed her; "oh, Alice, what is this?"

"Yes, aunt; it is very bad, I know," and poor Alice tried to make a jest of it. "Young ladies are very wicked when they don't know their own minds. But if they haven't known them and have been wicked, what can they do but repent?"

"Repent!" said Lady Macleod. "Yes; I hope you will repent. Poor Mr. Grey;—what must he think of it?"

"I can only hope, aunt, that he won't think of it at all for very long."

"That's nonsense, my dear, Of course he'll think of it, and of course you'll marry him."

"Shall I, aunt?"

"Of course you will. Why, Alice, hasn't it been all settled among families? Lady Midlothian knew all the particulars of it just as well as I did. And is not your word pledged to him? I really don't understand what you mean. I don't see how it is possible you should go back. Gentlemen when they do that kind of thing are put out of society;—but I really think it is worse in a woman."

"Then they may if they please put me out of society;—only that I don't know that I'm particularly in it."

"And the wickedness of the thing, Alice! I'm obliged to say so."

"When you talk to me about society, aunt, and about Lady Midlothian, I give up to you, willingly;—the more willingly, perhaps, because I don't care much for one or the other." Here Lady Macleod tried to say a word; but she failed, and Alice went on, boldly looking up into her aunt's face, which became a shade more bitter than ever. "But when you tell me about wickedness and my conscience, then I must be my own judge. It is my conscience, and the fear of committing wickedness, that has made me do this."

"You should submit to be guided by your elders, Alice."

"No; my elders in such a matter as this cannot teach me. It cannot be right that I should go to a man's house and be his wife, if I do not think that I can make him happy."

"Then why did you accept him?"

"Because I was mistaken. I am not going to defend that. If you choose to scold me for that, you may do so, aunt, and I will not answer you. But as to marrying him or not marrying him now,—as to that, I must judge for myself."

"It was a pity you did not know your own mind earlier."

"It was a pity,—a great pity. I have done myself an injury that is quite irretrievable;—I know that, and am prepared to bear it. I have done him, too, an injustice which I regret with my whole heart. I can only excuse myself by saying that I might have done him a worse injustice."

All this was said at the very moment of her arrival, and the greeting did not seem to promise much for the happiness of the next month; but perhaps it was better for them both that the attack and the defence should thus be made suddenly, at their first meeting. It is better to pull the string at once when you are in the shower-bath, and not to stand shivering, thinking of the inevitable shock which you can only postpone for a few minutes. Lady Macleod in this case had pulled the string, and thus reaped the advantage of her alacrity.

"Well, my dear," said her ladyship, "I suppose you will like to go up-stairs and take off your bonnet. Mary shall bring you some tea when you come down." So Alice escaped, and when she returned to the comfort of her cup of tea in the drawing-room, the fury of the storm had passed away. She sat talking of other things till dinner; and though Lady Macleod did during the evening make one allusion to "poor Mr. Grey," the subject was allowed to drop. Alice was very tender as to her aunt's ailments, was more than ordinarily attentive to the long list of Cheltenham iniquities which was displayed to her, and refrained from combating any of her aunt's religious views. After a while they got upon the subject of Aunt Greenow, for whose name Lady Macleod had a special aversion,—as indeed she had for all the Vavasor side of Alice's family; and then Alice offered to read, and did read to her aunt many pages out of one of those terrible books of wrath, which from time to time come forth and tell us that there is no hope for us. Lady Macleod liked to be so told; and as she now, poor woman, could not read at nights herself, she enjoyed her evening.

Lady Macleod no doubt did enjoy her niece's sojourn at Cheltenham, but I do not think it could have been pleasant to Alice. On the second day nothing was said about Mr. Grey, and Alice hoped that by her continual readings in the book of wrath her aunt's heart might be softened towards her. But it seemed that Lady Macleod measured the periods of respite, for on the third day and on the fifth she returned to the attack. "Did John Grey still wish that the match should go on?" she asked, categorically. It was in vain that Alice tried to put aside the question, and begged that the matter might not be discussed. Lady Macleod insisted on her right to carry on the examination, and Alice was driven to acknowledge that she believed he did wish it. She could hardly say otherwise, seeing that she had at that moment a letter from him in her pocket, in which he still spoke of his engagement as being absolutely binding on him, and expressed a hope that this change from London to Cheltenham would bring her round and set everything to rights. He certainly did, in a fashion, wave his hand over her, as Kate had said of him. This letter Alice had resolved that she would not answer. He would probably write again, and she would beg him to desist. Instead of Cheltenham bringing her round, Cheltenham had made her firmer than ever in her resolution. I am inclined to think that the best mode of bringing her round at this moment would have been a course of visits from her cousin George, and a series of letters from her cousin Kate. Lady Macleod's injunctions would certainly not bring her round.

After ten days, ten terrible days, devoted to discussions on matrimony in the morning, and to the book of wrath in the evening,—relieved by two tea-parties, in which the sins of Cheltenham were discussed at length,— Lady Macleod herself got a letter from Mr. Grey. Mr. Grey's kindest compliments to Lady Macleod. He believed that Lady Macleod was aware of the circumstances of his engagement with Miss Vavasor. Might he call on Miss Vavasor at Lady Macleod's house in Cheltenham? and might he also hope to have the pleasure of making Lady Macleod's acquaintance? Alice had been in the room when her aunt received this letter, but her aunt had said nothing, and Alice had not known from whom the letter had come. When her aunt crept away with it after breakfast she had suspected nothing, and had never imagined that Lady Macleod, in the privacy of her own room looking out upon the stables, had addressed a letter to Nethercoats. But such a letter had been addressed to Nethercoats, and Mr. Grey had been informed that he would be received in Paramount Crescent with great pleasure.

Mr. Grey had even indicated the day on which he would come, and on the morning of that day Lady Macleod had presided over the two teacups in a state of nervous excitement which was quite visible to Alice. More than once Alice asked little questions, not supposing that she was specially concerned in the matter which had caused her aunt's fidgety restlessness, but observing it so plainly that it was almost impossible not to allude to it. "There's nothing the matter, my dear, at all," at last Lady Macleod said; but as she said so she was making up her mind that the moment had not come in which she must apprise Alice of Mr. Grey's intended visit. As Alice had questioned her at the breakfast table she would say nothing about it then, but waited till the teacups were withdrawn, and till the maid had given her last officious poke to the fire. Then she began. She had Mr. Grey's letter in her pocket, and as she prepared herself to speak, she pulled it out and held it on the little table before her.

"Alice," she said, "I expect a visitor here to-day."

Alice knew instantly who was the expected visitor. Probably any girl under such circumstances would have known equally well. "A visitor, aunt," she said, and managed to hide her knowledge admirably.

"Yes, Alice, a visitor. I should have told you before, only I thought,—I thought I had better not. It is Mr.—Mr. Grey."

"Indeed, aunt! Is he coming to see you?"

"Well;—he is desirous no doubt of seeing you more especially; but he has expressed a wish to make my acquaintance, which I cannot, under the circumstances, think is unnatural. Of course, Alice, he must want to talk over this affair with your friends."

"I wish I could have spared them," said Alice,—"I wish I could."

"I have brought his letter here, and you can see it if you please. It is very nicely written, and as far as I am concerned I should not think of refusing to see him. And now comes the question. What are we to do with him? Am I to ask him to dinner? I take it for granted that he will not expect me to offer him a bed, as he knows that I live in lodgings."

"Oh no, aunt; he certainly will not expect that."

"But ought I to ask him to dinner? I should be most happy to entertain him, though you know how very scanty my means of doing so are;—but I really do not know how it might be,—between you and him, I mean."

"We should not fight, aunt."

"No, I suppose not;—but if you cannot be affectionate in your manner to him—"

"I will not answer for my manners, aunt; but you may be sure of this,—that I should be affectionate in my heart. I shall always regard him as a dearly loved friend; though for many years, no doubt, I shall be unable to express my friendship."

"That may be all very well, Alice, but it will not be what he will want. I think upon the whole that I had better not ask him to dinner."

"Perhaps not, aunt."

"It is a period of the day in which any special constraint among people is more disagreeable than at any other time, and then at dinner the servants must see it. I think there might be some awkwardness if he were to dine here."

"I really think there would," said Alice, anxious to have the subject dropped.

"I hope he won't think that I am inhospitable. I should be so happy to do the best I could for him, for I regard him, Alice, quite as though he were to be your husband. And when anybody at all connected with me has come to Cheltenham I always have asked them to dine, and then I have Gubbins's man to come and wait at table,—as you know."

"Of all men in the world Mr. Grey is the last to think about it."

"That should only make me the more careful. But I think it would perhaps be more comfortable if he were to come in the evening."

"Much more comfortable, aunt."

"I suppose he will be here in the afternoon, before dinner, and we had better wait at home for him. I dare say he'll want to see you alone, and therefore I'll retire to my own rooms,"—looking over the stables! Dear old lady. "But if you wish it, I will receive him first—and then Martha,"—Martha was Alice's maid—"can fetch you down."

This discussion as to the propriety or impropriety of giving her lover a dinner had not been pleasant to Alice, but, nevertheless, when it was over she felt grateful to Lady Macleod. There was an attempt in the arrangement to make Mr. Grey's visit as little painful as possible; and though such a discussion at such a time might as well have been avoided, the decision to which her ladyship had at last come with reference both to the dinner and the management of the visit was, no doubt, the right one.

Lady Macleod had been quite correct in all her anticipations. At three o'clock Mr. Grey was announced, and Lady Macleod, alone, received him in her drawing-room. She had intended to give him a great deal of good advice, to bid him still keep up his heart and as it were hold up his head, to confess to him how very badly Alice was behaving, and to express her entire concurrence with that theory of bodily ailment as the cause and origin of her conduct. But she found that Mr. Grey was a man to whom she could not give much advice. It was he who did the speaking at this conference, and not she. She was overawed by him after the first three minutes. Indeed her first glance at him had awed her. He was so handsome,—and then, in his beauty, he had so quiet and almost saddened an air! Strange to say that after she had seen him, Lady Macleod entertained for him an infinitely higher admiration than before, and yet she was less surprised than she had been at Alice's refusal of him. The conference was very short; and Mr. Grey had not been a quarter of an hour in the house before Martha attended upon her mistress with her summons.

Alice was ready and came down instantly. She found Mr. Grey standing in the middle of the room waiting to receive her, and the look of majesty which had cowed Lady Macleod had gone from his countenance. He could not have received her with a kinder smile, had she come to him with a promise that she would at this meeting name the day for their marriage. "At any rate it does not make him unhappy," she said to herself.

"You are not angry," he said, "that I should have followed you all the way here, to see you."

"No, certainly; not angry, Mr. Grey. All anger that there may be between us must be on your side. I feel that thoroughly."

"Then there shall be none on either side. Whatever may be done, I will not be angry with you. Your father advised me to come down here to you."

"You have seen him, then?"

"Yes, I have seen him. I was in London the day you left."

"It is so terrible to think that I should have brought upon you all this trouble."

"You will bring upon me much worse trouble than that unless—. But I have not now come down here to tell you that. I believe that according to rule in such matters I should not have come to you at all, but I don't know that I care much about such rules."

"It is I that have broken all rules."

"When a lady tells a gentleman that she does not wish to see more of him—"

"Oh, Mr. Grey, I have not told you that."

"Have you not? I am glad at any rate to hear you deny it. But you will understand what I mean. When a gentleman gets his dismissal from a lady he should accept it,—that is, his dismissal under such circumstances as I have received mine. But I cannot lay down my love in that way; nor, maintaining my love, can I give up the battle. It seems to me that I have a right at any rate to know something of your comings and goings as long as,—unless, Alice, you should take another name than mine."

"My intention is to keep my own." This she said in the lowest possible tone,—almost in a whisper,—with her eyes fixed upon the ground.

"And you will not deny me that right?"

"I cannot hinder you. Whatever you may do, I myself have sinned so against you that I can have no right to blame you."

"There shall be no question between us of injury from one to the other. In any conversation that we may have, or in any correspondence—"

"Oh, Mr. Grey, do not ask me to write."

"Listen to me. Should there be any on either side, there shall be no idea of any wrong done."

"But I have done you wrong;—great wrong."

"No, Alice; I will not have it so. When I asked you to accept my hand,—begging the greatest boon which it could ever come to my lot to ask from a fellow-mortal,—I knew well how great was your goodness to me when you told me that it should be mine. Now that you refuse it, I know also that you are good, thinking that in doing so you are acting for my welfare,—thinking more of my welfare than of your own."

"Oh yes, yes; it is so, Mr. Grey; indeed it is so."

"Believing that, how can I talk of wrong? That you are wrong in your thinking on this subject,—that your mind has become twisted by false impressions,—that I believe. But I cannot therefore love you less,—nor, so believing, can I consider myself to be injured. Nor am I even so little selfish as you are. I think if you were my wife that I could make you happy; but I feel sure that my happiness depends on your being my wife."

She looked up into his face, but it was still serene in all its manly beauty. Her cousin George, if he were moved to strong feeling, showed it at once in his eyes, — in his mouth, in the whole visage of his countenance. He glared in his anger, and was impassioned in his love. But Mr. Grey when speaking of the happiness of his entire life, when confessing that it was now at stake with a decision against him that would be ruinous to it, spoke without a quiver in his voice, and had no more sign of passion in his face than if he were telling his gardener to move a rose tree.

"I hope—and believe that you will find your happiness elsewhere, Mr. Grey."

"Well; we can but differ, Alice. In that we do differ. And now I will say one word to explain why I have come here. If I were to write to you against your will, it would seem that I were persecuting you. I cannot bring myself to do that, even though I had the right. But if I were to let you go from me, taking what you have said to me and doing nothing, it would seem that I had accepted your decision as final. I do not do so. I will not do so. I come simply to tell you that I am still your suitor. If you will let me, I will see you again early in January, — as soon as you have returned to town. You will hardly refuse to see me."

"No," she said; "I cannot refuse to see you."

"Then it shall be so," he said, "and I will not trouble you with letters, nor will I trouble you longer now with words. Tell your aunt that I have said what I came to say, and that I give her my kindest thanks." Then he took her hand and pressed it, — not as George Vavasor had pressed it, — and was gone. When Lady Macleod returned, she found that the question of the evening's tea arrangements had settled itself.

CHAPTER XVI
THE ROEBURY CLUB

It has been said that George Vavasor had a little establishment at Roebury, down in Oxfordshire, and thither he betook himself about the middle of November. He had been long known in this county, and whether or no men spoke well of him as a man of business in London, men spoke well of him down there, as one who knew how to ride to hounds. Not that Vavasor was popular among fellow-sportsmen. It was quite otherwise. He was not a man that made himself really popular in any social meetings of men. He did not himself care for the loose little talkings, half flat and half sharp, of men when they meet together in idleness. He was not open enough in his nature for such popularity. Some men were afraid of him, and some suspected him. There were others who made up to him, seeking his intimacy, but these he usually snubbed, and always kept at a distance. Though he had indulged in all the ordinary pleasures of young men, he had never been a jovial man. In his conversations with men he always seemed to think that he should use his time towards serving some purpose of business. With women he was quite the reverse. With women he could be happy. With women he could really associate. A woman he could really love;—but I doubt whether for all that he could treat a woman well.

But he was known in the Oxfordshire country as a man who knew what he was about, and such men are always welcome. It is the man who does not know how to ride that is made uncomfortable in the hunting field by cold looks or expressed censure. And yet it is very rarely that such men do any real harm. Such a one may now and then get among the hounds or override the hunt, but it is not often so. Many such complaints are made; but in truth the too forward man, who presses the dogs, is generally one who can ride, but is too eager or too selfish to keep in his proper place. The bad rider, like the bad whist player, pays highly for what he does not enjoy, and should be thanked. But at both games he gets cruelly snubbed. At both games George Vavasor was great and he never got snubbed.

There were men who lived together at Roebury in a kind of club,—four or five of them, who came thither from London, running backwards and forwards as hunting arrangements enabled them to do so,—a brewer or two and a banker, with a would-be fast attorney, a sporting literary gentleman, and a young unmarried Member of Parliament who had no particular home of his own in the country. These men formed the Roebury Club, and a jolly life they had of it. They had their own wine closet at the King's Head,—or Roebury Inn as the house had come to be popularly called,—and supplied their own game. The landlord found everything else; and as they were not very particular about their bills, they were allowed to do pretty much as they liked in the house. They were rather imperious, very late in their hours, sometimes, though not often, noisy, and once there had been a hasty quarrel which had made the landlord in his anger say that the club should be turned out of his house. But they paid well, chaffed the servants much oftener than they bullied them, and on the whole were very popular.

To this club Vavasor did not belong, alleging that he could not afford to live at their pace, and alleging, also, that his stays at Roebury were not long enough to make him a desirable member. The invitation to him was not repeated and he lodged elsewhere in the little town. But he occasionally went in of an evening, and would make up with the members a table at whist.

He had come down to Roebury by mail train, ready for hunting the next morning, and walked into the club-room just at midnight. There he found Maxwell the banker, Grindley the would-be fast attorney, and Calder Jones the Member of Parliament, playing dummy. Neither of the brewers were there, nor was the sporting literary gentleman.

"Here's Vavasor," said Maxwell, "and now we won't play this blackguard game any longer. Somebody told me, Vavasor, that you were gone away."

"Gone away;—what, like a fox?"

"I don't know what it was; that something had happened to you since last season; that you were married, or dead, or gone abroad. By George, I've lost the trick after all! I hate dummy like the devil. I never hold a card in dummy's hand. Yes, I know; that's seven points on each side. Vavasor, come and cut. Upon my word if any one had asked me, I should have said you were dead."

"But you see, nobody ever does think of asking you anything."

"What you probably mean," said Grindley, "is that Vavasor was not returned for Chelsea last February; but you've seen him since that. Are you going to try it again, Vavasor?"

"If you'll lend me the money I will."

"I don't see what on earth a man gains by going into the house," said Calder Jones. "I couldn't help myself as it happened, but, upon my word it's a deuce of a bore. A fellow thinks he can do as he likes about going, —but he can't. It wouldn't do for me to give it up, because—"

"Oh no, of course not; where should we all be?" said Vavasor.

"It's you and me, Grindems," said Maxwell. "D—— parliament, and now let's have a rubber."

They played till three and Mr. Calder Jones lost a good deal of money, —a good deal of money in a little way, for they never played above ten-shilling points, and no bet was made for more than a pound or two. But Vavasor was the winner, and when he left the room he became the subject of some ill-natured remarks.

"I wonder he likes coming in here," said Grindley, who had himself been the man to invite him to belong to the club, and who had at one time indulged the ambition of an intimacy with George Vavasor.

"I can't understand it," said Calder Jones, who was a little bitter about his money. "Last year he seemed to walk in just when he liked, as though he were one of us."

"He's a bad sort of fellow," said Grindley; "he's so uncommonly dark. I don't know where on earth he gets his money from. He was heir to some small property in the north, but he lost every shilling of that when he was in the wine trade."

"You're wrong there, Grindems," said Maxwell,—making use of a playful nickname which he had invented for his friend. "He made a pot of money at the wine business, and had he stuck to it he would have been a rich man."

"He's lost it all since then, and that place in the north into the bargain."

"Wrong again, Grindems, my boy. If old Vavasor were to die to-morrow, Vavasor Hall would go just as he might choose to leave it. George may be a ruined man for aught I know—"

"There's no doubt about that, I believe," said Grindley.

"Perhaps not, Grindems; but he can't have lost Vavasor Hall because he has never as yet had an interest in it. He's the natural heir, and will probably get it some day."

"All the same," said Calder Jones, "isn't it rather odd he should come in here?"

"We've asked him often enough," said Maxwell; "not because we like him, but because we want him so often to make up a rubber. I don't like George Vavasor, and I don't know who does; but I like him better than dummy. And I'd sooner play whist with men I don't like, Grindems, than I'd not play at all." A bystander might have thought from the tone of Mr. Maxwell's voice that he was alluding to Mr. Grindley himself, but Mr. Grindley didn't seem to take it in that light.

"That's true, of course," said he. "We can't pick men just as we please. But I certainly didn't think that he'd make it out for another season."

The club breakfasted the next morning at nine o'clock, in order that they might start at half-past for the meet at Edgehill. Edgehill is twelve miles from Roebury, and the hacks would do it in an hour and a half,—or perhaps a little less. "Does anybody know anything about that brown horse of Vavasor's?" said Maxwell. "I saw him coming into the yard yesterday with that old groom of his."

"He had a brown horse last season," said Grindley;—"a little thing that went very fast, but wasn't quite sound on the road."

"That was a mare," said Maxwell, "and he sold her to Cinquebars."*

[*Ah, my friend, from whom I have borrowed this scion
of the nobility! Had he been left with us he would have
forgiven me my little theft, and now that he has gone I will
not change the name.]

"For a hundred and fifty," said Calder Jones, "and she wasn't worth the odd fifty."

"He won seventy with her at Leamington," said Maxwell, "and I doubt whether he'd take his money now."

"Is Cinquebars coming down here this year?"

"I don't know," said Maxwell. "I hope not. He's the best fellow in the world, but he can't ride, and he don't care for hunting, and he makes more row than any fellow I ever met. I wish some fellow could tell me something about that fellow's brown horse."

"I'd never buy a horse of Vavasor's if I were you," said Grindley. "He never has anything that's all right all round."

"And who has?" said Maxwell, as he took into his plate a second mutton chop, which had just been brought up hot into the room especially for him. "That's the mistake men make about horses, and that's why there's so much cheating. I never ask for a warranty with a horse, and don't very often have a horse examined. Yet I do as well as others. You can't have perfect horses any more than you can perfect men, or perfect women. You put up with red hair, or bad teeth, or big feet,—or sometimes with the devil of a voice. But a man when he wants a horse won't put up with anything! Therefore those who've got horses to sell must lie. When I go into the market with three hundred pounds I expect a perfect animal. As I never do that now I never expect a perfect animal. I like 'em to see; I like 'em to have four legs; and I like 'em to have a little wind. I don't much mind anything else."

"By Jove you're about right," said Calder Jones. The reader will therefore readily see that Mr. Maxwell the banker reigned as king in that club.

Vavasor had sent two horses on in charge of Bat Smithers, and followed on a pony about fourteen hands high, which he had ridden as a cover hack for the last four years. He did not start till near ten, but he was able to catch Bat with his two horses about a mile and a half on that side of Edgehill. "Have you managed to come along pretty clean?" the master asked as he came up with his servant.

"They be the most beastly roads in all England," said Bat, who always found fault with any county in which he happened to be located. "But I'll warrant I'm cleaner than most on 'em. What for any county should make such roads as them I never could tell."

"The roads about there are bad, certainly;—very bad. But I suppose they would have been better had Providence sent better materials. And what do you think of the brown horse, Bat?"

"Well, sir." He said no more, and that he said with a drawl.

"He's as fine an animal to look at as ever I put my eye on," said George.

"He's all that," said Bat.

"He's got lots of pace too."

"I'm sure he has, sir."

"And they tell me you can't beat him at jumping."

"They can mostly do that, sir, if they're well handled."

"You see he's a deal over my weight."

"Yes, he is, Mr. Vavasor. He is a fourteen stoner."

"Or fifteen," said Vavasor.

"Perhaps he may, sir. There's no knowing what a 'orse can carry till he's tried."

George asked his groom no more questions, but felt sure that he had better sell his brown horse if he could. Now I here protest that there was nothing specially amiss with the brown horse. Towards the end of the preceding season he had overreached himself and had been lame, and had been sold by some owner with more money than brains who had not cared to wait for a cure. Then there had gone with him a bad character, and a vague suspicion had attached itself to him, as there does to hundreds of horses which are very good animals in their way. He had come thus to Tattersall's, and Vavasor had bought him cheap, thinking that he might make money of him, from his form and action. He had found nothing amiss with him,—nor, indeed, had Bat Smithers. But his character went with him, and therefore Bat Smithers thought it well to be knowing. George Vavasor knew as much of horses as most men can,—as, perhaps, as any man can who is not a dealer, or a veterinary surgeon; but he, like all men, doubted his own knowledge, though on that subject he would never admit that he doubted it. Therefore he took Bat's word and felt sure that the horse was wrong.

"We shall have a run from the big wood," said George.

"If they make un break, you will, sir," said Bat.

"At any rate I'll ride the brown horse," said George. Then, as soon as that was settled between them, the Roebury Club overtook them.

There was now a rush of horses on the road altogether, and they were within a quarter of a mile of Edgehill church, close to which was the meet. Bat with his two hunters fell a little behind, and the others trotted on together. The other grooms with their animals were on in advance, and were by this time employed in combing out forelocks, and rubbing stirrup leathers and horses' legs free from the dirt of the roads;—but Bat Smithers was like his master, and did not congregate much with other men, and Vavasor was sure to give orders to his servant different from the orders given by others.

"Are you well mounted this year?" Maxwell asked of George Vavasor.

"No, indeed; I never was what I call well mounted yet. I generally have one horse and three or four cripples. That brown horse behind there is pretty good, I believe."

"I see your man has got the old chestnut mare with him."

"She's one of the cripples,—not but what she's as sound as a bell, and as good a hunter as ever I wish to ride; but she makes a little noise when she's going."

"So that you can hear her three fields off," said Grindley.

"Five if the fields are small enough and your ears are sharp enough," said Vavasor. "All the same I wouldn't change her for the best horse I ever saw under you."

"Had you there, Grindems," said Maxwell.

"No, he didn't," said Grindley. "He didn't have me at all."

"Your horses, Grindley, are always up to all the work they have to do," said George; "and I don't know what any man wants more than that."

"Had you again, Grindems," said Maxwell.

"I can ride against him any day," said Grindley.

"Yes; or against a brick wall either, if your horse didn't know any better," said George.

"Had you again, Grindems," said Maxwell. Whereupon Mr. Grindley trotted on, round the corner by the church, and into the field in which the hounds were assembled. The fire had become too hot for him, and he thought it best to escape. Had it been Vavasor alone he would have turned upon him and snarled, but he could not afford to exhibit any ill temper to the king of the club. Mr. Grindley was not popular, and were Maxwell to turn openly against him his sporting life down at Roebury would decidedly be a failure.

The lives of such men as Mr. Grindley,—men who are tolerated in the daily society of others who are accounted their superiors, do not seem to have many attractions. And yet how many such men does one see in almost every set? Why Mr. Grindley should have been inferior to Mr. Maxwell the banker, or to Stone, or to Prettyman who were brewers, or even to Mr. Pollock the heavy-weight literary gentleman, I can hardly say. An attorney by his trade is at any rate as good as a brewer, and there are many attorneys who hold their heads high anywhere. Grindley was a rich man,—or at any rate rich enough for the life he led. I don't know much about his birth, but I believe it was as good as Maxwell's. He was not ignorant, or a fool;—whereas I rather think Maxwell was a fool. Grindley had made his own way in the world, but Maxwell would certainly not have made himself a banker if his father had not been a banker before him; nor could the bank have gone on and prospered had there not been partners there who were better men of business than our friend. Grindley knew that he had a better intellect than Maxwell; and yet he allowed Maxwell to snub him, and he toadied Maxwell in return. It was not on the score of riding that Maxwell claimed and held his superiority, for Grindley did not want pluck, and every one knew that Maxwell had lived freely and that his nerves were not what they had been. I think it had come from the outward look of the men, from the form of each, from the gait and visage which in one was good and in the other insignificant. The nature of such dominion of man over man is very singular, but this is certain that when once obtained in manhood it may be easily held.

Among boys at school the same thing is even more conspicuous, because boys have less of conscience than men, are more addicted to tyranny, and when weak are less prone to feel the misery and disgrace of succumbing. Who has been through a large school and does not remember the Maxwells and Grindleys,—the tyrants and the slaves,—those who domineered and those who submitted? Nor was it, even then, personal strength, nor always superior courage, that gave the power of command. Nor was it intellect, or thoughtfulness, nor by any means such qualities as make men and boys lovable. It is said by many who have had to deal with boys, that certain among them claim and obtain ascendancy by the spirit within them; but I doubt whether the ascendancy is not rather thrust on them than claimed by them. Here again I think the outward gait of the boy goes far towards obtaining for him the submission of his fellows.

But the tyrant boy does not become the tyrant man, or the slave boy the slave man, because the outward visage, that has been noble or mean in the one, changes and becomes so often mean or noble in the other.

"By George, there's Pollock!" said Maxwell, as he rode into the field by the church. "I'll bet half a crown that he's come down from London this morning, that he was up all night last night, and that he tells us so three times before the hounds go out of the paddock." Mr. Pollock was the heavy-weight sporting literary gentleman.

CHAPTER XVII
EDGEHILL

Of all sights in the world there is, I think, none more beautiful than that of a pack of fox-hounds seated, on a winter morning, round the huntsman, if the place of meeting has been chosen with anything of artistic skill. It should be in a grassy field, and the field should be small. It should not be absolutely away from all buildings, and the hedgerows should not have been clipped and pared, and made straight with reference to modern agricultural economy. There should be trees near, and the ground should be a little uneven, so as to mark some certain small space as the exact spot where the dogs and servants of the hunt should congregate.

There are well-known grand meets in England, in the parks of noblemen, before their houses, or even on what are called their lawns; but these magnificent affairs have but little of the beauty of which I speak. Such assemblies are too grand and too ornate, and, moreover, much too far removed from true sporting proprieties. At them, equipages are shining, and ladies' dresses are gorgeous, and crowds of tradesmen from the neighbouring town have come there to look at the grand folk. To my eye there is nothing beautiful in that. The meet I speak of is arranged with a view to sport, but the accident of the locality may make it the prettiest thing in the world.

Such, in a special degree, was the case at Edgehill. At Edgehill the whole village consisted of three or four cottages; but there was a small old church, with an old grey tower, and a narrow, green, almost dark, churchyard, surrounded by elm-trees. The road from Roebury to the meet passed by the church stile, and turning just beyond it came upon the gate which led into the little field in which the hounds felt themselves as much at home as in their kennels. There might be six or seven acres in the field, which was long and narrow, so that the huntsman had space to walk leisurely up and down with the pack clustering round him, when he considered that longer sitting might chill them. The church tower was close at hand, visible through the trees, and the field itself was green and soft, though never splashing with mud or heavy with holes.

Edgehill was a favourite meet in that country, partly because foxes were very abundant in the great wood adjacent, partly because the whole country around is grass-land, and partly, no doubt, from the sporting propensities of the neighbouring population. As regards my own taste, I do not know that I do like beginning a day with a great wood,—and if not beginning it, certainly not ending it. It is hard to come upon the cream of hunting, as it is upon the cream of any other delight. Who can always drink Lafitte of the finest, can always talk to a woman who is both beautiful and witty, or can always find the right spirit in the poetry he reads? A man has usually to work through much mud before he gets his nugget. It is so certainly in hunting, and a big wood too frequently afflicts the sportsman, as the mud does the miner. The small gorse cover is the happy, much-envied bit of ground in which the gold is sure to show itself readily. But without the woods the gorse would not hold the foxes, and without the mud the gold would not have found its resting-place.

But, as I have said, Edgehill was a popular meet, and, as regarded the meet itself, was eminently picturesque. On the present occasion the little field was full of horsemen, moving about slowly, chatting together, smoking cigars, getting off from their hacks and mounting their hunters, giving orders to their servants, and preparing for the day. There were old country gentlemen there, greeting each other from far sides of the county; sporting farmers who love to find themselves alongside their landlords, and to feel that the pleasures of the country are common to both; men down from town, like our friends of the Roebury club, who made hunting their chosen pleasure, and who formed, in number, perhaps the largest portion of the field; officers from garrisons round about; a cloud of servants, and a few nondescript stragglers who had picked up horses, hither and thither, round the country. Outside the gate on the road were drawn up a variety of vehicles, open carriages, dog-carts, gigs, and waggonettes, in some few of which were seated ladies who had come over to see the meet. But Edgehill was, essentially, not a ladies' meet. The distances to it were long, and the rides in Cranby Wood—the big wood—were not adapted for wheels. There were one or two ladies on horseback, as is always the case; but Edgehill was not a place popular, even with hunting ladies. One carriage, that of the old master of the hounds, had entered the sacred precincts of the field, and from this the old baronet was just descending, as Maxwell, Calder Jones, and Vavasor rode into the field.

Edgehill.

"I hope I see you well, Sir William," said Maxwell, greeting the master. Calder Jones also made his little speech, and so did Vavasor.

"Humph—well, yes, I'm pretty well, thank'ee. Just move on, will you? My mare can't stir here." Then some one else spoke to him, and he only grunted in answer. Having slowly been assisted up on to his horse,—for he was over seventy years of age,—he trotted off to the hounds, while all the farmers round him touched their hats to him. But his mind was laden with affairs of import, and he noticed no one. In a whispered voice he gave his instructions to his huntsman, who said, "Yes, Sir William," "No, Sir William," "No doubt, Sir William." One long-eared, long-legged fellow, in a hunting-cap and scarlet coat, hung listening by, anxious to catch something of the orders for the morning. "Who the devil's that fellow, that's all breeches and boots?" said Sir William aloud to some one near him, as the huntsman moved off with the hounds. Sir William knew the man well enough, but was minded to punish him for his discourtesy. "Where shall we find first, Sir William?" said Calder Jones, in a voice that was really very humble. "How the mischief am I to know where the foxes are?" said Sir William, with an oath; and Calder Jones retired unhappy, and for the moment altogether silenced.

And yet Sir William was the most popular man in the county, and no more courteous gentleman ever sat at the bottom of his own table. A mild man he was, too, when out of his saddle, and one by no means disposed to assume special supremacy. But a master of hounds, if he have long held the country,—and Sir William had held his for more than thirty years,—obtains a power which that of no other potentate can equal. He may say and do what he pleases, and his tyranny is always respected. No conspiracy against him has a chance of success; no sedition will meet with sympathy;—that is, if he be successful in showing sport. If a man be sworn at, abused, and put down without cause, let him bear it and think that he has been a victim for the public good. And let him never be angry with the master. That rough tongue is the necessity of the master's position. They used to say that no captain could manage a ship without swearing at his men. But what are the captain's troubles in comparison with those of the master of hounds? The captain's men are under discipline, and can be locked up, flogged, or have their grog stopped. The master of hounds cannot stop the grog of any offender, and he can only stop the tongue, or horse, of such an one by very sharp words.

"Well, Pollock, when did you come?" said Maxwell.

"By George," said the literary gentleman, "just down from London by the 8.30 from Euston Square, and got over here from Winslow in a trap, with two fellows I never saw in my life before. We came tandem in a fly, and did the nineteen miles in an hour."

"Come, Athenian, draw it mild," said Maxwell.

"We did, indeed. I wonder whether they'll pay me their share of the fly. I had to leave Onslow Crescent at a quarter before eight, and I did three hours' work before I started."

"Then you did it by candle-light," said Grindley.

"Of course I did; and why shouldn't I? Do you suppose no one can work by candle-light except a lawyer? I suppose you fellows were playing whist, and drinking hard. I'm uncommon glad I wasn't with you, for I shall be able to ride."

"I bet you a pound," said Jones, "if there's a run, I see more of it than you."

"I'll take that bet with Jones," said Grindley, "and Vavasor shall be the judge."

"Gentlemen, the hounds can't get out, if you will stop up the gate," said Sir William. Then the pack passed through, and they all trotted on for four miles, to Cranby Wood.

Vavasor, as he rode on to the wood, was alone, or speaking, from time to time, a few words to his servant. "I'll ride the chestnut mare in the wood," he said, "and do you keep near me."

"I bean't to be galloping up and down them rides, I suppose," said Bat, almost contemptuously.

"I shan't gallop up and down the rides, myself; but do you mark me, to know where I am, so that I can change if a fox should go away."

"You'll be here all day, sir. That's my belief."

"If so, I won't ride the brown horse at all. But do you take care to let me have him if there's a chance. Do you understand?"

"Oh, yes, I understand, sir. There ain't no difficulty in my understanding;—only I don't think, sir, you'll ever get a fox out of that wood to-day. Why, it stands to reason. The wind's from the north-east."

Cranby Wood is very large,—there being, in truth, two or three woods together. It was nearly twelve before they found; and then for an hour there was great excitement among the men, who rode up and down the rides as the hounds drove the fox from one end to another of the enclosure. Once or twice the poor animal did try to go away, and then there was great hallooing, galloping, and jumping over unnecessary fences; but he was headed back again, or changed his mind, not liking the north-east wind of which Bat Smithers had predicted such bad things. After one the crowd of men became rather more indifferent, and clustered together in broad spots, eating their lunch, smoking cigars, and chaffing each other. It was singular to observe the amazing quantity of ham sandwiches and of sherry that had been carried into Cranby Wood on that day. Grooms appeared to have been laden with cases, and men were as well armed with flasks at their saddle-bows as they used to be with pistols. Maxwell and Pollock formed the centre of one of these crowds, and chaffed each other with the utmost industry, till, tired of having inflicted no wounds, they turned upon Grindley and drove him out of the circle. "You'll make that man cut his throat, if you go on at that," said Pollock. "Shall I?" said Maxwell. "Then I'll certainly stick to him for the sake of humanity in general." During all this time Vavasor sat apart, quite alone, and Bat Smithers grimly kept his place, about three hundred yards from him.

"We shan't do any good to-day," said Grindley, coming up to Vavasor.

"I'm sure I don't know," said Vavasor.

"That old fellow has got to be so stupid, he doesn't know what he's about," said Grindley, meaning Sir William.

"How can he make the fox break?" said Vavasor; and as his voice was by no means encouraging Grindley rode away.

Lunch and cigars lasted till two, during which hour the hounds, the huntsmen, the whips, and old Sir William were hard at work, as also were some few others who persistently followed every chance of the game. From that till three there were two or three flashes in the pan, and false reports as to foxes which had gone away, which first set men galloping, and then made them very angry. After three, men began to say naughty things, to abuse Cranby Wood, to wish violently that they had remained at home or gone elsewhere, and to speak irreverently of their ancient master. "It's the cussidest place in all creation," said Maxwell. "I often said I'd not come here any more, and now I say it again."

"And yet you'll be here the next meet," said Grindley, who had sneaked back to his old companions in weariness of spirit.

"Grindems, you know a sight too much," said Maxwell; "you do indeed. An ordinary fellow has no chance with you."

Grindley was again going to catch it, but was on this time saved by the appearance of the huntsman, who came galloping up one of the rides, with a lot of the hounds at his heels.

"He isn't away, Tom, surely?" said Maxwell.

"He's out of the wood somewheres," said Tom;—and off they all went. Vavasor changed his horse, getting on to the brown one, and giving up his chestnut mare to Bat Smithers, who suggested that he might as well go home to Roebury now. Vavasor gave him no answer, but, trotting on to the point where the rides met, stopped a moment and listened carefully. Then he took a path diverging away from that by which the huntsmen and the crowd of horsemen had gone, and made the best of his way through the wood. At the end of this he came upon Sir William, who, with no one near him but his servant, was standing in the pathway of a little hunting-gate.

"Hold hard," said Sir William. "The hounds are not out of the wood yet."

"Is the fox away, sir?"

"What's the good of that if we can't get the hounds out?—Yes, he's away. He passed out where I'm standing." And then he began to blow his horn lustily, and by degrees other men and a few hounds came down the ride. Then Tom, with his horse almost blown, made his appearance outside the wood, and soon there came a rush of men, nearly on the top of one another, pushing on, not knowing whither, but keenly alive to the fact that the fox had at last consented to move his quarters.

Tom touched his hat, and looked at his master, inquiringly. "He's gone for Claydon's," said the master. "Try them up that hedgerow." Tom did try them up the hedgerow, and in half a minute the hounds came upon the scent. Then you might see men settling their hats on their heads, and feeling their feet in the stirrups. The moment for which they had so long waited had come, and yet there were many who would now have preferred that the fox should be headed back into cover. Some had but little confidence in their half-blown horses;—with many the waiting, though so abused and anathematized, was in truth more to their taste than the run itself;—with others the excitement had gone by, and a gallop over a field or two was necessary before it would be restored. With most men at such a moment there is a little nervousness, some fear of making a bad start, a dread lest others should have more of the success of the hunt than falls to them. But there was a great rush and a mighty bustle as the hounds made out their game, and Sir William felt himself called upon to use the rough side of his tongue to more than one delinquent.

And then certain sly old stagers might be seen turning off to the left, instead of following the course of the game as indicated by the hounds. They were men who had felt the air as they came out, and knew that the fox must soon run down wind, whatever he might do for the first half mile or so,—men who knew also which was the shortest way to Claydon's by the road. Ah, the satisfaction that there is when these men are thrown out, and their dead knowledge proved to be of no avail! If a fox will only run straight, heading from the cover on his real line, these very sagacious gentlemen seldom come to much honour and glory.

In the present instance the beast seemed determined to go straight enough, for the hounds ran the scent along three or four hedgerows in a line. He had managed to get for himself full ten minutes' start, and had been able to leave the cover and all his enemies well behind him before he bethought himself as to his best way to his purposed destination. And here, from field to field, there were little hunting-gates at which men crowded lustily, poking and shoving each other's horses, and hating each other with a bitterness of hatred which is, I think, known nowhere else. No hunting man ever wants to jump if he can help it, and the hedges near the gate were not alluring. A few there were who made lines for themselves, taking the next field to the right, or scrambling through the corners of the fences while the rush was going on at the gates; and among these was George Vavasor. He never rode in a crowd, always keeping himself somewhat away from men as well as hounds. He would often be thrown out, and then men would hear no more of him for that day. On such occasions he did not show himself, as other men do, twenty minutes after the fox had been killed or run to ground,—but betook himself home by himself, going through the byeways and lanes, thus leaving no report of his failure to be spoken of by his compeers.

As long as the line of gates lasted, the crowd continued as thick as ever, and the best man was he whose horse could shove the hardest. After passing some four or five fields in this way they came out upon a road, and, the scent holding strong, the dogs crossed it without any demurring. Then came doubt into the minds of men, many of whom, before they would venture away from their position on the lane, narrowly watched the leading hounds to see whether there was indication of a turn to the one side or the other. Sir William, whose seventy odd years excused him, turned sharp to the left, knowing that he could make Claydon's that way; and very many were the submissive horsemen who followed him; a few took the road to the right, having in their minds some little game of their own. The hardest riders there had already crossed from the road into the country, and were going well to the hounds, ignorant, some of them, of the brook before them, and others unheeding. Foremost among these was Burgo Fitzgerald,—Burgo Fitzgerald, whom no man had ever known to crane at a fence, or to hug a road, or to spare his own neck or his horse's. And yet poor Burgo seldom finished well,—coming to repeated grief in this matter of his hunting, as he did so constantly in other matters of his life.

But almost neck and neck with Burgo was Pollock, the sporting literary gentleman. Pollock had but two horses to his stud, and was never known to give much money for them;—and he weighed without his boots, fifteen stones! No one ever knew how Pollock did it;—more especially as all the world declared that he was as ignorant of hunting as any tailor. He could ride, or when he couldn't ride he could tumble,—men said that of him,—and he would ride as long as the beast under him could go. But few knew the sad misfortunes which poor Pollock sometimes encountered;—the muddy ditches in which he was left; the despair with which he would stand by his unfortunate horse when the poor brute could no longer move across some deep-ploughed field; the miles that he would walk at night beside a tired animal, as he made his way slowly back to Roebury!

Then came Tom the huntsman, with Calder Jones close to him, and Grindley intent on winning his sovereign. Vavasor had also crossed the road somewhat to the left, carrying with him one or two who knew that he was a safe man to follow. Maxwell had been ignominiously turned by the hedge, which, together with its ditch, formed a fence such as all men do not love at the beginning of a run. He had turned from it, acknowledging the cause. "By George!" said he, "that's too big for me yet awhile; and there's no end of a river at the bottom." So he had followed the master down the road.

All those whom we have named managed to get over the brook, Pollock's horse barely contriving to get up his hind legs from the broken edge of the bank. Some nags refused it, and their riders thus lost all their chance of sport for that day. Such is the lot of men who hunt. A man pays five or six pounds for his day's amusement, and it is ten to one that the occurrences of the day disgust rather than gratify him! One or two got in, and scrambled out on the other side, but Tufto Pearlings, the Manchester man from Friday Street, stuck in the mud at the bottom, and could not get his mare out till seven men had come with ropes to help him. "Where the devil is my fellow?" Pearlings asked of the countrymen; but the countrymen could not tell him that "his fellow" with his second horse was riding the hunt with great satisfaction to himself.

George Vavasor found that his horse went with him uncommonly well, taking his fences almost in the stride of his gallop, and giving unmistakeable signs of good condition. "I wonder what it is that's amiss with him," said George to himself, resolving, however, that he would sell him that day if he got an opportunity. Straight went the line of the fox, up from the brook, and Tom began to say that his master had been wrong about Claydon's.

"Where are we now?" said Burgo, as four or five of them dashed through the open gate of a farmyard.

"This is Bulby's farm," said Tom, "and we're going right away for Elmham Wood."

"Elmham Wood be d——," said a stout farmer, who had come as far as that with them. "You won't see Elmham Wood to-day."

"I suppose you know best," said Tom; and then they were through the yard, across another road, and down a steep ravine by the side of a little copse. "He's been through them firs, any way," said Tom. "To him, Gaylass!" Then up they went the other side of the ravine, and saw the body of the hounds almost a field before them at the top.

"I say,—that took some of the wind out of a fellow," said Pollock.

"You mustn't mind about wind now," said Burgo, dashing on.

"Wasn't the pace awful, coming up to that farmhouse?" said Calder Jones, looking round to see if Grindley was shaken off. But Grindley, with some six or seven others, was still there. And there, also, always in the next field to the left, was George Vavasor. He had spoken no word to any one since the hunt commenced, nor had he wished to speak to any one. He desired to sell his horse,—and he desired also to succeed in the run for other reasons than that, though I think he would have found it difficult to define them.

Now they had open grass land for about a mile, but with very heavy fences,—so that the hounds gained upon them a little, and Pollock's weight began to tell. The huntsman and Burgo were leading with some fortunate county gentleman whose good stars had brought him in upon them at the farmyard gate. It is the injustice of such accidents as this that breaks the heart of a man who has honestly gone through all the heat and work of the struggle! And the hounds had veered a little round to the left, making, after all, for Claydon's. "Darned if the Squire warn't right," said Tom. Sir William, though a baronet, was familiarly called the Squire throughout the hunt.

"We ain't going for Claydon's now?" asked Burgo.

"Them's Claydon's beeches we sees over there," said Tom. "'Tain't often the Squire's wrong."

Here they came to a little double rail and a little quick-set hedge. A double rail is a nasty fence always if it has been made any way strong, and one which a man with a wife and a family is justified in avoiding. They mostly can be avoided, having gates; and this could have been avoided. But Burgo never avoided anything, and went over it beautifully. The difficulty is to be discreet when the man before one has been indiscreet. Tom went for the gate, as did Pollock, who knew that he could have no chance at the double rails. But Calder Jones came to infinite grief, striking the top bar of the second rail, and going head-foremost out of his saddle, as though thrown by a catapult. There we must leave him. Grindley, rejoicing greatly at this discomfiture, made for the gate; but the country gentleman with the fresh horse accomplished the rails, and was soon alongside of Burgo.

"I didn't see you at the start," said Burgo.

"And I didn't see you," said the country gentleman; "so it's even."

Burgo did not see the thing in the same light, but he said no more. Grindley and Tom were soon after them, Tom doing his utmost to shake off the attorney. Pollock was coming on also; but the pace had been too much for him, and though the ground rode light his poor beast laboured and grunted sorely. The hounds were still veering somewhat to the left, and Burgo, jumping over a small fence into the same field with them, saw that there was a horseman ahead of him. This was George Vavasor, who was going well, without any symptom of distress.

And now they were at Claydon's, having run over some seven miles of ground in about thirty-five minutes. To those who do not know what hunting is, this pace does not seem very extraordinary; but it had been quite quick enough, as was testified by the horses which had gone the distance.

Our party entered Claydon's Park at back, through a gate in the park palings that was open on hunting days; but a much more numerous lot was there almost as soon as them, who had come in by the main entrance. This lot was headed by Sir William, and our friend Maxwell was with him.

"A jolly thing so far," said Burgo to Maxwell; "about the best we've had this year."

"I didn't see a yard of it," said Maxwell. "I hadn't nerve to get off the first road, and I haven't been off it ever since." Maxwell was a man who never lied about his hunting, or had the slightest shame in riding roads. "Who's been with you?" said he.

"There've been Tom and I;—and Calder Jones was there for a while. I think he killed himself somewhere. And there was Pollock, and your friend Grindley, and a chap whose name I don't know who dropped out of heaven about half-way in the run; and there was another man whose back I saw just now; there he is,—by heavens, it's Vavasor! I didn't know he was here."

They hung about the Claydon covers for ten minutes, and then their fox went off again,—their fox or another, as to which there was a great discussion afterwards; but he who would have suggested the idea of a new fox to Sir William would have been a bold man. A fox, however, went off, turning still to the left from Claydon's towards Roebury. Those ten minutes had brought up some fifty men; but it did not bring up Calder Jones nor Tufto Pearlings, nor some half-dozen others who had already come to serious misfortune; but Grindley was there, very triumphant in his own success, and already talking of Jones's sovereign. And Pollock was there also, thankful for the ten minutes' law, and trusting that wind might be given to his horse to finish the run triumphantly.

But the pace on leaving Claydon's was better than ever. This may have come from the fact that the scent was keener, as they got out so close upon their game. But I think they must have changed their fox. Maxwell, who saw him go, swore that he was fresh and clean. Burgo said that he knew it to be the same fox, but gave no reason. "Same fox! in course it was; why shouldn't it be the same?" said Tom. The country gentleman who had dropped from heaven was quite sure that they had changed, and so were most of those who had ridden the road. Pollock confined himself to hoping that he might soon be killed, and that thus his triumph for the day might be assured.

On they went, and the pace soon became too good for the poor author. His horse at last refused a little hedge, and there was not another trot to be got out of him. That night Pollock turned up at Roebury about nine o'clock, very hungry,—and it was known that his animal was alive;—but the poor horse ate not a grain of oats that night, nor on the next morning. Vavasor had again taken a line to himself, on this occasion a little to the right of the meet; but Maxwell followed him and rode close with him to the end. Burgo for a while still led the body of the field, incurring at first much condemnation from Sir William,—nominally for hurrying on among the hounds, but in truth because he got before Sir William himself. During this latter part of the run Sir William stuck to the hounds in spite of his seventy odd years. Going down into Marham Bottom, some four or five were left behind, for they feared the soft ground near the river, and did not know the pass through it. But Sir William knew it, and those who remained close to him got over that trouble. Burgo, who would still lead, nearly foundered in the bog;—but he was light, and his horse pulled him through,—leaving a fore-shoe in the mud. After that Burgo was contented to give Sir William the lead.

Then they came up by Marham Pits to Cleshey Small Wood, which they passed without hanging there a minute, and over the grass lands of Cleshey Farm. Here Vavasor and Maxwell joined the others, having gained some three hundred yards in distance by their course, but having been forced to jump the Marham Stream which Sir William had forded. The pace now was as good as the horses could make it,—and perhaps something better as regarded some of them. Sir William's servant had been with him, and he had got his second horse at Claydon's; Maxwell had been equally fortunate; Tom's second horse had not come up, and his beast was in great distress; Grindley had remained behind at Marham Bottom, being contented perhaps with having beaten Calder Jones,—from whom by-the-by I may here declare that he never got his sovereign. Burgo, Vavasor, and the country gentleman still held on; but it was devoutly desired by all of them that the fox might soon come to the end of his tether. Ah! that intense longing that the fox may fail, when the failings of the horse begin to make themselves known,—and the consciousness comes on that all that one has done will go for nothing unless the thing can be brought to a close in a field or two! So far you have triumphed, leaving scores of men behind; but of what good is all that, if you also are to be left behind at the last?

It was manifest now to all who knew the country that the fox was making for Thornden Deer Park, but Thornden Deer Park was still two miles ahead of them, and the hounds were so near to their game that the poor beast could hardly hope to live till he got there. He had tried a well-known drain near Cleshey Farm House; but it had been inhospitably, nay cruelly, closed against him. Soon after that he threw himself down in a ditch, and the eager hounds overran him, giving him a moment's law,—and giving also a moment's law to horses that wanted it as badly. "I'm about done for," said Burgo to Maxwell. "Luckily for you," said Maxwell, "the fox is much in the same way."

But the fox had still more power left in him than poor Burgo Fitzgerald's horse. He gained a minute's check and then he started again, being viewed away by Sir William himself. The country gentleman of whom mention has been made also viewed him, and holloa'd as he did so: "Yoicks, tally; gone away!" The unfortunate man! "What the d—— are you roaring at?" said Sir William. "Do you suppose I don't know where the fox is?" Whereupon the country gentleman retreated, and became less conspicuous than he had been.

Away they went again, off Cleshey and into Thornden parish, on the land of Sorrel Farm,—a spot well to be remembered by one or two ever afterwards. Here Sir William made for a gate which took him a little out of the line, but Maxwell and Burgo Fitzgerald, followed by Vavasor, went straight ahead. There was a huge ditch and boundary bank there which Sir William had known and had avoided. Maxwell, whose pluck had returned to him at last, took it well. His horse was comparatively fresh and made nothing of it. Then came poor Burgo! Oh, Burgo, hadst thou not have been a very child, thou shouldst have known that now, at this time of the day,—after all that thy gallant horse had done for thee,—it was impossible to thee or him. But when did Burgo Fitzgerald know anything? He rode at the bank as though it had been the first fence of the day, striking his poor beast with his spurs, as though muscle, strength, and new power could be imparted by their rowels. The animal rose at the bank and in some way got upon it, scrambling as he struck it with his chest, and then fell headlong into the ditch at the other side, a confused mass of head, limbs, and body. His career was at an end, and he had broken his heart! Poor noble beast, noble in vain! To his very last gasp he had done his best, and had deserved that he should have been in better hands. His master's ignorance had killed him. There are men who never know how little a horse can do,—or how much!

There was to some extent a gap in the fence when Maxwell had first ridden it and Burgo had followed him; a gap, or break in the hedge at the top, indicating plainly the place at which a horse could best get over. To this spot Vavasor followed, and was on the bank at Burgo's heels before he knew what had happened. But the man had got away and only the horse lay there in the ditch. "Are you hurt?" said Vavasor; "can I do anything?" But he did not stop, "If you can find a chap just send him to me," said Burgo in a melancholy tone. Then he sat down, with his feet in the ditch, and looked at the carcase of his horse.

There was no more need of jumping that day. The way was open into the next field,—a turnip field,—and there amidst the crisp breaking turnip-tops, with the breath of his enemies hot upon him, with their sharp teeth at his entrails, biting at them impotently in the agonies of his death struggle, poor Reynard finished his career. Maxwell was certainly the first there,— but Sir William and George Vavasor were close upon him. That taking of brushes of which we used to hear is a little out of fashion; but if such honour were due to any one it was due to Vavasor, for he and he only had ridden the hunt throughout. But he claimed no honour, and none was specially given to him. He and Maxwell rode homewards together, having sent assistance to poor Burgo Fitzgerald; and as they went along the road, saying but little to each other, Maxwell, in a very indifferent voice, asked him a question.

"What do you want for that horse, Vavasor?"

"A hundred and fifty," said Vavasor.

"He's mine," said Maxwell. So the brown horse was sold for about half his value, because he had brought with him a bad character.

CHAPTER XVIII
ALICE VAVASOR'S GREAT RELATIONS

Burgo Fitzgerald, of whose hunting experiences something has been told in the last chapter, was a young man born in the purple of the English aristocracy. He was related to half the dukes in the kingdom, and had three countesses for his aunts. When he came of age he was master of a sufficient fortune to make it quite out of the question that he should be asked to earn his bread; and though that, and other windfalls that had come to him, had long since been spent, no one had ever made to him so ridiculous a proposition as that. He was now thirty, and for some years past had been known to be much worse than penniless; but still he lived on in the same circles, still slept softly and drank of the best, and went about with his valet and his groom and his horses, and fared sumptuously every day. Some people said the countesses did it for him, and some said that it was the dukes;—while others, again, declared that the Jews were his most generous friends. At any rate he still seemed to live as he had always lived, setting tradesmen at defiance, and laughing to scorn all the rules which regulate the lives of other men.

About eighteen months before the time of which I am now speaking, a great chance had come in this young man's way, and he had almost succeeded in making himself one of the richest men in England. There had been then a great heiress in the land, on whom the properties of half-a-dozen ancient families had concentrated; and Burgo, who in spite of his iniquities still kept his position in the drawing-rooms of the great, had almost succeeded in obtaining the hand and the wealth,—as people still said that he had obtained the heart,—of the Lady Glencora M'Cluskie. But sundry mighty magnates, driven almost to despair at the prospect of such a sacrifice, had sagaciously put their heads together, and the result had been that the Lady Glencora had heard reason. She had listened,—with many haughty tossings indeed of her proud little head, with many throbbings of her passionate young heart; but in the end she listened and heard reason. She saw Burgo, for the last time, and told him that she was the promised bride of Plantagenet Palliser, nephew and heir of the Duke of Omnium.

He had borne it like a man,—never having groaned openly, or quivered once before any comrade at the name of the Lady Glencora. She had married Mr. Palliser at St. George's Square, and on the morning of the marriage he had hung about his club door in Pall Mall, listening to the bells, and saying a word or two about the wedding, with admirable courage. It had been for him a great chance,—and he had lost it. Who can say, too, that his only regret was for the money? He had spoken once of it to a married sister of his, in whose house he had first met Lady Glencora. "I shall never marry now,—that is all," he said—and then he went about, living his old reckless life, with the same recklessness as ever. He was one of those young men with dark hair and blue eyes,—who wear no beard, and are certainly among the handsomest of all God's creatures. No more handsome man than Burgo Fitzgerald lived in his days; and this merit at any rate was his,—that he thought nothing of his own beauty. But he lived ever without conscience, without purpose,—with no idea that it behoved him as a man to do anything but eat and drink,—or ride well to hounds till some poor brute, much nobler than himself, perished beneath him.

He chiefly concerns our story at this present time because the Lady Glencora who had loved him,—and would have married him had not those sagacious heads prevented it,—was a cousin of Alice Vavasor's. She was among those very great relations with whom Alice was connected by her mother's side,—being indeed so near to Lady Macleod, that she was first cousin to that lady, only once removed. Lady Midlothian was aunt to the Lady Glencora, and our Alice might have called cousins, and not been forbidden, with the old Lord of the Isles, Lady Glencora's father,—who was dead, however, some time previous to that affair with Burgo,—and with the Marquis of Auld Reekie, who was Lady Glencora's uncle, and had been her guardian. But Alice had kept herself aloof from her grand relations on her mother's side, choosing rather to hold herself as belonging to those who were her father's kindred. With Lady Glencora, however, she had for a short time—for some week or ten days,—been on terms of almost affectionate intimacy. It had been then, when the wayward heiress with the bright waving locks had been most strongly minded to give herself and her wealth to Burgo Fitzgerald. Burgo had had money dealings with George Vavasor, and knew him,—knew him intimately, and had learned the fact of his cousinship between the heiress and his friend's cousin. Whereupon in the agony of those weeks in which the sagacious heads were resisting her love, Lady Glencora came to her cousin in Queen Anne Street, and told Alice all that tale. "Was Alice," she asked, "afraid of the marquises and the countesses, or of all the rank and all the money which they boasted?" Alice answered that she was not at all afraid of them. "Then would she permit Lady Glencora and Burgo to see each other in the drawing-room at Queen Anne Street, just once!" Just once,—so that they might arrange that little plan of an elopement. But Alice could not do that for her newly found cousin. She endeavoured to explain that it was not the dignity of the sagacious heads which stood in her way, but her woman's feeling of what was right and wrong in such a matter.

"Why should I not marry him?" said Lady Glencora, with her eyes flashing. "He is my equal."

Alice explained that she had no word to say against such a marriage. She counselled her cousin to be true to her love if her love was in itself true. But she, an unmarried woman, who had hitherto not known her cousin, might not give such help as that! "If you will not help me, I am helpless!" said the Lady Glencora, and then she kneeled at Alice's knees and threw her wavy locks abroad on Alice's lap. "How shall I bribe you?" said Lady Glencora. "Next to him I will love you better than all the world." But Alice, though she kissed the fair forehead and owned that such reward would be worth much to her, could not take any bribe for such a cause. Then Lady Glencora had been angry with her, calling her heartless, and threatening her that she too might have sorrow of her own and want assistance. Alice told nothing of her own tale,—how she had loved her cousin and had been forced to give him up, but said what kind words she could, and she of the waving hair and light blue eyes had been pacified. Then she had come again,—had come daily while the sagacious heads were at work,—and Alice in her trouble had been a comfort to her.

But the sagacious heads were victorious, as we know, and Lady Glencora M'Cluskie became Lady Glencora Palliser with all the propriety in the world, instead of becoming wife to poor Burgo, with all imaginable impropriety. And then she wrote a letter to Alice, very short and rather sad; but still with a certain sweetness in it. "She had been counselled that it was not fitting for her to love as she had thought to love, and she had resolved to give up her dream. Her cousin Alice, she knew, would respect her secret. She was going to become the wife of the best man, she thought, in all the world; and it should be the one care of her life to make him happy." She said not a word in all her letter of loving this newly found lord. "She was to be married at once. Would Alice be one among the bevy of bridesmaids who were to grace the ceremony?"

Alice wished her joy heartily,—"heartily," she said, but had declined that office of bridesmaid. She did not wish to undergo the cold looks of the Lady Julias and Lady Janes who all would know each other, but none of whom would know her. So she sent her cousin a little ring, and asked her to keep it amidst all the wealthy tribute of marriage gifts which would be poured forth at her feet.

From that time to this present Alice had heard no more of Lady Glencora. She had been married late in the preceding season and had gone away with Mr. Palliser, spending her honeymoon amidst the softnesses of some Italian lake. They had not returned to England till the time had come for them to encounter the magnificent Christmas festivities of Mr. Palliser's uncle, the Duke. On this occasion Gatherum Castle, the vast palace which the Duke had built at a cost of nearly a quarter of a million, was opened, as it had never been opened before;—for the Duke's heir had married to the Duke's liking, and the Duke was a man who could do such things handsomely when he was well pleased. Then there had been a throng of bridal guests, and a succession of bridal gaieties which had continued themselves even past the time at which Mr. Palliser was due at Westminster;—and Mr. Palliser was a legislator who served his country with the utmost assiduity. So the London season commenced, progressed, and was consumed; and still Alice heard nothing more of her friend and cousin Lady Glencora.

But this had troubled her not at all. A chance circumstance, the story of which she had told to no one, had given her a short intimacy with this fair child of the gold mines, but she had felt that they two could not live together in habits of much intimacy. She had, when thinking of the young bride, only thought of that wild love episode in the girl's life. It had been strange to her that she should in one week have listened to the most passionate protestations from her friend of love for one man, and then have been told in the next that another man was to be her friend's husband! But she reflected that her own career was much the same,—only with the interval of some longer time.

But her own career was not the same. Glencora had married Mr. Palliser,—had married him without pausing to doubt;—but Alice had gone on doubting till at last she had resolved that she would not marry Mr. Grey. She thought of this much in those days at Cheltenham, and wondered often whether Glencora lived with her husband in the full happiness of conjugal love.

One morning, about three days after Mr. Grey's visit, there came to her two letters, as to neither of which did she know the writer by the handwriting. Lady Macleod had told her,—with some hesitation, indeed, for Lady Macleod was afraid of her,—but had told her, nevertheless, more than once, that those noble relatives had heard of the treatment to which Mr. Grey was being subjected, and had expressed their great sorrow,—if not dismay or almost anger. Lady Macleod, indeed, had gone as far as she dared, and might have gone further without any sacrifice of truth. Lady Midlothian had said that it would be disgraceful to the family, and Lady Glencora's aunt, the Marchioness of Auld Reekie, had demanded to be told what it was the girl wanted.

When the letters came Lady Macleod was not present, and I am disposed to think that one of them had been written by concerted arrangement with her. But if so she had not dared to watch the immediate effect of her own projectile. This one was from Lady Midlothian. Of the other Lady Macleod certainly knew nothing, though it also had sprung out of the discussions which had taken place as to Alice's sins in the Auld Reekie-Midlothian set. This other letter was from Lady Glencora. Alice opened the two, one without reading the other, very slowly. Lady Midlothian's was the first opened, and then came a spot of anger on Alice's cheeks as she saw the signature, and caught a word or two as she allowed her eye to glance down the page. Then she opened the other, which was shorter, and when she saw her cousin's signature, "Glencora Palliser," she read that letter first, —read it twice before she went back to the disagreeable task of perusing Lady Midlothian's lecture. The reader shall have both the letters, but that from the Countess shall have precedence.

Castle Reekie, N.B.
— Oct. 186—.

My dear Miss Vavasor,
I have not the pleasure of knowing you personally,
though I have heard of you very often from our dear
mutual friend and relative Lady Macleod, with whom
I understand that you are at present on a visit. Your
grandmother,—by the mother's side,—Lady Flora Macleod,
and my mother the Countess of Leith, were half-sisters;
and though circumstances since that have prevented our
seeing so much of each other as is desirable, I have always
remembered the connection, and have ever regarded you
as one in whose welfare I am bound by ties of blood to take
a warm interest.

"'Since that!' —what does she mean by 'since that'?" said Alice to herself. "She has never set eyes on me at all. Why does she talk of not having seen as much of me as is desirable?"

I had learned with great gratification that you were going
to be married to a most worthy gentleman, Mr. John Grey

of Nethercoats, in Cambridgeshire. When I first heard this I made it my business to institute some inquiries, and I was heartily glad to find that your choice had done you so much credit. [If the reader has read Alice's character as I have meant it should be read, it will thoroughly be understood that this was wormwood to her.] I was informed that Mr. Grey is in every respect a gentleman,— that he is a man of most excellent habits, and one to whom any young woman could commit her future happiness with security, that his means are very good for his position, and that there was no possible objection to such a marriage. All this gave great satisfaction to me, in which I was joined by the Marchioness of Auld Reekie, who is connected with you almost as nearly as I am, and who, I can assure you, feels a considerable interest in your welfare. I am staying with her now, and in all that I say, she agrees with me.

You may feel then how dreadfully we were dismayed when we were told by dear Lady Macleod that you had told Mr. Grey that you intended to change your mind! My dear Miss Vavasor, can this be true? There are things in which a young lady has no right to change her mind after it has been once made up; and certainly when a young lady has accepted a gentleman, that is one of them. He cannot legally make you become his wife, but he has a right to claim you before God and man. Have you considered that he has probably furnished his house in consequence of his intended marriage,—and perhaps in compliance with your own especial wishes? [I think that Lady Macleod must have told the Countess something that she had heard about the garden.] Have you reflected that he has of course told all his friends? Have you any reason to give? I am told, none! Nothing should ever be done without a reason; much less such a thing as this in which your own interests and, I may say, respectability are involved. I hope you will think of this before you persist in destroying your own happiness and perhaps that of a very worthy man.

I had heard, some years ago, when you were much younger, that you had become imprudently attached in another direction—with a gentleman with none of those qualities to recommend him which speak so highly for Mr. Grey. It would grieve me very much, as it would also the Marchioness, who in this matter thinks exactly as I do, if I were led to suppose that your rejection of Mr. Grey had been caused by any renewal of that project. Nothing, my dear Miss Vavasor, could be more unfortunate,—and I might almost add a stronger word.

I have been advised that a line from me as representing your poor mother's family, especially as I have at the present moment the opportunity of expressing Lady Auld Reekie's sentiments as well as my own, might be of service. I implore you, my dear Miss Vavasor, to remember what you owe to God and man, and to carry out an engagement made by yourself, that is in all respects comme il faut, and which will give entire satisfaction to your friends and relatives.

Margaret M. Midlothian.

I think that Lady Macleod had been wrong in supposing that this could do any good. She should have known Alice better; and should also have known the world better. But her own reverence for her own noble relatives was so great that she could not understand, even yet, that all such feeling was wanting to her niece. It was to her impossible that the expressed opinion of such an one as the Countess of Midlothian, owning her relationship and solicitude, and condescending at the same time to express friendship,— she could not, I say, understand that the voice of such an one, so speaking, should have no weight whatever. But I think that she had been quite right in keeping out of Alice's way at the moment of the arrival of the letter. Alice read it, slowly, and then replacing it in its envelope, leaned back quietly in her chair,—with her eyes fixed upon the teapot on the table. She had, however, the other letter on which to occupy her mind, and thus relieve her from the effects of too deep an animosity against the Countess.

The Lady Glencora's letter was as follows:

Matching Priory,
Thursday.

Dear Cousin,

I have just come home from Scotland, where they have been telling me something of your little troubles. I had little troubles once too, and you were so good to me! Will you come to us here for a few weeks? We shall be here till Christmas-time, when we go somewhere else. I have told my husband that you are a great friend of mine as well as a cousin, and that he must be good to you. He is very quiet, and works very hard at politics; but I think you will like him. Do come! There will be a good many people here, so that you will not find it dull. If you will name the day we will send the carriage for you at Matching Station, and I dare say I can manage to come myself.

Yours affectionately,

G. Palliser.

P.S. I know what will be in your mind. You will say, why did not she come to me in London? She knew the way to Queen Anne Street well enough. Dear Alice, don't say that. Believe me, I had much to do and think of in London. And if I was wrong, yet you will forgive me. Mr. Palliser says I am to give you his love,—as being a cousin,—and say that you must come!

This letter was certainly better than the other, but Alice, on reading it, came to a resolve that she would not accept the invitation. In the first place, even that allusion to her little troubles jarred upon her feelings; and then she thought that her rejection of Mr. Grey could be no special reason why she should go to Matching Priory. Was it not very possible that she had been invited that she might meet Lady Midlothian there, and encounter all the strength of a personal battery from the Countess? Lady Glencora's letter she would of course answer, but to Lady Midlothian she would not condescend to make any reply whatever.

About eleven o'clock Lady Macleod came down to her. For half-an-hour or so Alice said nothing; nor did Lady Macleod ask any question. She looked inquisitively at Alice, eyeing the letter which was lying by the side of her niece's workbasket, but she said no word about Mr. Grey or the Countess. At last Alice spoke.

"Aunt," she said, "I have had a letter this morning from your friend, Lady Midlothian."

"She is my cousin, Alice; and yours as much as mine."

"Your cousin then, aunt. But it is of more moment that she is your friend. She certainly is not mine, nor can her cousinship afford any justification for her interfering in my affairs."

"Alice,—from her position—"

"Her position can be nothing to me, aunt. I will not submit to it. There is her letter, which you can read if you please. After that you may burn it. I need hardly say that I shall not answer it."

"And what am I to say to her, Alice?"

"Nothing from me, aunt;—from yourself, whatever you please, of course." Then there was silence between them for a few minutes. "And I have had another letter, from Lady Glencora, who married Mr. Palliser, and whom I knew in London last spring."

"And has that offended you, too?"

"No, there is no offence in that. She asks me to go and see her at Matching Priory, her husband's house; but I shall not go."

But at last Alice agreed to pay this visit, and it may be as well to explain here how she was brought to do so. She wrote to Lady Glencora, declining, and explaining frankly that she did decline, because she thought it probable that she might there meet Lady Midlothian. Lady Midlothian, she said, had interfered very unwarrantably in her affairs, and she did not wish to make her acquaintance. To this Lady Glencora replied, post haste, that she had intended no such horrid treachery as that for Alice; that neither would Lady Midlothian be there, nor any of that set; by which Alice knew that Lady Glencora referred specially to her aunt the Marchioness; that no one would be at Matching who could torment Alice, either with right or without it, "except so far as I myself may do so," Lady Glencora said; and then she named an early day in November, at which she would herself undertake to meet Alice at the Matching Station. On receipt of this letter, Alice, after two days' doubt, accepted the invitation.

CHAPTER XIX
TRIBUTE FROM OILEYMEAD

Kate Vavasor, in writing to her cousin Alice, felt some little difficulty in excusing herself for remaining in Norfolk with Mrs. Greenow. She had laughed at Mrs. Greenow before she went to Yarmouth, and had laughed at herself for going there. And in all her letters since, she had spoken of her aunt as a silly, vain, worldly woman, weeping crocodile tears, for an old husband whose death had released her from the tedium of his company, and spreading lures to catch new lovers. But yet she agreed to stay with her aunt, and remain with her in lodgings at Norwich for a month.

But Mrs. Greenow had about her something more than Kate had acknowledged when she first attempted to read her aunt's character. She was clever, and in her own way persuasive. She was very generous, and possessed a certain power of making herself pleasant to those around her. In asking Kate to stay with her she had so asked as to make it appear that Kate was to confer the favour. She had told her niece that she was all alone in the world. "I have money," she had said, with more appearance of true feeling than Kate had observed before. "I have money, but I have nothing else in the world. I have no home. Why should I not remain here in Norfolk, where I know a few people? If you'll say that you'll go anywhere else with me, I'll go to any place you'll name." Kate had believed this to be hardly true. She had felt sure that her aunt wished to remain in the neighbourhood of her seaside admirers; but, nevertheless, she had yielded, and at the end of October the two ladies, with Jeannette, settled themselves in comfortable lodgings within the precincts of the Close at Norwich.

Mr. Greenow at this time had been dead very nearly six months, but his widow made some mistakes in her dates and appeared to think that the interval had been longer. On the day of their arrival at Norwich it was evident that this error had confirmed itself in her mind. "Only think," she said, as she unpacked a little miniature of the departed one, and sat with it for a moment in her hands, as she pressed her handkerchief to her eyes, "only think, that it is barely nine months since he was with me?"

"Six, you mean, aunt," said Kate, unadvisedly.

"Only nine months" repeated Mrs. Greenow, as though she had not heard her niece. "Only nine months!" After that Kate attempted to correct no more such errors. "It happened in May, Miss," Jeannette said afterwards to Miss Vavasor, "and that, as we reckons, it will be just a twelvemonth come Christmas." But Kate paid no attention to this.

And Jeannette was very ungrateful, and certainly should have indulged herself in no such sarcasms. When Mrs. Greenow made a slight change in her mourning, which she did on her arrival at Norwich, using a little lace among her crapes, Jeannette reaped a rich harvest in gifts of clothes. Mrs. Greenow knew well enough that she expected more from a servant than mere service;—that she wanted loyalty, discretion, and perhaps sometimes a little secrecy;—and as she paid for these things, she should have had them.

Kate undertook to stay a month with her aunt at Norwich, and Mrs. Greenow undertook that Mr. Cheesacre should declare himself as Kate's lover, before the expiration of the month. It was in vain that Kate protested that she wanted no such lover, and that she would certainly reject him if he came. "That's all very well, my dear," Aunt Greenow would say. "A girl must settle herself some day, you know;—and you'd have it all your own way at Oileymead."

But the offer certainly showed much generosity on the part of Aunt Greenow, inasmuch as Mr. Cheesacre's attentions were apparently paid to herself rather than to her niece. Mr. Cheesacre was very attentive. He had taken the lodgings in the Close, and had sent over fowls and cream from Oileymead, and had called on the morning after their arrival; but in all his attentions he distinguished the aunt more particularly than the niece. "I am all for Mr. Cheesacre, Miss," said Jeannette once. "The Captain is perhaps the nicerer-looking gentleman, and he ain't so podgy like; but what's good looks if a gentleman hasn't got nothing? I can't abide anything that's poor; neither can't Missus." From which it was evident that Jeannette gave Miss Vavasor no credit in having Mr. Cheesacre in her train.

Captain Bellfield was also at Norwich, having obtained some quasi-military employment there in the matter of drilling volunteers. Certain capacities in that line it may be supposed that he possessed, and, as his friend Cheesacre said of him, he was going to earn an honest penny once in his life. The Captain and Mr. Cheesacre had made up any little differences that had existed between them at Yarmouth, and were close allies again when they left that place. Some little compact on matters of business must have been arranged between them,—for the Captain was in funds again. He was in funds again through the liberality of his friend,—and no payment of former loans had been made, nor had there been any speech of such. Mr.

Cheesacre had drawn his purse-strings liberally, and had declared that if all went well the hospitality of Oileymead should not be wanting during the winter. Captain Bellfield had nodded his head and declared that all should go well.

"You won't see much of the Captain, I suppose," said Mr. Cheesacre to Mrs. Greenow on the morning of the day after her arrival at Norwich. He had come across the whole way from Oileymead to ask her if she found herself comfortable,—and perhaps with an eye to the Norwich markets at the same time. He now wore a pair of black riding boots over his trousers, and a round topped hat, and looked much more at home than he had done by the seaside.

"Not much, I dare say," said the widow. "He tells me that he must be on duty ten or twelve hours a day. Poor fellow!"

"It's a deuced good thing for him, and he ought to be very much obliged to me for putting him in the way of getting it. But he told me to tell you that if he didn't call, you were not to be angry with him."

"Oh, no;—I shall remember, of course."

"You see, if he don't work now he must come to grief. He hasn't got a shilling that he can call his own."

"Hasn't he really?"

"Not a shilling, Mrs. Greenow;—and then he's awfully in debt. He isn't a bad fellow, you know, only there's no trusting him for anything." Then after a few further inquiries that were almost tender, and a promise of further supplies from the dairy, Mr. Cheesacre took his leave, almost forgetting to ask after Miss Vavasor.

But as he left the house he had a word to say to Jeannette. "He hasn't been here, has he, Jenny?" "We haven't seen a sight of him yet, sir,—and I have thought it a little odd." Then Mr. Cheesacre gave the girl half-a-crown, and went his way. Jeannette, I think, must have forgotten that the Captain had looked in after leaving his military duties on the preceding evening.

The Captain's ten or twelve hours of daily work was performed, no doubt, at irregular intervals,—some days late and some days early,—for he might be seen about Norwich almost at all times, during the early part of that November;—and he might be very often seen going into the Close. In Norwich there are two weekly market-days, but on those days the Captain was no doubt kept more entirely to his military employment, for at such times he never was seen near the Close. Now Mr. Cheesacre's visits to the town were generally made on market-days, and so it happened that they did not meet. On such occasions Mr. Cheesacre always was driven to Mrs. Greenow's door in a cab,—for he would come into town by railway,—and he would deposit a basket bearing the rich produce of his dairy. It was in vain that Mrs. Greenow protested against these gifts,—for she did protest and declared that if they were continued, they would be sent back. They were, however, continued, and Mrs. Greenow was at her wits' end about them. Cheesacre would not come up with them; but leaving them, would go about his business, and would return to see the ladies. On such occasions he would be very particular in getting his basket from Jeannette. As he did so he would generally ask some question about the Captain, and Jeannette would give him answers confidentially,—so that there was a strong friendship between these two.

"What am I to do about it?" said Mrs. Greenow, as Kate came into the sitting-room one morning, and saw on the table a small hamper lined with a clean cloth. "It's as much as Jeannette has been able to carry."

"So it is, ma'am,—quite; and I'm strong in the arm, too, ma'am."

"What am I to do, Kate? He is such a good creature."

"And he do admire you both so much," said Jeannette.

"Of course I don't want to offend him for many reasons," said the aunt, looking knowingly at her niece.

"I don't know anything about your reasons, aunt, but if I were you, I should leave the basket just as it is till he comes in the afternoon."

"Would you mind seeing him yourself, Kate, and explaining to him that it won't do to get on in this way. Perhaps you wouldn't mind telling him that if he'll promise not to bring any more, you won't object to take this one."

"Indeed, aunt, I can't do that. They're not brought to me."

"Oh, Kate!"

"Nonsense, aunt;—I won't have you say so;—before Jeannette, too."

"I think it's for both, ma'am; I do indeed. And there certainly ain't any cream to be bought like it in Norwich:—nor yet eggs."

"I wonder what there is in the basket." And the widow lifted up the corner of the cloth. "I declare if there isn't a turkey poult already."

"My!" said Jeannette. "A turkey poult! Why, that's worth ten and sixpence in the market if it's worth a penny."

"It's out of the question that I should take upon myself to say anything to him about it," said Kate.

"Upon my word I don't see why you shouldn't, as well as I," said Mrs. Greenow.

"I'll tell you what, ma'am," said Jeannette: "let me just ask him who they're for;—he'll tell me anything."

"Don't do anything of the kind, Jeannette," said Kate. "Of course, aunt, they're brought for you. There's no doubt about that. A gentleman doesn't bring cream and turkeys to— I've never heard of such a thing!"

"I don't see why a gentleman shouldn't bring cream and turkeys to you just as well as to me. Indeed, he told me once as much himself."

"Then, if they're for me, I'll leave them down outside the front door, and he may find his provisions there." And Kate proceeded to lift the basket off the table.

"Leave it alone, Kate," said Mrs. Greenow, with a voice that was rather solemn; and which had, too, something of sadness in its tone. "Leave it alone. I'll see Mr. Cheesacre myself."

"And I do hope you won't mention my name. It's the most absurd thing in the world. The man never spoke two dozen words to me in his life."

"He speaks to me, though," said Mrs. Greenow.

"I dare say he does," said Kate.

"And about you, too, my dear."

"He doesn't come here with those big flowers in his button-hole for nothing," said Jeannette,—"not if I knows what a gentleman means."

"Of course he doesn't," said Mrs. Greenow.

"If you don't object, aunt," said Kate, "I will write to grandpapa and tell him that I will return home at once."

"What!—because of Mr. Cheesacre?" said Mrs. Greenow. "I don't think you'll be so silly as that, my dear."

On the present occasion Mrs. Greenow undertook that she would see the generous gentleman, and endeavour to stop the supplies from his farmyard. It was well understood that he would call about four o'clock, when his business in the town would be over; and that he would bring with him a little boy, who would carry away the basket. At that hour Kate of course was absent, and the widow received Mr. Cheesacre alone. The basket and cloth were there, in the sitting-room, and on the table were laid out the rich things which it had contained;—the turkey poult first, on a dish provided in the lodging-house, then a dozen fresh eggs in a soup plate, then the cream in a little tin can, which, for the last fortnight, had passed regularly between Oileymead and the house in the Close, and as to which Mr. Cheesacre was very pointed in his inquiries with Jeannette. Then behind the cream there were two or three heads of broccoli, and a stick of celery as thick as a man's wrist. Altogether the tribute was a very comfortable assistance to the housekeeping of a lady living in a small way in lodgings.

Mr. Cheesacre, when he saw the array on the long sofa-table, knew that he was to prepare himself for some resistance; but that resistance would give him, he thought, an opportunity of saying a few words that he was desirous of speaking, and he did not altogether regret it. "I just called in," he said, "to see how you were."

"We are not likely to starve," said Mrs. Greenow, pointing to the delicacies from Oileymead.

"Just a few trifles that my old woman asked me to bring in," said Cheesacre. "She insisted on putting them up."

"But your old woman is by far too magnificent," said Mrs. Greenow. "She really frightens Kate and me out of our wits."

Mr. Cheesacre had no wish that Miss Vavasor's name should be brought into play upon the occasion. "Dear Mrs. Greenow," said he, "there is no cause for you to be alarmed, I can assure you. Mere trifles;—light as air, you know. I don't think anything of such things as these."

"But I and Kate think a great deal of them,—a very great deal, I can assure you. Do you know, we had a long debate this morning whether or no we would return them to Oileymead?"

"Return them, Mrs. Greenow!"

"Yes, indeed: what are women, situated as we are, to do under such circumstances? When gentlemen will be too liberal, their liberality must be repressed."

"And have I been too liberal, Mrs. Greenow? What is a young turkey and a stick of celery when a man is willing to give everything that he has in the world?"

"You've got a great deal more in the world, Mr. Cheesacre, than you'd like to part with. But we won't talk of that, now."

"When shall we talk of it?"

"If you really have anything to say, you had by far better speak to Kate herself."

"Mrs. Greenow, you mistake me. Indeed, you mistake me." Just at this moment, as he was drawing close to the widow, she heard, or fancied that she heard, Jeannette's step, and, going to the sitting-room door, called to her maid. Jeannette did not hear her, but the bell was rung, and then Jeannette came. "You may take these things down, Jeannette," she said. "Mr. Cheesacre has promised that no more shall come."

"But I haven't promised," said Mr. Cheesacre.

"You will oblige me and Kate, I know;—and, Jeannette, tell Miss Vavasor that I am ready to walk with her."

Then Mr. Cheesacre knew that he could not say those few words on that occasion; and as the hour of his train was near, he took his departure, and went out of the Close, followed by the little boy, carrying the basket, the cloth, and the tin can.

CHAPTER XX
WHICH SHALL IT BE?

The next day was Sunday, and it was well known at the lodging-house in the Close that Mr. Cheesacre would not be seen there then. Mrs. Greenow had specially warned him that she was not fond of Sunday visitors, fearing that otherwise he might find it convenient to give them too much of his society on that idle day. In the morning the aunt and niece both went to the Cathedral, and then at three o'clock they dined. But on this occasion they did not dine alone. Charlie Fairstairs, who, with her family, had come home from Yarmouth, had been asked to join them; and in order that Charlie might not feel it dull, Mrs. Greenow had, with her usual good-nature, invited Captain Bellfield. A very nice little dinner they had. The captain carved the turkey, giving due honour to Mr. Cheesacre as he did so; and when he nibbled his celery with his cheese, he was prettily jocose about the richness of the farmyard at Oileymead.

"He is the most generous man I ever met," said Mrs. Greenow.

"So he is," said Captain Bellfield, "and we'll drink his health. Poor old Cheesy! It's a great pity he shouldn't get himself a wife."

"I don't know any man more calculated to make a young woman happy," said Mrs. Greenow.

"No, indeed," said Miss Fairstairs. "I'm told that his house and all about it is quite beautiful."

"Especially the straw-yard and the horse-pond," said the Captain. And then they drank the health of their absent friend.

It had been arranged that the ladies should go to church in the evening, and it was thought that Captain Bellfield would, perhaps, accompany them; but when the time for starting came, Kate and Charlie were ready, but the widow was not, and she remained,—in order, as she afterwards explained to Kate, that Captain Bellfield might not seem to be turned out of the house. He had made no offer churchwards, and,—"Poor man," as Mrs. Greenow said in her little explanation, "if I hadn't let him stay there, he would have had no resting-place for the sole of his foot, but some horrid barrack-room!"

Therefore the Captain was allowed to find a resting-place in Mrs. Greenow's drawing-room; but on the return of the young ladies from church, he was not there, and the widow was alone, "looking back," she said, "to things that were gone;—that were gone. But come, dears, I am not going to make you melancholy." So they had tea, and Mr. Cheesacre's cream was used with liberality.

Captain Bellfield had not allowed the opportunity to slip idly from his hands. In the first quarter of an hour after the younger ladies had gone, he said little or nothing, but sat with a wine-glass before him, which once or twice he filled from the decanter. "I'm afraid the wine is not very good," said Mrs. Greenow. "But one can't get good wine in lodgings."

"I'm not thinking very much about it, Mrs. Greenow; that's the truth," said the Captain. "I daresay the wine is very good of its kind." Then there was another period of silence between them.

"I suppose you find it rather dull, living in lodgings; don't you?" asked the Captain.

"I don't know quite what you mean by dull, Captain Bellfield; but a woman circumstanced as I am, can't find her life very gay. It's not a full twelvemonth yet since I lost all that made life desirable, and sometimes I wonder at myself for holding up as well as I do."

"It's wicked to give way to grief too much, Mrs. Greenow."

"That's what my dear Kate always says to me, and I'm sure I do my best to overcome it." Upon this soft tears trickled down her cheek, showing in their course that she at any rate used no paint in producing that freshness of colour which was one of her great charms. Then she pressed her handkerchief to her eyes, and removing it, smiled faintly on the Captain. "I didn't intend to treat you to such a scene as this, Captain Bellfield."

"There is nothing on earth, Mrs. Greenow, I desire so much, as permission to dry those tears."

"Time alone can do that, Captain Bellfield;—time alone."

"But cannot time be aided by love and friendship and affection?"

"By friendship, yes. What would life be worth without the solace of friendship?"

"And how much better is the warm glow of love?" Captain Bellfield, as he asked this question, deliberately got up, and moved his chair over to the widow's side. But the widow as deliberately changed her position to the corner of a sofa. The Captain did not at once follow her, nor did he in any way show that he was aware that she had fled from him.

"How much better is the warm glow of love?" he said again, contenting himself with looking into her face with all his eyes. He had hoped that he would have been able to press her hand by this time.

"The warm, glow of love, Captain Bellfield, if you have ever felt it—"

"If I have ever felt it! Do I not feel it now, Mrs. Greenow? There can be no longer any mask kept upon my feelings. I never could restrain the yearnings of my heart when they have been strong."

"Have they often been strong, Captain Bellfield?"

"Yes; often;—in various scenes of life; on the field of battle—"

"I did not know that you had seen active service."

"What!—not on the plains of Zuzuland, when with fifty picked men I kept five hundred Caffres at bay for seven weeks;—never knew the comfort of a bed, or a pillow to my head, for seven long weeks!"

"Not for seven weeks?" said Mrs. Greenow.

"No. Did I not see active service at Essiquebo, on the burning coast of Guiana, when all the wild Africans from the woods rose up to destroy the colony; or again at the mouth of the Kitchyhomy River, when I made good the capture of a slaver by my own hand and my own sword!"

"I really hadn't heard," said Mrs. Greenow.

"Ah, I understand. I know. Cheesy is the best fellow in the world in some respects, but he cannot bring himself to speak well of a fellow behind his back. I know who has belittled me. Who was the first to storm the heights of Inkerman?" demanded the Captain, thinking in the heat of the moment that he might as well be hung for a sheep as a lamb.

"But when you spoke of yearnings, I thought you meant yearnings of a softer kind."

"So I did. So I did. I don't know why I have been led away to speak of deeds that are very seldom mentioned, at any rate by myself. But I cannot bear that a slanderous backbiting tongue should make you think that I have seen no service. I have served her Majesty in the four quarters of the globe, Mrs. Greenow; and now I am ready to serve you in any way in which you will allow me to make my service acceptable." Whereupon he took one stride over to the sofa, and went down upon his knees before her.

"But, Captain Bellfield, I don't want any services. Pray get up now; the girl will come in."

"I care nothing for any girl. I am planted here till some answer shall have been made to me; till some word shall have been said that may give me a little hope." Then he attempted to get hold of her hand, but she put them behind her back and shook her head. "Arabella," he said, "will you not speak a word to me?"

"Not a word, Captain Bellfield, till you get up; and I won't have you call me Arabella. I am the widow of Samuel Greenow, than whom no man was more respected where he was known, and it is not fitting that I should be addressed in that way."

"But I want you to become my wife,—and then—"

"Ah, then indeed! But that then isn't likely to come. Get up, Captain Bellfield, or I'll push you over and then ring the bell. A man never looks so much like a fool as when he's kneeling down,—unless he's saying his prayers, as you ought to be doing now. Get up, I tell you. It's just half past seven, and I told Jeannette to come to me then."

There was that in the widow's voice which made him get up, and he rose slowly to his feet. "You've pushed all the chairs about, you stupid man," she said. Then in one minute she had restored the scattered furniture to their proper places, and had rung the bell. When Jeannette came she desired that tea might be ready by the time that the young ladies returned, and asked Captain Bellfield if a cup should be set for him. This he declined, and bade her farewell while Jeannette was still in the room. She shook hands with him without any sign of anger, and even expressed a hope that they might see him again before long.

"He's a very handsome man, is the Captain," said Jeannette, as the hero of the Kitchyhomy River descended the stairs.

"You shouldn't think about handsome men, child," said Mrs. Greenow.

"And I'm sure I don't," said Jeannette. "Not no more than anybody else; but if a man is handsome, ma'am, why it stands to reason that he is handsome."

"I suppose Captain Bellfield has given you a kiss and a pair of gloves."

"As for gloves and such like, Mr. Cheesacre is much better for giving than the Captain; as we all know; don't we, ma'am? But in regard to kisses, they're presents as I never takes from anybody. Let everybody pay his debts. If the Captain ever gets a wife, let him kiss her."

On the following Tuesday morning Mr. Cheesacre as usual called in the Close, but he brought with him no basket. He merely left a winter nosegay made of green leaves and laurestinus flowers, and sent up a message to say that he should call at half past three, and hoped that he might then be able to see Mrs. Greenow—on particular business.

"That means you, Kate," said Mrs. Greenow.

"No, it doesn't; it doesn't mean me at all. At any rate he won't see me."

"I dare say it's me he wishes to see. It seems to be the fashionable plan now for gentlemen to make offers by deputy. If he says anything, I can only refer him to you, you know."

"Yes, you can; you can tell him simply that I won't have him. But he is no more thinking of me than—"

"Than he is of me, you were going to say."

"No, aunt; I wasn't going to say that at all."

"Well, we shall see. If he does mean anything, of course you can please yourself; but I really think you might do worse."

"But if I don't want to do at all?"

"Very well; you must have your own way. I can only tell you what I think."

At half past three o'clock punctually Mr. Cheesacre came to the door, and was shown up-stairs. He was told by Jeannette that Captain Bellfield had looked in on the Sunday afternoon, but that Miss Fairstairs and Miss Vavasor had been there the whole time. He had not got on his black boots nor yet had his round topped hat. And as he did wear a new frock coat, and had his left hand thrust into a kid glove, Jeannette was quite sure that he intended business of some kind. With new boots, creaking loudly, he walked up into the drawing-room, and there he found the widow alone.

"Thanks for the flowers," she said at once. "It was so good of you to bring something that we could accept."

"As for that," said he, "I don't see why you should scruple about a trifle of cream, but I hope that any such feeling as that will be over before long." To this the widow made no answer, but she looked very sweetly on him as she bade him sit down.

He did sit down; but first he put his hat and stick carefully away in one corner, and then he pulled off his glove—somewhat laboriously, for his hand was warm. He was clearly prepared for great things. As he pushed up his hair with his hands there came from his locks an ambrosial perfume,—as of marrow-oil, and there was a fixed propriety of position of every hair of his whiskers, which indicated very plainly that he had been at a hairdresser's shop since he left the market. Nor do I believe that he had worn that coat when he came to the door earlier in the morning. If I were to say that he had called at his tailor's also, I do not think that I should be wrong.

"How goes everything at Oileymead?" said Mrs. Greenow, seeing that her guest wanted some little assistance in leading off the conversation.

"Pretty well, Mrs. Greenow; pretty well. Everything will go very well if I am successful in the object which I have on hand to-day."

"I'm sure I hope you'll be successful in all your undertakings."

"In all my business undertakings I am, Mrs. Greenow. There isn't a shilling due on my land to e'er a bank in Norwich; and I haven't thrashed out a quarter of last year's corn yet, which is more than many of them can say. But there ain't many of them who don't have to pay rent, and so perhaps I oughtn't to boast."

"I know that Providence has been very good to you, Mr. Cheesacre, as regards worldly matters."

"And I haven't left it all to Providence, either. Those who do, generally go to the wall, as far as I can see. I'm always at work late and early, and I know when I get a profit out of a man's labour and when I don't, as well as though it was my only chance of bread and cheese."

"I always thought you understood farming business, Mr. Cheesacre."

"Yes, I do. I like a bit of fun well enough, when the time for it comes, as you saw at Yarmouth. And I keep my three or four hunters, as I think a country gentleman should; and I shoot over my own ground. But I always stick to my work. There are men, like Bellfield, who won't work. What do they come to? They're always borrowing."

"But he has fought his country's battles, Mr. Cheesacre."

"He fight! I suppose he's been telling you some of his old stories. He was ten years in the West Indies, and all his fighting was with the mosquitoes."

"But he was in the Crimea. At Inkerman, for instance—"

"He in the Crimea! Well, never mind. But do you inquire before you believe that story. But as I was saying, Mrs. Greenow, you have seen my little place at Oileymead."

"A charming house. All you want is a mistress for it."

"That's it; that's just it. All I want is a mistress for it. And there's only one woman on earth that I would wish to see in that position. Arabella

Greenow, will you be that woman?" As he made the offer he got up and stood before her, placing his right hand upon his heart.

"Arabella Greenow, will you be that woman?"

"I, Mr. Cheesacre!" she said.

"Yes, you. Who else? Since I saw you what other woman has been anything to me; or, indeed, I may say before? Since the first day I saw you I felt that there my happiness depended."

"Oh, Mr. Cheesacre, I thought you were looking elsewhere."

"No, no, no. There never was such a mistake as that. I have the highest regard and esteem for Miss Vavasor, but really—"

"Mr. Cheesacre, what am I to say to you?"

"What are you to say to me? Say that you'll be mine. Say that I shall be yours. Say that all I have at Oileymead shall be yours. Say that the open carriage for a pair of ponies to be driven by a lady which I have been looking at this morning shall be yours. Yes, indeed; the sweetest thing you ever saw in your life,—just like one that the lady of the Lord Lieutenant drives about in always. That's what you must say. Come, Mrs. Greenow!"

"Ah, Mr. Cheesacre, you don't know what it is to have buried the pride of your youth hardly yet twelve months."

"But you have buried him, and there let there be an end of it. Your sitting here all alone, morning, noon, and night, won't bring him back. I'm sorry for him; I am indeed. Poor Greenow! But what more can I do?"

"I can do more, Mr. Cheesacre. I can mourn for him in solitude and in silence."

"No, no, no. What's the use of it,—breaking your heart for nothing,—and my heart too. You never think of that." And Mr. Cheesacre spoke in a tone that was full of reproach.

"It cannot be, Mr. Cheesacre."

"Ah, but it can be. Come, Mrs. Greenow. We understand each other well enough now, surely. Come, dearest." And he approached her as though to put his arm round her waist. But at that moment there came a knock at the door, and Jeannette, entering the room, told her mistress that Captain Bellfield was below and wanted to know whether he could see her for a minute on particular business.

"Show Captain Bellfield up, certainly," said Mrs. Greenow.

"D—— Captain Bellfield!" said Mr. Cheesacre.

CHAPTER XXI
ALICE IS TAUGHT TO GROW
UPWARDS, TOWARDS THE LIGHT

Before the day came on which Alice was to go to Matching Priory, she had often regretted that she had been induced to make the promise, and yet she had as often resolved that there was no possible reason why she should not go to Matching Priory. But she feared this commencement of a closer connection with her great relations. She had told herself so often that she was quite separated from them, that the slight accident of blood in no way tied her to them or them to her,—this lesson had been so thoroughly taught to her by the injudicious attempts of Lady Macleod to teach an opposite lesson, that she did not like the idea of putting aside the effect of that teaching. And perhaps she was a little afraid of the great folk whom she might probably meet at her cousin's house. Lady Glencora herself she had liked,—and had loved too with that momentary love which certain circumstances of our life will sometimes produce, a love which is strong while it lasts, but which can be laid down when the need of it is passed. She had liked and loved Lady Glencora, and had in no degree been afraid of her during those strange visitings in Queen Anne Street;—but she was by no means sure that she should like Lady Glencora in the midst of her grandeur and surrounded by the pomp of her rank. She would have no other friend or acquaintance in that house, and feared that she might find herself desolate, cold, and wounded in her pride. She had been tricked into the visit, too, or rather had tricked herself into it. She had been sure that there had been a joint scheme between her cousin and Lady Midlothian, and could not resist the temptation of repudiating it in her letter to Lady Glencora. But there had been no such scheme; she had wronged Lady Glencora, and had therefore been unable to resist her second request. But she felt unhappy, fearing that she would be out of her element, and more than once half made up her mind to excuse herself.

Her aunt had, from the first, thought well of her going, believing that it might probably be the means of reconciling her to Mr. Grey. Moreover, it was a step altogether in the right direction. Lady Glencora would, if she lived, become a Duchess, and as she was decidedly Alice's cousin, of course

Alice should go to her house when invited. It must be acknowledged that Lady Macleod was not selfish in her worship of rank. She had played out her game in life, and there was no probability that she would live to be called cousin by a Duchess of Omnium. She bade Alice go to Matching Priory, simply because she loved her niece, and therefore wished her to live in the best and most eligible way within her reach. "I think you owe it as a duty to your family to go," said Lady Macleod.

What further correspondence about her affairs had passed between Lady Macleod and Lady Midlothian Alice never knew. She steadily refused all entreaty made that she would answer the Countess's letter, and at last threatened her aunt that if the request were further urged she would answer it, — telling Lady Midlothian that she had been very impertinent.

"I am becoming a very old woman, Alice," the poor lady said, piteously, "and I suppose I had better not interfere any further. Whatever I have said I have always meant to be for your good." Then Alice got up, and kissing her aunt, tried to explain to her that she resented no interference from her, and felt grateful for all that she both said and did; but that she could not endure meddling from people whom she did not know, and who thought themselves entitled to meddle by their rank.

"And because they are cousins as well," said Lady Macleod, in a softly sad, apologetic voice.

Alice left Cheltenham about the middle of November on her road to Matching Priory. She was to sleep in London one night, and go down to Matching in Yorkshire with her maid on the following day. Her father undertook to meet her at the Great Western Station, and to take her on the following morning to the Great Northern. He said nothing in his letter about dining with her, but when he met her, muttered something about an engagement, and taking her home graciously promised that he would breakfast with her on the following morning.

"I'm very glad you are going, Alice," he said when they were in the cab together.

"Why, papa?"

"Why?—because I think it's the proper thing to do. You know I've never said much to you about these people. They're not connected with me, and I know that they hate the name of Vavasor;—not but what the name is a deal older than any of theirs, and the family too."

"And therefore I don't understand why you think I'm specially right. If you were to say I was specially wrong, I should be less surprised, and of course I shouldn't go."

"You should go by all means. Rank and wealth are advantages, let anybody say what they will to the contrary. Why else does everybody want to get them?"

"But I shan't get them by going to Matching Priory."

"You'll get part of their value. Take them as a whole, the nobility of England are pleasant acquaintances to have. I haven't run after them very much myself, though I married, as I may say, among them. That very thing rather stood in my way than otherwise. But you may be sure of this, that men and women ought to grow, like plants, upwards. Everybody should endeavour to stand as well as he can in the world, and if I had a choice of acquaintance between a sugar-baker and a peer, I should prefer the peer,— unless, indeed, the sugar-baker had something very strong on his side to offer. I don't call that tuft-hunting, and it does not necessitate toadying. It's simply growing up, towards the light, as the trees do."

Alice listened to her father's worldly wisdom with a smile, but she did not attempt to answer him. It was very seldom, indeed, that he took upon himself the labour of lecturing her, or that he gave her even as much counsel as he had given now. "Well, papa, I hope I shall find myself growing towards the light," she said as she got out of the cab. Then he had not entered the house, but had taken the cab on with him to his club.

On her table Alice found a note from her cousin George. "I hear you are going down to the Pallisers at Matching Priory to-morrow, and as I shall be glad to say one word to you before you go, will you let me see you this evening,—say at nine?—G. V." She felt immediately that she could not help seeing him, but she greatly regretted the necessity. She wished that she had gone directly from Cheltenham to the North,—regardless even of those changes of wardrobe which her purposed visit required. Then she set herself to considering. How had George heard of her visit to the Priory, and how had he learned the precise evening which she would pass in London? Why should he be so intent on watching all her movements as it seemed that he was? As to seeing him she had no alternative, so she completed her arrangements for her journey before nine, and then awaited him in the drawing-room.

"I'm so glad you're going to Matching Priory," were the first words he said. He, too, might have taught her to grow towards the light, if she had asked him for his reasons;—but this she did not do just then.

"How did you learn that I was going?" she said.

"I heard it from a friend of mine. Well;—from Burgo Fitzgerald, if you must know."

"From Mr. Fitzgerald?" said Alice, in profound astonishment: "How could Mr. Fitzgerald have heard of it?"

"That's more than I know, Alice. Not directly from Lady Glencora, I should say."

"That would be impossible."

"Yes; quite so, no doubt. I think she keeps up her intimacy with Burgo's sister, and perhaps it got round to him in that way."

"And did he tell you also that I was going to-morrow? He must have known all about it very accurately."

"No; then I asked Kate, and Kate told me when you were going. Yes; I know. Kate has been wrong, hasn't she? Kate was cautioned, no doubt, to say nothing about your comings and goings to so inconsiderable a person as myself. But you must not be down upon Kate. She never mentioned it till I showed by my question to her that I knew all about your journey to Matching. I own I do not understand why it should be necessary to keep me so much in the dark."

Alice felt that she was blushing. The caution had been given to Kate because Kate still transgressed in her letters, by saying little words about her brother. And Alice did not even now believe Kate to have been false to her; but she saw that she herself had been imprudent.

"I cannot understand it," continued George, speaking without looking at her. "It was but the other day that we were such dear friends! Do you remember the balcony at Basle? and now it seems that we are quite estranged;—nay, worse than estranged; that I am, as it were, under some ban. Have I done anything to offend you, Alice? If so, speak out, like a woman of spirit as you are."

"Nothing," said Alice.

"Then why am I tabooed? Why was I told the other day that I might not congratulate you on your happy emancipation? I say boldly, that had you resolved on that while we were together in Switzerland, you would have permitted me, as a friend, almost as a brother, to discuss it with you."

"I think not, George."

"I am sure you would. And why has Kate been warned not to tell me of this visit to the Pallisers? I know she has been warned though she has not confessed it."

Alice sat silent, not knowing what to say in answer to this charge brought against her,—thinking, perhaps, that the questioner would allow his question to pass without an answer. But Vavasor was not so complaisant. "If there be any reason, Alice, I think that I have a right to ask it."

For a few seconds she did not speak a word, but sat considering. He also remained silent with his eyes fixed upon her. She looked at him and saw nothing but his scar,—nothing but his scar and the brightness of his eyes, which was almost fierce. She knew that he was in earnest, and therefore resolved that she would be in earnest also. "I think that you have such a right," she said at last.

"Then let me exercise it."

"I think that you have such a right, but I think also that you are ungenerous to exercise it."

"I cannot understand that. By heavens, Alice, I cannot be left in this suspense! If I have done anything to offend you, perhaps I can remove the offence by apology."

"You have done nothing to offend me."

"Or if there be any cause why our friendship should be dropped,—why we should be on a different footing to each other in London than we were in Switzerland, I may acknowledge it, if it be explained to me. But I cannot put up with the doubt, when I am told that I have a right to demand its solution."

"Then I will be frank with you, George, though my being so will, as you may guess, be very painful." She paused again, looking at him to see if yet he would spare her; but he was all scar and eyes as before, and there was no mercy in his face.

"Your sister, George, has thought that my parting with Mr. Grey might lead to a renewal of a purpose of marriage between you and me. You know her eagerness, and will understand that it may have been necessary that I should require silence from her on that head. You ought now to understand it all."

"I then am being punished for her sins," he said; and suddenly the scar on his face was healed up again, and there was something of the old pleasantness in his eyes.

"I have said nothing about any sins, George, but I have found it necessary to be on my guard."

"Well," he said, after a short pause, "You are an honest woman, Alice,— the honestest I ever knew. I will bring Kate to order,—and, now, we may be friends again; may we not?" And he extended his hand to her across the table.

"Yes," she said, "certainly, if you wish it." She spoke doubtingly, with indecision in her voice, as though remembering at the moment that he had given her no pledge. "I certainly do wish it very much," said he; and then she gave him her hand.

"And I may now talk about your new freedom?"

"No," said she; "no. Do not speak of that. A woman does not do what I have done in that affair without great suffering. I have to think of it daily; but do not make me speak of it."

"But this other subject, this visit to Matching; surely I may speak of that?" There was something now in his voice so bright, that she felt the influence of it, and answered him cheerfully, "I don't see what you can have to say about it."

"But I have a great deal. I am so glad you are going. Mind you cement a close intimacy with Mr. Palliser."

"With Mr. Palliser?"

"Yes; with Mr. Palliser. You must read all the blue books about finance. I'll send them to you if you like it."

"Oh, George!"

"I'm quite in earnest. That is, not in earnest about the blue books, as you would not have time; but about Mr. Palliser. He will be the new Chancellor of the Exchequer without a doubt."

"Will he indeed? But why should I make a bosom friend of the Chancellor of the Exchequer. I don't want any public money."

"But I do, my girl. Don't you see?"

"No; I don't."

"I think I shall get returned at this next election."

"I'm sure I hope you will."

"And if I do, of course it will be my game to support the ministry;—or rather the new ministry; for of course there will be changes."

"I hope they will be on the right side."

"Not a doubt of that, Alice."

"I wish they might be changed altogether."

"Ah! that's impossible. It's very well as a dream; but there are no such men as you want to see,—men really from the people,—strong enough to take high office. A man can't drive four horses because he's a philanthropist,—or rather a philhorseophist, and is desirous that the team should be driven without any hurt to them. A man can't govern well, simply because he is genuinely anxious that men should be well governed."

"And will there never be any such men?"

"I won't say that. I don't mind confessing to you that it is my ambition to be such a one myself. But a child must crawl before he can walk. Such a one as I, hoping to do something in politics, must spare no chance. It would be something to me that Mr. Palliser should become the friend of any dear friend of mine,—especially of a dear friend bearing the same name."

"I'm afraid, George, you'll find me a bad hand at making any such friendship."

"They say he is led immensely by his wife, and that she is very clever. But I mean this chiefly, Alice, that I do hope I shall have all your sympathy in any political career that I may make, and all your assistance also."

"My sympathy I think I can promise you. My assistance, I fear, would be worthless."

"By no means worthless, Alice; not if I see you take that place in the world which I hope to see you fill. Do you think women nowadays have no bearing upon the politics of the times? Almost as much as men have." In answer to which Alice shook her head; but, nevertheless, she felt in some way pleased and flattered.

George left her without saying a word more about her marriage prospects past or future, and Alice as she went to bed felt glad that this explanation between them had been made.

CHAPTER XXII
DANDY AND FLIRT

Alice reached the Matching Road Station about three o'clock in the afternoon without adventure, and immediately on the stopping of the train became aware that all trouble was off her own hands. A servant in livery came to the open window, and touching his hat to her, inquired if she were Miss Vavasor. Then her dressing-bag and shawls and cloaks were taken from her, and she was conveyed through the station by the station-master on one side of her, the footman on the other, and by the railway porter behind. She instantly perceived that she had become possessed of great privileges by belonging even for a time to Matching Priory, and that she was essentially growing upwards towards the light.

Outside, on the broad drive before the little station, she saw an omnibus that was going to the small town of Matching, intended for people who had not grown upwards as had been her lot; and she saw also a light stylish-looking cart which she would have called a Whitechapel had she been properly instructed in such matters, and a little low open carriage with two beautiful small horses, in which was sitting a lady enveloped in furs. Of course this was Lady Glencora. Another servant was standing on the ground, holding the horses of the carriage and the cart.

"Dear Alice, I'm so glad you've come," said a voice from the furs. "Look here, dear; your maid can go in the dog-cart with your things,"—it wasn't a dog-cart, but Lady Glencora knew no better;—"she'll be quite comfortable there; and do you get in here. Are you very cold?"

"Oh, no; not cold at all."

"But it is awfully cold. You've been in the stuffy carriage, but you'll find it cold enough out here, I can tell you."

"Oh! Lady Glencora, I am so sorry that I've brought you out on such a morning," said Alice, getting in and taking the place assigned her next to the charioteer.

"What nonsense! Sorry! Why I've looked forward to meeting you all alone, ever since I knew you were coming. If it had snowed all the morning

I should have come just the same. I drive out almost every day when I'm down here,—that is, when the house is not too crowded, or I can make an excuse. Wrap these things over you; there are plenty of them. You shall drive if you like." Alice, however, declined the driving, expressing her gratitude in what prettiest words she could find.

"I like driving better than anything, I think. Mr. Palliser doesn't like ladies to hunt, and of course it wouldn't do as he does not hunt himself. I do ride, but he never gets on horseback. I almost fancy I should like to drive four-in-hand,—only I know I should be afraid."

"It would look very terrible," said Alice.

"Yes; wouldn't it? The look would be the worst of it; as it is all the world over. Sometimes I wish there were no such things as looks. I don't mean anything improper, you know; only one does get so hampered, right and left, for fear of Mrs. Grundy. I endeavour to go straight, and get along pretty well on the whole, I suppose. Baker, you must put Dandy in the bar; he pulls so, going home, that I can't hold him in the check." She stopped the horses, and Baker, a very completely-got-up groom of some forty years of age, who sat behind, got down and put the impetuous Dandy "in the bar," thereby changing the rein, so that the curb was brought to bear on him. "They're called Dandy and Flirt," continued Lady Glencora, speaking to Alice. "Ain't they a beautiful match? The Duke gave them to me and named them himself. Did you ever see the Duke?"

"Baker, you must put Dandy in the bar."

"Never," said Alice.

"He won't be here before Christmas, but you shall be introduced some day in London. He's an excellent creature and I'm a great pet of his; though, after all, I never speak half a dozen words to him when I see him. He's one of those people who never talk. I'm one of those who like talking, as you'll find out. I think it runs in families; and the Pallisers are non-talkers. That doesn't mean that they are not speakers, for Mr. Palliser has plenty to say in the House, and they declare that he's one of the few public men who've got lungs enough to make a financial statement without breaking down."

Alice was aware that she had as yet hardly spoken herself, and began to bethink herself that she didn't know what to say. Had Lady Glencora paused on the subject of Dandy and Flirt, she might have managed to be enthusiastic about the horses, but she could not discuss freely the general silence of the Palliser family, nor the excellent lungs, as regarded public purposes, of the one who was the husband of her present friend. So she asked how far it was to Matching Priory.

"You're not tired of me already, I hope," said Lady Glencora.

"I didn't mean that," said Alice. "I delight in the drive. But somehow one expects Matching Station to be near Matching."

"Ah, yes; that's a great cheat. It's not Matching Station at all but Matching Road Station, and it's eight miles. It is a great bore, for though the omnibus brings our parcels, we have to be constantly sending over, and it's very expensive, I can assure you. I want Mr. Palliser to have a branch, but he says he would have to take all the shares himself, and that would cost more, I suppose."

"Is there a town at Matching?"

"Oh, a little bit of a place. I'll go round by it if you like, and in at the further gate."

"Oh, no!" said Alice.

"Ah, but I should like. It was a borough once, and belonged to the Duke; but they put it out at the Reform Bill. They made some kind of bargain;— he was to keep either Silverbridge or Matching, but not both. Mr. Palliser sits for Silverbridge, you know. The Duke chose Silverbridge,—or rather his father did, as he was then going to build his great place in Barsetshire;— that's near Silverbridge. But the Matching people haven't forgiven him yet. He was sitting for Matching himself when the Reform Bill passed. Then his father died, and he hasn't lived there much since. It's a great deal nicer place than Gatherum Castle, only not half so grand. I hate grandeur; don't you?"

"I never tried much of it, as you have."

"Come now; that's not fair. There's no one in the world less grand than I am."

"I mean that I've not had grand people about me."

"Having cut all your cousins,—and Lady Midlothian in particular, like a naughty girl as you are. I was so angry with you when you accused me of selling you about that. You ought to have known that I was the last person in the world to have done such a thing."

"I did not think you meant to sell me, but I thought—"

"Yes, you did, Alice. I know what you thought; you thought that Lady Midlothian was making a tool of me that I might bring you under her thumb, so that she might bully you into Mr. Grey's arms. That's what you thought. I don't know that I was at all entitled to your good opinion, but I was not entitled to that special bad opinion."

"I had no bad opinion;—but it was so necessary that I should guard myself."

"You shall be guarded. I'll take you under my shield. Mr. Grey shan't be named to you, except that I shall expect you to tell me all about it; and you must tell me all about that dangerous cousin, too, of whom they were saying such terrible things down in Scotland. I had heard of him before." These last words Lady Glencora spoke in a lower voice and in an altered tone,—slowly, as though she were thinking of something that pained her. It was from Burgo Fitzgerald that she had heard of George Vavasor.

Alice did not know what to say. She found it impossible to discuss all the most secret and deepest of her feelings out in that open carriage, perhaps in the hearing of the servant behind, on this her first meeting with her cousin,—of whom, in fact, she knew very little. She had not intended to discuss these things at all, and certainly not in such a manner as this. So she remained silent. "This is the beginning of the park," said Lady Glencora, pointing to a grand old ruin of an oak tree, which stood on the wide margin of the road, outside the rounded corner of the park palings, propped up with a skeleton of supporting sticks all round it. "And that is Matching oak, under which Cœur de Lion or Edward the Third, I forget which, was met by Sir Guy de Palisere as he came from the war, or from hunting, or something of that kind. It was the king, you know, who had been fighting or whatever it was, and Sir Guy entertained him when he was very tired. Jeffrey Palliser, who is my husband's cousin, says that old Sir Guy luckily pulled out his brandy-flask. But the king immediately gave him all the lands of Matching,—only there was a priory then and a lot of monks, and I don't quite understand how that was. But I know one of the younger brothers always used to be abbot and sit in the House of Lords. And the king gave him Littlebury at the same time, which is about seven miles away from here. As Jeffrey Palliser says, it was a great deal of money for a pull at his flask. Jeffrey Palliser is here now, and I hope you'll like him. If I have no child, and Mr. Palliser were not to marry again, Jeffrey would be the heir." And here again her voice was low and slow, and altogether changed in its tone.

"I suppose that's the way most of the old families got their estates."

"Either so, or by robbery. Many of them were terrible thieves, my dear, and I dare say Sir Guy was no better than he should be. But since that they have always called some of the Pallisers Plantagenet. My husband's name is Plantagenet. The Duke is called George Plantagenet, and the king was his godfather. The queen is my godmother, I believe, but I don't know that I'm much the better for it. There's no use in godfathers and godmothers;—do you think there is?"

"Not much as it's managed now."

"If I had a child,— Oh, Alice, it's a dreadful thing not to have a child when so much depends on it!"

"But you're such a short time married yet."

"Ah, well; I can see it in his eyes when he asks me questions; but I don't think he'd say an unkind word, not if his own position depended on it. Ah, well; this is Matching. That other gate we passed, where Dandy wanted to turn in,—that's where we usually go up, but I've brought you round to show you the town. That's the inn,—whoever can possibly come to stay there I don't know; I never saw anybody go in or out. That's the baker who bakes our bread,—we baked it at the house at first, but nobody could eat it; and I know that that man there mends Mr. Palliser's shoes. He's very particular about his shoes. We shall see the church as we go in at the other gate. It is in the park, and is very pretty,—but not half so pretty as the priory ruins close to the house. The ruins are our great lion. I do so love to wander about them at moonlight. I often think of you when I do; I don't know why.—But I do know why, and I'll tell you some day. Come, Miss Flirt!"

As they drove up through the park, Lady Glencora pointed out first the church and then the ruins, through the midst of which the road ran, and then they were at once before the front door. The corner of the modern house came within two hundred yards of the gateway of the old priory. It was a large building, very pretty, with two long fronts; but it was no more than a house. It was not a palace, nor a castle, nor was it hardly to be called a mansion. It was built with gabled roofs, four of which formed the side from which the windows of the drawing-rooms opened out upon a lawn which separated the house from the old ruins, and which indeed surrounded the ruins, and went inside them, forming the present flooring of the old chapel, and the old refectory, and the old cloisters. Much of the cloisters indeed was standing, and there the stone pavement remained; but the square of the cloisters was all turfed, and in the middle of it stood a large modern stone vase, out of the broad basin of which hung flowering creepers and green tendrils.

As Lady Glencora drove up to the door, a gentleman, who had heard the sound of the wheels, came forth to meet them. "There's Mr. Palliser," said she; "that shows that you are an honoured guest, for you may be sure that he is hard at work and would not have come out for anybody else. Plantagenet, here is Miss Vavasor, perished. Alice, my husband." Then Mr. Palliser put forth his hand and helped her out of the carriage.

"I hope you've not found it very cold," said he. "The winter has come upon us quite suddenly."

He said nothing more to her than this, till he met her again before dinner. He was a tall thin man, apparently not more than thirty years of age, looking in all respects like a gentleman, but with nothing in his appearance that was remarkable. It was a face that you might see and forget, and see again and forget again; and yet when you looked at it and pulled it to pieces, you found that it was a fairly good face, showing intellect in the forehead, and much character in the mouth. The eyes too, though not to be called bright, had always something to say for themselves, looking as though they had a real meaning. But the outline of the face was almost insignificant, being too thin; and he wore no beard to give it character. But, indeed, Mr. Palliser was a man who had never thought of assisting his position in the world by his outward appearance. Not to be looked at, but to be read about in the newspapers, was his ambition. Men said that he was to be Chancellor of the Exchequer, and no one thought of suggesting that the insignificance of his face would stand in his way.

"Are the people all out?" his wife asked him.

"The men have not come in from shooting;—at least I think not;—and some of the ladies are driving, I suppose. But I haven't seen anybody since you went."

"Of course you haven't. He never has time, Alice, to see any one. But we'll go up-stairs, dear. I told them to let us have tea in my dressing-room, as I thought you'd like that better than going into the drawing-room before you had taken off your things. You must be famished, I know. Then you can come down, or if you want to avoid two dressings you can sit over the fire up-stairs till dinner-time." So saying she skipped up-stairs and Alice followed her. "Here's my dressing-room, and here's your room all but opposite. You look out into the park. It's pretty, isn't it? But come into my dressing-room, and see the ruins out of the window."

Alice followed Lady Glencora across the passage into what she called her dressing-room, and there found herself surrounded by an infinitude of feminine luxuries. The prettiest of tables were there;—the easiest of chairs;—the most costly of cabinets;—the quaintest of old china ornaments. It was bright with the gayest colours,—made pleasant to the eye with the binding of many books, having nymphs painted on the ceiling and little Cupids on the doors. "Isn't it pretty?" she said, turning quickly on Alice. "I call it my dressing-room because in that way I can keep people out of it, but I have my brushes and soap in a little closet there, and my clothes,—my clothes are everywhere I suppose, only there are none of them here. Isn't it pretty?"

"Very pretty."

"The Duke did it all. He understands such things thoroughly. Now to Mr. Palliser a dressing-room is a dressing-room, and a bedroom a bedroom. He cares for nothing being pretty; not even his wife, or he wouldn't have married me."

"You wouldn't say that if you meant it."

"Well, I don't know. Sometimes when I look at myself, when I simply am myself, with no making up or grimacing, you know, I think I'm the ugliest young woman the sun ever shone on. And in ten years' time I shall be the ugliest old woman. Only think,—my hair is beginning to get grey, and I'm not twenty-one yet. Look at it;" and she lifted up the wavy locks just above her ear. "But there's one comfort; he doesn't care about beauty. How old are you?"

"Over five-and-twenty," said Alice.

"Nonsense;—then I oughtn't to have asked you. I am so sorry."

"That's nonsense at any rate. Why should you think I should be ashamed of my age?"

"I don't know why, only somehow, people are; and I didn't think you were so old. Five-and-twenty seems so old to me. It would be nothing if you were married; only, you see, you won't get married."

"Perhaps I may yet; some day."

"Of course you will. You'll have to give way. You'll find that they'll get the better of you. Your father will storm at you, and Lady Macleod will preach at you, and Lady Midlothian will jump upon you."

"I'm not a bit afraid of Lady Midlothian."

"I know what it is, my dear, to be jumped upon. We talked with such horror of the French people giving their daughters in marriage, just as they might sell a house or a field, but we do exactly the same thing ourselves. When they all come upon you in earnest how are you to stand against them? How can any girl do it?"

"I think I shall be able."

"To be sure you're older,—and you are not so heavily weighted. But never mind; I didn't mean to talk about that;—not yet at any rate. Well, now, my dear, I must go down. The Duchess of St. Bungay is here, and Mr. Palliser will be angry if I don't do pretty to her. The Duke is to be the new President of the Council, or rather, I believe he is President now. I try to remember it all, but it is so hard when one doesn't really care two pence how it goes. Not but what I'm very anxious that Mr. Palliser should be Chancellor of the Exchequer. And now, will you remain here, or will you come down with me, or will you go to your own room, and I'll call for you when I go down to dinner? We dine at eight."

Alice decided that she would stay in her own room till dinner time, and was taken there by Lady Glencora. She found her maid unpacking her clothes, and for a while employed herself in assisting at the work; but that was soon done, and then she was left alone. "I shall feel so strange, ma'am, among all those people down-stairs," said the girl. "They all seem to look at me as though they didn't know who I was."

"You'll get over that soon, Jane."

"I suppose I shall; but you see, they're all like knowing each other, miss."

Alice, when she sat down alone, felt herself to be very much in the same condition as her maid. What would the Duchess of St. Bungay or Mr. Jeffrey Palliser,—who himself might live to be a duke if things went well for him,— care for her? As to Mr. Palliser, the master of the house, it was already evident to her that he would not put himself out of his way for her. Had she not done wrong to come there? If it were possible for her to fly away, back to the dullness of Queen Anne Street, or even to the preachings of Lady Macleod, would she not do so immediately? What business had she,—she asked herself,—to come to such a house as that? Lady Glencora was very kind to her, but frightened her even by her kindness. Moreover, she was aware that Lady Glencora could not devote herself especially to any such guest as she was. Lady Glencora must of course look after her duchesses, and do pretty, as she called it, to her husband's important political alliances.

And then she began to think about Lady Glencora herself. What a strange, weird nature she was,—with her round blue eyes and wavy hair, looking sometimes like a child and sometimes almost like an old woman! And how she talked! What things she said, and what terrible forebodings she uttered of stranger things that she meant to say! Why had she at their first meeting made that allusion to the mode of her own betrothal,—and then, checking herself for speaking of it so soon, almost declare that she meant to speak more of it hereafter? "She should never mention it to any one," said Alice to herself. "If her lot in life has not satisfied her, there is so much the more reason why she should not mention it." Then Alice protested to herself that no father, no aunt, no Lady Midlothian should persuade her into a marriage of which she feared the consequences. But Lady Glencora had made for herself excuses which were not altogether untrue. She had been very young, and had been terribly weighted with her wealth.

And it seemed to Alice that her cousin had told her everything in that hour and a half that they had been together. She had given a whole history of her husband and of herself. She had said how indifferent he was to her pleasures, and how vainly she strove to interest herself in his pursuits. And then, as yet, she was childless and without prospect of a child, when, as she herself had said,—"so much depended on it." It was very strange to Alice that all this should have been already told to her. And why should Lady Glencora think of Alice when she walked out among the priory ruins by moonlight?

The two hours seemed to her very long,—as though she were passing her time in absolute seclusion at Matching. Of course she did not dare to go down-stairs. But at last her maid came to dress her.

"How do you get on below, Jane?" her mistress asked her.

"Why, miss, they are uncommon civil, and I don't think after all it will be so bad. We had our teas very comfortable in the housekeeper's room. There are five or six of us altogether, all ladies'-maids, miss; and there's nothing on earth to do all the day long, only sit and do a little needlework over the fire."

A few minutes before eight Lady Glencora knocked at Alice's door, and took her arm to lead her to the drawing-room. Alice saw that she was magnificently dressed, with an enormous expanse of robe, and that her locks had been so managed that no one could suspect the presence of a grey hair. Indeed, with all her magnificence, she looked almost a child. "Let me see," she said, as they went down-stairs together. "I'll tell Jeffrey to take you in to dinner. He's about the easiest young man we have here. He rather turns up his nose at everything, but that doesn't make him the less agreeable; does it, dear?—unless he turns up his nose at you, you know."

"But perhaps he will."

"No; he won't do that. That would be uncourteous,—and he's the most courteous man in the world. There's nobody here, you see," she said as they entered the room, "and I didn't suppose there would be. It's always proper to be first in one's own house. I do so try to be proper,—and it is such trouble. Talking of people earning their bread, Alice;—I'm sure I earn mine. Oh dear!—what fun it would be to be sitting somewhere in Asia, eating a chicken with one's fingers, and lighting a big fire outside one's tent to keep off the lions and tigers. Fancy your being on one side of the fire and the lions and tigers on the other, grinning at you through the flames!" Then Lady Glencora strove to look like a lion, and grinned at herself in the glass.

"That sort of grin wouldn't frighten me," said Alice.

"I dare say not. I have been reading about it in that woman's travels. Oh, here they are, and I mustn't make any more faces. Duchess, do come to the fire. I hope you've got warm again. This is my cousin, Miss Vavasor."

The Duchess made a stiff little bow of condescension, and then declared that she was charmingly warm. "I don't know how you manage in your house, but the staircases are so comfortable. Now at Longroyston we've taken all the trouble in the world,—put down hot-water pipes all over the house, and everything else that could be thought of, and yet, you can't move about the place without meeting with draughts at every corner of the passages." The Duchess spoke with an enormous emphasis on every other word, sometimes putting so great a stress on some special syllable, as almost to bring her voice to a whistle. This she had done with the word "pipes" to a great degree,—so that Alice never afterwards forgot the hot-water pipes of Longroyston. "I was telling Lady Glencora, Miss Palliser, that I never knew a house so warm as this,—or, I'm sorry to say,"—and here the emphasis was very strong on the word sorry,—"so cold as Longroyston." And the tone in which Longroyston was uttered would almost have drawn tears from a critical audience in the pit of a playhouse. The Duchess was a woman of about forty, very handsome, but with no meaning in her beauty, carrying a good fixed colour in her face, which did not look like paint, but which probably had received some little assistance from art. She was a well-built, sizeable woman, with good proportions and fine health,—but a fool. She had addressed herself to one Miss Palliser; but two Miss Pallisers, cousins of Plantagenet Palliser, had entered the room at the same time, of whom I may say, whatever other traits of character they may have possessed, that at any rate they were not fools.

"It's always easy to warm a small house like this," said Miss Palliser, whose Christian names, unfortunately for her, were Iphigenia Theodata, and who by her cousin and sister was called Iphy—"and I suppose equally difficult to warm a large one such as Longroyston." The other Miss Palliser had been christened Euphemia.

"We've got no pipes, Duchess, at any rate," said Lady Glencora; and Alice, as she sat listening, thought she discerned in Lady Glencora's pronunciation of the word pipes an almost hidden imitation of the Duchess's whistle. It must have been so, for at the moment Lady Glencora's eye met Alice's for an instant, and was then withdrawn, so that Alice was compelled to think that her friend and cousin was not always quite successful in those struggles she made to be proper.

Then the gentlemen came in one after another, and other ladies, till about thirty people were assembled. Mr. Palliser came up and spoke another word to Alice in a kind voice,—meant to express some sense of connection if not cousinship. "My wife has been thinking so much of your coming. I hope we shall be able to amuse you." Alice, who had already begun to feel desolate, was grateful, and made up her mind that she would try to like Mr. Palliser.

Jeffrey Palliser was almost the last in the room, but directly he entered Lady Glencora got up from her seat, and met him as he was coming into the crowd. "You must take my cousin, Alice Vavasor, in to dinner," she said, "and;—will you oblige me to-day?"

"Yes;—as you ask me like that."

"Then try to make her comfortable." After that she introduced them, and Jeffrey Palliser stood opposite to Alice, talking to her, till dinner was announced.

CHAPTER XXIII
DINNER AT MATCHING PRIORY

Alice found herself seated near to Lady Glencora's end of the table, and, in spite of her resolution to like Mr. Palliser, she was not sorry that such an arrangement had been made. Mr. Palliser had taken the Duchess out to dinner, and Alice wished to be as far removed as possible from her Grace. She found herself seated between her bespoken friend Jeffrey Palliser and the Duke, and as soon as she was seated Lady Glencora introduced her to her second neighbour. "My cousin, Duke," Lady Glencora said, "and a terrible Radical."

"Oh, indeed; I'm glad of that. We're sadly in want of a few leading Radicals, and perhaps I may be able to gain one now."

Alice thought of her cousin George, and wished that he, instead of herself, was sitting next to the Duke of St. Bungay. "But I'm afraid I never shall be a leading Radical," she said.

"You shall lead me at any rate, if you will," said he.

"As the little dogs lead the blind men," said Lady Glencora.

"No, Lady Glencora, not so. But as the pretty women lead the men who have eyes in their head. There is nothing I want so much, Miss Vavasor, as to become a Radical;—if I only knew how."

"I think it's very easy to know how," said Alice.

"Do you? I don't. I've voted for every liberal measure that has come seriously before Parliament since I had a seat in either House, and I've not been able to get beyond Whiggery yet."

"Have you voted for the ballot?" asked Alice, almost trembling at her own audacity as she put the question.

"Well; no, I've not. And I suppose that is the crux. But the ballot has never been seriously brought before any House in which I have sat. I hate it with so keen a private hatred, that I doubt whether I could vote for it."

"But the Radicals love it," said Alice.

"Palliser," said the Duke, speaking loudly from his end of the table, "I'm told you can never be entitled to call yourself a Radical till you've voted for the ballot."

"I don't want to be called a Radical," said Mr. Palliser,—"or to be called anything at all."

"Except Chancellor of the Exchequer," said Lady Glencora in a low voice.

"And that's about the finest ambition by which a man can be moved," said the Duke. "The man who can manage the purse-strings of this country can manage anything." Then that conversation dropped and the Duke ate his dinner.

"I was especially commissioned to amuse you," said Mr. Jeffrey Palliser to Alice. "But when I undertook the task I had no conception that you would be calling Cabinet Ministers over the coals about their politics."

"I did nothing of the kind, surely, Mr. Palliser. I suppose all Radicals do vote for the ballot, and that's why I said it."

"Your definition was perfectly just, I dare say, only—"

"Only what?"

"Lady Glencora need not have been so anxious to provide specially for your amusement. Not but what I'm very much obliged to her,—of course. But Miss Vavasor, unfortunately I'm not a politician. I haven't a chance of a seat in the House, and so I despise politics."

"Women are not allowed to be politicians in this country."

"Thank God, they can't do much in that way;—not directly, I mean. Only think where we should be if we had a feminine House of Commons, with feminine debates, carried on, of course, with feminine courtesy. My cousins Iphy and Phemy there would of course be members. You don't know them yet?"

"No; not yet. Are they politicians?"

"Not especially. They have their tendencies, which are decidedly liberal. There has never been a Tory Palliser known, you know. But they are too clever to give themselves up to anything in which they can do nothing. Being women they live a depressed life, devoting themselves to literature, fine arts, social economy, and the abstract sciences. They write wonderful letters; but I believe their correspondence lists are quite full, so that you have no chance at present of getting on either of them."

"I haven't the slightest pretension to ask for such an honour."

"Oh! if you mean because you don't know them, that has nothing to do with it."

"But I have no claim either private or public."

"That has nothing to do with it either. They don't at all seek people of note as their correspondents. Free communication with all the world is their motto, and Rowland Hill is the god they worship. Only they have been forced to guard themselves against too great an accession of paper and ink. Are you fond of writing letters, Miss Vavasor?"

"Yes, to my friends; but I like getting them better."

"I shrewdly suspect they don't read half what they get. Is it possible any one should go through two sheets of paper filled by our friend the Duchess there? No; their delight is in writing. They sit each at her desk after breakfast, and go on till lunch. There is a little rivalry between them, not expressed to each other, but visible to their friends. Iphy certainly does get off the greater number, and I'm told crosses quite as often as Phemy, but then she has the advantage of a bolder and larger hand."

"Do they write to you?"

"Oh, dear no. I don't think they ever write to any relative. They don't discuss family affairs and such topics as that. Architecture goes a long way with them, and whether women ought to be clerks in public offices. Iphy has certain American correspondents that take up much of her time, but she acknowledges she does not read their letters."

"Then I certainly shall not write to her."

"But you are not American, I hope. I do hate the Americans. It's the only strong political feeling I have. I went there once, and found I couldn't live with them on any terms."

"But they please themselves. I don't see they are to be hated because they don't live after our fashion."

"Oh; it's jealousy of course. I know that. I didn't come across a cab-driver who wasn't a much better educated man than I am. And as for their women, they know everything. But I hated them, and I intend to hate them. You haven't been there?"

"Oh no."

"Then I will make bold to say that any English lady who spent a month with them and didn't hate them would have very singular tastes. I begin to think they'll eat each other up, and then there'll come an entirely new set of people of a different sort. I always regarded the States as a Sodom and

Gomorrah, prospering in wickedness, on which fire and brimstone were sure to fall sooner or later."

"I think that's wicked."

"I am wicked, as Topsy used to say. Do you hunt?"

"No."

"Do you shoot?"

"Shoot! What; with a gun?"

"Yes. I was staying in a house last week with a lady who shot a good deal."

"No; I don't shoot."

"Do you ride?"

"No; I wish I did. I have never ridden because I've no one to ride with me."

"Do you drive?"

"No; I don't drive either."

"Then what do you do?"

"I sit at home, and—"

"Mend your stockings?"

"No; I don't do that, because it's disagreeable; but I do work a good deal. Sometimes I have amused myself by reading."

"Ah; they never do that here. I have heard that there is a library, but the clue to it has been lost, and nobody now knows the way. I don't believe in libraries. Nobody ever goes into a library to read, any more than you would into a larder to eat. But there is this difference;—the food you consume does come out of the larders, but the books you read never come out of the libraries."

"Except Mudie's," said Alice.

"Ah, yes; he is the great librarian. And you mean to read all the time you are here, Miss Vavasor?"

"I mean to walk about the priory ruins sometimes."

"Then you must go by moonlight, and I'll go with you. Only isn't it rather late in the year for that?"

"I should think it is,—for you, Mr. Palliser."

Then the Duke spoke to her again, and she found that she got on very well during dinner. But she could not but feel angry with herself in that she had any fear on the subject;—and yet she could not divest herself of that fear. She acknowledged to herself that she was conscious of a certain inferiority to Lady Glencora and to Mr. Jeffrey Palliser, which almost made her unhappy. As regarded the Duke on the other side of her, she had no such feeling. He was old enough to be her father, and was a Cabinet Minister; therefore he was entitled to her reverence. But how was it that she could not help accepting the other people round her as being indeed superior to herself? Was she really learning to believe that she could grow upwards by their sunlight?

"Jeffrey is a pleasant fellow, is he not?" said Lady Glencora to her as they passed back through the billiard-room to the drawing-room.

"Very pleasant;—a little sarcastic, perhaps."

"I should think you would soon find yourself able to get the better of that if he tries it upon you," said Lady Glencora; and then the ladies were all in the drawing-room together.

"It is quite deliciously warm, coming from one room to another," said the Duchess, putting her emphasis on the "one" and the "other."

"Then we had better keep continually moving," said a certain Mrs. Conway Sparkes, a literary lady, who had been very handsome, who was still very clever, who was not perhaps very good-natured, and of whom the Duchess of St. Bungay was rather afraid.

"I hope we may be warm here too," said Lady Glencora.

"But not deliciously warm," said Mrs. Conway Sparkes.

"It makes me tremble in every limb when Mrs. Sparkes attacks her," Lady Glencora said to Alice in Alice's own room that night, "for I know she'll tell the Duke; and he'll tell that tall man with red hair whom you see standing about, and the tall man with red hair will tell Mr. Palliser, and then I shall catch it."

"And who is the tall man with red hair?"

"He's a political link between the Duke and Mr. Palliser. His name is Bott, and he's a Member of Parliament."

"But why should he interfere?"

"I suppose it's his business. I don't quite understand all the ins and outs of it. I believe he's to be one of Mr. Palliser's private secretaries if he becomes Chancellor of the Exchequer. Perhaps he doesn't tell;—only I think he does all the same. He always calls me Lady Glen-cowrer. He comes out of Lancashire, and made calico as long as he could get any cotton." But this happened in the bedroom, and we must go back for a while to the drawing-room.

The Duchess had made no answer to Mrs. Sparkes, and so nothing further was said about the warmth. Nor, indeed, was there any conversation that was comfortably general. The number of ladies in the room was too great for that, and ladies do not divide themselves nicely into small parties, as men and women do when they are mixed. Lady Glencora behaved pretty by telling the Duchess all about her pet pheasants; Mrs. Conway Sparkes told ill-natured tales of some one to Miss Euphemia Palliser; one of the Duchess's daughters walked off to a distant piano with an admiring friend and touched a few notes; while Iphigenia Palliser boldly took up a book, and placed herself at a table. Alice, who was sitting opposite to Lady Glencora, began to speculate whether she might do the same; but her courage failed her, and she sat on, telling herself that she was out of her element. "Alice Vavasor," said Lady Glencora after a while, suddenly, and in a somewhat loud voice, "can you play billiards?"

"No," said Alice, rather startled.

"Then you shall learn to-night, and if nobody else will teach you, you shall be my pupil." Whereupon Lady Glencora rang the bell and ordered that the billiard-table might be got ready. "You'll play, Duchess, of course," said Lady Glencora.

"It is so nice and warm, that I think I will," said the Duchess; but as she spoke she looked suspiciously to that part of the room where Mrs. Conway Sparkes was sitting.

"Let us all play," said Mrs. Conway Sparkes, "and then it will be nicer, — and perhaps warmer, too."

The gentlemen joined them just as they were settling themselves round the table, and as many of them stayed there, the billiard-room became full. Alice had first a cue put into her hand, and making nothing of that was permitted to play with a mace. The duty of instructing her devolved on Jeffrey Palliser, and the next hour passed pleasantly;—not so pleasantly, she thought afterwards, as did some of those hours in Switzerland when her cousins were with her. After all, she could get more out of her life with such associates as them, than she could with any of these people at Matching. She felt quite sure of that;—though Jeffrey Palliser did take great trouble to teach her the game, and once or twice made her laugh heartily by quizzing the Duchess's attitude as she stood up to make her stroke.

"I wish I could play billiards," said Mrs. Sparkes, on one of these occasions; "I do indeed."

"I thought you said you were coming to play," said the Duchess, almost majestically, and with a tone of triumph evidently produced by her own successes.

"Only to see your Grace," said Mrs. Sparkes.

"I don't know that there is anything more to see in me than in anybody else," said the Duchess. "Mr. Palliser, that was a cannon. Will you mark that for our side?"

"Mr. Palliser, that was a cannon."

"Oh no, Duchess, you hit the same ball twice."

"Very well;—then I suppose Miss Vavasor plays now. That was a miss. Will you mark that, if you please?" This latter demand was made with great stress, as though she had been defrauded in the matter of the cannon, and was obeyed. Before long, the Duchess, with her partner, Lady Glencora, won the game,—which fact, however, was, I think, owing rather to Alice's ignorance than to her Grace's skill. The Duchess, however, was very triumphant, and made her way back into the drawing-room with a step which seemed to declare loudly that she had trumped Mrs. Sparkes at last.

Not long after this the ladies went up-stairs on their way to bed. Many of them, perhaps, did not go to their pillows at once, as it was as yet not eleven o'clock, and it was past ten when they all came down to breakfast. At any rate, Alice, who had been up at seven, did not go to bed then, nor for the next two hours. "I'll come into your room just for one minute," Lady Glencora said as she passed on from the door to her own room; and in about five minutes she was back with her cousin. "Would you mind going into my room—it's just there, and sitting with Ellen for a minute?" This Lady Glencora said in the sweetest possible tone to the girl who was waiting on Alice; and then, when they were alone together, she got into a little chair by the fireside and prepared herself for conversation.

"I must keep you up for a quarter of an hour while I tell you something. But first of all, how do you like the people? Will you be able to be comfortable with them?" Alice of course said that she thought she would; and then there came that little discussion in which the duties of Mr. Bott, the man with the red hair, were described.

"But I've got something to tell you," said Lady Glencora, when they had already been there some twenty minutes. "Sit down opposite to me, and look at the fire while I look at you."

"Is it anything terrible?"

"It's nothing wrong."

"Oh, Lady Glencora, if it's—"

"I won't have you call me Lady Glencora. Don't I call you Alice? Why are you so unkind to me? I have not come to you now asking you to do for me anything that you ought not to do."

"But you are going to tell me something." Alice felt sure that the thing to be told would have some reference to Mr. Fitzgerald, and she did not wish to hear Mr. Fitzgerald's name from her cousin's lips.

"Tell you something;—of course I am. I'm going to tell you that,—that in writing to you the other day I wrote a fib. But it wasn't that I wished to deceive you;—only I couldn't say it all in a letter."

"Say all what?"

"You know I confessed that I had been very bad in not coming to you in London last year."

"I never thought of it for a moment."

"You did not care whether I came or not: was that it? But never mind. Why should you have cared? But I cared. I told you in my letter that I didn't come because I had so many things on hand. Of course that was a fib."

"Everybody makes excuses of that kind," said Alice.

"But they don't make them to the very people of all others whom they want to know and love. I was longing to come to you every day. But I feared I could not come without speaking of him;—and I had determined never to speak of him again." This she said in that peculiar low voice which she assumed at times.

"Then why do it now, Lady Glencora?"

"I won't be called Lady Glencora. Call me Cora. I had a sister once, older than I, and she used to call me Cora. If she had lived—. But never mind that now. She didn't live. I'll tell you why I do it now. Because I cannot help it. Besides, I've met him. I've been in the same room with him, and have spoken to him. What's the good of any such resolution now?"

"And you have met him?"

"Yes; he—Mr. Palliser—knew all about it. When he talked of taking me to the house, I whispered to him that I thought Burgo would be there."

"Do not call him by his Christian name," said Alice, almost with a shudder.

"Why not?—why not his Christian name? I did when I told my husband. Or perhaps I said Burgo Fitzgerald."

"Well."

"And he bade me go. He said it didn't signify, and that I had better learn to bear it. Bear it, indeed! If I am to meet him, and speak to him, and look at him, surely I may mention his name." And then she paused for an answer. "May I not?"

"What am I to say?" exclaimed Alice.

"Anything you please, that's not a falsehood. But I've got you here because I don't think you will tell a falsehood. Oh, Alice, I do so want to go right, and it is so hard!"

Hard, indeed, poor creature, for one so weighted as she had been, and sent out into the world with so small advantages of previous training or of present friendship! Alice began to feel now that she had been enticed to Matching Priory because her cousin wanted a friend, and of course she could not refuse to give the friendship that was asked from her. She got up from her chair, and kneeling down at the other's feet put up her face and kissed her.

"I knew you would be good to me," said Lady Glencora. "I knew you would. And you may say whatever you like. But I could not bear that you should not know the real reason why I neither came to you nor sent for you after we went to London. You'll come to me now; won't you, dear?"

"Yes;—and you'll come to me," said Alice, making in her mind a sort of bargain that she was not to be received into Mr. Palliser's house after the fashion in which Lady Midlothian had proposed to receive her. But it struck her at once that this was unworthy of her, and ungenerous. "But I'll come to you," she added, "whether you come to me or not."

"I will go to you," said Lady Glencora, "of course,—why shouldn't I? But you know what I mean. We shall have dinners and parties and lots of people."

"And we shall have none," said Alice, smiling.

"And therefore there is so much more excuse for your coming to me;— or rather I mean so much more reason, for I don't want excuses. Well, dear, I'm so glad I've told you. I was afraid to see you in London. I should hardly have known how to look at you then. But I've got over that now." Then she smiled and returned the kiss which Alice had given her. It was singular to see her standing on the bedroom rug with all her magnificence of dress, but with her hair pushed back behind her ears, and her eyes red with tears,—as though the burden of the magnificence remained to her after its purpose was over.

"I declare it's ever so much past twelve. Good night, now, dear. I wonder whether he's come up. But I should have heard his step if he had. He never treads lightly. He seldom gives over work till after one, and sometimes goes on till three. It's the only thing he likes, I believe. God bless you! good night. I've such a deal more to say to you; and Alice, you must tell me something about yourself, too; won't you, dear?" Then without waiting for an answer Lady Glencora went, leaving Alice in a maze of bewilderment. She could hardly believe that all she had heard, and all she had done, had happened since she left Queen Anne Street that morning.

CHAPTER XXIV
THREE POLITICIANS

Mr. Palliser was one of those politicians in possessing whom England has perhaps more reason to be proud than of any other of her resources, and who, as a body, give to her that exquisite combination of conservatism and progress which is her present strength and best security for the future. He could afford to learn to be a statesman, and had the industry wanted for such training. He was born in the purple, noble himself, and heir to the highest rank as well as one of the greatest fortunes of the country, already very rich, surrounded by all the temptations of luxury and pleasure; and yet he devoted himself to work with the grinding energy of a young penniless barrister labouring for a penniless wife, and did so without any motive more selfish than that of being counted in the roll of the public servants of England. He was not a brilliant man, and understood well that such was the case. He was now listened to in the House, as the phrase goes; but he was listened to as a laborious man, who was in earnest in what he did, who got up his facts with accuracy, and who, dull though he be, was worthy of confidence. And he was very dull. He rather prided himself on being dull, and on conquering in spite of his dullness. He never allowed himself a joke in his speeches, nor attempted even the smallest flourish of rhetoric. He was very careful in his language, labouring night and day to learn to express himself with accuracy, with no needless repetition of words, perspicuously with regard to the special object he might have in view. He had taught himself to believe that oratory, as oratory, was a sin against that honesty in politics by which he strove to guide himself. He desired to use words for the purpose of teaching things which he knew and which others did not know; and he desired also to be honoured for his knowledge. But he had no desire to be honoured for the language in which his knowledge was conveyed. He was an upright, thin, laborious man; who by his parts alone could have served no political party materially, but whose parts were sufficient to make his education, integrity, and industry useful in the highest degree. It is the trust which such men inspire which makes them so serviceable;—trust not only in their labour,—for any man rising from the mass of the people may be equally laborious; nor yet simply in their honesty and patriotism. The confidence is given to their labour, honesty, and patriotism joined to such a personal stake in the country as gives them a weight and ballast which no politician in England can possess without it.

If he was dull as a statesman he was more dull in private life, and it may be imagined that such a woman as his wife would find some difficulty in making his society the source of her happiness. Their marriage, in a point of view regarding business, had been a complete success,—and a success, too, when on the one side, that of Lady Glencora, there had been terrible dangers of shipwreck, and when on his side also there had been some little fears of a mishap. As regards her it has been told how near she went to throwing herself, with all her vast wealth, into the arms of a young man, whom no father, no guardian could have regarded as a well-chosen husband for any girl;—one who as yet had shown no good qualities, who had been a spendthrift, unprincipled, and debauched. Alas, she had loved him! It is possible that her love and her wealth might have turned him from evil to good. But who would have ventured to risk her,—I will not say her and her vast inheritances,—on such a chance? That evil, however, had been prevented, and those about her had managed to marry her to a young man, very steady by nature, with worldly prospects as brilliant as her own, and with a station than which the world offers nothing higher. His little threatened mischance,—a passing fancy for a married lady who was too wise to receive vows which were proffered not in the most ardent manner,—had, from special reasons, given some little alarm to his uncle, which had just sufficed at the time to make so very judicious a marriage doubly pleasant to that noble duke. So that all things and all people had conspired to shower substantial comforts on the heads of this couple, when they were joined together, and men and women had not yet ceased to declare how happy were both in the accumulated gifts of fortune.

And as regards Mr. Palliser, I think that his married life, and the wife, whom he certainly had not chosen, but who had dropped upon him, suited him admirably. He wanted great wealth for that position at which he aimed. He had been rich before his marriage with his own wealth,—so rich that he could throw thousands away if he wished it; but for him and his career was needed that colossal wealth which would make men talk about it,—which would necessitate an expansive expenditure, reaching far and wide, doing nothing, or less than nothing, for his own personal comfort, but giving to him at once that rock-like solidity which is so necessary to our great aristocratic politicians. And his wife was, as far as he knew, all that he desired. He had not dabbled much in the fountains of Venus, though he had forgotten himself once, and sinned in coveting another man's wife. But his sin then had hardly polluted his natural character, and his desire had been of a kind which was almost more gratified in its disappointment than it would have been in its fruition. On the morning after the lady had frowned on him he had told himself that he was very well out of that trouble. He knew that it would never be for him to hang up on the walls of a temple a well-worn lute as a votive offering when leaving the pursuits of love. *Idoneus puellis* he never could have been. So he married Lady Glencora and was satisfied. The story of Burgo Fitzgerald was told to him, and he supposed that most girls had some such story to tell. He thought little about it, and by no means understood her when she said to him, with all the impressiveness which she could throw into the words, "You must know that I have really loved him." "You must love me now," he had replied with a smile; and then as regarded his mind, the thing was over. And since his marriage he had thought that things matrimonial had gone well with him, and with her too. He gave her almost unlimited power of enjoying her money, and interfered but little in her way of life. Sometimes he would say a word of caution to her with reference to those childish ways which hardly became the dull dignity of his position; and his words then would have in them something of unintentional severity,—whether instigated or not by the red-haired Radical Member of Parliament, I will not pretend to say;—but on the whole he was contented and loved his wife, as he thought, very heartily, and at least better than he loved any one else. One cause of unhappiness, or rather one doubt as to his entire good fortune, was beginning to make itself felt, as his wife had to her sorrow already discovered. He had hoped that before this he might have heard that she would give him a child. But the days were young yet for that trouble, and the care had not become a sorrow.

But this judicious arrangement as to properties, this well-ordered alliance between families, had not perhaps suited her as well as it had suited him. I think that she might have learned to forget her early lover, or to look back upon it with a soft melancholy hardly amounting to regret, had her new lord been more tender in his ways with her. I do not know that Lady Glencora's heart was made of that stern stuff which refuses to change its impressions; but it was a heart, and it required food. To love and fondle someone,—to be loved and fondled, were absolutely necessary to her happiness. She wanted the little daily assurance of her supremacy in the man's feelings, the constant touch of love, half accidental half contrived, the passing glance of the eye telling perhaps of some little joke understood only between them two rather than of love, the softness of an occasional kiss given here and there when chance might bring them together, some half-pretended interest in her little doings, a nod, a wink, a shake of the head, or even a pout. It should have been given to her to feed upon such food as this daily, and then she would have forgotten Burgo Fitzgerald. But Mr.

Palliser understood none of these things; and therefore the image of Burgo Fitzgerald in all his beauty was ever before her eyes.

But not the less was Mr. Palliser a prosperous man, as to the success of whose career few who knew him had much doubt. It might be written in the book of his destiny that he would have to pass through some violent domestic trouble, some ruin in the hopes of his home, of a nature to destroy then and for ever the worldly prospects of other men. But he was one who would pass through such violence, should it come upon him, without much scathe. To lose his influence with his party would be worse to him than to lose his wife, and public disgrace would hit him harder than private dishonour.

And the present was the very moment in which success was, as was said, coming to him. He had already held laborious office under the Crown, but had never sat in the Cabinet. He had worked much harder than Cabinet Ministers generally work,—but hitherto had worked without any reward that was worth his having. For the stipend which he had received had been nothing to him,—as the great stipend which he would receive, if his hopes were true, would also be nothing to him. To have ascendancy over other men, to be known by his countrymen as one of their real rulers, to have an actual and acknowledged voice in the management of nations,—those were the rewards for which he looked; and now in truth it seemed as though they were coming to him. It was all but known that the existing Chancellor of the Exchequer would separate himself from the Government, carrying various others with him, either before or immediately consequent on the meeting of Parliament;—and it was all but known, also, that Mr. Palliser would fill his place, taking that high office at once, although he had never hitherto sat in that august assembly which men call the Cabinet. He could thus afford to put up with the small everyday calamity of having a wife who loved another man better than she loved him.

The presence of the Duke of St. Bungay at Matching was assumed to be a sure sign of Mr. Palliser's coming triumph. The Duke was a statesman of a very different class, but he also had been eminently successful as an aristocratic pillar of the British Constitutional Republic. He was a minister of very many years' standing, being as used to cabinet sittings as other men are to their own armchairs; but he had never been a hard-working man. Though a constant politician, he had ever taken politics easy whether in office or out. The world had said before now that the Duke might be Premier, only that he would not take the trouble. He had been consulted by a very distinguished person,—so the papers had said more than once,— as to the making of Prime Ministers. His voice in council was esteemed to be very great. He was regarded as a strong rock of support to the liberal cause, and yet nobody ever knew what he did; nor was there much record of what he said. The offices which he held, or had held, were generally those to which no very arduous duties were attached. In severe debates he never took upon himself the brunt of opposition oratory. What he said in the House was generally short and pleasant,—with some slight, drolling, undercurrent of uninjurious satire running through it. But he was a walking miracle of the wisdom of common sense. He never lost his temper. He never made mistakes. He never grew either hot or cold in a cause. He was never reckless in politics, and never cowardly. He snubbed no man, and took snubbings from no man. He was a Knight of the Garter, a Lord Lieutenant of his county, and at sixty-two had his digestion unimpaired and his estate in excellent order. He was a great buyer of pictures, which, perhaps, he did not understand, and a great collector of books which certainly he never read. All the world respected him, and he was a man to whom the respect of all the world was as the breath of his nostrils.

But even he was not without his peacock on the wall, his skeleton in the closet, his thorn in his side; though the peacock did not scream loud, the skeleton was not very terrible in his anatomical arrangement, nor was the thorn likely to fester to a gangrene. The Duke was always in awe about his wife.

He was ever uneasy about his wife, but it must not be supposed that he feared the machinations of any Burgo Fitzgerald as being destructive of his domestic comfort. The Duchess was and always had been all that is proper. Ladies in high rank, when gifted with excelling beauty, have often been made the marks of undeserved calumny;—but no breath of slander had ever touched her name. I doubt if any man alive had ever had the courage even to wink at her since the Duke had first called her his own. Nor was she a spendthrift, or a gambler. She was not fast in her tastes, or given to any pursuit that was objectionable. She was simply a fool, and as a fool was ever fearing that she was the mark of ridicule. In all such miseries she would complain sorrowfully, piteously, and occasionally very angrily, to her dear Duke and protector; till sometimes her dear Duke did not quite know what to do with her or how to protect her. It did not suit him, a Knight of the Garter and a Duke of St. Bungay, to beg mercy for that poor wife of his from such a one as Mrs. Conway Sparkes; nor would it be more in his way to lodge a formal complaint against that lady before his host or hostess,—as one boy at school may sometimes do as regards another. "If you don't like the people, my dear, we will go away," he said to her late on that evening of which we have spoken. "No," she replied, "I do not wish to go away. I have said that we would stay till December, and Longroyston won't be ready before that. But I think that something ought to be done to silence that woman." And the accent came strong upon "something," and then again with terrific violence upon "woman."

The Duke did not know how to silence Mrs. Conway Sparkes. It was a great principle of his life never to be angry with any one. How could he get at Mrs. Conway Sparkes? "I don't think she is worth your attention," said the husband. "That's all very well, Duke," said the wife, "and perhaps she is not. But I find her in this house, and I don't like to be laughed at. I think Lady Glencora should make her know her place."

"Lady Glencora is very young, my dear."

"I don't know about being so very young," said the Duchess, whose ear had perhaps caught some little hint of poor Lady Glencora's almost unintentional mimicry. Now as appeals of this kind were being made frequently to the Duke, and as he was often driven to say some word, of which he himself hardly approved, to some one in protection of his Duchess, he was aware that the matter was an annoyance, and at times almost wished that her Grace was at—Longroyston.

And there was a third politician staying at Matching Priory who had never yet risen to the rank of a statesman, but who had his hopes. This was Mr. Bott, the member for St. Helens, whom Lady Glencora had described as a man who stood about, with red hair,—and perhaps told tales of her to her husband. Mr. Bott was a person who certainly had had some success in life and who had won it for himself. He was not very young, being at this time only just on the right side of fifty. He was now enjoying his second session in Parliament, having been returned as a pledged disciple of the Manchester school. Nor had he apparently been false to his pledges. At St. Helens he was still held to be a good man and true. But they who sat on the same side with him in the House and watched his political manœuvres, knew that he was striving hard to get his finger into the public pie. He was not a rich man, though he had made calico and had got into Parliament. And though he claimed to be a thoroughgoing Radical, he was a man who liked to live with aristocrats, and was fond of listening to the whispers of such as the Duke of St. Bungay or Mr. Palliser. It was supposed that he did understand something of finance. He was at any rate great in figures; and as he was possessed of much industry, and was obedient withal, he was a man who might make himself useful to a Chancellor of the Exchequer ambitious of changes.

There are men who get into such houses as Matching Priory and whose presence there is a mystery to many;—as to whom the ladies of the house never quite understand why they are entertaining such a guest. "And Mr. Bott is coming," Mr. Palliser had said to his wife. "Mr. Bott!" Lady Glencora had answered. "Goodness me! who is Mr. Bott?" "He is member for St. Helens," said Mr. Palliser. "A very serviceable man in his way." "And what am I to do with him?" asked Lady Glencora. "I don't know that you can do anything with him. He is a man who has a great deal of business, and I dare say he will spend most of his time in the library." So Mr. Bott arrived. But though a huge pile of letters and papers came to him every morning by post, he unfortunately did not seem to spend much of his time in the library. Perhaps he had not found the clue to that lost apartment. Twice he went out shooting, but as on the first day he shot the keeper, and on the second very nearly shot the Duke, he gave that up. Hunting he declined, though much pressed to make an essay in that art by Jeffrey Palliser. He seemed to spend his time, as Lady Glencora said, in standing about,—except at certain times when he was closeted with Mr. Palliser, and when, it may be presumed, he made himself useful. On such days he would be seen at the hour of lunch with fingers much stained with ink, and it was generally supposed that on those occasions he had been counting up taxes and calculating the effect of great financial changes. He was a tall, wiry, strong man, with a bald head and bristly red beard, which, however, was cut off from his upper and under lip. This was unfortunate, as had he hidden his mouth he would not have been in so marked a degree an ugly man. His upper lip was very long, and his mouth was mean. But he had found that without the help of a razor to these parts he could not manage his soup to his satisfaction, and preferring cleanliness to beauty had shaved himself accordingly.

"I shouldn't dislike Mr. Bott so much," Lady Glencora said to her husband, "if he didn't rub his hands and smile so often, and seem to be going to say something when he really is not going to say anything."

"I don't think you need trouble yourself about him, my dear," Mr. Palliser had answered.

"But when he looks at me in that way, I can't help stopping, as I think he is going to speak; and then he always says, 'Can I do anything for you, Lady Glen-cowrer?'"

She instantly saw that her husband did not like this. "Don't be angry with me, dear," she said. "You must admit that he is rather a bore."

"I am not at all angry, Glencora," said the husband; "and if you insist upon it, I will see that he leaves;—and in such case will of course never ask him again. But that might be prejudicial to me, as he is a man whom I trust in politics, and who may perhaps be serviceable to me."

Of course Lady Glencora declared that Mr. Bott might remain as long as he and her husband desired, and of course she mentioned his name no more to Mr. Palliser; but from that time forth she regarded Mr. Bott as an enemy, and felt also that Mr. Bott regarded her in the same light.

When it was known among outside politicians that the Duke of St. Bungay was staying at Matching Priory, outside politicians became more sure than ever that Mr. Palliser would be the new Chancellor of the Exchequer. The old minister and the young minister were of course arranging matters together. But I doubt whether Mr. Palliser and the Duke ever spoke on any such topic during the entire visit. Though Mr. Bott was occasionally closeted with Mr. Palliser, the Duke never troubled himself with such closetings. He went out shooting—on his pony, read his newspaper, wrote his notes, and looked with the eye of a connoisseur over all Mr. Palliser's farming apparatus. "You seem to have a good man, I should say," said the Duke. "What! Hubbings? Yes;—he was a legacy from my uncle when he gave me up the Priory." "A very good man, I should say. Of course he won't make it pay; but he'll make it look as though it did;—which is the next best thing. I could never get rent out of land that I farmed myself,—never." "I suppose not," said Mr. Palliser, who did not care much about it. The Duke would have talked to him by the hour together about farming had Mr. Palliser been so minded; but he talked to him very little about politics. Nor during the whole time of his stay at Matching did the Duke make any other allusion to Mr. Palliser's hopes as regarded the ministry, than that in which he had told Lady Glencora at the dinner-table that her husband's ambition was the highest by which any man could be moved.

But Mr. Bott was sometimes honoured by a few words with the Duke.

"We shall muster pretty strong, your Grace," Mr. Bott had said to him one day before dinner.

"That depends on how the changes go," said the Duke.

"I suppose there will be a change?"

"Oh yes; there'll be a change,—certainly, I should say. And it will be in your direction."

"And in Palliser's?"

"Yes; I should think so;—that is, if it suits him. By-the-by, Mr. Bott—" Then there was a little whispered communication, in which perhaps Mr. Bott was undertaking some commission of that nature which Lady Glencora had called "telling."

CHAPTER XXV
IN WHICH MUCH OF THE HISTORY
OF THE PALLISERS IS TOLD

At the end of ten days Alice found herself quite comfortable at Matching Priory. She had now promised to remain there till the second week of December, at which time she was to go to Vavasor Hall,—there to meet her father and Kate. The Pallisers were to pass their Christmas with the Duke of Omnium in Barsetshire. "We always are to do that," said Glencora. "It is the state occasion at Gatherum Castle, but it only lasts for one week. Then we go somewhere else. Oh dear!"

"Why do you say 'oh dear'?"

"Because—; I don't think I mean to tell you."

"Then I'm sure I won't ask."

"That's so like you, Alice. But I can be as firm as you, and I'm sure I won't tell you unless you do ask." But Alice did not ask, and it was not long before Lady Glencora's firmness gave way.

But, as I have said, Alice had become quite comfortable at Matching Priory. Perhaps she was already growing upwards towards the light. At any rate she could listen with pleasure to the few words the Duke would say to her. She could even chat a little to the Duchess,—so that her Grace had observed to Lady Glencora that "her cousin was a very nice person,—a very nice person indeed. What a pity it was that she had been so ill-treated by that gentleman in Oxfordshire!" Lady Glencora had to explain that the gentleman lived in Cambridgeshire, and that he, at any rate, had not treated anybody ill. "Do you mean that she—jilted him?" said the Duchess, almost whistling, and opening her eyes very wide. "Dear me, I'm sorry for that. I shouldn't have thought it." And when she next spoke to Alice she assumed rather a severe tone of emphasis;—but this was soon abandoned when Alice listened to her with complacency.

Alice also had learned to ride,—or rather had resumed her riding, which for years had been abandoned. Jeffrey Palliser had been her squire, and she had become intimate with him so as to learn to quarrel with him and to like him,—to such an extent that Lady Glencora had laughingly told her that she was going to do more.

"I rather think not," said Alice.

"But what has thinking to do with it? Who ever thinks about it?"

"I don't just at present,—at any rate."

"Upon my word it would be very nice;—and then perhaps some day you'd be the Duchess."

"Glencora, don't talk such nonsense."

"Those are the speculations which people make. Only I should spite you by killing myself, so that he might marry again."

"How can you say such horrid things?"

"I think I shall,—some day. What right have I to stand in his way? He spoke to me the other day about Jeffrey's altered position, and I knew what he meant;—or rather what he didn't mean to say, but what he thought. But I shan't kill myself."

"I should think not."

"I only know one other way," said Lady Glencora.

"You are thinking of things which should never be in your thoughts," said Alice vehemently. "Have you no trust in God's providence? Cannot you accept what has been done for you?"

Mr. Bott had gone away, much to Lady Glencora's delight, but had unfortunately come back again. On his return Alice heard more of the feud between the Duchess and Mrs. Conway Sparkes. "I did not tell you," said Lady Glencora to her friend;—"I did not tell you before he went that I was right about his tale-bearing."

"And did he bear tales?"

"Yes; I did get the scolding, and I know very well that it came through him, though Mr. Palliser did not say so. But he told me that the Duchess had felt herself hurt by that other woman's way of talking."

"But it was not your fault."

"No; that's what I said. It was he who desired me to ask Mrs. Conway Sparkes to come here. I didn't want her. She goes everywhere, and it is thought a catch to get her; but if she had been drowned in the Red Sea I shouldn't have minded. When I told him that, he said it was nonsense,—which of course it was; and then he said I ought to make her hold her tongue. Of course I said I couldn't. Mrs. Conway Sparkes wouldn't care for me. If she quizzed me, myself, I told him that I could take care of myself, though she were ten times Mrs. Conway Sparkes, and had written finer poetry than Tennyson."

"It is fine;—some of it," said Alice.

"Oh, I dare say! I know a great deal of it by heart, only I wouldn't give her the pleasure of supposing that I had ever thought so much about her poetry. And then I told him that I couldn't take care of the Duchess,—and he told me that I was a child."

"He only meant that in love."

"I am a child; I know that. Why didn't he marry some strong-minded, ferocious woman that could keep his house in order, and frown Mrs. Sparkes out of her impudence? It wasn't my fault."

"You didn't tell him that."

"But I did. Then he kissed me, and said it was all right, and told me that I should grow older. 'And Mrs. Sparkes will grow more impudent,' I said, 'and the Duchess more silly.' And after that I went away. Now this horrid Mr. Bott has come back again, and only that it would be mean in me to condescend so far, I would punish him. He grins and smiles at me, and rubs his big hands more than ever, because he feels that he has behaved badly. Is it not horrid to have to live in the house with such people?"

"I don't think you need mind him much."

"Yes; but I am the mistress here, and am told that I am to entertain the people. Fancy entertaining the Duchess of St. Bungay and Mr. Bott!"

Alice had now become so intimate with Lady Glencora that she did not scruple to read her wise lectures,—telling her that she allowed herself to think too much of little things,—and too much also of some big things. "As regards Mr. Bott," said Alice, "I think you should bear it as though there were no such person."

"But that would be pretence,—especially to you."

"No; it would not be pretence; it would be the reticence which all women should practise,—and you, in your position, more almost than any other woman." Then Lady Glencora pouted, told Alice that it was a pity she had not married Mr. Palliser, and left her.

That evening,—the evening of Mr. Bott's return to Matching, that gentleman found a place near to Alice in the drawing-room. He had often come up to her, rubbing his hands together, and saying little words, as though there was some reason from their positions that they two should be friends. Alice had perceived this, and had endeavoured with all her force to shake him off; but he was a man, who if he understood a hint, never took it. A cold shoulder was nothing to him, if he wanted to gain the person who showed it him. His code of perseverance taught him that it was a virtue to overcome cold shoulders. The man or woman who received his first overtures with grace would probably be one on whom it would be better that he should look down and waste no further time; whereas he or she who could afford to treat him with disdain would no doubt be worth gaining. Such men as Mr. Bott are ever gracious to cold shoulders. The colder the shoulders, the more gracious are the Mr. Botts.

"What a delightful person is our dear friend, Lady Glencora!" said Mr. Bott, having caught Alice in a position from which she could not readily escape.

Alice had half a mind to differ, or to make any remark that might rid her from Mr. Bott. But she did not dare to say a word that might seem to have been said playfully. "Yes, indeed," she replied. "How very cold it is to-night!" She was angry with herself for her own stupidity as soon as the phrase was out of her mouth, and then she almost laughed as she thought of the Duchess and the hot-water pipes at Longroyston.

"Yes, it is cold. You and her ladyship are great friends, I believe, Miss Vavasor."

"She is my cousin," said Alice.

"Ah! yes; that is so pleasant. I have reason to know that Mr. Palliser is very much gratified that you should be so much with her."

This was unbearable. Alice could not quite assume sufficient courage to get up from her chair and walk away from him, and yet she felt that she must escape further conversation. "I don't know that I am very much with her, and if I were I can't think it would make any difference to Mr. Palliser."

But Mr. Bott was not a man to be put down when he had a purpose in hand. "I can assure you that those are his sentiments. Of course we all know that dear Lady Glencora is young. She is very young."

"Mr. Bott, I really would rather not talk about my cousin."

"But, dear Miss Vavasor;—when we both have her welfare in view—?"

"I haven't her welfare in view, Mr. Bott; not in the least. There is no reason why I should. You must excuse me if I say I cannot talk about her welfare with a perfect stranger." Then she did get up, and went away from the Member of Parliament, leaving him rather astonished at her audacity.

But he was a constant man, and his inner resolve was simply to the effect that he would try it again.

I wonder whether Jeffrey Palliser did think much of the difference between his present position and that which would have been his had Lady Glencora been the happy possessor of a cradle up-stairs with a boy in it. I suppose he must have done so. It is hardly possible that any man should not be alive to the importance of such a chance. His own present position was one of the most unfortunate which can fall to the lot of a man. His father, the Duke's youngest brother, had left him about six hundred a year, and had left him also a taste for living with people of six thousand. The propriety of earning his bread had never been put before him. His father had been in Parliament, and had been the most favoured son of the old Duke, who for some years before his death had never spoken to him who now reigned over the house of the Pallisers. Jeffrey's father had been brought up at Matching Priory as scions of ducal houses are brought up, and on the old man's death had been possessed of means sufficient to go on in the same path, though with difficulty. His brother had done something for him, and at various times he had held some place near the throne. But on his death, when the property left behind him was divided between his son and three daughters, Jeffrey Palliser became possessed of the income above stated. Of course he could live on it,—and as during the winter months of the year a home was found for him free of cost, he could keep hunters, and live as rich men live. But he was a poor, embarrassed man, without prospects,—until this fine ducal prospect became opened to him by the want of that cradle at Matching Priory.

But the prospect was no doubt very distant. Lady Glencora might yet have as many sons as Hecuba. Or she might die, and some other more fortunate lady might become the mother of his cousin's heir. Or the Duke might marry and have a son. And, moreover, his cousin was only one year older than himself, and the great prize, if it came his way, might not come for forty years as yet. Nevertheless his hand might now be acceptable in quarters where it would certainly be rejected had Lady Glencora possessed that cradle up-stairs. We cannot but suppose that he must have made some calculations of this nature.

"It is a pity you should do nothing all your life," his cousin Plantagenet said to him one morning just at this time. Jeffrey had sought the interview in his cousin's room, and I fear had done so with some slight request for ready money.

"What am I to do?" said Jeffrey.

"At any rate you might marry."

"Oh, yes;—I could marry. There's no man so poor but what he can do that. The question would be how I might like the subsequent starvation."

"I don't see that you need starve. Though your own fortune is small, it is something,—and many girls have fortunes of their own."

Jeffrey thought of Lady Glencora, but he made no allusion to her in speech. "I don't think I'm very good at that kind of thing," he said. "When the father and mother came to ask of my house and my home I should break down. I don't say it as praising myself;—indeed, quite the reverse; but I fear I have not a mercenary tendency."

"That's nonsense."

"Oh, yes; quite so. I admit that."

"Men must have mercenary tendencies or they would not have bread. The man who ploughs that he may live does so because he, luckily, has a mercenary tendency."

"Just so. But you see I am less lucky than the ploughman."

"There is no vulgar error so vulgar,—that is to say, common or erroneous, as that by which men have been taught to say that mercenary tendencies are bad. A desire for wealth is the source of all progress. Civilization comes from what men call greed. Let your mercenary tendencies be combined with honesty and they cannot take you astray." This the future Chancellor of the Exchequer said with much of that air and tone of wisdom which a Chancellor of the Exchequer ought to possess.

"But I haven't got any such tendencies," said Jeffrey.

"Would you like to occupy a farm in Scotland?" said Plantagenet Palliser.

"And pay rent?"

"You would have to pay rent of course."

"Thank you, no. It would be dishonest, as I know I should never pay it."

"You are too old, I fear, for the public service."

"You mean a desk in the Treasury,—with a hundred a year. Yes; I think I am too old."

"But have you no plan of your own?"

"Not much of one. Sometimes I have thought I would go to New Zealand."

"You would have to be a farmer there."

"No;—I shouldn't do that. I should get up an opposition to the Government and that sort of thing, and then they would buy me off and give me a place."

"That does very well here, Jeffrey, if a man can get into Parliament and has capital enough to wait; but I don't think it would do out there. Would you like to go into Parliament?"

"What; here? Of course I should. Only I should be sure to get terribly into debt. I don't owe very much, now,—not to speak of,—except what I owe you."

"You owe nothing to me," said Plantagenet, with some little touch of magniloquence in his tone. "No; don't speak of it. I have no brother, and between you and me it means nothing. You see, Jeffrey, it may be that I shall have to look to you as my—my—my heir, in short." Hereupon Jeffrey muttered something as to the small probability of such necessity, and as to the great remoteness of any result even if it were so.

"That's all true," said the elder heir of the Pallisers, "but still—. In short, I wish you would do something. Do you think about it; and then some day speak to me again."

Jeffrey, as he left his cousin with a cheque for £500 in his waist-coat pocket, thought that the interview which had at one time taken important dimensions, had not been concluded altogether satisfactorily. A seat in Parliament! Yes, indeed! If his cousin would so far use his political, monetary, or ducal interest as to do that for him;—as to give him something of the status properly belonging to the younger son of the House, then indeed life would have some charms for him! But as for the farm in Scotland, or a desk at an office in London,—his own New Zealand plan would be better than those. And then as he went along of course he bethought himself that it might be his lot yet to die, and at least to be buried, in the purple, as a Duke of Omnium. If so, certainly it would be his duty to prepare another heir, and leave a duke behind him,—if it were possible.

"Are you going to ride with us after lunch?" said Lady Glencora to him as he strolled into the drawing-room.

"No," said Jeffrey; "I'm going to study."

"To do what?" said Lady Glencora.

"To study;—or rather I shall spend to-day in sitting down and considering what I will study. My cousin has just been telling me that I ought to do something."

"So you ought," said Iphigenia energetically from her writing-desk.

"But he didn't seem to have any clear opinion what it ought to be. You see there can't be two Chancellors of the Exchequer at the same time. Mrs. Sparkes, what ought a young man like me to set about doing?"

"Go into Parliament, I should say," said Mrs. Sparkes.

"Ah, yes; exactly. He had some notion of that kind, too, but he didn't name any particular place. I think I'll try the City of London. They've four there, and of course the chance of getting in would thereby be doubled."

"I thought that commercial men were generally preferred in the City," said the Duchess, taking a strong and good-natured interest in the matter.

"Mr. Palliser means to make a fortune in trade as a preliminary," said Mrs. Sparkes.

"I don't think he meant anything of the kind," said the Duchess.

"At any rate I have got to do something, so I can't go and ride," said Jeffrey.

"And you ought to do something," said Iphigenia from her desk.

Twice during this little conversation Lady Glencora had looked up, catching Alice's eye, and Alice had well known what she had meant. "You see," the glance had said, "Plantagenet is beginning to take an interest in his cousin, and you know why. The man who is to be the father of the future dukes must not be allowed to fritter away his time in obscurity. Had I that cradle up-stairs Jeffrey might be as idle as he pleased." Alice understood it well.

Of course Jeffrey did join the riding party. "What is a man like me to do who wants to do something?" he said to Alice. Alice was quite aware that Lady Glencora had contrived some little scheme that Mr. Palliser should be riding next to her. She liked Mr. Palliser, and therefore had no objection; but she declared to herself that her cousin was a goose for her pains.

"Mrs. Sparkes says you ought to go into Parliament."

"Yes;—and the dear Duchess would perhaps suggest a house in Belgrave Square. I want to hear your advice now."

"I can only say ditto to Miss Palliser."

"What! Iphy? About procrastination? But you see the more of my time he steals the better it is for me."

"That's the evil you have got to cure."

"My cousin Plantagenet suggested—marriage."

"A very good thing too, I'm sure," said Alice; "only it depends something on the sort of wife you get."

"You mean, of course, how much money she has."

"Not altogether."

"Looking at it from my cousin's point of view, I suppose that it is the only important point. Who are there coming up this year,—in the way of heiresses?"

"Upon my word I don't know. In the first place, how much money makes an heiress?"

"For such a fellow as me, I suppose ten thousand pounds ought to do."

"That's not much," said Alice, who had exactly that amount of her own.

"No—; perhaps that's too moderate. But the lower one went in the money speculation, the greater would be the number to choose from, and the better the chance of getting something decent in the woman herself. I have something of my own,—not much you know; so with the lady's ten thousand pounds we might be able to live,—in some second-rate French town perhaps."

"But I don't see what you would gain by that."

"My people here would have got rid of me. That seems to be the great thing. If you hear of any girl with about that sum, moderately good-looking, not too young so that she might know something of the world, decently born, and able to read and write, perhaps you will bear me in mind."

"Yes, I will," said Alice, who was quite aware that he had made an accurate picture of her own position. "When I meet such a one, I will send for you at once."

"You know no such person now?"

"Well, no; not just at present."

"I declare I don't think he could do anything better," her cousin said to her that night. Lady Glencora was now in the habit of having Alice with her in what she called her dressing-room every evening, and then they would sit till the small hours came upon them. Mr. Palliser always burnt the midnight oil and came to bed with the owls. They would often talk of him and his prospects till Alice had perhaps inspired his wife with more of interest in him and them than she had before felt. And Alice had managed generally to drive her friend away from those topics which were so dangerous,—those allusions to her childlessness, and those hints that Burgo Fitzgerald was still in her thoughts. And sometimes, of course, they had spoken of Alice's own prospects, till she got into a way of telling her cousin freely all that she felt. On such occasions Lady Glencora would always tell her that she had been right,—if she did not love the man. "Though your finger were put out for the ring," said Lady Glencora on one such occasion, "you should go back, if you did not love him."

"But I did love him," said Alice.

"Then I don't understand it," said Lady Glencora; and, in truth, close as was their intimacy, they did not perfectly understand each other.

But on this occasion they were speaking of Jeffrey Palliser. "I declare I don't think he could do any better," said Lady Glencora.

"If you talk such nonsense, I will not stay," said Alice.

"But why should it be nonsense? You would be very comfortable with your joint incomes. He is one of the best fellows in the world. It is clear that he likes you; and then we should be so near to each other. I am sure Mr. Palliser would do something for him if he married,—and especially if I asked him."

"I only know of two things against it."

"And what are they?"

"That he would not take me for his wife, and that I would not take him for my husband."

"Why not? What do you dislike in him?"

"I don't dislike him at all. I like him very much indeed. But one can't marry all the people one likes."

"But what reason is there why you shouldn't marry him?"

"This chiefly," said Alice, after a pause; "that I have just separated myself from a man whom I certainly did love truly, and that I cannot transfer my affections quite so quickly as that."

As soon as the words were out of her mouth she knew that they should not have been spoken. It was exactly what Glencora had done. She had loved a man and had separated herself from him and had married another all within a month or two. Lady Glencora first became red as fire over her whole face and shoulders, and Alice afterwards did the same as she looked up, as though searching in her cousin's eyes for pardon.

"It is an unmaidenly thing to do, certainly," said Lady Glencora very slowly, and in her lowest voice. "Nay, it is unwomanly; but one may be driven. One may be so driven that all gentleness of womanhood is driven out of one."

"Oh, Glencora!"

"I did not propose that you should do it as a sudden thing."

"Glencora!"

"I did do it suddenly. I know it. I did it like a beast that is driven as its owner chooses. I know it. I was a beast. Oh, Alice, if you know how I hate myself!"

"But I love you with all my heart," said Alice. "Glencora, I have learned to love you so dearly!"

"Then you are the only being that does. He can't love me. How is it possible? You,—and perhaps another."

"There are many who love you. He loves you. Mr. Palliser loves you."

"It is impossible. I have never said a word to him that could make him love me. I have never done a thing for him that can make him love me. The mother of his child he might have loved, because of that. Why should he love me? We were told to marry each other and did it. When could he have learned to love me? But, Alice, he requires no loving, either to take it or to give it. I wish it were so with me."

Alice said what she could to comfort her, but her words were but of little avail as regarded those marriage sorrows.

"Forgive you!" at last Glencora said. "What have I to forgive? You don't suppose I do not know it all, and think of it all without the chance of some stray word like that! Forgive you! I am so grateful that you love me! Some one's love I must have found,—or I could not have remained here."

CHAPTER XXVI
LADY MIDLOTHIAN

A week or ten days after this, Alice, when she came down to the breakfast-parlour one morning, found herself alone with Mr. Bott. It was the fashion at Matching Priory for people to assemble rather late in the day. The nominal hour for breakfast was ten, and none of the ladies of the party were ever seen before that. Some of the gentlemen would breakfast earlier, especially on hunting mornings; and on some occasions the ladies, when they came together, would find themselves altogether deserted by their husbands and brothers. On this day it was fated that Mr. Bott alone should represent the sterner sex, and when Alice entered the room he was standing on the rug with his back to the fire, waiting till the appearance of some other guest should give him the sanction necessary for the commencement of his morning meal. Alice, when she saw him, would have retreated had it been possible, for she had learned to dislike him greatly, and was, indeed, almost afraid of him; but she could not do so without making her flight too conspicuous.

"Do you intend to prolong your stay here, Miss Vavasor?" said Mr. Bott, taking advantage of the first moment at which she looked up from a letter which she was reading.

"For a few more days, I think," said Alice.

"Ah—I'm glad of that. Mr. Palliser has pressed me so much to remain till he goes to the Duke's, that I cannot get away sooner. As I am an unmarried man myself, I can employ my time as well in one place as in another;—at this time of the year at least."

"You must find that very convenient," said Alice.

"Yes, it is convenient. You see in my position,—Parliamentary position, I mean,—I am obliged, as a public man, to act in concert with others. A public man can be of no service unless he is prepared to do that. We must give and take, you know, Miss Vavasor."

As Miss Vavasor made no remark in answer to this, Mr. Bott continued—"I always say to the men of my party,—of course I regard myself as belonging to the extreme Radicals."

"Oh, indeed!" said Alice.

"Yes. I came into Parliament on that understanding; and I have never seen any occasion as yet to change any political opinion that I have expressed. But I always say to the gentlemen with whom I act, that nothing can be done if we don't give and take. I don't mind saying to you, Miss Vavasor, that I look upon our friend, Mr. Palliser, as the most rising public man in the country. I do, indeed."

"I am happy to hear you say so," said his victim, who found herself driven to make some remark.

"And I, as an extreme Radical, do not think I can serve my party better than by keeping in the same boat with him, as long as it will hold the two. 'He'll make a Government hack of you,' a friend of mine said to me the other day. 'And I'll make a Manchester school Prime Minister of him,' I replied. I rather think I know what I'm about, Miss Vavasor."

"No doubt," said Alice.

"And so does he;—and so does he. Mr. Palliser is not the man to be led by the nose by any one. But it's a fair system of give and take. You can't get on in politics without it. What a charming woman is your relative, Lady Glencowrer! I remember well what you said to me the other evening."

"Do you?" said Alice.

"And I quite agree with you that confidential intercourse regarding dear friends should not be lightly made."

"Certainly not," said Alice.

"But there are occasions, Miss Vavasor; there are occasions when the ordinary laws by which we govern our social conduct must be made somewhat elastic."

"I don't think this one of them, Mr. Bott."

"Is it not? Just listen to me for one moment, Miss Vavasor. Our friend, Mr. Palliser, I am proud to say, relies much upon my humble friendship. Our first connection has, of course, been political; but it has extended beyond that, and has become pleasantly social;—I may say, very pleasantly social."

"What a taste Mr. Palliser must have!" Alice thought to herself.

"But I need not tell you that Lady Glencowrer is—very young; we may say, very young indeed."

"Mr. Bott, I will not talk to you about Lady Glencora Palliser."

This Alice said in a determined voice, and with all the power of resistance at her command. She frowned too, and looked savagely at Mr. Bott. But he was a man of considerable courage, and knew how to bear such opposition without flinching.

"When I tell you, Miss Vavasor, that I speak solely with a view to her domestic happiness!"

"I don't think that she wishes to have any such guardian of her happiness."

"But if he wishes it, Miss Vavasor! Now I have the means of knowing that he has the greatest reliance on your judgement."

Hereupon Alice got up with the intention of leaving the room, but she was met at the door by Mrs. Conway Sparkes.

"Are you running from your breakfast, Miss Vavasor?" said she.

"No, Mrs. Sparkes; I am running from Mr. Bott," said Alice, who was almost beside herself with anger.

"Mr. Bott, what is this?" said Mrs. Sparkes. "Ha, ha, ha," laughed Mr. Bott.

Alice returned to the room, and Mrs. Sparkes immediately saw that she had in truth been running from Mr. Bott. "I hope I shall be able to keep the peace," said she. "I trust his offence was not one that requires special punishment."

"Ha, ha, ha," again laughed Mr. Bott, who rather liked his position.

Alice was very angry with herself, feeling that she had told more of the truth to Mrs. Sparkes than she should have done, unless she was prepared to tell the whole. As it was, she wanted to say something, and did not know what to say; but her confusion was at once stopped by the entrance of Lady Glencora.

"Mrs. Sparkes, good morning," said Lady Glencora. "I hope nobody has waited breakfast. Good morning, Mr. Bott. Oh, Alice!"

"What is the matter?" said Alice, going up to her.

"Oh, Alice, such a blow!" But Alice could see that her cousin was not quite in earnest;—that the new trouble, though it might be vexatious, was no great calamity. "Come here," said Lady Glencora; and they both went into an embrasure of the window. "Now I shall have to put your confidence in me to the test. This letter is from,—whom do you think?"

"How can I guess?"

"From Lady Midlothian! and she's coming here on Monday, on her road to London. Unless you tell me that you are quite sure this is as unexpected by me as by you, I will never speak to you again."

"I am quite sure of that."

"Ah! then we can consult. But first we'll go and have some breakfast." Then more ladies swarmed into the room,—the Duchess and her daughter, and the two Miss Pallisers, and others; and Mr. Bott had his hands full in attending,—or rather in offering to attend, to their little wants.

The morning was nearly gone before Alice and her cousin had any further opportunity of discussing in private the approach of Lady Midlothian; but Mr. Palliser had come in among them, and had been told of the good thing which was in store for him. "We shall be delighted to see Lady Midlothian," said Mr. Palliser.

"But there is somebody here who will not be at all delighted to see her," said Lady Glencora to her husband.

"Is there, indeed?" said he. "Who is that?"

"Her most undutiful cousin, Alice Vavasor. But, Alice, Mr. Palliser knows nothing about it, and it is too long to explain."

"I am extremely sorry—" began Mr. Palliser.

"I can assure you it does not signify in the least," said Alice. "It will only be taking me away three days earlier."

Upon hearing this Mr. Palliser looked very serious. What quarrel could Miss Vavasor have had with Lady Midlothian which should make it impossible for them to be visitors at the same house?

"It will do no such thing," said Lady Glencora. "Do you mean to say that you are coward enough to run away from her?"

"I'm afraid, Miss Vavasor, that we can hardly bid her not come," said Mr. Palliser. In answer to this, Alice protested that she would not for worlds have been the means of keeping Lady Midlothian away from Matching. "I should tell you, Mr. Palliser, that I have never seen Lady Midlothian, though she is my far-away cousin. Nor have I ever quarrelled with her. But she has given me advice by letter, and I did not answer her because I thought she had no business to interfere. I shall go away, not because I am afraid of her, but because, after what has passed, our meeting would be unpleasant to her."

"You could tell her that Miss Vavasor is here," said Mr. Palliser. "And then she need not come unless she pleased."

The matter was so managed at last that Alice found herself unable to leave Matching without making more of Lady Midlothian's coming than it was worth. It would undoubtedly be very disagreeable,—this unexpected meeting with her relative; but, as Lady Glencora said, Lady Midlothian would not eat her. In truth, she felt ashamed of herself in that she was afraid of her relative. No doubt she was afraid of her. So much she was forced to admit to herself. But she resolved at last that she would not let her drive her out of the house.

"Is Mr. Bott an admirer of your cousin?" Mrs. Sparkes said that evening to Lady Glencora.

"A very distant one I should think," said Lady Glencora.

"Goodness gracious!" exclaimed an old lady who had been rather awed by Alice's intimacy and cousinship with Lady Glencora; "it's the very last thing I should have dreamt of."

"But I didn't dream it, first or last," said Mrs. Sparkes.

"Why do you ask?" said Lady Glencora.

"Don't suppose that I am asking whether Miss Vavasor is an admirer of his," said Mrs. Sparkes. "I have no suspicion of that nature. I rather think that when he plays Bacchus she plays Ariadne, with full intention of flying from him in earnest."

"Is Mr. Bott inclined to play Bacchus?" asked Lady Glencora.

"I rather thought he was this morning. If you observe, he has something of a godlike and triumphant air about him."

"I don't think his godship will triumph there," said Lady Glencora.

"I really think she would be throwing herself very much away," said the old lady.

"Miss Vavasor is not at all disposed to do that," said Mrs. Sparkes. Then that conversation was allowed to drop.

On the following Monday, Lady Midlothian arrived. The carriage was sent to meet her at the station about three o'clock in the afternoon, and Alice had to choose whether she would undergo her first introduction immediately on her relative's arrival, or whether she would keep herself out of the way till she should meet her in the drawing-room before dinner.

"I shall receive her when she comes," said Lady Glencora, "and of course will tell her that you are here."

"Yes, that will be best; and—; dear me, I declare I don't know how to manage it."

"I'll bring her to you in my room if you like it."

"No; that would be too solemn," said Alice. "That would make her understand that I thought a great deal about her."

"Then we'll let things take their chance, and you shall come across her just as you would any other stranger." It was settled at last that this would be the better course, but that Lady Midlothian was to be informed of Alice's presence at the Priory as soon as she should arrive.

Alice was in her own room when the carriage in which sat the unwelcome old lady was driven up to the hall-door. She heard the wheels plainly, and knew well that her enemy was within the house. She had striven hard all the morning to make herself feel indifferent to this arrival, but had not succeeded; and was angry with herself at finding that she sat up-stairs with an anxious heart, because she knew that her cousin was in the room down-stairs. What was Lady Midlothian to her that she should be afraid of her? And yet she was very much afraid of Lady Midlothian. She questioned herself on the subject over and over again, and found herself bound to admit that such was the fact. At last, about five o'clock, having reasoned much with herself, and rebuked herself for her own timidity, she descended into the drawing-room,—Lady Glencora having promised that she would at that hour be there, and on opening the door became immediately conscious that she was in the presence of her august relative. There sat Lady Midlothian in a great chair opposite the fire, and Lady Glencora sat near to her on a stool. One of the Miss Pallisers was reading in a further part of the room, and there was no one else present in the chamber.

The Countess of Midlothian was a very little woman, between sixty and seventy years of age, who must have been very pretty in her youth. At present she made no pretension either to youth or beauty,—as some ladies above sixty will still do,—but sat confessedly an old woman in all her external relations. She wore a round bonnet which came much over her face,—being accustomed to continue the use of her bonnet till dinner time when once she had been forced by circumstances to put it on. She wore a short cloak which fitted close to her person, and, though she occupied a great arm-chair, sat perfectly upright, looking at the fire. Very small she was, but she carried in her grey eyes and sharp-cut features a certain look of importance which saved her from being considered as small in importance. Alice, as soon as she saw her, knew that she was a lady over whom no easy victory could be obtained.

"Here is Alice," said Lady Glencora, rising as her cousin entered the room. "Alice, let me introduce you to Lady Midlothian."

Alice, as she came forward, was able to assume an easy demeanour, even though her heart within was failing her. She put out her hand, leaving it to the elder lady to speak the first words of greeting.

"I am glad at last to be able to make your acquaintance, my dear," said Lady Midlothian; "very glad." But still Alice did not speak. "Your aunt, Lady Macleod, is one of my oldest friends, and I have heard her speak of you very often."

"And Lady Macleod has often spoken to me of your ladyship," said Alice.

"Then we know each other's names," said the Countess; "and it will be well that we should be acquainted with each other's persons. I am becoming an old woman, and if I did not learn to know you now, or very shortly, I might never do so."

Alice could not help thinking that even under those circumstances neither might have had, so far as that was concerned, much cause of sorrow, but she did not say so. She was thinking altogether of Lady Midlothian's letter to her, and trying to calculate whether or no it would be well for her to rush away at once to the subject. That Lady Midlothian would mention the letter, Alice felt well assured; and when could it be better mentioned than now, in Glencora's presence,—when no other person was near them to listen to her? "You are very kind," said Alice.

"I would wish to be so," said Lady Midlothian. "Blood is thicker than water, my dear; and I know no earthly ties that can bind people together if those of family connection will not do so. Your mother, when she and I were young, was my dearest friend."

"I never knew my mother," said Alice,—feeling, however, as she spoke, that the strength of her resistance to the old woman was beginning to give way.

"No, my dear, you never did; and that is to my thinking another reason why they who loved her should love you. But Lady Macleod is your nearest relative,—on your mother's side, I mean,—and she has done her duty by you well."

"Indeed she has, Lady Midlothian."

"She has, and others, therefore, have been the less called upon to interfere. I only say this, my dear, in my own vindication,—feeling, perhaps, that my conduct needs some excuse."

"I'm sure Alice does not think that," said Lady Glencora.

"It is what I think rather than what Alice thinks that concerns my own shortcomings," said Lady Midlothian, with a smile which was intended to be pleasant. "But I have wished to make up for former lost opportunities." Alice knew that she was about to refer to her letter, and trembled. "I am very anxious now to be reckoned one of Alice Vavasor's friends, if she will allow me to become so."

"I can only be too proud,—if—"

"If what, my dear?" said the old lady. I believe that she meant to be gracious, but there was something in her manner, or, perhaps, rather in her voice, so repellant, that Alice felt that they could hardly become true friends. "If what, my dear?"

"Alice means—" began Lady Glencora.

"Let Alice say what she means herself," said Lady Midlothian.

"I hardly know how to say what I do mean," said Alice, whose spirit within her was rising higher as the occasion for using it came upon her. "I am assured that you and I, Lady Midlothian, differ very much as to a certain matter; and as it is one in which I must be guided by my own opinion, and not that of any other person, perhaps—"

"You mean about Mr. Grey?"

"Yes," said Alice; "I mean about Mr. Grey."

"I think so much about that matter, and your happiness as therein concerned, that when I heard that you were here I was determined to take Matching in my way to London, so that I might have an opportunity of speaking to you."

"Then you knew that Alice was here," said Lady Glencora.

"Of course I did. I suppose you have heard all the history, Glencora?"

Lady Glencora was forced to acknowledge that she had heard the history,—"the history" being poor Alice's treatment of Mr. Grey.

"And what do you think of it?" Both Alice and her hostess looked round to the further end of the room in which Miss Palliser was reading, intending thus to indicate that the lady knew as yet none of the circumstances, and that there could be no good reason why she should be instructed in them at this moment. "Perhaps another time and another place may be better," said Lady Midlothian; "but I must go the day after to-morrow,—indeed, I thought of going to-morrow."

"Oh, Lady Midlothian!" exclaimed Lady Glencora.

"You must regard this as merely a passing visit, made upon business. But, as I was saying, when shall I get an opportunity of speaking to Alice where we need not be interrupted?"

Lady Glencora suggested her room up-stairs, and offered the use of it then, or on that night when the world should be about to go to bed. But the idea of this premeditated lecture was terrible to Alice, and she determined that she would not endure it.

"Lady Midlothian, it would really be of no use."

"Of no use, my dear!"

"No, indeed. I did get your letter, you know."

"And as you have not answered it, I have come all this way to see you."

"I shall be so sorry if I give offence, but it is a subject which I cannot bring myself to discuss"—she was going to say with a stranger, but she was able to check herself before the offensive word was uttered,—"which I cannot bring myself to discuss with any one."

"But you don't mean to say that you won't see me?"

"I will not talk upon that matter," said Alice. "I will not do it even with Lady Macleod."

"No," said Lady Midlothian, and her sharp grey eyes now began to kindle with anger; "and therefore it is so very necessary that other friends should interfere."

"But I will endure no interference," said Alice, "either from persons who are friends or who are not friends." And as she spoke she rose from her chair. "You must forgive me, Lady Midlothian, if I say that I can have no conversation with you on this matter." Then she walked out of the room, leaving the Countess and Lady Glencora together. As she went Miss Palliser lifted her eyes from her book, and knew that there had been a quarrel, but I doubt if she had heard any of the words which had been spoken.

"The most self-willed young woman I ever met in my life," said Lady Midlothian, as soon as Alice was gone.

"The most self-willed young woman I ever met in my life."

"I knew very well how it would be," said Lady Glencora.

"But it is quite frightful, my dear. She has been engaged, with the consent of all her friends, to this young man."

"I know all about it."

"But you must think she is very wrong."

"I don't quite understand her, but I suppose she fears they would not be happy together."

"Understand her! I should think not; nobody can understand her. A young woman to become engaged to a gentleman in that way,—before all the world, as one may say;—to go to his house, as I am told, and talk to the servants, and give orders about the furniture and then turn round and simply say that she has changed her mind! She hasn't given the slightest reason to my knowledge." And Lady Midlothian, as she insisted on the absolute iniquity of Alice's proceedings, almost startled Lady Glencora by the eagerness of her countenance. Lady Midlothian had been one of those who, even now not quite two years ago, had assisted in obtaining the submission of Lady Glencora herself. Lady Midlothian seemed on the present occasion to remember nothing of this, but Lady Glencora remembered it very exactly. "I shall not give it up," continued Lady Midlothian. "I have the greatest possible objection to her father, who contrived to connect himself with our family in a most shameful manner, without the slightest encouragement. I don't think I have spoken to him since, but I shall see him now and tell him my opinion."

Alice held her ground, and avoided all further conversation with Lady Midlothian. A message came to her through Lady Glencora imploring her to give way, but she was quite firm.

"Good-bye to you," Lady Midlothian said to her as she went. "Even yet I hope that things may go right, and if so you will find that I can forget and forgive."

"If perseverance merits success," said Lady Glencora to Alice, "she ought to succeed." "But she won't succeed," said Alice.

CHAPTER XXVII
THE PRIORY RUINS

Lady Midlothian went away on her road to London on the Wednesday morning, and Alice was to follow her on the next day. It was now December, and the weather was very clear and frosty, but at night there was bright moonlight. On this special night the moon would be full, and Lady Glencora had declared that she and Alice would go out amidst the ruins. It was no secret engagement, having been canvassed in public, and having been met with considerable discouragement by some of the party. Mr. Palliser had remarked that the night air would be very cold, and Mr. Bott had suggested all manner of evil consequences. Had Mr. Palliser alone objected, Lady Glencora might have given way, but Mr. Bott's word riveted her purpose.

"We are not going to be frightened," Lady Glencora said.

"People do not generally walk out at night in December," Mr. Palliser observed.

"That's just the reason why we want to do it," said Lady Glencora. "But we shall wrap ourselves up, and nobody need be afraid. Jeffrey, we shall expect you to stand sentinel at the old gate, and guard us from the ghosts."

Jeffrey Palliser, bargaining that he might be allowed a cigar, promised that he would do as he was bidden.

The party at Matching Priory had by this time become very small. There were indeed no guests left, not counting those of the Palliser family, excepting Miss Vavasor, Mr. Bott, and an old lady who had been a great friend of Mr. Palliser's mother. It was past ten in the evening when Lady Glencora declared that the time had arrived for them to carry out their purpose. She invited the two Miss Pallisers to join her, but they declined, urging their fear of the night air, and showing by their manner that they thought the proposition a very imprudent one. Mr. Bott offered to accompany them, but Lady Glencora declined his attendance very stoutly.

"No, indeed, Mr. Bott; you were one of those who preached a sermon against my dissipation in the morning, and I'm not going to allow you to join it, now the time for its enjoyment has come."

"My dear Lady Glencora, if I were you, indeed I wouldn't," said the old lady, looking round towards Mr. Palliser.

"My dear Mrs. Marsham, if you were me, indeed you would," and Lady Glencora also looked at her husband.

"I think it a foolish thing to do," said Mr. Palliser, sternly.

"If you forbid it, of course we won't go," said Lady Glencora.

"Forbid it:—no; I shall not forbid it."

"Allons donc," said Lady Glencora.

She and Alice were already muffled in cloaks and thick shawls, and Alice now followed her out of the room. There was a door which opened from the billiard-room out on to the grand terrace, which ran in front of the house, and here they found Jeffrey Palliser already armed with his cigar. Alice, to tell the truth, would much have preferred to abandon the expedition, but she had felt that it would be cowardly in her to desert Lady Glencora. There had not arisen any very close intimacy between her and Mr. Palliser, but she entertained a certain feeling that Mr. Palliser trusted her, and liked her to be with his wife. She would have wished to justify this supposed confidence, and was almost sure that Mr. Palliser expected her to do so in this instance. She did say a word or two to her cousin up-stairs, urging that perhaps her husband would not like it.

"Let him say so plainly," said Lady Glencora, "and I'll give it up instantly. But I'm not going to be lectured out of my purposes secondhand by Mr. Bott or old Mother Marsham. I understand all these people, my dear. And if you throw me over, Alice, I'll never forgive you," Lady Glencora added.

After this Alice resolved that she would not throw her friend over. She was afraid to do so. But she was also becoming a little afraid of her friend,— afraid that she would be driven some day either to throw her over, or to say words to her that would be very unpalatable.

"Now, Jeffrey," said Lady Glencora as they walked abreast along the broad terrace towards the ruins, "when we get under the old gateway you must let me and Alice go round the dormitory and the chapel alone. Then we'll come back by the cloisters, and we'll take another turn outside with you. The outside is the finest by this light,—only I want to show Alice something by ourselves."

"You're not afraid, I know, and if Miss Vavasor is not—"

"Miss Vavasor,—who, I think, would have allowed you to call her by her other name on such an occasion as this,—is never afraid."

"Glencora, how dare you say so?" said Alice. "I really think we had better go back."

She felt herself to be very angry with her cousin. She almost began to fear that she had mistaken her, and had thought better of her than she had deserved. What she had now said struck Alice as being vulgar,—as being premeditated vulgarity, and her annoyance was excessive. Of course Mr. Palliser would think that she was a consenting party to the proposition made to him.

"Go back!" said Glencora. "No, indeed. We'll go on, and leave him here. Then he can call nobody anything. Don't be angry with me," she said, as soon as they were out of hearing. "The truth is this;—if you choose to have him for your husband, you may."

"But if I do not choose."

"Then there can be no harm done, and I will tell him so. But, Alice,— think of this. Whom will you meet that would suit you better? And you need not decide now. You need not say a word, but leave me to tell him, that if it is to be thought of at all, it cannot be thought of till he meets you in London. Trust me, you will be safe with me."

"You shall tell him nothing of the kind," said Alice. "I believe you to be joking throughout, and I think the joke is a bad one." "No; there you wrong me. Indeed I am not joking. I know that in what I am saying I am telling you the simple truth. He has said enough to me to justify me in saying so. Alice, think of it all. It would reconcile me to much, and it would be something to be the mother of the future Duke of Omnium."

"To me it would be nothing," said Alice; "less than nothing. I mean to say that the temptation is one so easily resisted that it acts in the other way. Don't say anything more about it, Glencora."

"If you don't wish it, I will not."

"No;—I do not wish it. I don't think I ever saw moonlight so bright as this. Look at the lines of that window against the light. They are clearer than you ever see them in the day."

They were now standing just within the gateway of the old cruciform chapel, having entered the transept from a ruined passage which was supposed to have connected the church with the dormitory. The church was altogether roofless, but the entire walls were standing. The small clerestory windows of the nave were perfect, and the large windows of the two transepts and of the west end were nearly so. Of the opposite window, which had formed the back of the choir, very little remained. The top of it, with all its tracery, was gone, and three broken upright mullions of uneven heights alone remained. This was all that remained of the old window, but a transom or cross-bar of stone had been added to protect the carved stonework of the sides, and save the form of the aperture from further ruin. That this transom was modern was to be seen from the magnificent height and light grace of the workmanship in the other windows, in which the long slender mullions rose from the lower stage or foundation of the whole up into the middle tracery of the arch without protection or support, and then lost themselves among the curves, not running up into the roof or soffit, and there holding on as though unable to stand alone. Such weakness as that had not as yet shown itself in English church architecture when Matching Priory was built.

The Priory Ruins.

"Is it not beautiful!" said Glencora. "I do love it so! And there is a peculiar feeling of cold about the chill of the moon, different from any other cold. It makes you wrap yourself up tight, but it does not make your teeth chatter; and it seems to go into your senses rather than into your bones. But I suppose that's nonsense," she added, after a pause.

"Not more so than what people are supposed to talk by moonlight."

"That's unkind. I'd like what I say on such an occasion to be more poetical or else more nonsensical than what other people say under the same circumstances. And now I'll tell you why I always think of you when I come here by moonlight."

"But I suppose you don't often come."

"Yes, I do; that is to say, I did come very often when we had the full moon in August. The weather wasn't like this, and I used to run out through the open windows and nobody knew where I was gone. I made him come once, but he didn't seem to care about it. I told him that part of the refectory wall was falling; so he looked at that, and had a mason sent the next day. If anything is out of order he has it put to rights at once. There would have been no ruins if all the Pallisers had been like him."

"So much the better for the world."

"No;—I say no. Things may live too long. But now I'm going to tell you. Do you remember that night I brought you home from the play to Queen Anne Street?"

"Indeed I do,—very well."

Alice had occasion to remember it, for it had been in the carriage on that evening that she had positively refused to give any aid to her cousin in that matter relating to Burgo Fitzgerald.

"And do you remember how the moon shone then?"

"Yes, I think I do."

"I know I do. As we came round the corner out of Cavendish Square he was standing there,—and a friend of yours was standing with him."

"What friend of mine?"

"Never mind that; it does not matter now."

"Do you mean my cousin George?"

"Yes, I do mean your cousin; and oh, Alice! dear Alice! I don't know why I should love you, for if you had not been hardhearted that night,—stony cruel in your hard propriety, I should have gone with him then, and all this icy coldness would have been prevented."

She was standing quite close to Alice, and as she spake she shook with shivering and wrapped her furs closer and still closer about her.

"You are very cold," said Alice. "We had better go in."

"No, I am not cold,—not in that way. I won't go in yet. Jeffrey will come to us directly. Yes;—we should have escaped that night if you would have allowed him to come into your house. Ah, well! we didn't, and there's an end of it."

"But Glencora,—you cannot regret it."

"Not regret it! Alice, where can your heart be? Or have you a heart? Not regret it! I would give everything I have in the world to have been true to him. They told me that he would spend my money. Though he should have spent every farthing of it, I regret it; though he should have made me a beggar, I regret it. They told me that he would ill-use me, and desert me,— perhaps beat me. I do not believe it; but even though that should have been so, I regret it. It is better to have a false husband than to be a false wife."

"Glencora, do not speak like that. Do not try to make me think that anything could tempt you to be false to your vows."

"Tempt me to be false! Why, child, it has been all false throughout. I never loved him. How can you talk in that way, when you know that I never loved him? They browbeat me and frightened me till I did as I was told;— and now;—what am I now?"

"You are his honest wife. Glencora, listen to me." And Alice took hold of her arm.

"No," she said, "no; I am not honest. By law I am his wife; but the laws are liars! I am not his wife. I will not say the thing that I am. When I went to him at the altar, I knew that I did not love the man that was to be my husband. But him,—Burgo,—I love him with all my heart and soul. I could stoop at his feet and clean his shoes for him, and think it no disgrace!"

"Oh, Cora, my friend, do not say such words as those! Remember what you owe your husband and yourself, and come away."

"I do know what I owe him, and I will pay it him. Alice, if I had a child I think I would be true to him. Think! I know I would;—though I had no hour of happiness left to me in my life. But what now is the only honest thing that I can do? Why, leave him;—so leave him that he may have another wife and be the father of a child. What injury shall I do him by leaving him? He does not love me; you know yourself that he does not love me."

"I know that he does."

"Alice, that is untrue. He does not; and you have seen clearly that it is so. It may be that he can love no woman. But another woman would give him a son, and he would be happy. I tell you that every day and every night,—

every hour of every day and of every night,—I am thinking of the man I love. I have nothing else to think of. I have no occupation,—no friends,—no one to whom I care to say a word. But I am always talking to Burgo in my thoughts; and he listens to me. I dream that his arm is round me—"

"Oh, Glencora!"

"Well!—Do you begrudge me that I should tell you the truth? You have said that you would be my friend, and you must bear the burden of my friendship. And now,—this is what I want to tell you.—Immediately after Christmas, we are to go to Monkshade, and he will be there. Lady Monk is his aunt."

"You must not go. No power should take you there."

"That is easily said, child; but all the same I must go. I told Mr. Palliser that he would be there, and he said it did not signify. He actually said that it did not signify. I wonder whether he understands what it is for people to love each other;—whether he has ever thought about it."

"You must tell him plainly that you will not go."

"I did. I told him plainly as words could tell him. 'Glencora,' he said,—and you know the way he looks when he means to be lord and master, and put on the very husband indeed,—'This is an annoyance which you must bear and overcome. It suits me that we should go to Monkshade, and it does not suit me that there should be any one whom you are afraid to meet.' Could I tell him that he would lose his wife if I did go? Could I threaten him that I would throw myself into Burgo's arms if that opportunity were given to me? You are very wise, and very prudent. What would you have had me say?"

"I would have you now tell him everything, rather than go to that house."

"Alice, look here. I know what I am, and what I am like to become. I loathe myself, and I loathe the thing that I am thinking of. I could have clung to the outside of a man's body, to his very trappings, and loved him ten times better than myself!—ay, even though he had ill-treated me,—if I had been allowed to choose a husband for myself. Burgo would have spent my money,—all that it would have been possible for me to give him. But there would have been something left, and I think that by that time I could have won even him to care for me. But with that man—! Alice you are very wise. What am I to do?"

Alice had no doubt as to what her cousin should do. She should be true to her marriage-vow, whether that vow when made were true or false.

She should be true to it as far as truth would now carry her. And in order that she might be true, she should tell her husband as much as might be necessary to induce him to spare her the threatened visit to Monkshade. All that she said to Lady Glencora, as they walked slowly across the chapel. But Lady Glencora was more occupied with her own thoughts than with her friend's advice. "Here's Jeffrey!" she said. "What an unconscionable time we have kept him!"

"Don't mention it," he said. "And I shouldn't have come to you now, only that I thought I should find you both freezing into marble."

"We are not such cold-blooded creatures as that,—are we, Alice?" said Lady Glencora. "And now we'll go round the outside; only we must not stay long, or we shall frighten those two delicious old duennas, Mrs. Marsham and Mr. Bott."

These last words were said as it were in a whisper to Alice; but they were so whispered that there was no real attempt to keep them from the ears of Mr. Jeffrey Palliser. Glencora, Alice thought, should not have allowed the word duenna to have passed her lips in speaking to any one; but, above all, she should not have done so in the hearing of Mr. Palliser's cousin.

They walked all round the ruin, on a raised gravel-path which had been made there; and Alice, who could hardly bring herself to speak,—so full was her mind of that which had just been said to her,—was surprised to find that Glencora could go on, in her usual light humour, chatting as though there were no weight within her to depress her spirits.

CHAPTER XXVIII
ALICE LEAVES THE PRIORY

As they came in at the billiard-room door, Mr. Palliser was there to meet them. "You must be very cold," he said to Glencora, who entered first. "No, indeed," said Glencora;—but her teeth were chattering, and her whole appearance gave the lie to her words. "Jeffrey," said Mr. Palliser, turning to his cousin, "I am angry with you. You, at least, should have known better than to have allowed her to remain so long." Then Mr. Palliser turned away, and walked his wife off, taking no notice whatsoever of Miss Vavasor.

Alice felt the slight, and understood it all. He had told her plainly enough, though not in words, that he had trusted his wife with her, and that she had betrayed the trust. She might have brought Glencora in within five or six minutes, instead of allowing her to remain out there in the freezing night air for nearly three-quarters of an hour. That was the accusation which Mr. Palliser made against her, and he made it with the utmost severity. He asked no question of her whether she were cold. He spoke no word to her, nor did he even look at her. She might get herself away to her bedroom as she pleased. Alice understood all this completely, and though she knew that she had not deserved such severity, she was not inclined to resent it. There was so much in Mr. Palliser's position that was to be pitied, that Alice could not find it in her heart to be angry with him.

"He is provoked with us, now," said Jeffrey Palliser, standing with her for a moment in the billiard-room, as he handed her a candle.

"He is afraid that she will have caught cold."

"Yes; and he thinks it wrong that she should remain out at night so long. You can easily understand, Miss Vavasor, that he has not much sympathy for romance."

"I dare say he is right," said Alice, not exactly knowing what to say, and not being able to forget what had been said about herself and Jeffrey Palliser when they first left the house. "Romance usually means nonsense, I believe."

"That is not Glencora's doctrine."

"No; but she is younger than I am. My feet are very cold, Mr. Palliser, and I think I will go up to my room."

"Good night," said Jeffrey, offering her his hand. "I think it so hard that you should have incurred his displeasure."

"It will not hurt me," said Alice, smiling.

"No;—but he does not forget."

"Even that will not hurt me. Good night, Mr. Palliser."

"As it is the last night, may I say good night, Alice? I shall be away to-morrow before you are up."

He still held her hand; but it had not been in his for half a minute, and she had thought nothing of that, nor did she draw it away even now suddenly. "No," said she, "Glencora was very wrong there,—doing an injury without meaning it to both of us. There can be no possible reason why you should call me otherwise than is customary."

"Can there never be a reason?"

"No, Mr. Palliser. Good night;—and if I am not to see you to-morrow morning, good-bye."

"You will certainly not see me to-morrow morning."

"Good-bye. Had it not been for this folly of Glencora's, our acquaintance would have been very pleasant."

"To me it has been very pleasant. Good night."

Then she left him, and went up alone to her own room. Whether or no other guests were still left in the drawing-room she did not know; but she had seen that Mr. Palliser took his wife up-stairs, and therefore she considered herself right in presuming that the party was broken up for the night. Mr. Palliser,—Plantagenet Palliser, according to all rules of courtesy should have said a word to her as he went; but, as I have said before, Alice was disposed to overlook his want of civility on this occasion. So she went up alone to her room, and was very glad to find herself able to get close to a good fire. She was, in truth, very cold—cold to her bones, in spite of what Lady Glencora had said on behalf of the moonlight. They two had been standing all but still during the greater part of the time that they had been talking, and Alice, as she sat herself down, found that her feet were numbed with the damp that had penetrated through her boots. Certainly Mr. Palliser had reason to be angry that his wife should have remained out in the night air so long,—though perhaps not with Alice.

And then she began to think of what had been told her; and to try to think of what, under such circumstances, it behoved her to do. She could not doubt that Lady Glencora had intended to declare that, if opportunity offered itself, she would leave her husband, and put herself under the protection of Mr. Fitzgerald; and Alice, moreover, had become painfully conscious that the poor deluded unreasoning creature had taught herself to think that she might excuse herself for this sin to her own conscience by the fact that she was childless, and that she might thus give to the man who had married her an opportunity of seeking another wife who might give him an heir. Alice well knew how insufficient such an excuse would be even to the wretched woman who had framed it for herself. But still it would operate, — manifestly had already operated, on her mind, teaching her to hope that good might come out of evil. Alice, who was perfectly clearsighted as regarded her cousin, however much impaired her vision might have been with reference to herself, saw nothing but absolute ruin, ruin of the worst and most intolerable description, in the plan which Lady Glencora seemed to have formed. To her it was black in the depths of hell; and she knew that to Glencora also it was black. "I loathe myself," Glencora had said, "and the thing that I am thinking of."

What was Alice to do under these circumstances? Mr. Palliser, she was aware, had quarrelled with her; for in his silent way he had first shown that he had trusted her as his wife's friend; and then, on this evening, he had shown that he had ceased to trust her. But she cared little for this. If she told him that she wished to speak to him, he would listen, let his opinion of her be what it might; and having listened he would surely act in some way that would serve to save his wife. What Mr. Palliser might think of herself, Alice cared but little.

But then there came to her an idea that was in every respect feminine, — that in such a matter she had no right to betray her friend. When one woman tells the story of her love to another woman, the confidant always feels that she will be a traitor if she reveals the secret. Had Lady Glencora made Alice believe that she meditated murder, or robbery, Alice would have had no difficulty in telling the tale, and thus preventing the crime. But now she hesitated, feeling that she would disgrace herself by betraying her friend. And, after all, was it not more than probable that Glencora had no intention of carrying out a threat the very thought of which must be terrible to herself?

As she was thinking of all this, sitting in her dressing-gown close over the fire, there came a loud knock at the door, which, as she had turned the key, she was forced to answer in person. She opened the door, and there was Iphigenia Palliser, Jeffrey's cousin, and Mr. Palliser's cousin. "Miss Vavasor," she said, "I know that I am taking a great liberty, but may I come into your room for a few minutes? I so much wish to speak to you!" Alice of course bade her enter, and placed a chair for her by the fire.

Alice Vavasor had made very little intimacy with either of the two Miss Pallisers. It had seemed to herself as though there had been two parties in the house, and that she had belonged to the one which was headed by the wife, whereas the Miss Pallisers had been naturally attached to that of the husband. These ladies, as she had already seen, almost idolized their cousin; and though Plantagenet Palliser had till lately treated Alice with the greatest personal courtesy, there had been no intimacy of friendship between them, and consequently none between her and his special adherents. Nor was either of these ladies prone to sudden friendship with such a one as Alice Vavasor. A sudden friendship, with a snuffy president of a foreign learned society, with some personally unknown lady employed on female emigration, was very much in their way. But Alice had not shown herself to be useful or learned, and her special intimacy with Lady Glencora had marked her out as in some sort separated from them and their ways.

"I know that I am intruding," said Miss Palliser, as though she were almost afraid of Alice.

"Oh dear, no," said Alice. "If I can do anything for you I shall be very happy."

"You are going to-morrow, and if I did not speak to you now I should have no other opportunity. Glencora seems to be very much attached to you, and we all thought it so good a thing that she should have such a friend."

"I hope you have not all changed your minds," said Alice, with a faint smile, thinking as she spoke that the "all" must have been specially intended to include the master of the house.

"Oh, no;—by no means. I did not mean that. My cousin, Mr. Palliser, I mean, liked you so much when you came."

"And he does not like me quite so much now, because I went out in the moonlight with his wife. Isn't that it?"

"Well;—no, Miss Vavasor. I had not intended to mention that at all. I had not indeed. I have seen him certainly since you came in,—just for a minute, and he is vexed. But it is not about that that I would speak to you."

"I saw plainly enough that he was angry with me."

"He thought you would have brought her in earlier."

"And why should he think that I can manage his wife? She was the mistress out there as she is in here. Mr. Palliser has been unreasonable. Not that it signifies."

"I don't think he has been unreasonable; I don't, indeed, Miss Vavasor. He has certainly been vexed. Sometimes he has much to vex him. You see, Glencora is very young."

Mr. Bott also had declared that Lady Glencora was very young. It was probable, therefore, that that special phrase had been used in some discussion among Mr. Palliser's party as to Glencora's foibles. So thought Alice as the remembrance of the word came upon her.

"She is not younger than when Mr. Palliser married her," Alice said.

"You mean that if a man marries a young wife he must put up with the trouble. That is a matter of course. But their ages, in truth, are very suitable. My cousin himself is not yet thirty. When I say that Glencora is young—"

"You mean that she is younger in spirit, and perhaps in conduct, than he had expected to find her."

"But you are not to suppose that he complains, Miss Vavasor. He is much too proud for that."

"I should hope so," said Alice, thinking of Mr. Bott.

"I hardly know how to explain to you what I wish to say, or how far I may be justified in supposing that you will believe me to be acting solely on Glencora's behalf. I think you have some influence with her;—and I know no one else that has any."

"My friendship with her is not of very long date, Miss Palliser."

"I know it, but still there is the fact. Am I not right in supposing—"

"In supposing what?"

"In supposing that you had heard the name of Mr. Fitzgerald as connected with Glencora's before her marriage with my cousin?"

Alice paused a moment before she answered.

"Yes, I had," she then said.

"And I think you were agreed, with her other relations, that such a marriage would have been very dreadful."

"I never spoke of the matter in the presence of any relatives of Glencora's. You must understand, Miss Palliser, that though I am her far-away cousin, I do not even know her nearest connections. I never saw Lady Midlothian till she came here the other day."

"But you advised her to abandon Mr. Fitzgerald."

"Never!"

"I know she was much with you, just at that time."

"I used to see her, certainly."

Then there was a pause, and Miss Palliser, in truth, scarcely knew how to go on. There had been a hardness about Alice which her visitor had not expected,—an unwillingness to speak or even to listen, which made Miss Palliser almost wish that she were out of the room. She had, however, mentioned Burgo Fitzgerald's name, and out of the room now she could not go without explaining why she had done so. But at this point Alice came suddenly to her assistance.

"Just then she was often with me," said Alice, continuing her reply; "and there was much talk between us about Mr. Fitzgerald. What was my advice then can be of little matter; but in this we shall be both agreed, Miss Palliser, that Glencora now should certainly not be called upon to be in his company."

"She has told you, then?"

"Yes;—she has told me."

"That he is to be at Lady Monk's?"

"She has told me that Mr. Palliser expects her to meet him at the place to which they are going when they leave the Duke's, and that she thinks it hard that she should be subjected to such a trial."

"It should be no trial, Miss Vavasor."

"How can it be otherwise? Come, Miss Palliser; if you are her friend, be fair to her."

"I am her friend;—but I am, above everything, my cousin's friend. He has told me that she has complained of having to meet this man. He declares that it should be nothing to her, and that the fear is an idle folly. It should be nothing to her, but still the fear may not be idle. Is there any reason,—any real reason,—why she should not go? Miss Vavasor, I conjure you to tell me,—even though in doing so you must cast so deep reproach upon her name! Anything will be better than utter disgrace and sin!"

"I conceive that I cast no reproach upon her in saying that there is great reason why she should not go to Monkshade."

"You think there is absolute grounds for interference? I must tell him, you know, openly what he would have to fear."

"I think,—nay, Miss Palliser, I know,—that there is ample reason why you should save her from being taken to Monkshade, if you have the power to do so."

"I can only do it, or attempt to do it, by telling him just what you tell me."

"Then tell him. You must have thought of that, I suppose, before you came to me."

"Yes;—yes, Miss Vavasor. I had thought of it. No doubt I had thought of it. But I had believed all through that you would assure me that there was no danger. I believed that you would have said that she was innocent."

"And she is innocent," said Alice, rising from her chair, as though she might thus give emphasis to words which she hardly dared to speak above a whisper. "She is innocent. Who accuses her of guilt? You ask me a question on his behalf—"

"On hers—and on his, Miss Vavasor."

"A question which I feel myself bound to answer truly,—to answer with reference to the welfare of them both; but I will not have it said that I accuse her. She had been attached to Mr. Fitzgerald when your cousin married her. He knew that this had been the case. She told him the whole truth. In a worldly point of view her marriage with Mr. Fitzgerald would probably have been very imprudent."

"It would have been utterly ruinous."

"Perhaps so; I say nothing about that. But as it turned out, she gave up her own wishes and married your cousin."

"I don't know about her own wishes, Miss Vavasor."

"It is what she did. She would have married Mr. Fitzgerald, had she not been hindered by the advice of those around her. It cannot be supposed that she has forgotten him in so short a time. There can be no guilt in her remembrance."

"There is guilt in loving any other than her husband."

"Then, Miss Palliser, it was her marriage that was guilty, and not her love. But all that is done and past. It should be your cousin's object to teach her to forget Mr. Fitzgerald, and he will not do that by taking her to a house where that gentleman is staying."

"She has said so much to you herself?"

"I do not know that I need declare to you what she has said herself. You have asked me a question, and I have answered it, and I am thankful to you for having asked it. What object can either of us have but to assist her in her position?"

"And to save him from dishonour. I had so hoped that this was simply a childish dread on her part."

"It is not so. It is no childish dread. If you have the power to prevent her going to Lady Monk's, I implore you to use it. Indeed, I will ask you to promise me that you will do so."

"After what you have said, I have no alternative."

"Exactly. There is no alternative. Either for his sake or for hers, there is none."

Thereupon Miss Palliser got up, and wishing her companion good night, took her departure. Throughout the interview there had been no cordiality of feeling between them. There was no pretence of friendship, even as they were parting. They acknowledged that their objects were different. That of Alice was to save Lady Glencora from ruin. That of Miss Palliser was to save her cousin from disgrace,—with perhaps some further honest desire to prevent sorrow and sin. One loved Lady Glencora, and the other clearly did not love her. But, nevertheless, Alice felt that Miss Palliser, in coming to her, had acted well, and that to herself this coming had afforded immense relief. Some step would now be taken to prevent that meeting which she had so deprecated, and it would be taken without any great violation of confidence on her part. She had said nothing as to which Lady Glencora could feel herself aggrieved.

On the next morning she was down in the breakfast-room soon after nine, and had not been in the room many minutes before Mr. Palliser entered. "The carriage is ordered for you at a quarter before ten," he said, "and I have come down to give you your breakfast." There was a smile on his face as he spoke, and Alice could see that he intended to make himself pleasant.

"Will you allow me to give you yours instead?" said she. But as it happened, no giving on either side was needed, as Alice's breakfast was brought to her separately.

"Glencora bids me say that she will be down immediately," said Mr. Palliser.

Alice then made some inquiry with reference to the effects of last night's imprudence, which received only a half-pronounced reply. Mr. Palliser was willing to be gracious, but did not intend to be understood as having forgiven the offence. The Miss Pallisers then came in together, and after them Mr. Bott, closely followed by Mrs. Marsham, and all of them made inquiries after Lady Glencora, as though it was to be supposed that she might probably be in a perilous state after what she had undergone on the previous evening. Mr. Bott was particularly anxious. "The frost was so uncommonly severe," said he, "that any delicate person like Lady Glencora must have suffered in remaining out so long."

The insinuation that Alice was not a delicate person and that, as regarded her, the severity of the frost was of no moment, was very open, and was duly appreciated. Mr. Bott was aware that his great patron had in some sort changed his opinion about Miss Vavasor, and he was of course disposed to change his own. A fortnight since Alice might have been as delicate as she pleased in Mr. Bott's estimation.

"I hope you do not consider Lady Glencora delicate," said Alice to Mr. Palliser.

"She is not robust," said the husband.

"By no means," said Mrs. Marsham.

"Indeed, no," said Mr. Bott.

Alice knew that she was being accused of being robust herself; but she bore it in silence. Ploughboys and milkmaids are robust, and the accusation was a heavy one. Alice, however, thought that she would not have minded it, if she could have allowed herself to reply; but this at the moment of her going away she could not do.

"I think she is as strong as the rest of us," said Iphigenia Palliser, who felt that after last night she owed something to Miss Vavasor.

"As some of us," said Mr. Bott, determined to persevere in his accusation.

At this moment Lady Glencora entered, and encountered the eager inquiries of her two duennas. These, however, she quickly put aside, and made her way up to Alice. "The last morning has come, then," she said.

"Yes, indeed," said Alice. "Mr. Palliser must have thought that I was never going."

"On the other hand," said he, "I have felt much obliged to you for staying." But he said it coldly; and Alice began to wish that she had never seen Matching Priory.

"Obliged!" exclaimed Lady Glencora. "I can't tell you how much obliged I am. Oh, Alice, I wish you were going to stay with us!"

"We are leaving this in a week's time," said Mr. Palliser.

"Of course we are," said Lady Glencora. "With all my heart I wish we were not. Dear Alice! I suppose we shall not meet till we are all in town."

"You will let me know when you come up," said Alice.

"I will send to you instantly; and, Alice, I will write to you from Gatherum,—or from Monkshade."

Alice could not help looking around and catching Miss Palliser's eye. Miss Palliser was standing with her foot on the fender, but was so placed that she could see Alice. She made a slight sign with her head, as much as to say that Lady Glencora must have no opportunity of writing from the latter place; but she said nothing.

Then the carriage was announced, and Mr. Palliser took Alice out on his arm. "Don't come to the door, Glencora," he said. "I especially wish you not to do so." The two cousins then kissed each other, and Alice went away to the carriage.

"Good-bye, Miss Vavasor," said Mr. Palliser; but he expressed no wish that he might see her again as his guest at Matching Priory.

Alice, as she was driven in solitary grandeur to the railway station, could not but wish that she had never gone there.

CHAPTER XXIX
BURGO FITZGERALD

On the night before Christmas Eve two men were sitting together in George Vavasor's rooms in Cecil Street. It was past twelve o'clock, and they were both smoking; there were square bottles on the table containing spirits, with hot water and cold water in jugs, and one of the two men was using, and had been using, these materials for enjoyment. Vavasor had not been drinking, nor did it appear as though he intended to begin. There was a little weak brandy and water in a glass by his side, but there it had remained untouched for the last twenty minutes. His companion, however, had twice in that time replenished his beaker, and was now puffing out the smoke of his pipe with the fury of a steamer's funnel when she has not yet burned the black off her last instalment of fresh coals. This man was Burgo Fitzgerald. He was as handsome as ever;—a man whom neither man nor woman could help regarding as a thing beautiful to behold;—but not the less was there in his eyes and cheeks a look of haggard dissipation,—of riotous living, which had become wearisome, by its continuance, even to himself,—that told to all who saw him much of the history of his life. Most men who drink at nights, and are out till cockcrow doing deeds of darkness, become red in their faces, have pimpled cheeks and watery eyes, and are bloated and not comfortable to be seen. It is a kind dispensation of Providence who thus affords to such sinners a visible sign, to be seen day by day, of the injury which is being done. The first approach of a carbuncle on the nose, about the age of thirty, has stopped many a man from drinking. No one likes to have carbuncles on his nose, or to appear before his female friends with eyes which look as though they were swimming in grog. But to Burgo Fitzgerald Providence in her anger had not afforded this protection. He became at times pale, sallow, worn, and haggard. He grew thin, and still thinner. At times he had been ill to death's door. Among his intimate friends there were those who heard him declare frequently that his liver had become useless to him; and that, as for gastric juices, he had none left to him. But still his beauty remained. The perfect form of his almost god-like face was the same as ever, and the brightness of his bright blue eye was never quenched.

On the present occasion he had come to Vavasor's room with the object of asking from him certain assistance, and perhaps also some amount of advice. But as regarded the latter article he was, I think, in the state of most men when they seek for counsellors who shall counsel them to do evil. Advice administered in accordance with his own views would give him comfortable encouragement, but advice on the other side he was prepared to disregard altogether. These two men had known each other long, and a close intimacy had existed between them in the days past, previous to Lady Glencora's engagement with Mr. Palliser. When Lady Glencora endeavoured, vainly as we know, to obtain aid from Alice Vavasor, Burgo had been instigated to believe that Alice's cousin might assist him. Any such assistance George Vavasor would have been quite ready to give. Some pecuniary assistance he had given, he at that time having been in good funds. Perhaps he had for a moment induced Burgo to think that he could obtain for the pair the use of the house in Queen Anne Street as a point at which they might meet, and from whence they might start on their journey of love. All that was over. Those hopes had been frustrated, and Lady Glencora M'Cluskie had become Lady Glencora Palliser and not Lady Glencora Fitzgerald. But now other hopes had sprung up, and Burgo was again looking to his friend for assistance.

"I believe she would," Burgo said, as he lifted the glass to his mouth. "It's a thing of that sort that a man can only believe,—perhaps only hope,— till he has tried. I know that she is not happy with him, and I have made up my mind that I will at least ask her."

"But he would have her fortune all the same?"

"I don't know how that would be. I haven't inquired, and I don't mean to inquire. Of course I don't expect you or any one else to believe me, but her money has no bearing on the question now. Heaven knows I want money bad enough, but I wouldn't take away another man's wife for money."

"You don't mean to say you think it would be wicked. I supposed you to be above those prejudices."

"It's all very well for you to chaff."

"It's no chaff at all. I tell you fairly I wouldn't run away with any man's wife. I have an old-fashioned idea that when a man has got a wife he ought to be allowed to keep her. Public opinion, I know, is against me."

"I think he ran away with my wife," said Burgo, with emphasis; "that's the way I look at it. She was engaged to me first; and she really loved me, while she never cared for him."

"Nevertheless, marriage is marriage, and the law is against you. But if I did go in for such a troublesome job at all, I certainly should keep an eye upon the money."

"It can make no difference."

"It did make a difference, I suppose, when you first thought of marrying her?"

"Of course it did. My people brought us together because she had a large fortune and I had none. There's no doubt in the world about that. And I'll tell you what; I believe that old harridan of an aunt of mine is willing to do the same thing now again. Of course she doesn't say as much. She wouldn't dare do that, but I do believe she means it. I wonder where she expects to go to!"

"That's grateful on your part."

"Upon my soul I hate her. I do indeed. It isn't love for me now so much as downright malice against Palliser, because he baulked her project before. She is a wicked old woman. Some of us fellows are wicked enough—you and I for instance—"

"Thank you. I don't know, however, that I am qualified to run in a curricle with you."

"But we are angels to such an old she-devil as that. You may believe me or not, as you like.—I dare say you won't believe me."

"I'll say I do, at any rate."

"The truth is, I want to get her, partly because I love her; but chiefly because I do believe in my heart that she loves me."

"It's for her sake then! You are ready to sacrifice yourself to do her a good turn."

"As for sacrificing myself, that's done. I'm a man utterly ruined and would cut my throat to-morrow for the sake of my relations, if I cared enough about them. I know my own condition pretty well. I have made a shipwreck of everything, and have now only got to go down among the breakers."

"Only you would like to take Lady Glencora with you."

"No, by heavens! But sometimes, when I do think about it at all,—which I do as seldom as I can,—it seems to me that I might still become a different fellow if it were possible for me to marry her."

"Had you married her when she was free to marry any one and when her money was her own, it might have been so."

"I think it would be quite as much so now. I do, indeed. If I could get her once, say to Italy, or perhaps to Greece, I think I could treat her well, and live with her quietly. I know that I would try."

"Without the assistance of brandy and cigars."

"Yes."

"And without any money."

"With only a little. I know you'll laugh at me; but I make pictures to myself of a sort of life which I think would suit us, and be very different from this hideous way of living, with which I have become so sick that I loathe it."

"Something like Juan and Haidée, with Planty Pall coming after you, like old Lambro." By the nickname of Planty Pall George Vavasor intended to designate Lady Glencora's present husband.

"He'd get a divorce, of course, and then we should be married. I really don't think he'd dislike it, when it was all done. They tell me he doesn't care for her."

"You have seen her since her marriage?"

"Yes; twice."

"And have spoken to her?"

"Once only,—so as to be able to do more than ask her if she were well. Once, for about two minutes, I did speak to her."

"And what did she say?"

"She said it would be better that we should not meet. When she said that, I knew that she was still fond of me. I could have fallen at her feet that moment, only the room was full of people. I do think that she is fond of me."

Vavasor paused a few minutes. "I dare say she is fond of you," he then said; "but whether she has pluck for such a thing as this, is more than I can say. Probably she has not. And if she has, probably you would fail in carrying out your plan."

"I must get a little money first," said Burgo.

"And that's an operation which no doubt you find more difficult every day, as you grow older."

"It seems to be much the same sort of thing. I went to Magruin this morning."

"He's the fellow that lives out near Gray's Inn Lane?"

"Just beyond the Foundling Hospital. I went to him, and he was quite civil about it. He says I owe him over three thousand pounds, but that doesn't seem to make any difference."

"How much did you ever have from him?"

"I don't recollect that I ever absolutely had any money. He got a bill of mine from a tailor who went to smash, and he kept on renewing that till it grew to be ever so many bills. I think he did once let me have twenty-four pounds,—but certainly never more than that."

"And he says he'll give you money now? I suppose you told him why you wanted it."

"I didn't name her,—but I told him what would make him understand that I hoped to get off with a lady who had a lot of tin. I asked him for two hundred and fifty. He says he'll let me have one hundred and fifty on a bill at two months for five hundred,—with your name to it."

"With my name to it! That's kind on his part,—and on yours too."

"Of course I can't take it up at the end of two months."

"I dare say not," said Vavasor.

"But he won't come upon you then,—nor for a year or more afterwards. I did pay you what you lent me before."

"Yes, you did. I always thought that to be a special compliment on your part."

"And you'll find I'll pull you through now in some way. If I don't succeed in this I shall go off the hooks altogether soon; and if I were dead my people would pay my debts then."

Before the evening was over Vavasor promised the assistance asked of him. He knew that he was lending his name to a man who was utterly ruined, and putting it into the hands of another man who was absolutely without conscience in the use he would make of it. He knew that he was creating for himself trouble, and in all probability loss, which he was ill able to bear. But the thing was one which came within the pale of his laws. Such assistance as that he might ask of others, and had asked and received before now. It was a reckless deed on his part, but then all his doings were reckless. It was consonant with his mode of life.

"I thought you would, old fellow," said Burgo, as he got up to go away. "Perhaps, you know, I shall pull through in this; and perhaps, after all, some part of her fortune will come with her. If so you'll be all right."

"Perhaps I may. But look here, Burgo,—don't you give that fellow up the bill till you've got the money into your fist."

"You may be quite easy about that. I know their tricks. He and I will go to the bank together, and we shall squabble there at the door about four or five odd sovereigns,—and at last I shall have to give him up two or three. Beastly old robber! I declare I think he's worse than I am myself." Then Burgo Fitzgerald took a little more brandy and water and went away.

He was living at this time in the house of one of his relatives in Cavendish Square, north of Oxford Street. His uncles and his aunts, and all those who were his natural friends, had clung to him with a tenacity that was surprising; for he had never been true to any of them, and did not even pretend to like them. His father, with whom for many years he had not been on speaking terms, was now dead; but he had sisters whose husbands would still open their houses to him, either in London or in the country;— would open their houses to him, and lend him their horses, and provide him with every luxury which the rich enjoy,—except ready money. When the uttermost stress of pecuniary embarrassment would come upon him, they would pay something to stave off the immediate evil. And so Burgo went on. Nobody now thought of saying much to reproach him. It was known to be waste of words, and trouble in vain. They were still fond of him because he was beautiful and never vain of his beauty;—because in the midst of his recklessness there was always about him a certain kindliness which made him pleasant to those around him. He was soft and gracious with children, and would be very courteous to his lady cousins. They knew that as a man he was worthless, but nevertheless they loved him. I think the secret of it was chiefly in this,—that he seemed to think so little of himself.

But now as he walked home in the middle of the night from Cecil Street to Cavendish Square he did think much of himself. Indeed such self-thoughts come naturally to all men, be their outward conduct ever so reckless. Every man to himself is the centre of the whole world;—the axle on which it all turns. All knowledge is but his own perception of the things around him. All love, and care for others, and solicitude for the world's welfare, are but his own feelings as to the world's wants and the world's merits.

He had played his part as a centre of all things very badly. Of that he was very well aware. He had sense enough to know that it should be a man's lot to earn his bread after some fashion, and he often told himself that never as yet had he earned so much as a penny roll. He had learned to comprehend that the world's progress depends on the way in which men do their duty by each other,—that the progress of one generation depends on the discharge of such duties by that which preceded it;—and he knew that he, in his generation, had done nothing to promote such progress. He thoroughly despised himself,—if there might be any good in that! But on such occasions as these, when the wine he had drunk was sufficient only to drive away from him the numbness of despair, when he was all alone with the cold night air upon his face, when the stars were bright above him and the world around him was almost quiet, he would still ask himself whether there might not yet be, even for him, some hope of a redemption,—some chance of a better life in store for him. He was still young,—wanting some years of thirty. Could there be, even for him, some mode of extrication from his misery?

We know what was the mode which now, at this moment, was suggesting itself to him. He was proposing to himself, as the best thing that he could do, to take away another man's wife and make himself happy with her! What he had said to Vavasor as to disregarding Lady Glencora's money had been perfectly true. That in the event of her going off with him, some portion of her enormous wealth would still cling to her, he did believe. Seeing that she had no children he could not understand where else it should all go. But he thought of this as it regarded her, not as it regarded him. When he had before made his suit to her,—a suit which was then honourable, however disadvantageous it might have seemed to be to her—he had made in his mind certain calculations as to the good things which would result to him if he were successful. He would keep hounds, and have three or four horses every day for his own riding, and he would have no more interviews with Magruin, waiting in that rogue's dingy back parlour for many a weary wretched half-hour, till the rogue should be pleased to show himself. So far he had been mercenary; but he had learned to love the girl, and to care more for her than for her money, and when the day of disappointment came upon him,—the day on which she had told him that all between them was to be over for ever,—he had, for a few hours, felt the loss of his love more than the loss of his money.

Then he had had no further hope. No such idea as that which now filled his mind had then come upon him. The girl had gone from him and married another man, and there was an end of it. But by degrees tidings had reached him that she was not happy,—reaching him through the mouths of people who were glad to exaggerate all that they had heard. A whole tribe of his female relatives had been anxious to promote his marriage with Lady Glencora M'Cluskie, declaring that, after all that was come and gone, Burgo would come forth from his troubles as a man of great wealth. So great was the wealth of the heiress that it might withstand even his propensities for spending. That whole tribe had been bitterly disappointed; and when they heard that Mr. Palliser's marriage had given him no child, and that

Lady Glencora was unhappy,—they made their remarks in triumph rather than in sorrow. I will not say that they looked forward approvingly to such a step as that which Burgo now wished to take,—though as regarded his aunt, Lady Monk, he himself had accused her; but they whispered that such things had been done and must be expected, when marriages were made up as had been that marriage between Mr. Palliser and his bride.

As he walked on, thinking of his project, he strove hard to cheat himself into a belief that he would do a good thing in carrying Lady Glencora away from her husband. Bad as had been his life he had never before done aught so bad as that. The more fixed his intention became, the more thoroughly he came to perceive how great and grievous was the crime which he contemplated. To elope with another man's wife no longer appeared to him to be a joke at which such men as he might smile. But he tried to think that in this case there would be special circumstances which would almost justify him, and also her. They had loved each other and had sworn to love each other with constancy. There had been no change in the feelings or even in the wishes of either of them. But cold people had come between them with cold calculations, and had separated them. She had been, he told himself, made to marry a man she did not love. If they two loved each other truly, would it not still be better that they should come together? Would not the sin be forgiven on account of the injustice which had been done to them? Had Mr. Palliser a right to expect more from a wife who had been made to marry him without loving him? Then he reverted to those dreams of a life of love, in some sunny country, of which he had spoken to Vavasor, and he strove to nourish them. Vavasor had laughed at him, talking of Juan and Haidée. But Vavasor, he said to himself, was a hard cold man, who had no touch of romance in his character. He would not be laughed out of his plan by such as he,—nor would he be frightened by the threat of any Lambro who might come after him, whether he might come in the guise of indignant uncle or injured husband.

He had crossed from Regent Street through Hanover Square, and as he came out by the iron gates into Oxford Street, a poor wretched girl, lightly clad in thin raiment, into whose bones the sharp freezing air was penetrating, asked him for money. Would he give her something to get drink, so that for a moment she might feel the warmth of her life renewed? Such midnight petitions were common enough in his ears, and he was passing on without thinking of her. But she was urgent, and took hold of him. "For love of God," she said, "if it's only a penny to get a glass of gin! Feel my hand,— how cold it is." And she strove to put it up against his face.

He looked round at her and saw that she was very young,—sixteen, perhaps, at the most, and that she had once,—nay very lately,—been exquisitely pretty. There still lingered about her eyes some remains of that look of perfect innocency and pure faith which had been hers not more than twelve months since. And now, at midnight, in the middle of the streets, she was praying for a pennyworth of gin, as the only comfort she knew, or could expect!

"You are cold!" said he, trying to speak to her cheerily.

"Cold!" said she, repeating the word, and striving to wrap herself closer in her rags, as she shivered—"Oh God! if you knew what it was to be as cold as I am! I have nothing in the world,—not one penny,—not a hole to lie in!"

"We are alike then," said Burgo, with a slight low laugh. "I also have nothing. You cannot be poorer than I am."

"You poor!" she said. And then she looked up into his face. "Gracious; how beautiful you are! Such as you are never poor."

He laughed again,—in a different tone. He always laughed when any one told him of his beauty. "I am a deal poorer than you, my girl," he said. "You have nothing. I have thirty thousand pounds worse than nothing. But come along, and I will get you something to eat."

"Will you?" said she, eagerly. Then looking up at him again, she exclaimed—"Oh, you are so handsome!"

He took her to a public-house and gave her bread and meat and beer, and stood by her while she ate it. She was shy with him then, and would fain have taken it to a corner by herself, had he allowed her. He perceived this, and turned his back to her, but still spoke to her a word or two as she ate. The woman at the bar who served him looked at him wonderingly, staring into his face; and the pot-boy woke himself thoroughly that he might look at Burgo; and the waterman from the cab-stand stared at him; and women who came in for gin looked almost lovingly up into his eyes. He regarded them all not at all, showing no feeling of disgrace at his position, and no desire to carry himself as a ruffler. He quietly paid what was due when the girl had finished her meal, and then walked with her out of the shop. "And now," said he, "what must I do with you? If I give you a shilling can you get a bed?" She told him that she could get a bed for sixpence. "Then keep the other sixpence for your breakfast," said he. "But you must promise me that you will buy no gin to-night." She promised him, and then he gave her his hand as he wished her good night;—his hand, which it had been the dearest wish of Lady Glencora to call her own. She took it and pressed it to her lips. "I wish I might once see you again," she said, "because you are so good and so beautiful." He laughed again cheerily, and walked on, crossing the street towards Cavendish Square. She stood looking at him till he was out of sight, and then as she moved away,—let us hope to the bed which his bounty had provided, and not to a gin-shop,—she exclaimed to herself again and again—"Gracious, how beautiful he was!" "He's a good un," the woman at the public-house had said as soon as he left it; "but, my! did you ever see a man's face handsome as that fellow's?"

Burgo Fitzgerald.

Poor Burgo! All who had seen him since life had begun with him had loved him and striven to cherish him. And with it all, to what a state had he come! Poor Burgo! had his eyes been less brightly blue, and his face less godlike in form, it may be that things would have gone better with him. A sweeter-tempered man than he never lived,—nor one who was of a kinder nature. At this moment he had barely money about him to take him down to his aunt's house at Monkshade, and as he had promised to be there before Christmas Day, he was bound to start on the next morning, before help from Mr. Magruin was possible. Nevertheless, out of his very narrow funds he had given half a crown to comfort the poor creature who had spoken to him in the street.

CHAPTER XXX
CONTAINING A LOVE LETTER

Vavasor, as he sat alone in his room, after Fitzgerald had left him, began to think of the days in which he had before wished to assist his friend in his views with reference to Lady Glencora;—or rather he began to think of Alice's behaviour then, and of Alice's words. Alice had steadfastly refused to give any aid. No less likely assistant for such a purpose could have been selected. But she had been very earnest in declaring that it was Glencora's duty to stand by her promise to Burgo. "He is a desperate spendthrift," Kate Vavasor had said to her. "Then let her teach him to be otherwise," Alice had answered. "That might have been a good reason for refusing his offer when he first made it; but it can be no excuse for untruth, now that she has told him that she loves him!" "If a woman," she had said again, "won't venture her fortune for the man she loves, her love is not worth having." All this George Vavasor remembered now; and as he remembered it he asked himself whether the woman that had once loved him would venture her fortune for him still.

Though his sister had pressed him on the subject with all the vehemence that she could use, he had hardly hitherto made up his mind that he really desired to marry Alice. There had grown upon him lately certain Bohemian propensities,—a love of absolute independence in his thoughts as well as actions,—which were antagonistic to marriage. He was almost inclined to think that marriage was an old-fashioned custom, fitted indeed well enough for the usual dull life of the world at large,—as many men both in heathen and in Christian ages have taught themselves to think of religion,—but which was not adapted to his advanced intelligence. If he loved any woman he loved his cousin Alice. If he thoroughly respected any woman he respected her. But that idea of tying himself down to a household was in itself distasteful to him. "It is a thing terrible to think of," he once said to a congenial friend in these days of his life, "that a man should give permission to a priest to tie him to another human being like a Siamese twin, so that all power of separate and solitary action should be taken from him for ever! The beasts of the field do not treat each other so badly. They neither drink themselves drunk, nor eat themselves stupid;—nor do they bind themselves together in a union which both would have to hate." In this way George Vavasor, trying to imitate the wisdom of the brutes, had taught himself some theories of a peculiar nature. But, nevertheless, as he thought of Alice Vavasor on this occasion, he began to feel that if a Siamese twin were necessary for him, she of all others was the woman to whom he would wish to be so bound.

And if he did it at all, he must do it now. Under the joint instigation of himself and his sister,—as he thought, and perhaps not altogether without reason,—she had broken her engagement with Mr. Grey. That she would renew it again if left to herself, he believed probable. And then, despite that advanced intelligence which had taught him to regard all forms and ceremonies with the eye of a philosopher, he had still enough of human frailty about him to feel keenly alive to the pleasure of taking from John Grey the prize which John Grey had so nearly taken from him. If Alice could have been taught to think as he did as to the absurdity of those indissoluble ties, that would have been better. But nothing would have been more impossible than the teaching of such a lesson to his cousin Alice. George Vavasor was a man of courage, and dared do most things;—but he would not have dared to commence the teaching of such a lesson to her.

And now, at this moment, what was his outlook into life generally? He had very high ambition, and a fair hope of gratifying it if he could only provide that things should go well with him for a year or so. He was still a poor man, having been once nearly a rich man; but still so much of the result of his nearly acquired riches remained to him, that on the strength of them he might probably find his way into Parliament. He had paid the cost of the last attempt, and might, in a great degree, carry on this present attempt on credit. If he succeeded there would be open to him a mode of life, agreeable in itself, and honourable among men. But how was he to bear the cost of this for the next year, or the next two years? His grandfather was still alive, and would probably live over that period. If he married Alice he would do so with no idea of cheating her out of her money. She should learn,—nay, she had already learned from his own lips,—how perilous was his enterprise. But he knew her to be a woman who would boldly risk all in money, though no consideration would induce her to stir a hair's breadth towards danger in reputation. Towards teaching her that doctrine at which I have hinted, he would not have dared to make an attempt; but he felt that he should have no repugnance to telling her that he wanted to spend all her money in the first year or two of their married life!

He was still in his arm-chair, thinking of all this, with that small untasted modicum of brandy and water beside him, when he heard some distant Lambeth clock strike three from over the river. Then he rose from his seat, and taking the candles in his hand, sat himself down at a writing-desk on the other side of the room. "I needn't send it when it's written," he said to himself, "and the chances are that I won't." Then he took his paper, and wrote as follows:—

Dear Alice,

The time was when the privilege was mine of beginning my letters to you with a warmer show of love than the above word contains,—when I might and did call you dearest; but I lost that privilege through my own folly, and since that it has been accorded to another. But you have found,— with a thorough honesty of purpose than which I know nothing greater,—that it has behoved you to withdraw that privilege also. I need hardly say that I should not have written as I now write, had you not found it expedient to do as you have done. I now once again ask you to be my wife. In spite of all that passed in those old days,—of all the selfish folly of which I was then guilty, I think you know, and at the time knew, that I ever loved you. I claim to say for myself that my love to you was true from first to last, and I claim from you belief for that statement. Indeed I do not think that you ever doubted my love.

Nevertheless, when you told me that I might no longer hope to make you my wife, I had no word of remonstrance that I could utter. You acted as any woman would act whom love had not made a fool. Then came the episode of Mr. Grey; and bitter as have been my feelings whilst that engagement lasted, I never made any attempt to come between you and the life you had chosen. In saying this I do not forget the words which I spoke last summer at Basle, when, as far as I knew, you still intended that he should be your husband. But what I said then was nothing to that which, with much violence, I refrained from saying. Whether you remember those few words I cannot tell; but certainly you would not have remembered them,—would not even have noticed them,—had your heart been at Nethercoats.

But all this is nothing. You are now again a free woman; and once again I ask you to be my wife. We are both older than we were when we loved before, and will both be prone to think of marriage in a somewhat different light. Then personal love for each other was most in our thoughts. God forbid that it should not be much in our thoughts now! Perhaps I am deceiving myself in saying that it is not even now stronger in mine than any other consideration. But we have both reached that time of life, when it is probable that in any proposition of marriage we should think more of our adaptability to each other than we did before. For myself I know that there is much in my character and disposition to make me unfit to marry a woman of the common stamp. You know my mode of life, and what are my hopes and my chances of success. I run great risk of failing. It may be that I shall encounter ruin where I look for reputation and a career of honour. The chances are perhaps more in favour of ruin than of success. But, whatever may be the chances, I shall go on as long as any means of carrying on the fight are at my disposal. If you were my wife to-morrow I should expect to use your money, if it were needed, in struggling to obtain a seat in Parliament and a hearing there. I will hardly stoop to tell you that I do not ask you to be my wife for the sake of this aid;—but if you were to become my wife I should expect all your cooperation;—with your money, possibly, but certainly with your warmest spirit.

And now, once again, Alice,—dearest Alice, will you be my wife? I have been punished, and I have kissed the rod,—as I never kissed any other rod. You cannot accuse my love. Since the time in which I might sit with my arm round your waist, I have sat with it round no other waist. Since your lips were mine, no other lips have been dear to me. Since you were my counsellor, I have had no other counsellor,—unless it be poor Kate, whose wish that we may at length be married is second in earnestness only to my own. Nor do I think you will doubt my repentance. Such repentance indeed claims no merit, as it has been the natural result of the loss which I have suffered. Providence has hitherto been very good to me in not having made that loss irremediable by your marriage with Mr. Grey. I wish you now to consider the matter well, and to tell me whether you can pardon me and still love me. Do I flatter myself when I feel that I doubt your pardon almost more than I doubt your love?

Think of this thing in all its bearings before you answer me. I am so anxious that you should think of it that I will not expect your reply till this day week. It can hardly be your desire to go through life unmarried. I should say that it must be essential to your ambition that you should join your lot to that of some man the nature of whose aspirations would be like to your own. It is because this was not so as regarded him whose suit you had accepted, that you found yourself at last obliged to part from him. May I not say that with us there would be no such difference? It is because I believe that in this respect we are fitted for each other, as man and woman seldom are fitted, that I once again ask you to be my wife.

This will reach you at Vavasor, where you will now be with the old squire and Kate. I have told her nothing of my purpose in writing this letter. If it should be that your answer is such as I desire, I should use the opportunity of our re-engagement to endeavour to be reconciled to my grandfather. He has misunderstood me and has ill-used me. But I am ready to forgive that, if he will allow me to do so. In such case you and Kate would arrange that, and I would, if possible, go down to Vavasor while you are there. But I am galloping on a-head foolishly in thinking of this, and am counting up my wealth while the crockery in my basket is so very fragile. One word from you will decide whether or no I shall ever bring it into market.

If that word is to be adverse do not say anything of a meeting between me and the Squire. Under such circumstances it would be impossible. But, oh, Alice! do not let it be adverse. I think you love me. Your woman's pride towards me has been great and good and womanly; but it has had its way; and, if you love me, might now be taught to succumb.

Dear Alice, will you be my wife?

Yours, in any event, most affectionately,

George Vavasor.

Vavasor, when he had finished his letter, went back to his seat over the fire, and there he sat with it close at his hand for nearly an hour. Once or twice he took it up with fingers almost itching to throw it into the fire. He took it up and held the corners between his forefinger and thumb, throwing forward his hand towards the flame, as though willing that the letter should escape from him and perish if chance should so decide. But chance did not so decide, and the letter was put back upon the table at his elbow. Then when the hour was nearly over he read it again. "I'll bet two to one that she gives way," he said to himself, as he put the sheet of paper back into the envelope. "Women are such out-and-out fools." Then he took his candle, and carrying his letter with him, went into his bedroom.

The next morning was the morning of Christmas Eve. At about nine o'clock a boy came into his room who was accustomed to call for orders for the day. "Jem," he said to the boy, "there's half a crown lying there on the looking-glass." Jem looked and acknowledged the presence of the half-crown. "Is it a head or a tail, Jem?" asked the boy's master. Jem scrutinized the coin, and declared that the uppermost surface showed a tail. "Then take that letter and post it," said George Vavasor. Whereupon Jem, asking no question and thinking but little of the circumstances under which the command was given, did take the letter and did post it. In due accordance with postal regulations it reached Vavasor Hall and was delivered to Alice on the Christmas morning.

A merry Christmas did not fall to the lot of George Vavasor on the present occasion. An early Christmas-box he did receive in the shape of a very hurried note from his friend Burgo. "This will be brought to you by Stickling," the note said; but who Stickling was Vavasor did not know. "I send the bill. Couldn't you get the money and send it me, as I don't want to go up to town again before the thing comes off? You're a trump; and will do the best you can. Don't let that rogue off for less than a hundred and twenty.—Yours, B. F." Vavasor, therefore, having nothing better to do, spent his Christmas morning in calling on Mr. Magruin.

"Oh, Mr. Vavasor," said Magruin; "really this is no morning for business!"

"Time and tide wait for no man, Mr. Magruin, and my friend wants his money to-morrow."

"Oh, Mr. Vavasor,—to-morrow!"

"Yes, to-morrow. If time and tide won't wait, neither will love. Come, Mr. Magruin, out with your cheque-book, and don't let's have any nonsense."

"But is the lady sure, Mr. Vavasor?" asked Mr. Magruin, anxiously.

"Ladies never are sure," said Vavasor; "hardly more sure than bills made over to money-lenders. I'm not going to wait here all day. Are you going to give him the money?"

"Christmas-day, Mr. Vavasor! There's no getting money in the city to-day."

But Vavasor before he left did get the money from Mr. Magruin,—£122 10s.—for which an acceptance at two months for £500 was given in exchange,—and carried it off in triumph. "Do tell him to be punctual," said

Mr. Magruin, when Vavasor took his leave. "I do so like young men to be punctual. But I really think Mr. Fitzgerald is the most unpunctual young man I ever did know yet."

"I think he is," said George Vavasor, as he went away.

He ate his Christmas dinner in absolute solitude at an eating-house near his lodgings. It may be supposed that no man dares to dine at his club on a Christmas Day. He at any rate did not so dare;—and after dinner he wandered about through the streets, wondering within his mind how he would endure the restraints of married life. And the same dull monotony of his days was continued for a week, during which he waited, not impatiently, for an answer to his letter. And before the end of the week the answer came.

CHAPTER XXXI
AMONG THE FELLS

Alice came down to breakfast on that Christmas morning at Vavasor Hall without making any sign as to the letter she had received. The party there consisted of her grandfather, her father, her cousin Kate, and herself. They all made their Christmas salutations as is usual, and Alice received and made hers as did the others, without showing that anything had occurred to disturb her tranquillity. Kate remarked that she had heard that morning from Aunt Greenow, and promised to show Alice the letter after breakfast. But Alice said no word of her own letter.

"Why didn't your aunt come here to eat her Christmas dinner?" said the Squire.

"Perhaps, sir, because you didn't ask her," said Kate, standing close to her grandfather,—for the old man was somewhat deaf.

"And why didn't you ask her;—that is, if she stands upon asking to come to her old home?"

"Nay, sir, but I couldn't do that without your bidding. We Vavasors are not always fond of meeting each other."

"Hold your tongue, Kate. I know what you mean, and you should be the last to speak of it. Alice, my dear, come and sit next to me. I am much obliged to you for coming down all this way to see your old grandfather at Christmas. I am indeed. I only wish you had brought better news about your sweetheart."

"She'll think better of it before long, sir," said her father.

"Papa, you shouldn't say that. You would not wish me to marry against my own judgement."

"I don't know much about ladies' judgements," said the old man. "It does seem to me that when a lady makes a promise she ought to keep it."

"According to that," said Kate, "if I were engaged to a man, and found that he was a murderer, I still ought to marry him."

"But Mr. Grey is not a murderer," said the Squire.

"Pray,—pray, don't talk about it," said Alice. "If you do I really cannot sit and hear it."

"I have given over saying anything on the subject," said John Vavasor, speaking as though he had already expended upon it a vast amount of paternal eloquence. He had, however, never said more than has been recorded in these pages. Alice during this conversation, sat with her cousin's letter in her pocket, and as yet had not even begun to think what should be the nature of her reply.

The Squire of Vavasor Hall was a stout old man, with a red face and grey eyes, which looked fiercely at you, and with long grey hair, and a rough grey beard, which gave him something of the appearance of an old lion. He was passionate, unreasoning, and specially impatient of all opposition; but he was affectionate, prone to forgive when asked to do so, unselfish, and hospitable. He was, moreover, guided strictly by rules, which he believed to be rules of right. His grandson George had offended him very deeply,— had offended him and never asked his pardon. He was determined that such pardon should never be given, unless it were asked for with almost bended knees; but, nevertheless, this grandson should be his heir. That was his present intention. The right of primogeniture could not, in accordance with his theory, be abrogated by the fact that it was, in George Vavasor's case, protected by no law. The Squire could leave Vavasor Hall to whom he pleased, but he could not have hoped to rest quietly in his grave should it be found that he had left it to any one but the eldest son of his own eldest son. Though violent, and even stern, he was more prone to love than to anger; and though none of those around him dared to speak to him of his grandson, yet he longed in his heart for some opportunity of being reconciled to him.

The whole party went to church on this Christmas morning. The small parish church of Vavasor, an unpretending wooden structure, with a single bell which might be heard tinkling for a mile or two over the fells, stood all alone about half a mile from the Squire's gate. Vavasor was a parish situated on the intermediate ground between the mountains of the lake country and the plains. Its land was unproductive, ill-drained, and poor, and yet it possessed little or none of the beauty which tourists go to see. It was all amidst the fells, and very dreary. There were long skirtings of dark pines around a portion of the Squire's property, and at the back of the house there was a thick wood of firs running up to the top of what was there called the Beacon Hill. Through this there was a wild steep walk which came out upon the moorland, and from thence there was a track across the mountain to Hawes Water and Naddale, and on over many miles to the further beauties of Bowness and Windermere. They who knew the country, and whose legs were of use to them, could find some of the grandest scenery in England within reach of a walk from Vavasor Hall; but to others the place was very desolate. For myself, I can find I know not what of charm in wandering over open, unadorned moorland. It must be more in the softness of the grass to the feet, and the freshness of air to the lungs, than in anything that meets the eye. You might walk for miles and miles to the north-east, or east, or south-east of Vavasor without meeting any object to arrest the view. The great road from Lancaster to Carlisle crossed the outskirts of the small parish about a mile from the church, and beyond that the fell seemed to be interminable. Towards the north it rose, and towards the south it fell, and it rose and fell very gradually. Here and there some slight appearance of a valley might be traced which had been formed by the action of the waters; but such breakings of ground were inconsiderable, and did not suffice to interrupt the stern sameness of the everlasting moorland.

The daily life at Vavasor was melancholy enough for such a one as the Squire's son, who regarded London as the only place on the earth's surface in which a man could live with comfort. The moors offered no charms to him. Nor did he much appreciate the homely comforts of the Hall; for the house, though warm, was old-fashioned and small, and the Squire's cook was nearly as old as the Squire himself. John Vavasor's visits to Vavasor were always visits of duty rather than of pleasure. But it was not so with Alice. She could be very happy there with Kate; for, like herself, Kate was a good walker and loved the mountains. Their regard for each other had grown and become strong because they had gone together o'er river and moor, and because they had together disregarded those impediments of mud and wet which frighten so many girls away from the beauties of nature.

On this Christmas Day they all went to church, the Squire being accompanied by Alice in a vehicle which in Ireland is called an inside jaunting-car, and which is perhaps the most uncomfortable kind of vehicle yet invented; while John Vavasor walked with his niece. But the girls had arranged that immediately after church they would start for a walk up the Beacon Hill, across the fells, towards Hawes Water. They always dined at the Hall at the vexatious hour of five; but as their church service, with the sacrament included, would be completed soon after twelve, and as lunch was a meal which the Squire did not himself attend, they could have full four hours for their excursion. This had all been planned before Alice received her letter; but there was nothing in that to make her change her mind about the walk.

"Alice, my dear," said the old man to her when they were together in the jaunting-car, "you ought to get married." The Squire was hard of hearing, and under any circumstances an inside jaunting-car is a bad place for conversation, as your teeth are nearly shaken out of your head by every movement which the horse makes. Alice therefore said nothing, but smiled faintly, in reply to her grandfather. On returning from church he insisted that Alice should again accompany him, telling her specially that he desired to speak to her. "My dear child," he said, "I have been thinking a great deal about you, and you ought to get married."

"Well, sir, perhaps I shall some day."

"Not if you quarrel with all your suitors," said the old man. "You quarrelled with your cousin George, and now you have quarrelled with Mr. Grey. You'll never get married, my dear, if you go on in that way."

"Why should I be married more than Kate?"

"Oh, Kate! I don't know that anybody wants to marry Kate. I wish you'd think of what I say. If you don't get married before long, perhaps you'll never get married at all. Gentlemen won't stand that kind of thing for ever."

The two girls took a slice of cake each in her hand, and started on their walk. "We shan't be able to get to the lake," said Kate.

"No," said Alice; "but we can go as far as the big stone on Swindale Fell, where we can sit down and see it."

"Do you remember the last time we sat there?" said Kate. "It is nearly three years ago, and it was then that you told me that all was to be over between you and George. Do you remember what a fool I was, and how I screamed in my sorrow? I sometimes wonder at myself and my own folly. How is it that I can never get up any interest about my own belongings? And then we got soaking wet through coming home."

"I remember that very well."

"And how dark it was! That was in September, but we had dined early. If we go as far as Swindale we shall have it very dark coming home to-day;—but I don't mind that through the Beacon Wood, because I know my way so well. You won't be afraid of half an hour's dark?"

"Oh, no," said Alice.

"Yes; I do remember that day. Well; it's all for the best, I suppose. And now I must read you my aunt's letter." Then, while they were still in the wood, Kate took out the letter from her aunt and read it, while they still walked slowly up the hill. It seemed that hitherto neither of her two suitors had brought the widow to terms. Indeed, she continued to write of Mr. Cheesacre as though that gentleman were inconsolable for the loss of Kate, and gave her niece much serious advice as to the expedience of returning to Norfolk, in order that she might secure so eligible a husband. "You must understand all the time, Alice," said Kate, pausing as she read the letter, "that the dear man has never given me the slightest ground for the faintest hope, and that I know to a certainty that he makes an offer to her twice a week,—that is, on every market day. You can't enjoy half the joke if you won't bear that in mind." Alice promised that she would bear it all in mind, and then Kate went on with her reading. Poor Bellfield was working very hard at his drill, Mrs. Greenow went on to say; so hard that sometimes she really thought the fatigue would be too much for his strength. He would come in sometimes of an evening and just take a cup of tea;—generally on Mondays and Thursdays. "These are not market days at Norwich," said Kate; "and thus unpleasant meetings are avoided." "He comes in," said Mrs. Greenow, "and takes a little tea; and sometimes I think that he will faint at my feet." "That he kneels there on every occasion," said Kate, "and repeats his offer also twice a week, I have not the least doubt in the world."

"And will she accept him at last?"

"Really I don't know what to think of it. Sometimes I fancy that she likes the fun of the thing, but that she is too wide-awake to put herself in any man's power. I have no doubt she lends him money, because he wants it sadly and she is very generous. She gives him money, I feel sure, but takes his receipt on stamped paper for every shilling. That's her character all over."

The letter then went on to say that the writer had made up her mind to remain at Norwich certainly through the winter and spring, and that she was anxiously desirous that her dear Kate should go back to her. "Come and have one other look at Oileymead," said the letter, "and then, if you make up your mind that you don't like it or him, I won't ask you to think of them ever again. I believe him to be a very honest fellow." "Did you ever know such a woman?" said Kate; "with all her faults I believe she would go through fire and water to serve me. I think she'd lend me money without any stamped paper." Then Aunt Greenow's letter was put up, and the two girls had come out upon the open fell.

It was a delicious afternoon for a winter's walk. The air was clear and cold, but not actually frosty. The ground beneath their feet was dry, and the sky, though not bright, had that appearance of enduring weather which gives no foreboding of rain. There is a special winter's light, which is very clear though devoid of all brilliancy, — through which every object strikes upon the eye with well-marked lines, and under which almost all forms of nature seem graceful to the sight if not actually beautiful. But there is a certain melancholy which ever accompanies it. It is the light of the afternoon, and gives token of the speedy coming of the early twilight. It tells of the shortness of the day, and contains even in its clearness a promise of the gloom of night. It is absolute light, but it seems to contain the darkness which is to follow it. I do not know that it is ever to be seen and felt so plainly as on the wide moorland, where the eye stretches away over miles, and sees at the world's end the faint low lines of distant clouds settling themselves upon the horizon. Such was the light of this Christmas afternoon, and both the girls had felt the effects of it before they reached the big stone on Swindale Fell, from which they intended to look down upon the loveliness of Hawes Water. As they went up through the wood there had been some laughter between them over Aunt Greenow's letter; and they had discussed almost with mirth the merits of Oileymead and Mr. Cheesacre; but as they got further on to the fell, and as the half-melancholy wildness of the place struck them, their words became less light, and after a while they almost ceased to speak.

Alice had still her letter in her pocket. She had placed it there when she came down to breakfast, and had carried it with her since. She had come to no resolution as yet as to her answer to it, nor had she resolved whether or no she would show it to Kate. Kate had ever been regarded by her as her steadfast friend. In all these affairs she had spoken openly to Kate. We know that Kate had in part betrayed her, but Alice suspected no such treason. She had often quarrelled with Kate; but she had quarrelled with her not on account of any sin against the faith of their friendship. She believed in her cousin perfectly, though she found herself often called upon to disagree with her almost violently. Why should she not show this letter to Kate, and discuss it in all its bearings before she replied to it? This was in her mind as she walked silently along over the fell.

The reader will surmise from this that she was already half inclined to give way, and to join her lot to that of her cousin George. Alas, yes! The reader will be right in his surmise. And yet it was not her love for the man that prompted her to run so terrible a risk. Had it been so, I think that it would be easier to forgive her. She was beginning to think that love,—the love of which she had once thought so much,—did not matter. Of what use was it, and to what had it led? What had love done for her friend Glencora? What had love done for her? Had she not loved John Grey, and had she not felt that with all her love life with him would have been distasteful to her? It would have been impossible for her to marry a man whom personally she disliked; but she liked her cousin George,—well enough, as she said to herself almost indifferently.

Upon the whole it was a grievous task to her in these days,—this having to do something with her life. Was it not all vain and futile? As for that girl's dream of the joys of love which she had once dreamed,—that had gone from her slumbers, never to return. How might she best make herself useful,—useful in some sort that might gratify her ambition;—that was now the question which seemed to her to be of most importance.

Her cousin's letter to her had been very crafty. He had studied the whole of her character accurately as he wrote it. When he had sat down to write it he had been indifferent to the result; but he had written it with that care to attain success which a man uses when he is anxious not to fail in an attempt. Whether or no he cared to marry his cousin was a point so little interesting to him that chance might decide it for him; but when chance had decided that he did wish it, it was necessary for his honour that he should have that for which he condescended to ask.

His letter to her had been clever and very crafty. "At any rate he does me justice," she said to herself, when she read those words about her money, and the use which he proposed to make of it. "He is welcome to it all if it will help him in his career, whether he has it as my friend or as my husband." Then she thought of Kate's promise of her little mite, and declared to herself that she would not be less noble than her cousin Kate. And would it not be well that she should be the means of reconciling George to his grandfather? George was the representative of the family,—of a family so old that no one now knew which had first taken the ancient titular name of some old Saxon landowner,—the parish, or the man. There had been in old days some worthy Vavaseurs, as Chaucer calls them, whose rank and bearing had been adopted on the moorland side. Of these things Alice thought much, and felt that it should be her duty so to act, that future Vavasors might at any rate not be less in the world than they who had passed away. In a few years at furthest, George Vavasor must be Vavasor of Vavasor. Would it not be right that she should help him to make that position honourable?

They walked on, exchanging now and again a word or two, till the distant Cumberland mountains began to form themselves in groups of beauty before their eyes. "There's Helvellyn at last," said Kate. "I'm always happy when I see that." "And isn't that Kidsty Pike?" asked Alice. "No; you don't see Kidsty yet. But you will when you get up to the bank there. That's Scaw Fell on the left;—the round distant top. I can distinguish it, though I doubt whether you can." Then they went on again, and were soon at the bank from whence the sharp top of the mountain which Alice had named was visible. "And now we are on Swindale, and in five minutes we shall get to the stone."

In less than five minutes they were there; and then, but not till then, the beauty of the little lake, lying down below them in the quiet bosom of the hills, disclosed itself. A lake should, I think, be small, and should be seen from above, to be seen in all its glory. The distance should be such that the shadows of the mountains on its surface may just be traced, and that some faint idea of the ripple on the waters may be present to the eye. And the form of the lakes should be irregular, curving round from its base among the lower hills, deeper and still deeper into some close nook up among the mountains from which its head waters spring. It is thus that a lake should be seen, and it was thus that Hawes Water was seen by them from the flat stone on the side of Swindale Fell. The basin of the lake has formed itself into the shape of the figure of 3, and the top section of the figure lies embosomed among the very wildest of the Westmoreland mountains. Altogether it is not above three miles long, and every point of it was to be seen from the spot on which the girls sat themselves down. The water beneath was still as death, and as dark,—and looked almost as cold. But the slow clouds were passing over it, and the shades of darkness on its surface changed themselves with gradual changes. And though no movement was visible, there was ever and again in places a slight sheen upon the lake, which indicated the ripple made by the breeze.

"I'm so glad I've come here," said Alice, seating herself. "I cannot bear the idea of coming to Vavasor without seeing one of the lakes at least."

"We'll get over to Windermere one day," said Kate.

"I don't think we shall. I don't think it possible that I should stay long. Kate, I've got a letter to show you." And there was that in the tone of her voice which instantly put Kate upon her mettle.

Kate seated herself also, and put up her hand for the letter. "Is it from Mr. Grey?" she asked.

"No," said Alice; "it is not from Mr. Grey." And she gave her companion the paper. Kate before she had touched it had seen that it was from her brother George; and as she opened it looked anxiously into Alice's face. "Has he offended you?" Kate asked.

Swindale Fell.

"Read it," said Alice, "and then we'll talk of it afterwards,—as we go home." Then she got up from the stone and walked a step or two towards the brow of the fell, and stood there looking down upon the lake, while Kate read the letter. "Well!" she said, when she returned to her place.

"Well," said Kate. "Alice, Alice, it will, indeed, be well if you listen to him. Oh, Alice, may I hope? Alice, my own Alice, my darling, my friend! Say that it shall be so." And Kate knelt at her friend's feet upon the heather, and looked up into her face with eyes full of tears. What shall we say of a woman who could be as false as she had been, and yet could be so true?

Alice made no immediate answer, but still continued to gaze down over her friend upon the lake. "Alice," continued Kate, "I did not think I should be made so happy this Christmas Day. You could not have the heart to bring me here and show me this letter in this way, and bid me read it so calmly, and then tell me that it is all for nothing. No; you could not do that? Alice, I am so happy. I will so love this place. I hated it before." And then she put her face down upon the boulder-stone and kissed it. Still Alice said nothing, but she began to feel that she had gone further than she had intended. It was almost impossible for her now to say that her answer to George must be a refusal.

Then Kate again went on speaking. "But is it not a beautiful letter? Say, Alice,—is it not a letter of which if you were his brother you would feel proud if another girl had shown it to you? I do feel proud of him. I know that he is a man with a manly heart and manly courage, who will yet do manly things. Here out on the mountain, with nobody near us, with Nature all round us, I ask you on your solemn word as a woman, do you love him?"

"Love him!" said Alice.

"Yes;—love him: as a woman should love her husband. Is not your heart his? Alice, there need be no lies now. If it be so, it should be your glory to say so, here, to me, as you hold that letter in your hand."

"I can have no such glory, Kate. I have ever loved my cousin; but not so passionately as you seem to think."

"Then there can be no passion in you."

"Perhaps not, Kate. I would sometimes hope that it is so. But come; we shall be late; and you will be cold sitting there."

"I would sit here all night to be sure that your answer would be as I would have it. But, Alice, at any rate you shall tell me before I move what your answer is to be. I know you will not refuse him; but make me happy by saying so with your own lips."

"I cannot tell you before you move, Kate."

"And why not?"

"Because I have not as yet resolved."

"Ah, that is impossible. That is quite impossible. On such a subject and under such circumstances a woman must resolve at the first moment. You had resolved, I know, before you had half read the letter;—though, perhaps, it may not suit you to say so."

"You are quite mistaken. Come along and let us walk, and I will tell you all." Then Kate arose, and they turned their back to the lake, and began to make their way homewards. "I have not made up my mind as to what answer I will give him; but I have shown you his letter in order that I might have some one with whom I might speak openly. I knew well how it would be, and that you would strive to hurry me into an immediate promise."

"No;—no; I want nothing of the kind."

"But yet I could not deny myself the comfort of your friendship."

"No, Alice, I will not hurry you. I will do nothing that you do not wish. But you cannot be surprised that I should be very eager. Has it not been the longing of all my life? Have I not passed my time plotting and planning and thinking of it till I have had time to think of nothing else? Do you know what I suffered when, through George's fault, the engagement was broken off? Was it not martyrdom to me,—that horrid time in which your Crichton from Cambridgeshire was in the ascendant? Did I not suffer the tortures of purgatory while that went on;—and yet, on the whole, did I not bear them with patience? And, now, can you be surprised that I am wild with joy when I begin to see that everything will be as I wish;—for it will be as I wish, Alice. It may be that you have not resolved to accept him. But you would have resolved to refuse him instantly had that been your destined answer to his letter." There was but little more said between them on the subject as they were passing over the fell, but when they were going down the path through the Beacon Wood, Kate again spoke: "You will not answer him without speaking to me first?" said Kate.

"I will, at any rate, not send my answer without telling you," said Alice.

"And you will let me see it?"

"Nay," said Alice; "I will not promise that. But if it is unfavourable I will show it you."

"Then I shall never see it," said Kate, laughing. "But that is quite enough for me. I by no means wish to criticise the love-sweet words in which you tell him that his offences are all forgiven. I know how sweet they will be. Oh, heavens! how I envy him!"

Then they were at home; and the old man met them at the front door, glowering at them angrily from out his old leonine eyes, because the roast beef was already roasted. He had his great uncouth silver watch in his hand, which was always a quarter of an hour too fast, and he pointed at it fiercely, showing them the minute hand at ten minutes past the hour.

"But, grandpapa, you are always too fast," said Kate.

"And you are always too slow, miss," said the hungry old squire.

"Indeed, it is not five yet. Is it, Alice?"

"And how long are you going to be dressing?"

"Not ten minutes;—are we, Alice? And, grandpapa, pray don't wait."

"Don't wait! That's what they always say," he muttered, peevishly. "As if one would be any better waiting for them after the meat is on the table." But neither Kate nor Alice heard this, as they were already in their rooms.

Nothing more was said that evening between Alice and Kate about the letter; but Kate, as she wished her cousin good night inside her bedroom door, spoke to her just one word—"Pray for him to-night," she said, "as you pray for those you love best." Alice made no answer, but we may believe that she did as she was desired to do.

CHAPTER XXXII
CONTAINING AN ANSWER
TO THE LOVE LETTER

Alice had had a week allowed to her to write her answer; but she sent it off before the full week was past. "Why should I keep him in suspense?" she said. "If it is to be so, there can be no good in not saying so at once." Then she thought, also, that if this were to be her destiny it might be well for Mr. Grey that all his doubts on the matter should be dispelled. She had treated him badly,—very badly. She had so injured him that the remembrance of the injury must always be a source of misery to her; but she owed to him above everything to let him know what were her intentions as soon as they were settled. She tried to console herself by thinking that the wound to him would be easy to cure. "He also is not passionate," she said. But in so saying she deceived herself. He was a man in whom Love could be very passionate;—and was, moreover, one in whom Love could hardly be renewed.

Each morning Kate asked her whether her answer was written; and on the third day after Christmas, just before dinner, Alice said that she had written it, and that it was gone.

"But it isn't post-day," said Kate;—for the post illuminated Vavasor but three days a week.

"I have given a boy sixpence to take it to Shap," said Alice, blushing.

"And what have you said?" asked Kate, taking hold of the other's arm.

"I have kept my promise," said Alice; "and do you keep yours by asking no further questions."

"My sister,—my own sister," said Kate. And then, as Alice met her embrace, there was no longer any doubt as to the nature of the reply.

After this there was of course much close discussion between them as to what other steps should now be taken. Kate wanted her cousin to write immediately to Mr. Grey, and was somewhat frightened when Alice declined to do so till she had received a further letter from George. "You have not proposed any horrid stipulations to him?" exclaimed Kate.

"I don't know what you may call horrid stipulations," said Alice, gravely. "My conditions have not been very hard, and I do not think you would have disapproved them."

"But he!—He is so impetuous! Will he disapprove them?"

"I have told him— But, Kate, this is just what I did not mean to tell you."

"Why should there be secrets between us?" said Kate.

"There shall be none, then. I have told him that I cannot bring myself to marry him instantly;—that he must allow me twelve months to wear off, if I can in that time, much of sadness and of self-reproach which has fallen to my lot."

"Twelve months, Alice?"

"Listen to me. I have said so. But I have told him also that if he wishes it still, I will at once tell papa and grandpapa that I hold myself as engaged to him, so that he may know that I bind myself to him as far as it is possible that I should do so. And I have added something else, Kate," she continued to say after a slight pause,—"something else which I can tell you, though I could tell it to no other person. I can tell you because you would do, and will do the same. I have told him that any portion of my money is at his service which may be needed for his purposes before that twelve months is over."

"Oh, Alice! No;—no. You shall not do that. It is too generous." And Kate perhaps felt at the moment that her brother was a man to whom such an offer could hardly be made with safety.

"But I have done it. Mercury, with sixpence in his pocket, is already posting my generosity at Shap. And, to tell the truth, Kate, it is no more than fair. He has honestly told me that while the old Squire lives he will want my money to assist him in a career of which I do much more than approve. It has been my earnest wish to see him in Parliament. It will now be the most earnest desire of my heart;—the one thing as to which I shall feel an intense anxiety. How then can I have the face to bid him wait twelve months for that which is specially needed in six months' time? It would be like the workhouses which are so long in giving bread, that in the mean time the wretches starve."

"But the wretch shan't starve," said Kate. "My money, small as it is, will carry him over this bout. I have told him that he shall have it, and that I expect him to spend it. Moreover, I have no doubt that Aunt Greenow would lend me what he wants."

"But I should not wish him to borrow from Aunt Greenow. She would advance him the money, as you say, upon stamped paper, and then talk of it."

"He shall have mine," said Kate.

"And who are you?" said Alice, laughing. "You are not going to be his wife?"

"He shall not touch your money till you are his wife," said Kate, very seriously. "I wish you would consent to change your mind about this stupid tedious year, and then you might do as you pleased. I have no doubt such a settlement might be made as to the property here, when my grandfather hears of it, as would make you ultimately safe."

"And do you think I care to be ultimately safe, as you call it? Kate, my dear, you do not understand me."

"I suppose not. And yet I thought that I had known something about you."

"It is because I do not care for the safety of which you speak that I am now going to become your brother's wife. Do you suppose that I do not see that I must run much risk?"

"You prefer the excitement of London to the tranquillity, may I say, of Cambridgeshire."

"Exactly;—and therefore I have told George that he shall have my money whenever he wants it."

Kate was very persistent in her objection to this scheme till George's answer came. His answer to Alice was accompanied by a letter to his sister, and after that Kate said nothing more about the money question. She said no more then; but it must not therefore be supposed that she was less determined than she had been that no part of Alice's fortune should be sacrificed to her brother's wants;—at any rate before Alice should become her brother's wife. But her brother's letter for the moment stopped her mouth. It would be necessary that she should speak to him before she again spoke to Alice.

In what words Alice had written her assent it will be necessary that the reader should know, in order that something may be understood of the struggle which she made upon the occasion; but they shall be given presently, when I come to speak of George Vavasor's position as he received them. George's reply was very short and apparently very frank. He deprecated the delay of twelve months, and still hoped to be able to induce her to be more lenient to him. He advised her to write to Mr. Grey at once,—and as regarded the Squire he gave her *carte blanche* to act as she pleased. If the Squire required any kind of apology, expression of sorrow,—and asking for pardon, or such like, he, George, would, under the circumstances as they now existed, comply with the requisition most willingly. He would regard it as a simple form, made necessary by his coming marriage. As to Alice's money, he thanked her heartily for her confidence. If the nature of his coming contest at Chelsea should make it necessary, he would use her offer as frankly as it had been made. Such was his letter to Alice. What was contained in his letter to Kate, Alice never knew.

Then came the business of telling this new love tale,—the third which poor Alice had been forced to tell her father and grandfather;—and a grievous task it was. In this matter she feared her father much more than her grandfather, and therefore she resolved to tell her grandfather first;—or, rather, she determined that she would tell the Squire, and that in the mean time Kate should talk to her father.

"Grandpapa," she said to him the morning after she had received her cousin's second letter.—The old man was in the habit of breakfasting alone in a closet of his own, which was called his dressing-room, but in which he kept no appurtenances for dressing, but in lieu of them a large collection of old spuds and sticks and horse's-bits. There was a broken spade here, and a hoe or two; and a small table in the corner was covered with the debris of tradesmen's bills from Penrith, and dirty scraps which he was wont to call his farm accounts.—"Grandpapa," said Alice, rushing away at once into the middle of her subject, "you told me the other day that you thought I ought to be—married."

"Did I, my dear? Well, yes; so I did. And so you ought;—I mean to that Mr. Grey."

"That is impossible, sir."

"Then what's the use of your coming and talking to me about it?"

This made Alice's task not very easy; but, nevertheless, she persevered. "I am come, grandpapa, to tell you of another engagement."

"Another!" said he. And by the tone of his voice he accused his granddaughter of having a larger number of favoured suitors than ought to fall to the lot of any young lady. It was very hard upon her, but still she went on.

"You know," said she, "that some years ago I was to have been married to my cousin George;"—and then she paused.

"Well," said the old man.

"And I remember you told me then that you were much pleased."

"So I was. George was doing well then; or,—which is more likely,—had made us believe that he was doing well. Have you made it up with him again?"

"Yes, sir."

"And that's the meaning of your jilting Mr. Grey, is it?"

Poor Alice! It is hard to explain how heavy a blow fell upon her from the open utterance of that word! Of all words in the language it was the one which she now most dreaded. She had called herself a jilt, with that inaudible voice which one uses in making self-accusations;—but hitherto no lips had pronounced the odious word to her ears. Poor Alice! She was a jilt; and perhaps it may have been well that the old man should tell her so.

"Grandpapa!" she said; and there was that in the tone of her voice which somewhat softened the Squire's heart.

"Well, my dear, I don't want to be ill-natured. So you are going at last to marry George, are you? I hope he'll treat you well; that's all. Does your father approve of it?"

"I have told you first, sir;—because I wish to obtain your consent to seeing George again here as your grandson."

"Never," said the old man, snarling;—"never!"

"If he has been wrong, he will beg your pardon."

"If he has been wrong! Didn't he want to squander every shilling of the property,—property which has never belonged to him;—property which I could give to Tom, Dick, or Harry to-morrow, if I liked?—If he has been wrong!"

"I am not defending him, sir;—but I thought that, perhaps, on such an occasion as this—"

"A Tom Fool's occasion! You've got money of your own. He'll spend all that now."

"He will be less likely to do so if you will recognise him as your heir. Pray believe, sir, that he is not the sort of man that he was."

"He must be a very clever sort of man, I think, when he has talked you out of such a husband as John Grey. It's astounding to me,—with that ugly mug of his! Well, my dear, if your father approves of it, and if George will ask my pardon,—but I don't think he ever will—"

"He will, sir. I am his messenger for as much as that."

"Oh, you are, are you? Then you may also be my messenger to him, and tell him that, for your sake, I will let him come back here. I know he'll insult me the first day; but I'll try and put up with it,—for your sake, my dear. Of course I must know what your father thinks about it."

It may be imagined that Kate's success was even less than that which Alice achieved. "I knew it would be so," said John Vavasor, when his niece first told him;—and as he spoke he struck his hand upon the table. "I knew all along how it would be."

"And why should it not be so, Uncle John?"

"He is your brother, and I will not tell you why."

"You think that he is a spendthrift?"

"I think that he is as unsafe a man as ever I knew to be intrusted with the happiness of any young woman. That is all."

"You are hard upon him, uncle."

"Perhaps so. Tell Alice this from me,—that as I have never yet been able to get her to think anything of my opinion, I do not at all expect that I shall be able to induce her to do so now. I will not even make the attempt. As my son-in-law I will not receive George Vavasor. Tell Alice that."

Alice was told her father's message; but Kate in telling it felt no deep regret. She well knew that Alice would not be turned back from her present intention by her father's wishes. Nor would it have been very reasonable that she should. Her father had for many years relieved himself from the burden of a father's cares, and now had hardly the right to claim a father's privileges.

We will now go once again to George Vavasor's room in Cecil Street, in which he received Alice's letter. He was dressing when it was first brought to him; and when he recognised the handwriting he put it down on his toilet table unopened. He put it down, and went on brushing his hair, as though he were determined to prove to himself that he was indifferent as to the tidings which it might contain. He went on brushing his hair, and cleaning his teeth, and tying his cravat carefully over his turned-down collar, while the unopened letter lay close to his hand. Of course he was thinking of it,—of course he was anxious,—of course his eye went to it from moment to moment. But he carried it with him into the sitting-room still unopened, and so it remained until after the girl had brought him his tea and his toast. "And now," said he, as he threw himself into his arm-chair, "let us see what the girl of my heart says to me." The girl of his heart said to him as follows:—

My dear George,

I feel great difficulty in answering your letter. Could I have my own way, I should make no answer to it at present, but leave it for the next six months, so that then such answer might hereafter be made as circumstances should seem to require. This will be little flattering to you, but it is less flattering to myself. Whatever answer I may make, how can anything in this affair be flattering either to you or to me? We have been like children who have quarrelled over our game of play, till now, at the close of our little day of pleasure, we are fain to meet each other in tears, and acknowledge that we have looked for delights where no delights were to be found.

Kate, who is here, talks to me of passionate love. There is no such passion left to me;—nor, as I think, to you either. It would not now be possible that you and I should come together on such terms as that. We could not stand up together as man and wife with any hope of a happy marriage, unless we had both agreed that such happiness might be had without passionate love.

You will see from all this that I do not refuse your offer. Without passion, I have for you a warm affection, which enables me to take a livelier interest in your career than in any other of the matters which are around me. Of course, if I become your wife that interest will be still closer and dearer, and I do feel that I can take in it that concern which a wife should have in her husband's affairs.

If it suits you, I will become your wife;—but it cannot be quite at once. I have suffered much from the past conflicts of my life, and there has been very much with which I must reproach myself. I know that I have behaved badly. Sometimes I have to undergo the doubly bitter self-accusation of having behaved in a manner which the world will call unfeminine. You must understand that I have not passed through this unscathed, and I must beg you to allow me some time for a cure. A perfect cure I may never expect, but I think that in twelve months from this time I may so far have recovered my usual spirit and ease of mind as to enable me to devote myself to your happiness. Dear George, if you will accept me under such circumstances, I will be your wife, and will endeavour to do my duty by you faithfully.

I have said that even now, as your cousin, I take a lively interest in your career,—of course I mean your career as a politician,—and especially in your hopes of entering Parliament. I understand, accurately as I think, what you have said about my fortune, and I perfectly appreciate your truth and frankness. If I had nothing of my own you, in your circumstances, could not possibly take me as your wife. I know, moreover, that your need of assistance from my means is immediate rather than prospective. My money may be absolutely necessary to you within this year, during which, as I tell you most truly, I cannot bring myself to become a married woman. But my money shall be less cross-grained than myself. You will take it as frankly as I mean it when I say, that whatever you want for your political purposes shall be forthcoming at your slightest wish. Dear George, let me have the honour and glory of marrying a man who has gained a seat in the Parliament of Great Britain! Of all positions which a man may attain that, to me, is the grandest.

I shall wait for a further letter from you before I speak either to my father or to my grandfather. If you can tell me that you accede to my views, I will at once try to bring about a reconciliation between you and the Squire. I think that that will be almost easier than inducing my father to look with favour upon our marriage. But I need hardly say that should either one or the other oppose it,—or should both do so,—that would not turn me from my purpose.

I also wait for your answer to write a last line to Mr. Grey.

Your affectionate cousin,

George Vavasor when he had read the letter threw it carelessly from him on to the breakfast table, and began to munch his toast. He threw it carelessly from him, as though taking a certain pride in his carelessness. "Very well," said he; "so be it. It is probably the best thing that I could do, whatever the effect may be on her." Then he took up his newspaper. But before the day was over he had made many plans,—plans made almost unconsciously,—as to the benefit which might accrue to him from the offer which she had made of her money. And before night he had written that reply to her of which we have heard the contents; and had written also to his sister Kate a letter, of which Kate had kept the contents to herself.

CHAPTER XXXIII
MONKSHADE

When the first of the new year came round Lady Glencora was not keeping her appointment at Lady Monk's house. She went to Gatherum Castle, and let us hope that she enjoyed the magnificent Christmas hospitality of the Duke; but when the time came for moving on to Monkshade, she was indisposed, and Mr. Palliser went thither alone. Lady Glencora returned to Matching and remained at home, while her husband was away, in company with the two Miss Pallisers.

When the tidings reached Monkshade that Lady Glencora was not to be expected, Burgo Fitzgerald was already there, armed with such pecuniary assistance as George Vavasor had been able to wrench out of the hands of Mr. Magruin. "Burgo," said his aunt, catching him one morning near his bedroom door as he was about to go down-stairs in hunting trim, "Burgo, your old flame, Lady Glencora, is not coming here."

"Lady Glencora not coming!" said Burgo, betraying by his look and the tone of his voice too clearly that this change in the purpose of a married lady was to him of more importance than it should have been. Such betrayal, however, to Lady Monk was not perhaps matter of much moment.

"No; she is not coming. It can't be matter of any moment to you now."

"But, by heavens, it is," said he, putting his hand up to his forehead, and leaning back against the wall of the passage as though in despair. "It is matter of moment to me. I am the most unfortunate devil that ever lived."

"Fie, Burgo, fie! You must not speak in that way of a married woman. I begin to think it is better that she should not come." At this moment another man booted and spurred came down the passage, upon whom Lady Monk smiled sweetly, speaking some pretty little word as he passed. Burgo spoke never a word, but still stood leaning against the wall, with his hand to his forehead, showing that he had heard something which had moved him greatly. "Come back into your room, Burgo," said his aunt; and they both went in at the door that was nearest to them, for Lady Monk had been on the look-out for him, and had caught him as soon as he appeared in the passage. "If this does annoy you, you should keep it to yourself! What will people say?"

"How can I help what they say?"

"But you would not wish to injure her, I suppose? I thought it best to tell you, for fear you should show any special sign of surprise if you heard of it first in public. It is very weak in you to allow yourself to feel that sort of regard for a married woman. If you cannot constrain yourself I shall be afraid to let you meet her in Brook Street."

Burgo looked for a moment into his aunt's face without answering her, and then turned away towards the door. "You can do as you please about that," said he; "but you know as well as I do what I have made up my mind to do."

"Nonsense, Burgo; I know nothing of the kind. But do you go down-stairs to breakfast, and don't look like that when you go among the people there."

Lady Monk was a woman now about fifty years of age, who had been a great beauty, and who was still handsome in her advanced age. Her figure was very good. She was tall and of fine proportion, though by no means verging to that state of body which our excellent American friend and critic Mr. Hawthorne has described as beefy and has declared to be the general condition of English ladies of Lady Monk's age. Lady Monk was not beefy. She was a comely, handsome, upright, dame,—one of whom, as regards her outward appearance, England might be proud,—and of whom Sir Cosmo Monk was very proud. She had come of the family of the Worcestershire Fitzgeralds, of whom it used to be said that there never was one who was not beautiful and worthless. Looking at Lady Monk you would hardly think that she could be a worthless woman; but there were one or two who professed to know her, and who declared that she was a true scion of the family to which she belonged;—that even her husband's ample fortune had suffered from her extravagance, that she had quarrelled with her only son, and had succeeded in marrying her daughter to the greatest fool in the peerage. She had striven very hard to bring about a marriage between her nephew and the great heiress, and was a woman not likely to pardon those who had foiled her.

At this moment Burgo felt very certain that his aunt was aware of his purpose, and could not forgive her for pretending to be innocent of it. In this he was most ungrateful, as well as unreasonable,—and very indiscreet also. Had he been a man who ever reflected he must have known that such a woman as his aunt could only assist him as long as she might be presumed to be ignorant of his intention. But Burgo never reflected. The Fitzgeralds never reflected till they were nearer forty than thirty, and then people began to think worse of them than they had thought before.

When Burgo reached the dining-room there were many men there, but no ladies. Sir Cosmo Monk, a fine bald-headed hale man of about sixty, was standing up at the sideboard, cutting a huge game pie. He was a man also who did not reflect much, but who contrived to keep straight in his course through the world without much reflection. "Palliser is coming without her," he said in his loud clear voice, thinking nothing of his wife's nephew. "She's ill, she says."

"I'm sorry for it," said one man. "She's a deal the better fellow of the two."

"She has twice more go in her than Planty Pall," said another.

"Planty is no fool, I can tell you," said Sir Cosmo, coming to the table with his plate full of pie. "We think he's about the most rising man we have." Sir Cosmo was the member for his county, and was a Liberal. He had once, when a much younger man, been at the Treasury, and had since always spoken of the Whig Government as though he himself were in some sort a part of it.

"Burgo, do you hear that Palliser is coming without his wife?" said one man,—a very young man, who hardly knew what had been the circumstances of the case. The others, when they saw Burgo enter, had been silent on the subject of Lady Glencora.

"I have heard,—and be d——d to him," said Burgo. Then there was suddenly a silence in the room, and everyone seemed to attend assiduously to his breakfast. It was very terrible, this clear expression of a guilty meaning with reference to the wife of another man! Burgo regarded neither his plate nor his cup, but thrusting his hands into his breeches pockets, sat back in his chair with the blackness as of a thunder cloud upon his brow.

"I have heard," said Burgo.

"Burgo, you had better eat your breakfast," said Sir Cosmo.

"I don't want any breakfast." He took, however, a bit of toast, and crumbling it up in his hand as he put a morsel into his mouth, went away to the sideboard and filled for himself a glass of cherry brandy.

"If you don't eat any breakfast the less of that you take the better," said Sir Cosmo.

"I'm all right now," said he, and coming back to the table, went through some form of making a meal with a roll and a cup of tea.

They who were then present used afterwards to say that they should never forget that breakfast. There had been something, they declared, in the tone of Burgo's voice when he uttered his curse against Mr. Palliser, which had struck them all with dread. There had, too, they said, been a blackness in his face, so terrible to be seen, that it had taken from them all the power of conversation. Sir Cosmo, when he had broken the ominous silence, had done so with a manifest struggle. The loud clatter of glasses with which Burgo had swallowed his dram, as though resolved to show that he was regardless who might know that he was drinking, added to the feeling. It may easily be understood that there was no further word spoken at that breakfast-table about Planty Pall or his wife.

On that day Burgo Fitzgerald startled all those who saw him by the mad way in which he rode. Early in the day there was no excuse for any such rashness. The hounds went from wood to wood, and men went in troops along the forest sides as they do on such occasions. But Burgo was seen to cram his horse at impracticable places, and to ride at gates and rails as though resolved to do himself and his uncle's steed a mischief. This was so apparent that some friend spoke to Sir Cosmo Monk about it. "I can do nothing," said Sir Cosmo. "He is a man whom no one's words will control. Something has ruffled him this morning, and he must run his chance till he becomes quiet." In the afternoon there was a good run, and Burgo again rode as hard as he could make his horse carry him;—but then there was the usual excuse for hard riding; and such riding in a straight run is not dangerous, as it is when the circumstances of the occasion do not warrant it, But, be that as it may, Burgo went on to the end of the day without accident, and as he went home, assured Sir Cosmo, in a voice which was almost cheery, that his mare Spinster was by far the best thing in the Monkshade stables. Indeed Spinster made quite a character that day, and was sold at the end of the season for three hundred guineas on the strength of it. I am, however, inclined to believe that there was nothing particular about the mare. Horses always catch the temperament of their riders, and when a man wishes to break his neck, he will generally find a horse willing to assist him in appearance, but able to save him in the performance. Burgo, at any rate, did not break his neck, and appeared at the dinner-table in a better humour than that which he had displayed in the morning.

On the day appointed Mr. Palliser reached Monkshade. He was, in a manner, canvassing for the support of the Liberal party, and it would not have suited him to show any indifference to the invitation of so influential a man as Sir Cosmo. Sir Cosmo had a little party of his own in the House, consisting of four or five other respectable country gentlemen, who troubled themselves little with thinking, and who mostly had bald heads. Sir Cosmo was a man with whom it was quite necessary that such an aspirant as Mr. Palliser should stand well, and therefore Mr. Palliser came to Monkshade, although Lady Glencora was unable to accompany him.

"We are so sorry," said Lady Monk. "We have been looking forward to having Lady Glencora with us beyond everything."

Mr. Palliser declared that Lady Glencora herself was overwhelmed with grief in that she should have been debarred from making this special visit. She had, however, been so unwell at Gatherum, the anxious husband declared, as to make it unsafe for her to go again away from home.

"I hope it is nothing serious," said Lady Monk, with a look of grief so well arranged that any stranger would have thought that all the Pallisers must have been very dear to her heart. Then Mr. Palliser went on to explain that Lady Glencora had unfortunately been foolish. During one of those nights of hard frost she had gone out among the ruins at Matching, to show them by moonlight to a friend. The friend had thoughtlessly, foolishly, and in a manner which Mr. Palliser declared to be very reprehensible, allowed Lady Glencora to remain among the ruins till she had caught cold.

"How very wrong!" said Lady Monk with considerable emphasis.

"It was very wrong," said Mr. Palliser, speaking of poor Alice almost maliciously. "However, she caught a cold which, unfortunately, has become worse at my uncle's, and so I was obliged to take her home."

Lady Monk perceived that Mr. Palliser had in truth left his wife behind because he believed her to be ill, and not because he was afraid of Burgo Fitzgerald. So accomplished a woman as Lady Monk felt no doubt that the wife's absence was caused by fear of the lover, and not by any cold caught in viewing ruins by moonlight. She was not to be deceived in such a matter. But she became aware that Mr. Palliser had been deceived. As she was right in this we must go back for a moment, and say a word of things as they went on at Matching after Alice Vavasor had left that place.

Alice had told Miss Palliser that steps ought to be taken, whatever might be their cost, to save Lady Glencora from the peril of a visit to Monkshade. To this Miss Palliser had assented, and, when she left Alice, was determined to tell Mr. Palliser the whole story. But when the time for doing so had come, her courage failed her. She could not find words in which to warn the husband that his wife would not be safe in the company of her old lover. The task with Lady Glencora herself, bad as that would be, might be easier, and this task she at last undertook,—not without success.

"Glencora," she said, when she found a fitting opportunity, "you won't be angry, I hope, if I say a word to you?"

"That depends very much upon what the word is," said Lady Glencora. And here it must be acknowledged that Mr. Palliser's wife had not done much to ingratiate herself with Mr. Palliser's cousins;—not perhaps so much as she should have done, seeing that she found them in her husband's house. She had taught herself to think that they were hard, stiff, and too proud of bearing the name of Palliser. Perhaps some little attempt may have been made by one or both of them to teach her something, and it need hardly be said that such an attempt on the part of a husband's unmarried female relations would not be forgiven by a young bride. She had undoubtedly been ungracious, and of this Miss Palliser was well aware.

"Well,—the word shall be as little unpleasant as I can make it," said Miss Palliser, already appreciating fully the difficulty of her task.

"But why say anything that is unpleasant? However, if it is to be said, let us have it over at once."

"You are going to Monkshade, I believe, with Plantagenet."

"Well;—and what of that?"

"Dear Glencora, I think you had better not go. Do you not think so yourself?"

"Who has been talking to you?" said Lady Glencora, turning upon her very sharply.

"Nobody has been talking to me;—not in the sense you mean."

"Plantagenet has spoken to you?"

"Not a word," said Miss Palliser. "You may be sure that he would not utter a word on such a subject to anyone unless it were to yourself. But, dear Glencora, you should not go there;—I mean it in all kindness and love,—I do indeed." Saying this she offered her hand to Glencora, and Glencora took it.

"Perhaps you do," said she in a low voice.

"Indeed I do. The world is so hard and cruel in what it says."

"I do not care two straws for what the world says."

"But he might care."

"It is not my fault. I do not want to go to Monkshade. Lady Monk was my friend once, but I do not care if I never see her again. I did not arrange this visit. It was Plantagenet who did it."

"But he will not take you there if you say you do not wish it."

"I have said so, and he told me that I must go. You will hardly believe me,—but I condescended even to tell him why I thought it better to remain away. He told me, in answer, that it was a silly folly which I must live down, and that it did not become me to be afraid of any man."

"Of course you are not afraid, but—"

"I am afraid. That is just the truth. I am afraid;—but what can I do more than I have done?"

This was very terrible to Miss Palliser. She had not thought that Lady Glencora would say so much, and she felt a true regret in having been made to hear words which so nearly amounted to a confession. But for this there was no help now. There were not many more words between them, and we already know the result of the conversation. Lady Glencora became so ill from the effects of her imprudent lingering among the ruins that she was unable to go to Monkshade.

Mr. Palliser remained three days at Monkshade, and cemented his political alliance with Sir Cosmo much in the same way as he had before done with the Duke of St. Bungay. There was little or nothing said about politics, and certainly not a word that could be taken as any definite party understanding between the men; but they sat at dinner together at the same table, drank a glass of wine or two out of the same decanters, and dropped a chance word now and again about the next session of Parliament. I do not know that anything more had been expected either by Mr. Palliser or by Sir Cosmo; but it seemed to be understood when Mr. Palliser went away that Sir Cosmo was of opinion that that young scion of a ducal house ought to become the future Chancellor of the Exchequer in the Whig Government.

"I can't see that there's so much in him," said one young member of Parliament to Sir Cosmo.

"I rather think that there is, all the same," said the baronet. "There's a good deal in him, I believe! I dare say he's not very bright, but I don't know that we want brightness. A bright financier is the most dangerous man in the world. We've had enough of that already. Give me sound common sense, with just enough of the gab in a man to enable him to say what he's got to say! We don't want more than that nowadays." From which it became evident that Sir Cosmo was satisfied with the new political candidate for high place.

Lady Monk took an occasion to introduce Mr. Palliser to Burgo Fitzgerald; with what object it is difficult to say, unless she was anxious to make mischief between the men. Burgo scowled at him; but Mr. Palliser did not notice the scowl, and put out his hand to his late rival most affably. Burgo was forced to take it, and as he did so made a little speech. "I'm sorry that we have not the pleasure of seeing Lady Glencora with you," said he.

"She is unfortunately indisposed," said Mr. Palliser.

"I am sorry for it," said Burgo—"very sorry indeed." Then he turned his back and walked away. The few words he had spoken, and the manner in which he had carried himself, had been such as to make all those around them notice it. Each of them knew that Lady Glencora's name should not have been in Burgo's mouth, and all felt a fear not easily to be defined that something terrible would come of it. But Mr. Palliser himself did not seem to notice anything, or to fear anything; and nothing terrible did come of it during that visit of his to Monkshade.

CHAPTER XXXIV
MR. VAVASOR SPEAKS TO HIS DAUGHTER

Alice Vavasor returned to London with her father, leaving Kate at Vavasor Hall with her grandfather. The journey was not a pleasant one. Mr. Vavasor knew that it was his duty to do something,—to take some steps with the view of preventing the marriage which his daughter meditated; but he did not know what that something should be, and he did know that, whatever it might be, the doing of it would be thoroughly disagreeable. When they started from Vavasor he had as yet hardly spoken to her a word upon the subject. "I cannot congratulate you," he had simply said. "I hope the time may come, papa, when you will," Alice had answered; and that had been all.

The squire had promised that he would consent to a reconciliation with his grandson, if Alice's father would express himself satisfied with the proposed marriage. John Vavasor had certainly expressed nothing of the kind. "I think so badly of him," he had said, speaking to the old man of George, "that I would rather know that almost any other calamity was to befall her, than that she should be united to him." Then the squire, with his usual obstinacy, had taken up the cudgels on behalf of his grandson; and had tried to prove that the match after all would not be so bad in its results as his son seemed to expect. "It would do very well for the property," he said. "I would settle the estate on their eldest son, so that he could not touch it; and I don't see why he shouldn't reform as well as another." John Vavasor had then declared that George was thoroughly bad, that he was an adventurer; that he believed him to be a ruined man, and that he would never reform. The squire upon this had waxed angry, and in this way George obtained aid and assistance down at the old house, which he certainly had no right to expect. When Alice wished her grandfather good-bye the old man gave her a message to his grandson. "You may tell him," said he, "that I will never see him again unless he begs my pardon for his personal bad conduct to me, but that if he marries you, I will take care that the property is properly settled upon his child and yours. I shall always be glad to see you, my dear; and for your sake, I will see him if he will humble himself to me." There was no word spoken then about her father's consent; and Alice, when she left

Vavasor, felt that the squire was rather her friend than her enemy in regard to this thing which she contemplated. That her father was and would be an uncompromising enemy to her,—uncompromising though probably not energetical,—she was well aware; and, therefore, the journey up to London was not comfortable.

Alice had resolved, with great pain to herself, that in this matter she owed her father no obedience. "There cannot be obedience on one side," she said to herself, "without protection and support on the other." Now it was quite true that John Vavasor had done little in the way of supporting or protecting his daughter. Early in life, before she had resided under the same roof with him in London, he had, as it were, washed his hands of all solicitude regarding her; and having no other ties of family, had fallen into habits of life which made it almost impossible for him to live with her as any other father would live with his child. Then, when there first sprang up between them that manner of sharing the same house without any joining together of their habits of life, he had excused himself to himself by saying that Alice was unlike other girls, and that she required no protection. Her fortune was her own, and at her own disposal. Her character was such that she showed no inclination to throw the burden of such disposal on her father's shoulders. She was steady, too, and given to no pursuits which made it necessary that he should watch closely over her. She was a girl, he thought, who could do as well without surveillance as with it,—as well, or perhaps better. So it had come to pass that Alice had been the free mistress of her own actions, and had been left to make the most she could of her own hours. It cannot be supposed that she had eaten her lonely dinners in Queen Anne Street night after night, week after week, month after month, without telling herself that her father was neglecting her. She could not perceive that he spent every evening in society, but never an evening in her society, without feeling that the tie between her and him was not the strong bond which usually binds a father to his child. She was well aware that she had been ill-used in being thus left desolate in her home. She had uttered no word of complaint; but she had learned, without being aware that she was doing so, to entertain a firm resolve that her father should not guide her in her path through life. In that affair of John Grey they had both for a time thought alike, and Mr. Vavasor had believed that his theory with reference to Alice had been quite correct. She had been left to herself, and was going to dispose of herself in a way than which nothing could be more eligible. But evil days were now coming, and Mr. Vavasor, as he travelled up to London, with his daughter seated opposite to him in the railway carriage, felt that now, at last, he must interfere. In part of the journey they had the carriage to themselves, and Mr. Vavasor thought that he would begin what he had to say; but he put it off till others joined them, and then there was no further opportunity for such conversation as that which would be necessary between them. They reached home about eight in the evening, having dined on the road. "She will be tired to-night," he said to himself, as he went off to his club, "and I will speak to her to-morrow." Alice specially felt his going on this evening. When two persons had together the tedium of such a journey as that from Westmoreland up to London, there should be some feeling between them to bind them together while enjoying the comfort of the evening. Had he stayed and sat with her at her tea-table, Alice would at any rate have endeavoured to be soft with him in any discussion that might have been raised; but he went away from her at once, leaving her to think alone over the perils of the life before her. "I want to speak to you after breakfast to-morrow," he said as he went out. Alice answered that she should be there,—as a matter of course. She scorned to tell him that she was always there,—always alone at home. She had never uttered a word of complaint, and she would not begin now.

The discussion after breakfast the next day was commenced with formal and almost ceremonial preparation. The father and daughter breakfasted together, with the knowledge that the discussion was coming. It did not give to either of them a good appetite, and very little was said at table.

"Will you come up-stairs?" said Alice, when she perceived that her father had finished his tea.

"Perhaps that will be best," said he. Then he followed her into the drawing-room in which the fire had just been lit.

"Alice," said he, "I must speak to you about this engagement of yours."

"Won't you sit down, papa? It does look so dreadful, your standing up over one in that way." He had placed himself on the rug with his back to the incipient fire, but now, at her request, he sat himself down opposite to her.

"I was greatly grieved when I heard of this at Vavasor."

"I am sorry that you should be grieved, papa."

"I was grieved. I must confess that I never could understand why you treated Mr. Grey as you have done."

"Oh, papa, that's done and past. Pray let that be among the bygones."

"Does he know yet of your engagement with your cousin?"

"He will know it by this time to-morrow."

"Then I beg of you, as a great favour, to postpone your letter to him." To this Alice made no answer. "I have not troubled you with many such requests, Alice. Will you tell me that this one shall be granted?"

"I think that I owe it to him as an imperative duty to let him know the truth."

"But you may change your mind again." Alice found that this was hard to bear and hard to answer; but there was a certain amount of truth in the grievous reproach conveyed in her father's words, which made her bow her neck to it. "I have no right to say that it is impossible," she replied, in words that were barely audible.

"No;—exactly so," said her father. "And therefore it will be better that you should postpone any such communication."

"For how long do you mean?"

"Till you and I shall have agreed together that he should be told."

"No, papa; I will not consent to that. I consider myself bound to let him know the truth without delay. I have done him a great injury, and I must put an end to that as soon as possible."

"You have done him an injury certainly, my dear;—a very great injury," said Mr. Vavasor, going away from his object about the proposed letter; "and I believe he will feel it as such to the last day of his life, if this goes on."

"I hope not. I believe that it will not be so. I feel sure that it will not be so."

"But of course what I am thinking of now is your welfare,—not his. When you simply told me that you intended to—." Alice winced, for she feared to hear from her father that odious word which her grandfather had used to her; and indeed the word had been on her father's lips, but he had refrained and spared her—"that you intended to break your engagement with Mr. Grey," he continued, "I said little or nothing to you. I would not ask you to marry any man, even though you had yourself promised to marry him. But when you tell me that you are engaged to your cousin George, the matter is very different. I do not think well of your cousin. Indeed I think anything but well of him. It is my duty to tell you that the world speaks very ill of him." He paused, but Alice remained silent. "When you were about to travel with him," he continued, "I ought perhaps to have told you the same. But I did not wish to pain you or his sister; and, moreover, I have heard worse of him since then,—much worse than I had heard before."

"As you did not tell me before, I think you might spare me now," said Alice.

"No, my dear; I cannot allow you to sacrifice yourself without telling you that you are doing so. If it were not for your money he would never think of marrying you."

"Of that I am well aware," said Alice. "He has told me so himself very plainly."

"And yet you will marry him?"

"Certainly I will. It seems to me, papa, that there is a great deal of false feeling about this matter of money in marriage,—or rather, perhaps, a great deal of pretended feeling. Why should I be angry with a man for wishing to get that for which every man is struggling? At this point of George's career the use of money is essential to him. He could not marry without it."

"You had better then give him your money without yourself," said her father, speaking in irony.

"That is just what I mean to do, papa," said Alice.

"What!" said Mr. Vavasor, jumping up from his seat. "You mean to give him your money before you marry him?"

"Certainly I do;—if he should want it;—or, I should rather say, as much as he may want of it."

"Heavens and earth!" exclaimed Mr. Vavasor. "Alice, you must be mad."

"To part with my money to my friend?" said she. "It is a kind of madness of which I need not at any rate be ashamed."

"Tell me this, Alice; has he got any of it as yet?"

"Not a shilling. Papa, pray do not look at me like that. If I had no thought of marrying him you would not call me mad because I lent to my cousin what money he might need."

"I should only say that so much of your fortune was thrown away, and if it were not much that would be an end of it. I would sooner see you surrender to him the half of all you have, without any engagement to marry him, than know that he had received a shilling from you under such a promise."

"You are prejudiced against him, sir."

"Was it prejudice that made you reject him once before? Did you condemn him then through prejudice? Had you not ascertained that he was altogether unworthy of you?"

"We were both younger, then," said Alice, speaking very softly, but very seriously. "We were both much younger then, and looked at life with other eyes than those which we now use. For myself I expected much then, which I now seem hardly to regard at all; and as for him, he was then attached to pleasures to which I believe he has now learned to be indifferent."

"Psha!" ejaculated the father.

"I can only speak as I believe," continued Alice. "And I think I may perhaps know more of his manner of life than you do, papa. But I am prepared to run risks now which I feared before. Even though he were all that you think him to be, I would still endeavour to do my duty to him, and to bring him to other things."

"What is it you expect to get by marrying him?" asked Mr. Vavasor.

"A husband whose mode of thinking is congenial to my own," answered Alice. "A husband who proposes to himself a career in life with which I can sympathize. I think that I may perhaps help my cousin in the career which he has chosen, and that alone is a great reason why I should attempt to do so."

"With your money?" said Mr. Vavasor with a sneer.

"Partly with my money," said Alice, disdaining to answer the sneer. "Though it were only with my money, even that would be something."

"Well, Alice, as your father, I can only implore you to pause before you commit yourself to his hands. If he demands money from you, and you are minded to give it to him, let him have it in moderation. Anything will be better than marrying him. I know that I cannot hinder you; you are as much your own mistress as I am my own master,—or rather a great deal more, as my income depends on my going to that horrid place in Chancery Lane. But yet I suppose you must think something of your father's wishes and your father's opinion. It will not be pleasant for you to stand at the altar without my being there near you."

To this Alice made no answer; but she told herself that it had not been pleasant to her to have stood at so many places during the last four years,—and to have found herself so often alone,—without her father being near to her. That had been his fault, and it was not now in her power to remedy the ill-effects of it.

"Has any day been fixed between you and him?" he asked.

"No, papa."

"Nothing has been said about that?"

"Yes; something has been said. I have told him that it cannot be for a year yet. It is because I told him that, that I told him also that he should have my money when he wanted it."

"Not all of it?" said Mr. Vavasor.

"I don't suppose he will need it all. He intends to stand again for Chelsea, and it is the great expense of the election which makes him want money. You are not to suppose that he has asked me for it. When I made him understand that I did not wish to marry quite yet, I offered him the use of that which would be ultimately his own."

"And he has accepted it?"

"He answered me just as I had intended,—that when the need came he would take me at my word."

"Then, Alice, I will tell you what is my belief. He will drain you of every shilling of your money, and when that is gone, there will be no more heard of the marriage. We must take a small house in some cheap part of the town and live on my income as best we may. I shall go and insure my life, so that you may not absolutely starve when I die." Having said this, Mr. Vavasor went away, not immediately to the insurance office, as his words seemed to imply, but to his club where he sat alone, reading the newspaper, very gloomily, till the time came for his afternoon rubber of whist, and the club dinner bill for the day was brought under his eye.

Alice had no such consolations in her solitude. She had fought her battle with her father tolerably well, but she was now called upon to fight a battle with herself, which was one much more difficult to win. Was her cousin, her betrothed as she now must regard him, the worthless, heartless, mercenary rascal which her father painted him? There had certainly been a time, and that not very long distant, in which Alice herself had been almost constrained so to regard him. Since that any change for the better in her opinion of him had been grounded on evidence given either by himself or by his sister Kate. He had done nothing to inspire her with any confidence, unless his reckless daring in coming forward to contest a seat in Parliament could be regarded as a doing of something. And he had owned himself to be a man almost penniless; he had spoken of himself as being utterly reckless,—as being one whose standing in the world was and must continue to be a perch on the edge of a precipice, from which any accident might knock him headlong. Alice believed in her heart that this last profession or trade to which he had applied himself, was becoming as nothing to him,— that he received from it no certain income;—no income that a man could make to appear respectable to fathers or guardians when seeking a girl in marriage. Her father declared that all men spoke badly of him. Alice knew her father to be an idle man, a man given to pleasure, to be one who thought by far too much of the good things of the world; but she had never found him to be either false or malicious. His unwonted energy in this matter was in itself evidence that he believed himself to be right in what he said.

To tell the truth, Alice was frightened at what she had done, and almost repented of it already. Her acceptance of her cousin's offer had not come of love;—nor had it, in truth, come chiefly of ambition. She had not so much asked herself why she should do this thing, as why she should not do it,—seeing that it was required of her by her friend. What after all did it matter? That was her argument with herself. It cannot be supposed that she looked back on the past events of her life with any self-satisfaction. There was no self-satisfaction, but in truth there was more self-reproach than she deserved. As a girl she had loved her cousin George passionately, and that love had failed her. She did not tell herself that she had been wrong when she gave him up, but she thought herself to have been most unfortunate in the one necessity. After such an experience as that, would it not have been better for her to have remained without further thought of marriage?

Then came that terrible episode in her life for which she never could forgive herself. She had accepted Mr. Grey because she liked him and honoured him. "And I did love him," she said to herself, now on this morning. Poor, wretched, heart-wrung woman! As she sat there thinking of it all in her solitude she was to be pitied at any rate, if not to be forgiven. Now, as she thought of Nethercoats, with its quiet life, its gardens, its books, and the peaceful affectionate ascendancy of him who would have been her lord and master, her feelings were very different from those which had induced her to resolve that she would not stoop to put her neck beneath that yoke. Would it not have been well for her to have a master who by his wisdom and strength could save her from such wretched doubtings as these? But she had refused to bend, and then she had found herself desolate and alone in the world.

"If I can do him good why should I not marry him?" In that feeling had been the chief argument which had induced her to return such an answer as she had sent to her cousin. "For myself, what does it matter? As to this life of mine and all that belongs to it, why should I regard it otherwise than to make it of some service to some one who is dear to me?" He had been ever dear to her from her earliest years. She believed in his intellect, even if she could not believe in his conduct. Kate, her friend, longed for this thing. As for that dream of love, it meant nothing; and as for those arguments of prudence,—that cold calculation about her money, which all people seemed to expect from her,—she would throw it to the winds. What if she were ruined! There was always the other chance. She might save him from ruin, and help him to honour and fortune.

But then, when the word was once past her lips, there returned to her that true woman's feeling which made her plead for a long day,—which made her feel that that long day would be all too short,—which made her already dread the coming of the end of the year. She had said that she would become George Vavasor's wife, but she wished that the saying so might be the end of it. When he came to her to embrace her how should she receive him? The memory of John Grey's last kiss still lingered on her lips. She had told herself that she scorned the delights of love; if it were so, was she not bound to keep herself far from them; if it were so,—would not her cousin's kiss pollute her?

"It may be as my father says," she thought. "It may be that he wants my money only; if so, let him have it. Surely when the year is over I shall know." Then a plan formed itself in her head, which she did not make willingly, with any voluntary action of her mind,—but which came upon her as plans do come,—and recommended itself to her in despite of herself. He should have her money as he might call for it,—all of it excepting some small portion of her income, which might suffice to keep her from burdening her father. Then, if he were contented, he should go free, without reproach, and there should be an end of all question of marriage for her.

As she thought of this, and matured it in her mind, the door opened, and the servant announced her cousin George.

CHAPTER XXXV
PASSION VERSUS PRUDENCE

It had not occurred to Alice that her accepted lover would come to her so soon. She had not told him expressly of the day on which she would return, and had not reflected that Kate would certainly inform him. She had been thinking so much of the distant perils of this engagement, that this peril, so sure to come upon her before many days or hours could pass by, had been forgotten. When the name struck her ear, and George's step was heard outside on the landing-place, she felt the blood rush violently to her heart, and she jumped up from her seat panic-stricken and in utter dismay. How should she receive him? And then again, with what form of affection would she be accosted by him? But he was there in the room with her before she had had a moment allowed to her for thought.

She hardly ventured to look up at him; but, nevertheless, she became aware that there was something in his appearance and dress brighter, more lover-like, perhaps newer, than was usual with him. This in itself was an affliction to her. He ought to have understood that such an engagement as theirs not only did not require, but absolutely forbade, any such symptom of young love as this. Even when their marriage came, if it must come, it should come without any customary sign of smartness, without any outward mark of exaltation. It would have been very good in him to have remained away from her for weeks and months; but to come upon her thus, on the first morning of her return, was a cruelty not to be forgiven. These were the feelings with which Alice regarded her betrothed when he came to see her.

"Alice," said he, coming up to her with his extended hand,—"Dearest Alice!"

She gave him her hand, and muttered some word which was inaudible even to him; she gave him her hand, and immediately endeavoured to resume it, but he held it clenched within his own, and she felt that she was his prisoner. He was standing close to her now, and she could not escape from him. She was trembling with fear lest worse might betide her even than this. She had promised to marry him, and now she was covered with dismay as she felt rather than thought how very far she was from loving the man to whom she had given this promise.

"Alice," he said, "I am a man once again. It is only now that I can tell you what I have suffered during these last few years." He still held her hand, but he had not as yet attempted any closer embrace. She knew that she was standing away from him awkwardly, almost showing her repugnance to him; but it was altogether beyond her power to assume an attitude of ordinary ease. "Alice," he continued, "I feel that I am a strong man again, armed to meet the world at all points. Will you not let me thank you for what you have done for me?"

She must speak to him! Though the doing so should be ever so painful to her, she must say some word to him which should have in it a sound of kindness. After all, it was his undoubted right to come to her, and the footing on which he assumed to stand was simply that which she herself had given to him. It was not his fault if at this moment he inspired her with disgust rather than with love.

"I have done nothing for you, George," she said, "nothing at all." Then she got her hand away from him, and retreated back to a sofa where she seated herself, leaving him still standing in the space before the fire. "That you may do much for yourself is my greatest hope. If I can help you, I will do so most heartily." Then she became thoroughly ashamed of her words, feeling that she was at once offering to him the use of her purse.

"Of course you will help me," he said. "I am full of plans, all of which you must share with me. But now, at this moment, my one great plan is that in which you have already consented to be my partner. Alice, you are my wife now. Tell me that it will make you happy to call me your husband."

Not for worlds could she have said so at this moment. It was ill-judged in him to press her thus. He should already have seen, with half an eye, that no such triumph as that which he now demanded could be his on this occasion. He had had his triumph when, in the solitude of his own room, with quiet sarcasm he had thrown on one side of him the letter in which she had accepted him, as though the matter had been one almost indifferent to him. He had no right to expect the double triumph. Then he had frankly told himself that her money would be useful to him. He should have been contented with that conviction, and not have required her also to speak to him soft winning words of love.

"That must be still distant, George," she said. "I have suffered so much!"

"And it has been my fault that you have suffered; I know that. These years of misery have been my doing." It was, however, the year of coming misery that was the most to be dreaded.

"I do not say that," she replied, "nor have I ever thought it. I have myself and myself only to blame." Here he altogether misunderstood her, believing her to mean that the fault for which she blamed herself had been committed in separating herself from him on that former occasion.

"Alice, dear, let bygones be bygones."

"Bygones will not be bygones. It may be well for people to say so, but it is never true. One might as well say so to one's body as to one's heart. But the hairs will grow grey, and the heart will grow cold."

"I do not see that one follows upon the other," said George. "My hair is growing very grey;"—and to show that it was so, he lifted the dark lock from the side of his forehead, and displayed the incipient grizzling of the hair from behind. "If grey hairs make an old man, Alice, you will marry an old husband; but even you shall not be allowed to say that my heart is old."

That word "husband," which her cousin had twice used, was painful to Alice's ear. She shrunk from it with palpable bodily suffering. Marry an old husband! His age was nothing to the purpose, though he had been as old as Enoch. But she was again obliged to answer him. "I spoke of my own heart," said she: "I sometimes feel that it has grown very old."

"Alice, that is hardly cheering to me."

"You have come to me too quickly, George, and do not reflect how much there is that I must remember. You have said that bygones should be bygones. Let them be so, at any rate as far as words are concerned. Give me a few months in which I may learn,—not to forget them, for that will be impossible,—but to abstain from speaking of them."

There was something in her look as she spoke, and in the tone of her voice that was very sad. It struck him forcibly, but it struck him with anger rather than with sadness. Doubtless her money had been his chief object when he offered to renew his engagement with her. Doubtless he would have made no such offer had she been penniless, or even had his own need been less pressing. But, nevertheless, he desired something more than money. The triumph of being preferred to John Grey,—of having John Grey sent altogether adrift, in order that his old love might be recovered, would have been too costly a luxury for him to seek, had he not in seeking it been able to combine prudence with the luxury. But though his prudence had been undoubted, he desired the luxury also. It was on a calculation of the combined advantage that he had made his second offer to his cousin. As he would by no means have consented to proceed with the arrangement without the benefit of his cousin's money, so also did he feel unwilling to dispense with some expression of her love for him, which would be to him triumphant. Hitherto in their present interview there had certainly been no expression of her love.

"Alice," he said, "your greeting to me is hardly all that I had hoped."

"Is it not?" said she. "Indeed, George, I am sorry that you should be disappointed; but what can I say? You would not have me affect a lightness of spirit which I do not feel?"

"If you wish," said he, very slowly, —"if you wish to retract your letter to me, you now have my leave to do so."

What an opportunity was this of escape! But she had not the courage to accept it. What girl, under such circumstances, would have had such courage? How often are offers made to us which we would almost give our eyes to accept, but dare not accept because we fear the countenance of the offerer? "I do not wish to retract my letter," said she, speaking as slowly as he had spoken; "but I wish to be left awhile, that I may recover my strength of mind. Have you not heard doctors say, that muscles which have been strained, should be allowed rest, or they will never entirely renew their tension? It is so with me now; if I could be quiet for a few months, I think I could learn to face the future with a better courage."

"And is that all you can say to me, Alice?"

"What would you have me say?"

"I would fain hear one word of love from you; is that unreasonable? I would wish to know from your own lips that you have satisfaction in the renewed prospect of our union; is that too ambitious? It might have been that I was over-bold in pressing my suit upon you again; but as you accepted it, have I not a right to expect that you should show me that you have been happy in accepting it?"

But she had not been happy in accepting it. She was not happy now that she had accepted it. She could not show to him any sign of such joy as that which he desired to see. And now, at this moment, she feared with an excessive fear that there would come some demand for an outward demonstration of love, such as he in his position might have a right to make. She seemed to be aware that this might be prevented only by such demeanour on her part as that which she had practised, and she could not, therefore, be stirred to the expression of any word of affection. She listened to his appeal, and when it was finished she made no reply. If he chose to take her in dudgeon, he must do so. She would make for him any sacrifice that was possible to her, but this sacrifice was not possible.

"And you have not a word to say to me?" he asked. She looked up at him, and saw that the cicatrice on his face was becoming ominous; his eyes were bent upon her with all their forbidding brilliance, and he was assuming that look of angry audacity which was so peculiar to him, and which had so often cowed those with whom he was brought in contact.

"No other word, at present, George; I have told you that I am not at ease. Why do you press me now?"

He had her letter to him in the breast-pocket of his coat, and his hand was on it, that he might fling it back to her, and tell her that he would not hold her to be his promised wife under such circumstances as these. The anger which would have induced him to do so was the better part of his nature. Three or four years since, this better part would have prevailed, and he would have given way to his rage. But now, as his fingers played upon the paper, he remembered that her money was absolutely essential to him,—that some of it was needed by him almost instantly,—that on this very morning he was bound to go where money would be demanded from him, and that his hopes with regard to Chelsea could not be maintained unless he was able to make some substantial promise of providing funds. His sister Kate's fortune was just two thousand pounds. That, and no more, was now the capital at his command, if he should abandon this other source of aid. Even that must go, if all other sources should fail him; but he would fain have that untouched, if it were possible. Oh, that that old man in Westmoreland would die and be gathered to his fathers, now that he was full of years and ripe for the sickle! But there was no sign of death about the old man. So his fingers released their hold on the letter, and he stood looking at her in his anger.

"You wish me then to go from you?" he said.

"Do not be angry with me, George!"

"Angry! I have no right to be angry. But, by heaven, I am wrong there. I have the right, and I am angry. I think you owed it me to give me some warmer welcome. Is it to be thus with us always for the next accursed year?"

"Oh, George!"

"To me it will be accursed. But is it to be thus between us always? Alice, I have loved you above all women. I may say that I have never loved any woman but you; and yet I am sometimes driven to doubt whether you have a heart in you capable of love. After all that has passed, all your old protestations, all my repentance, and your proffer of forgiveness, you should have received me with open arms. I suppose I may go now, and feel that I have been kicked out of your house like a dog."

"If you speak to me like that, and look at me like that, how can I answer you?"

"I want no answer. I wanted you to put your hand in mine, to kiss me, and to tell me that you are once more my own. Alice, think better of it; kiss me, and let me feel my arm once more round your waist."

She shuddered as she sat, still silent, on her seat, and he saw that she shuddered. With all his desire for her money,—his instant need of it,—this was too much for him; and he turned upon his heel, and left the room without another word. She heard his quick step as he hurried down the stairs, but she did not rise to arrest him. She heard the door slam as he left the house, but still she did not move from her seat. Her immediate desire had been that he should go,—and now he was gone. There was in that a relief which almost comforted her. And this was the man from whom, within the last few days, she had accepted an offer of marriage.

George, when he left the house, walked hurriedly into Cavendish Square, and down along the east side, till he made his way out along Princes Street, into the Circus in Oxford Street. Close to him there, in Great Marlborough Street, was the house of his parliamentary attorney, Mr. Scruby, on whom he was bound to call on that morning. As he had walked away from Queen Anne Street, he had thought of nothing but that too visible shudder which his cousin Alice had been unable to repress. He had been feeding on his anger, and indulging it, telling himself at one moment that he would let her and her money go from him whither they list,—and making inward threats in the next that the time should come in which he would punish her for this ill-usage. But there was the necessity of resolving what he would say to Mr. Scruby. To Mr. Scruby was still due some trifle on the cost of the last election; but even if this were paid, Mr. Scruby would make no heavy advance towards the expense of the next election. Whoever might come out at the end of such affairs without a satisfactory settlement of his little bill, as had for a while been the case with Mr. Grimes, from the "Handsome Man,"—and as, indeed, still was the case with him, as that note of hand at three months' date was not yet paid,—Mr. Scruby seldom allowed himself to suffer. It was true that the election would not take place till the summer; but there were preliminary expenses which needed ready money. Metropolitan voters, as Mr. Scruby often declared, required to be kept in good humour,—so that Mr. Scruby wanted the present payment of some five hundred pounds, and a well-grounded assurance that he would be put in full funds by the beginning of next June. Even Mr. Scruby might not be true as perfect steel, if he thought that his candidate at the last moment would not come forth properly prepared. Other candidates, with money in their pockets, might find their way into Mr. Scruby's offices. As George Vavasor crossed Regent Street, he gulped down his anger, and applied his mind to business. Should he prepare himself to give orders that Kate's little property should be sold out, or would he resolve to use his cousin's money? That his cousin's money would still be at his disposal, in spite of the stormy mood in which he had retreated from her presence, he felt sure; but the asking for it on his part would be unpleasant. That duty he must entrust to Kate. But as he reached Mr. Scruby's door, he had decided that for such purposes as those now in hand, it was preferable that he should use his wife's fortune. It was thus that in his own mind he worded the phrase, and made for himself an excuse. Yes;—he would use his wife's fortune, and explain to Mr. Scruby that he would be justified in doing so by the fact that his own heritage would be settled on her at her marriage. I do not suppose that he altogether liked it. He was not, at any rate as yet, an altogether heartless swindler. He could not take his cousin's money without meaning,—without thinking that he meant, to repay her in full all that he took. Her behaviour to him this very morning had no doubt made the affair more difficult to his mind, and more unpleasant than it would have been had she smiled on him; but even as it was, he managed to assure himself that he was doing her no wrong, and with this self-assurance he entered Mr. Scruby's office.

The clerks in the outer office were very civil to him, and undertook to promise him that he should not be kept waiting an instant. There were four gentlemen in the little parlour, they said, waiting to see Mr. Scruby, but there they should remain till Mr. Vavasor's interview was over. One gentleman, as it seemed, was even turned out to make way for him; for as George was ushered into the lawyer's room, a little man, looking very meek, was hurried away from it.

"You can wait, Smithers," said Mr. Scruby, speaking from within. "I shan't be very long." Vavasor apologized to his agent for the injury he was doing Smithers; but Mr. Scruby explained that he was only a poor devil of a printer, looking for payment of his little account. He had printed and posted 30,000 placards for one of the late Marylebone candidates, and found some difficulty in getting his money. "You see, when they're in a small way of business, it ruins them," said Scruby. "Now that poor devil,—he hasn't had a shilling of his money yet, and the greater part has been paid out of his pocket to the posters. It is hard."

It comforted Vavasor when he thus heard that there were others who were more backward in their payments, even than himself, and made him reflect that a longer credit than had yet been achieved by him, might perhaps be within his reach. "It is astonishing how much a man may get done for him," said he, "without paying anything for years."

"Yes; that's true. So he may, if he knows how to go about it. But when he does pay, Mr. Vavasor, he does it through the nose;—cent. per cent., and worse, for all his former shortcomings."

"How many there are who never pay at all," said George.

"Yes, Mr. Vavasor;—that's true, too. But see what a life they lead. It isn't a pleasant thing to be afraid of coming into your agent's office; not what you would like, Mr. Vavasor;—not if I know you."

"I never was afraid of meeting anyone yet," said Vavasor; "but I don't know what I may come to."

"Nor never will, I'll go bail. But, Lord love you, I could tell you such tales! I've had Members of Parliament, past, present, and future, almost down on their knees to me in this little room. It's about a month or six weeks before the elections come on when they're at their worst. There is so much you see, Mr. Vavasor, for which a gentleman must pay ready money. It isn't like a business in which a lawyer is supposed to find the capital. If I had money enough to pay out of my own pocket all the cost of all the metropolitan gentlemen for whom I act, why, I could live on the interest without any trouble, and go into Parliament myself like a man."

George Vavasor perfectly understood that Mr. Scruby was explaining to him, with what best attempt at delicacy he could make, that funds for the expense of the Chelsea election were not to be forthcoming from the Great Marlborough Street establishment.

"I suppose so," said he. "But you do do it sometimes."

"Never, Mr. Vavasor," said Mr. Scruby, very solemnly. "As a rule, never. I may advance the money, on interest, of course, when I receive a guarantee from the candidate's father, or from six or seven among the committee, who must all be very substantial,—very substantial indeed. But in a general way I don't do it. It isn't my place."

"I thought you did;—but at any rate I don't want you to do it for me."

"I'm quite sure you don't," said Mr. Scruby, with a brighter tone of voice than that he had just been using. "I never thought you did, Mr. Vavasor. Lord bless you, Mr. Vavasor, I know the difference between gentlemen as soon as I see them."

Then they went to business, and Vavasor became aware that it would be thought convenient that he should lodge with Mr. Scruby, to his own account, a sum not less than six hundred pounds within the next week, and it would be also necessary that he should provide for taking up that bill, amounting to ninety-two pounds, which he had given to the landlord of the "Handsome Man." In short, it would be well that he should borrow a thousand pounds from Alice, and as he did not wish that the family attorney of the Vavasors should be employed to raise it, he communicated to Mr. Scruby as much of his plans as was necessary,—feeling more hesitation in doing it than might have been expected from him. When he had done so, he was very intent on explaining also that the money taken from his cousin, and future bride, would be repaid to her out of the property in Westmoreland, which was,—did he say settled on himself? I am afraid he did.

"Yes, yes;—a family arrangement," said Mr. Scruby, as he congratulated him on his proposed marriage. Mr. Scruby did not care a straw from what source the necessary funds might be drawn.

CHAPTER XXXVI
JOHN GREY GOES A SECOND TIME TO LONDON

Early in that conversation which Mr. Vavasor had with his daughter, and which was recorded a few pages back, he implored her to pause a while before she informed Mr. Grey of her engagement with her cousin. Nothing, however, on that point had been settled between them. Mr. Vavasor had wished her to say that she would not write till he should have assented to her doing so. She had declined to bind herself in this way, and then they had gone off to other things;—to George Vavasor's character and the disposition of her money. Alice, however, had felt herself bound not to write to Mr. Grey quite at once. Indeed, when her cousin left her she had no appetite for writing such a letter as hers was to be. A day or two passed by her in this way, and nothing more was said by her or her father. It was now the middle of January, and the reader may remember that Mr. Grey had promised that he would come to her in London in that month, as soon as he should know that she had returned from Westmoreland. She must at any rate do something to prevent that visit. Mr. Grey would not come without giving her notice. She knew enough of the habits of the man to be sure of that. But she desired that her letter to him should be in time to prevent his to her; so when those few days were gone, she sat down to write without speaking to her father again upon the subject.

It was a terrible job;—perhaps the most difficult of all the difficult tasks which her adverse fate had imposed upon her. She found when she did attempt it, that she could have done it better if she had done it at the moment when she was writing the other letter to her cousin George. Then Kate had been near her, and she had been comforted by Kate's affectionate happiness. She had been strengthened at that moment by a feeling that she was doing the best in her power, if not for herself, at any rate for others. All that comfort and all that strength had left her now. The atmosphere of the fells had buoyed her up, and now the thick air of London depressed her. She sat for hours with the pen in her hand, and could not write the letter. She let a day go by and a night, and still it was not written. She hardly knew herself in her unnatural weakness. As the mental photographs of the two men forced themselves upon her, she could not force herself to forget those words—"Look here, upon this picture—and on this." How was it that she now knew how great was the difference between the two men, how immense the pre-eminence of him whom she had rejected;—and that she had not before been able to see this on any of those many previous occasions on which she had compared the two together? As she thought of her cousin George's face when he left her room a few days since, and remembered Mr. Grey's countenance when last he held her hand at Cheltenham, the quiet dignity of his beauty which would submit to show no consciousness of injury, she could not but tell herself that when Paradise had been opened to her, she had declared herself to be fit only for Pandemonium. In that was her chief misery; that now,—now when it was too late,—she could look at it aright.

But the letter must be written, and on the second day she declared to herself that she would not rise from her chair till it was done. The letter was written on that day and was posted. I will now ask the reader to go down with me to Nethercoats that we may be present with John Grey when he received it. He was sitting at breakfast in his study there, and opposite to him, lounging in an arm-chair, with a *Quarterly* in his hand, was the most intimate of his friends, Frank Seward, a fellow of the college to which they had both belonged. Mr. Seward was a clergyman, and the tutor of his college, and a man who worked very hard at Cambridge. In the days of his leisure he spent much of his time at Nethercoats, and he was the only man to whom Grey had told anything of his love for Alice and of his disappointment. Even to Seward he had not told the whole story. He had at first informed his friend that he was engaged to be married, and as he had told this as no secret,—having even said that he hated secrets on such matters,—the engagement had been mentioned in the common room of their college, and men at Cambridge knew that Mr. Grey was going to take to himself a wife. Then Mr. Seward had been told that trouble had come, and that it was not improbable that there would be no such marriage. Even when saying this Mr. Grey told none of the particulars, though he owned to his friend that a heavy blow had struck him. His intimacy with Seward was of that thorough kind which is engendered only out of such young and lasting friendship as had existed between them; but even to such a friend as this Mr. Grey could not open his whole heart. It was only to a friend who should also be his wife that he could do that,—as he himself thoroughly understood. He had felt that such a friend was wanting to him, and he had made the attempt.

"Don't speak of this as yet," he had said to Mr. Seward. "Of course when the matter is settled, those few people who know me must know it. But perhaps there may be a doubt as yet, and as long as there is a doubt, it is better that it should not be discussed."

He had said no more than this,—had imputed no blame to Alice,—had told none of the circumstances; but Seward had known that the girl had jilted his friend, and had made up his mind that she must be heartless and false. He had known also that his friend would never look for any other such companion for his home.

Letters were brought to each of them on this morning, and Seward's attention was of course occupied by those which he received. Grey, as soon as the envelopes had touched his hand, became aware that one of them was from Alice, and this he at once opened. He did it very calmly, but without any of that bravado of indifference with which George Vavasor had received Alice's letter from Westmoreland. "It is right that I should tell you at once," said Alice, rushing into the middle of her subject without even the formality of the customary address—"It is right that I should tell you at once that—." Oh, the difficulty which she had encountered when her words had carried her as far as this!—"that my cousin, George Vavasor, has repeated to me his offer of marriage, and that I have accepted it. I tell you, chiefly in order that I may save you from the trouble which you purposed to take when I last saw you at Cheltenham. I will not tell you any of the circumstances of this engagement, because I have no right to presume that you will care to hear them. I hardly dare to ask you to believe of me that in all that I have done, I have endeavoured to act with truth and honesty. That I have been very ignorant, foolish,—what you will that is bad, I know well; otherwise there could not have been so much in the last few years of my life on which I am utterly ashamed to look back. For the injury that I have done you, I can only express deep contrition. I do not dare to ask you to forgive me.—ALICE VAVASOR." She had tormented herself in writing this,—had so nearly driven herself distracted with attempts which she had destroyed, that she would not even read once to herself these last words. "He'll know it, and that is all that is necessary," she said to herself as she sent the letter away from her.

Mr. Grey read it twice over, leaving the other letters unnoticed on the table by his tea-cup. He read it twice over, and the work of reading it was one to him of intense agony. Hitherto he had fed himself with hope. That Alice should have been brought to think of her engagement with him in a spirit of doubt and with a mind so troubled, that she had been inclined to attempt an escape from it, had been very grievous to him; but it had been in his mind a fantasy, a morbid fear of himself, which might be cured by time. He, at any rate, would give all his energies towards achieving such a cure. There had been one thing, however, which he most feared;—which he had chiefly feared, though he had forbidden himself to think that it could be probable, and this thing had now happened.

He had ever disliked and feared George Vavasor;—not from any effect which the man had upon himself, for as we know his acquaintance with Vavasor was of the slightest;—but he had feared and disliked his influence upon Alice. He had also feared the influence of her cousin Kate. To have cautioned Alice against her cousins would have been to him impossible. It was not his nature to express suspicion to one he loved. Is the tone of that letter remembered in which he had answered Alice when she informed him that her cousin George was to go with Kate and her to Switzerland? He had written, with a pleasant joke, words which Alice had been able to read with some little feeling of triumph to her two friends. He had not so written because he liked what he knew of the man. He disliked all that he knew of him. But it had not been possible for him to show that he distrusted the prudence of her, whom, as his future wife, he was prepared to trust in all things.

I have said that he read Alice's letter with an agony of sorrow; as he sat with it in his hand he suffered as, probably, he had never suffered before. But there was nothing in his countenance to show that he was in pain. Seward had received some long epistle, crossed from end to end,—indicative, I should say, of a not far distant termination to that college tutorship,—and was reading it with placid contentment. It did not occur to him to look across at Grey, but had he done so, I doubt whether he would have seen anything to attract his attention. But Grey, though he was wounded, would not allow himself to be dismayed. There was less hope now than before, but there might still be hope;—hope for her, even though there might be none for him. Tidings had reached his ears also as to George Vavasor, which had taught him to believe that the man was needy, reckless, and on the brink of ruin. Such a marriage to Alice Vavasor would be altogether ruinous. Whatever might be his own ultimate fate he would still seek to save her from that. Her cousin, doubtless, wanted her money. Might it not be possible that he would be satisfied with her money, and that thus the woman might be saved?

"Seward," he said at last, addressing his friend, who had not yet come to the end of the last crossed page.

"Is there anything wrong?" said Seward.

"Well;—yes; there is something a little wrong. I fear I must leave you, and go up to town to-day."

"Nobody ill, I hope?"

"No;—nobody is ill. But I must go up to London. Mrs. Bole will take care of you, and you must not be angry with me for leaving you."

Seward assured him that he would not be in the least angry, and that he was thoroughly conversant with the capabilities and good intentions of Mrs. Bole the housekeeper; but added, that as he was so near his own college, he would of course go back to Cambridge. He longed to say some word as to the purpose of Grey's threatened journey; to make some inquiry as to this new trouble; but he knew that Grey was a man who did not well bear close inquiries, and he was silent.

"Why not stay here?" said Grey, after a minute's pause. "I wish you would, old fellow; I do, indeed." There was a tone of special affection in his voice which struck Seward at once. "If I can be of the slightest service or comfort to you, I will of course."

Grey again sat silent for a little while. "I wish you would; I do, indeed."

"Then I will." And again there was a pause.

"I have got a letter here from—Miss Vavasor," said Grey.

"May I hope that—"

"No;—it does not bring good news to me. I do not know that I can tell it you all. I would if I could, but the whole story is one not to be told in a hurry. I should leave false impressions. There are things which a man cannot tell."

"Indeed there are," said Seward.

"I wish with all my heart that you knew it all as I know it; but that is impossible. There are things which happen in a day which it would take a lifetime to explain." Then there was another pause. "I have heard bad news this morning, and I must go up to London at once. I shall go into Ely so as to be there by twelve; and if you will, you shall drive me over. I may be back in a day; certainly in less than a week; but it will be a comfort to me to know that I shall find you here."

The matter was so arranged, and at eleven they started. During the first two miles not a word was spoken between them. "Seward," Grey said at last, "if I fail in what I am going to attempt, it is probable that you will never hear Alice Vavasor's name mentioned by me again; but I want you always to bear this in mind;—that at no moment has my opinion of her ever been changed, nor must you in such case imagine from my silence that it has changed. Do you understand me?"

"I think I do."

"To my thinking she is the finest of God's creatures that I have known. It may be that in her future life she will be severed from me altogether; but I shall not, therefore, think the less well of her; and I wish that you, as my friend, should know that I so esteem her, even though her name should never be mentioned between us." Seward, in some few words, assured him that it should be so, and then they finished their journey in silence.

From the station at Ely, Grey sent a message by the wires up to John Vavasor, saying that he would call on him that afternoon at his office in Chancery Lane. The chances were always much against finding Mr. Vavasor at his office; but on this occasion the telegram did reach him there, and he remained till the unaccustomed hour of half past four to meet the man who was to have been his son-in-law.

"Have you heard from her?" he asked as soon as Grey entered the dingy little room, not in Chancery Lane, but in its neighbourhood, which was allocated to him for his signing purposes.

"Yes," —said Grey; "she has written to me."

"And told you about her cousin George. I tried to hinder her from writing, but she is very wilful."

"Why should you have hindered her? If the thing was to be told, it is better that it should be done at once."

"But I hoped that there might be an escape. I don't know what you think of all this, Grey, but to me it is the bitterest misfortune that I have known. And I've had some bitter things, too," he added, —thinking of that period of his life, when the work of which he was ashamed was first ordained as his future task.

"What is the escape that you hoped?" asked Grey.

"I hardly know. The whole thing seems to me to be so mad, that I partly trusted that she would see the madness of it. I am not sure whether you know anything of my nephew George?" asked Mr. Vavasor.

"Very little," said Grey.

"I believe him to be utterly an adventurer, —a man without means and without principle, —upon the whole about as bad a man as you may meet. I give you my word, Grey, that I don't think I know a worse man. He's going to marry her for her money; then he will beggar her, after that he'll ill-treat her, and yet what can I do?"

"Prevent the marriage."

"But how, my dear fellow? Prevent it! It's all very well to say that, and it's the very thing I want to do. But how am I to prevent it? She's as much her own master as you are yours. She can give him every shilling of her fortune to-morrow. How am I to prevent her from marrying him?"

"Let her give him every shilling of her fortune to-morrow," said Grey.

"And what is she to do then?" asked Mr. Vavasor.

"Then—then,—then,—then let her come to me," said John Grey; and as he spoke there was the fragment of a tear in his eye, and the hint of quiver in his voice.

"Then—then,—then let her come to me

Even the worldly, worn-out, unsympathetic nature of John Vavasor was struck, and, as it were, warmed by this.

"God bless you; God bless you, my dear fellow. I heartily wish for her sake that I could look forward to any such an end to this affair."

"And why not look forward to it? You say that he merely wants her money. As he wants it let him have it!"

"But Grey, you do not know Alice; you do not understand my girl. When she had lost her fortune nothing would induce her to become your wife."

"Leave that to follow as it may," said John Grey. "Our first object must be to sever her from a man, who is, as you say, himself on the verge of ruin; and who would certainly make her wretched. I am here now, not because I wish her to be my own wife, but because I wish that she should not become the wife of such a one as your nephew. If I were you I would let him have her money."

"If you were I, you would have nothing more to do with it than the man that is as yet unborn. I know that she will give him her money because she has said so; but I have no power as to her giving it or as to her withholding it. That's the hardship of my position;—but it is of no use to think of that now."

John Grey certainly did not think about it. He knew well that Alice was independent, and that she was not inclined to give up that independence to anyone. He had not expected that her father would be able to do much towards hindering his daughter from becoming the wife of George Vavasor, but he had wished that he himself and her father should be in accord in their views, and he found that this was so. When he left Mr. Vavasor's room nothing had been said about the period of the marriage. Grey thought it improbable that Alice would find herself able to give herself in marriage to her cousin immediately,—so soon after her breach with him; but as to this he had no assurance, and he determined to have the facts from her own lips, if she would see him. So he wrote to her, naming a day on which he would call upon her early in the morning; and having received from her no prohibition, he was in Queen Anne Street at the hour appointed.

He had conceived a scheme which he had not made known to Mr. Vavasor, and as to the practicability of which he had much doubt; but which, nevertheless, he was resolved to try if he should find the attempt possible. He himself would buy off George Vavasor. He had ever been a prudent man, and he had money at command. If Vavasor was such a man as they, who knew him best, represented him, such a purchase might be possible. But then, before this was attempted, he must be quite sure that he knew his man, and he must satisfy himself also that in doing so he would not, in truth, add to Alice's misery. He could hardly bring himself to think it possible that she did, in truth, love her cousin with passionate love. It seemed to him, as he remembered what Alice had been to himself, that this must be impossible. But if it were so, that of course must put an end to his interference. He thought that if he saw her he might learn all this, and therefore he went to Queen Anne Street.

"Of course he must come if he will," she said to herself when she received his note. "It can make no matter. He will say nothing half so hard to me as what I say to myself all day long." But when the morning came, and the hour came, and the knock at the door for which her ears were on the alert, her heart misgave her, and she felt that the present moment of her punishment, though not the heaviest, would still be hard to bear.

He came slowly up-stairs,—his step was ever slow,—and gently opened the door for himself. Then, before he even looked at her, he closed it again. I do not know how to explain that it was so; but it was this perfect command of himself at all seasons which had in part made Alice afraid of him, and drove her to believe that they were not fitted for each other. She, when he thus turned for a moment from her, and then walked slowly towards her, stood with both her hands leaning on the centre table of the room, and with her eyes fixed upon its surface.

"Alice," he said, walking up to her very slowly.

Her whole frame shuddered as she heard the sweetness of his voice. Had I not better tell the truth of her at once? Oh, if she could only have been his again! What madness during these last six months had driven her to such a plight as this! The old love came back upon her. Nay; it had never gone. But that trust in his love returned to her,—that trust which told her that such love and such worth would have sufficed to make her happy. But this confidence in him was worthless now! Even though he should desire it, she could not change again.

"Alice," he said again. And then, as slowly she looked up at him, he asked her for her hand. "You may give it me," he said, "as to an old friend." She put her hand in his hand, and then, withdrawing it, felt that she must never trust herself to do so again.

"Alice," he continued, "I do not expect you to say much to me; but there is a question or two which I think you will answer. Has a day been fixed for this marriage?"

"No," she said.

"Will it be in a month?"

"Oh, no;—not for a year," she replied hurriedly;—and he knew at once by her voice that she already dreaded this new wedlock. Whatever of anger he might before have felt for her was banished. She had brought herself by her ill-judgement,—by her ignorance, as she had confessed,—to a sad pass; but he believed that she was still worthy of his love.

"And now one other question, Alice;—but if you are silent, I will not ask it again. Can you tell me why you have again accepted your cousin's offer?"

"Because—," she said very quickly, looking up as though she were about to speak with all her old courage. "But you would never understand me," she said,—"and there can be no reason why I should dare to hope that you should ever think well of me again."

He knew that there was no love,—no love for that man to whom she had pledged her hand. He did not know, on the other hand, how strong, how unchanged, how true was her love for himself. Indeed, of himself he was thinking not at all. He desired to learn whether she would suffer, if by any scheme he might succeed in breaking off this marriage. When he had asked her whether she were to be married at once, she had shuddered at the thought. When he asked her why she had accepted her cousin, she had faltered, and hinted at some excuse which he might fail to understand. Had she loved George Vavasor, he could have understood that well enough.

"Alice," he said, speaking still very slowly, "nothing has ever yet been done which need to a certainty separate you and me. I am a persistent man, and I do not even yet give up all hope. A year is a long time. As you say yourself, I do not as yet quite understand you. But, Alice,—and I think that the position in which we stood a few months since justifies me in saying so without offence,—I love you now as well as ever, and should things change with you, I cannot tell you with how much joy and eagerness I should take you back to my bosom. My heart is yours now as it has been since I knew you."

Then he again just touched her hand, and left her before she had been able to answer a word.

CHAPTER XXXVII
MR. TOMBE'S ADVICE

Alice sat alone for an hour without moving when John Grey had left her, and the last words which he had uttered were sounding in her ears all the time, "My heart is still yours, as it has been since I knew you." There had been something in his words which had soothed her spirits, and had, for the moment, almost comforted her. At any rate, he did not despise her. He could not have spoken such words as these to her had he not still held her high in his esteem. Nay;—had he not even declared that he would yet take her as his own if she would come to him? "I cannot tell you with how much joy I would take you back to my bosom!" Ah! that might never be. But yet the assurance had been sweet to her;—dangerously sweet, as she soon told herself. She knew that she had lost her Eden, but it was something to her that the master of the garden had not himself driven her forth. She sat there, thinking of her fate, as though it belonged to some other one,— not to herself; as though it were a tale that she had read. Herself she had shipwrecked altogether; but though she might sink, she had not been thrust from the ship by hands which she loved.

But would it not have been better that he should have scorned her and reviled her? Had he been able to do so, he at least would have escaped the grief of disappointed love. Had he learned to despise her, he would have ceased to regret her. She had no right to feel consolation in the fact that his sufferings were equal to her own. But when she thought of this, she told herself that it could not be that it was so. He was a man, she said, not passionate by nature. Alas! it was the mistake she had ever made when summing up the items of his character! He might be persistent, she thought, in still striving to do that upon which he had once resolved. He had said so, and that which he said was always true to the letter. But, nevertheless, when this thing which he still chose to pursue should have been put absolutely beyond his reach, he would not allow his calm bosom to be harassed by a vain regret. He was a man too whole at every point,—so Alice told herself,— to allow his happiness to be marred by such an accident.

But must the accident occur? Was there no chance that he might be saved, even from such trouble as might follow upon such a loss? Could it not be possible that he might be gratified,—since it would gratify him,— and that she might be saved! Over and over again she considered this,—but always as though it were another woman whom she would fain save, and not herself.

But she knew that her own fate was fixed. She had been mad when she had done the thing, but the thing was not on that account the less done. She had been mad when she had trusted herself abroad with two persons, both of whom, as she had well known, were intent on wrenching her happiness from out of her grasp. She had been mad when she had told herself, whilst walking over the Westmoreland fells, that after all she might as well marry her cousin, since that other marriage was then beyond her reach! Her two cousins had succeeded in blighting all the hopes of her life;—but what could she now think of herself in that she had been so weak as to submit to such usage from their hands? Alas!—she told herself, admitting in her misery all her weakness,—alas, she had no mother. She had gloried in her independence, and this had come of it! She had scorned the prudence of Lady Macleod, and her scorn had brought her to this pass!

Was she to give herself bodily,—body and soul, as she said aloud in her solitary agony,—to a man whom she did not love? Must she submit to his caresses,—lie on his bosom,—turn herself warmly to his kisses? "No," she said, "no,"—speaking audibly, as she walked about the room; "no;—it was not in my bargain; I never meant it." But if so what had she meant;—what had been her dream? Of what marriage had she thought, when she was writing that letter back to George Vavasor? How am I to analyse her mind, and make her thoughts and feelings intelligible to those who may care to trouble themselves with the study? Any sacrifice she would make for her cousin which one friend could make for another. She would fight his battles with her money, with her words, with her sympathy. She would sit with him if he needed it, and speak comfort to him by the hour. His disgrace should be her disgrace;—his glory her glory;—his pursuits her pursuits. Was not that the marriage to which she had consented? But he had come to her and asked her for a kiss, and she had shuddered before him, when he made the demand. Then that other one had come and had touched her hand, and the fibres of her body had seemed to melt within her at the touch, so that she could have fallen at his feet.

She had done very wrong. She knew that she had done wrong. She knew that she had sinned with that sin which specially disgraces a woman. She had said that she would become the wife of a man to whom she could not cleave with a wife's love; and, mad with a vile ambition, she had given up the man for whose modest love her heart was longing. She had thrown off from her that wondrous aroma of precious delicacy, which is the greatest treasure of womanhood. She had sinned against her sex; and, in an agony of despair, as she crouched down upon the floor with her head against her chair, she told herself that there was no pardon for her. She understood it now, and knew that she could not forgive herself.

But can you forgive her, delicate reader? Or am I asking the question too early in my story? For myself, I have forgiven her. The story of the struggle has been present to my mind for many years,—and I have learned to think that even this offence against womanhood may, with deep repentance, be forgiven. And you also must forgive her before we close the book, or else my story will have been told amiss.

But let us own that she had sinned,—almost damnably, almost past forgiveness. What;—think that she knew what love meant, and not know which of two she loved! What;—doubt, of two men for whose arms she longed, of which the kisses would be sweet to bear; on which side lay the modesty of her maiden love! Faugh! She had submitted to pollution of heart and feeling before she had brought herself to such a pass as this. Come;—let us see if it be possible that she may be cleansed by the fire of her sorrow.

"What am I to do?" She passed that whole day in asking herself that question. She was herself astounded at the rapidity with which the conviction had forced itself upon her that a marriage with her cousin would be to her almost impossible; and could she permit it to be said of her that she had thrice in her career jilted a promised suitor,—that three times she would go back from her word because her fancy had changed? Where could she find the courage to tell her father, to tell Kate, to tell even George himself, that her purpose was again altered? But she had a year at her disposal. If only during that year he would take her money and squander it, and then require nothing further of her hands, might she not thus escape the doom before her? Might it not be possible that the refusal should this time come from him? But she succeeded in making one resolve. She thought at least that she succeeded. Come what might, she would never stand with him at the altar. While there was a cliff from which she might fall, water that would cover her, a death-dealing grain that might be mixed in her cup, she could not submit herself to be George Vavasor's wife. To no ear could she tell of this resolve. To no friend could she hint her purpose. She owed her money to the man after what had passed between them. It was his right to count upon such assistance as that would give him, and he should have it. Only as his betrothed she could give it him, for she understood well that if there were any breach between them, his accepting of such aid would be impossible. He should have her money, and then, when the day came, some escape should be found.

In the afternoon her father came to her, and it may be as well to explain that Mr. Grey had seen him again that day. Mr. Grey, when he left Queen Anne Street, had gone to his lawyer, and from thence had made his way to Mr. Vavasor. It was between five and six when Mr. Vavasor came back to his house, and he then found his daughter sitting over the drawing-room fire, without lights, in the gloom of the evening. Mr. Vavasor had returned with Grey to the lawyer's chambers, and had from thence come direct to his own house. He had been startled at the precision with which all the circumstances of his daughter's position had been explained to a mild-eyed old gentleman, with a bald head, who carried on his business in a narrow, dark, clean street, behind Doctors' Commons. Mr. Tombe was his name. "No;" Mr. Grey had said, when Mr. Vavasor had asked as to the peculiar nature of Mr. Tombe's business; "he is not specially an ecclesiastical lawyer. He had a partner at Ely, and was always employed by my father, and by most of the clergy there." Mr. Tombe had evinced no surprise, no dismay, and certainly no mock delicacy, when the whole affair was under discussion. George Vavasor was to get present moneys, but,—if it could be so arranged—from John Grey's stores rather than from those belonging to Alice. Mr. Tombe could probably arrange that with Mr. Vavasor's lawyer, who would no doubt be able to make difficulty as to raising ready money. Mr. Tombe would be able to raise ready money without difficulty. And then, at last, George Vavasor was to be made to surrender his bride, taking or having taken the price of his bargain. John Vavasor sat by in silence as the arrangement was being made, not knowing how to speak. He had no money with which to give assistance. "I wish you to understand from the lady's father," Grey said to the lawyer, "that the marriage would be regarded by him with as much dismay as by myself."

"Certainly;—it would be ruinous," Mr. Vavasor had answered.

"And you see, Mr. Tombe," Mr. Grey went on, "we only wish to try the man. If he be not such as we believe him to be, he can prove it by his conduct. If he is worthy of her, he can then take her."

"You merely wish to open her eyes, Mr. Grey," said the mild-eyed lawyer.

"I wish that he should have what money he wants, and then we shall find what it is he really wishes."

"Yes; we shall know our man," said the lawyer. "He shall have the money, Mr. Grey," and so the interview had been ended.

Mr. Vavasor, when he entered the drawing-room, addressed his daughter in a cheery voice. "What; all in the dark?"

"Yes, papa. Why should I have candles when I am doing nothing? I did not expect you."

"No; I suppose not. I came here because I want to say a few words to you about business."

"What business, papa?" Alice well understood the tone of her father's voice. He was desirous of propitiating her; but was at the same time desirous of carrying some point in which he thought it probable that she would oppose him.

"Well; my love, if I understood you rightly, your cousin George wants some money."

"I did not say that he wants it now; but I think he will want it before the time for the election comes."

"If so, he will want it at once. He has not asked you for it yet?"

"No; he has merely said that should he be in need he would take me at my word."

"I think there is no doubt that he wants it. Indeed, I believe that he is almost entirely without present means of his own."

"I can hardly think so; but I have no knowledge about it. I can only say that he has not asked me yet, and that I should wish to oblige him whenever he may do so."

"To what extent, Alice?"

"I don't know what I have. I get about four hundred a year, but I do not know what it is worth, or how far it can all be turned into money. I should wish to keep a hundred a year and let him have the rest."

"What; eight thousand pounds!" said the father who in spite of his wish not to oppose her, could not but express his dismay.

"I do not imagine that he will want so much; but if he should, I wish that he should have it."

"Heaven and earth!" said John Vavasor. "Of course we should have to give up the house." He could not suppress his trouble, or refrain from bursting out in agony at the prospect of such a loss.

"But he has asked me for nothing yet, papa."

"No, exactly; and perhaps he may not; but I wish to know what to do when the demand is made. I am not going to oppose you now; your money is your own, and you have a right to do with it as you please;—but would you gratify me in one thing?"

"What is it, papa?"

"When he does apply, let the amount be raised through me?"

"How through you?"

"Come to me; I mean, so that I may see the lawyer, and have the arrangements made." Then he explained to her that in dealing with large sums of money, it could not be right that she should do so without his knowledge, even though the property was her own. "I will promise you that I will not oppose your wishes," he said. Then Alice undertook that when such case should arise the money should be raised through his means.

The day but one following this she received a letter from Lady Glencora, who was still at Matching Priory. It was a light-spirited, chatty, amusing letter, intended to be happy in its tone,—intended to have a flavour of happiness, but just failing through the too apparent meaning of a word here and there. "You will see that I am at Matching," the letter said, "whereas you will remember that I was to have been at Monkshade. I escaped at last by a violent effort, and am now passing my time innocently,—I fear not so profitably as she would induce me to do,—with Iphy Palliser. You remember Iphy. She is a good creature, and would fain turn even me to profit, if it were possible. I own that I am thinking of them all at Monkshade, and am in truth delighted that I am not there. My absence is entirely laid upon your shoulders. That wicked evening amidst the ruins! Poor ruins. I go there alone sometimes and fancy that I hear such voices from the walls, and see such faces through the broken windows! All the old Pallisers come and frown at me, and tell me that I am not good enough to belong to them. There is a particular window to which Sir Guy comes and makes faces at me. I told Iphy the other day, and she answered me very gravely, that I might, if I chose, make myself good enough for the Pallisers. Even for the Pallisers! Isn't that beautiful?"

Then Lady Glencora went on to say, that her husband intended to come up to London early in the session, and that she would accompany him. "That is," added Lady Glencora, "if I am still good enough for the Pallisers at that time."

CHAPTER XXXVIII
THE INN AT SHAP

When George Vavasor left Mr. Scruby's office—the attentive reader will remember that he did call upon Mr. Scruby, the Parliamentary lawyer, and there recognised the necessity of putting himself in possession of a small sum of money with as little delay as possible;—when he left the attorney's office, he was well aware that the work to be done was still before him. And he knew also that the job to be undertaken was a very disagreeable job. He did not like the task of borrowing his cousin Alice's money.

We all of us know that swindlers and rogues do very dirty tricks, and we are apt to picture to ourselves a certain amount of gusto and delight on the part of the swindlers in the doing of them. In this, I think we are wrong. The poor, broken, semi-genteel beggar, who borrows half-sovereigns apiece from all his old acquaintances, knowing that they know that he will never repay them, suffers a separate little agony with each petition that he makes. He does not enjoy pleasant sailing in this journey which he is making. To be refused is painful to him. To get his half sovereign with scorn is painful. To get it with apparent confidence in his honour is almost more painful. "D—— it," he says to himself on such rare occasions, "I will pay that fellow;" and yet, as he says it, he knows that he never will pay even that fellow. It is a comfortless unsatisfying trade, that of living upon other people's money.

How was George Vavasor to make his first step towards getting his hand into his cousin's purse? He had gone to her asking for her love, and she had shuddered when he asked her. That had been the commencement of their life under their new engagement. He knew very well that the money would be forthcoming when he demanded it,—but under their present joint circumstances, how was he to make the demand? If he wrote to her, should he simply ask for money, and make no allusion to his love? If he went to her in person, should he make his visit a mere visit of business,—as he might call on his banker?

He resolved at last that Kate should do the work for him. Indeed, he had felt all along that it would be well that Kate should act as ambassador between him and Alice in money matters, as she had long done in other things. He could talk to Kate as he could not talk to Alice;—and then, between the women, those hard money necessities would be softened down by a romantic phraseology which he would not himself know how to use with any effect. He made up his mind to see Kate, and with this view he went down to Westmoreland; and took himself to a small wayside inn at Shap among the fells, which had been known to him of old. He gave his sister notice that he would be there, and begged her to come over to him as early as she might find it possible on the morning after his arrival. He himself reached the place late in the evening by train from London. There is a station at Shap, by which the railway company no doubt conceives that it has conferred on that somewhat rough and remote locality all the advantages of a refined civilization; but I doubt whether the Shappites have been thankful for the favour. The landlord at the inn, for one, is not thankful. Shap had been a place owing all such life as it had possessed to coaching and posting. It had been a stage on the high road from Lancaster to Carlisle, and though it lay high and bleak among the fells, and was a cold, windy, thinly-populated place,—filling all travellers with thankfulness that they had not been made Shappites, nevertheless, it had had its glory in its coaching and posting. I have no doubt that there are men and women who look back with a fond regret to the palmy days of Shap.

Vavasor reached the little inn about nine in the evening on a night that was pitchy dark, and in a wind which made it necessary for him to hold his hat on to his head. "What a beastly country to live in," he said to himself, resolving that he would certainly sell Vavasor Hall in spite of all family associations, if ever the power to do so should be his. "What trash it is," he said, "hanging on to such a place as that without the means of living like a gentleman, simply because one's ancestors have done so." And then he expressed a doubt to himself whether all the world contained a more ignorant, opinionated, useless old man than his grandfather,—or, in short, a greater fool.

"Well, Mr. George," said the landlord as soon as he saw him, "a sight of you's guid for sair een. It's o'er lang since you've been doon amang the fells." But George did not want to converse with the innkeeper, or to explain how it was that he did not visit Vavasor Hall. The innkeeper, no doubt, knew all about it,—knew that the grandfather had quarrelled with his grandson, and knew the reason why; but George, if he suspected such knowledge, did not choose to refer to it. So he simply grunted something in reply, and getting himself in before a spark of fire which hardly was burning in a public room with a sandy floor, begged that the little sitting-room up-stairs might be got ready for him. There he passed the evening in solitude, giving no encouragement to the landlord, who, nevertheless, looked him up three or four times,—till at last George said that his head ached, and that he would wish to be alone. "He was always one of them cankery chiels as never have a kindly word for man nor beast," said the landlord. "Seems as though that raw slash in his face had gone right through into his heart." After that George was left alone, and sat thinking whether it would not be better to ask Alice for two thousand pounds at once,—so as to save him from the disagreeable necessity of a second borrowing before their marriage. He was very uneasy in his mind. He had flattered himself through it all that his cousin had loved him. He had felt sure that such was the case while they were together in Switzerland. When she had determined to give up John Grey, of course he had told himself the same thing. When she had at once answered his first subsequent overture with an assent, he had of course been certain that it was so. Dark, selfish, and even dishonest as he was, he had, nevertheless, enjoyed something of a lover's true pleasure in believing that Alice had still loved him through all their mischances. But his joy had in a moment been turned into gall during that interview in Queen Anne Street. He had read the truth at a glance. A man must be very vain, or else very little used to such matters, who at George Vavasor's age cannot understand the feelings with which a woman receives him. When Alice contrived as she had done to escape the embrace he was so well justified in asking, he knew the whole truth. He was sore at heart, and very angry withal. He could have readily spurned her from him, and rejected her who had once rejected him. He would have done so had not his need for her money restrained him. He was not a man who could deceive himself in such matters. He knew that this was so, and he told himself that he was a rascal.

Vavasor Hall was, by the road, about five miles from Shap, and it was not altogether an easy task for Kate to get over to the village without informing her grandfather that the visit was to be made, and what was its purport. She could, indeed, walk, and the walk would not be so long as that she had taken with Alice to Swindale fell;—but walking to an inn on a high road, is not the same thing as walking to a point on a hill side over a lake. Had she been dirty, draggled, and wet through on Swindale fell, it would have simply been matter for mirth; but her brother she knew would not have liked to see her enter the Lowther Arms at Shap in such a condition. It, therefore, became necessary that she should ask her grandfather to lend her the jaunting car.

"Where do you want to go?" he asked sharply. In such establishments as that at Vavasor Hall the family horse is generally used for double duties. Though he draws the lady of the house one day, he is not too proud to draw manure on the next. And it will always be found that the master of the house gives a great preference to the manure over the lady. The squire at Vavasor had come to do so to such an extent that he regarded any application for the animal's services as an encroachment.

"Only to Shap, grandpapa."

"To Shap! what on earth can take you to Shap? There are no shops at Shap."

"I am not going to do shopping. I want to see some one there."

"Whom can you want to see at Shap?"

Then it occurred to Kate on the spur of the moment that she might as well tell her grandfather the fact. "My brother has come down," she said; "and is at the inn there. I had not intended to tell you, as I did not wish to mention his name till you had consented to receive him here."

"And he expects to come here now;—does he?" said the squire.

"Oh, no, sir. I think he has no expectation of the kind. He has come down simply to see me;—about business I believe."

"Business! what business? I suppose he wants to get your money from you?"

"I think it is with reference to his marriage. I think he wants me to use my influence with Alice that it may not be delayed."

"Look here, Kate; if ever you lend him your money, or any of it,—that is, of the principal I mean,—I will never speak to him again under any circumstance. And more than that! Look here, Kate. In spite of all that has past and gone, the property will become his for his life when I die,—unless I change my will. If he gets your money from you, I will change it, and he shall not be a shilling richer at my death than he is now. You can have the horse to go to Shap."

What unlucky chance had it been which had put this idea into the old squire's head on this especial morning? Kate had resolved that she would entreat her brother to make use of her little fortune. She feared that he was now coming with some reference to his cousin's money,—that something was to be done to enable him to avail himself of his cousin's offer; and Kate, almost blushing in the solitude of her chamber at the thought, was determined that her brother must be saved from such temptation. She knew that money was necessary to him. She knew that he could not stand a second contest without assistance. With all their confidences, he had never told her much of his pecuniary circumstances in the world, but she was almost sure that he was a poor man. He had said as much as that to her, and in his letter desiring her to come to him at Shap, he had inserted a word or two purposely intended to prepare her mind for monetary considerations.

As she was jogged along over the rough road to Shap, she made up her mind that Aunt Greenow would be the proper person to defray the expense of the coming election. To give Kate her due she would have given up every shilling of her own money without a moment's hesitation, or any feeling that her brother would be wrong to accept it. Nor would she, perhaps, have been unalterably opposed to his taking Alice's money, had Alice simply been his cousin. She felt that as Vavasors they were bound to stand by the future head of the family in an attempt which was to be made, as she felt, for the general Vavasor interest. But she could not endure to think that her brother should take the money of the girl whom he was engaged to marry. Aunt Greenow's money she thought was fair game. Aunt Greenow herself had made various liberal offers to herself which Kate had declined, not caring to be under pecuniary obligations even to Aunt Greenow without necessity; but she felt that for such a purpose as her brother's contest, she need not hesitate to ask for assistance, and she thought also that such assistance would be forthcoming.

"Grandpapa knows that you are here, George," said Kate, when their first greeting was over.

"The deuce he does! and why did you tell him?"

"I could not get the car to come in without letting him know why I wanted it."

"What nonsense! as if you couldn't have made any excuse! I was particularly anxious that he should not guess that I am here."

"I don't see that it can make any difference, George."

"But I see that it can,—a very great difference. It may prevent my ever being able to get near him again before he dies. What did he say about my coming?"

"He didn't say much."

"He made no offer as to my going there?"

"No."

"I should not have gone if he had. I don't know now that I ever shall go. To be there to do any good,—so as to make him alter his will, and leave me in the position which I have a right to expect, would take more time than the whole property is worth. And he would endeavour to tie me down in some way I could not stand;—perhaps ask me to give up my notion for going into Parliament."

"He might ask you, but he would not make it ground for another quarrel, if you refused."

"He is so unreasonable and ignorant that I am better away from him. But, Kate, you have not congratulated me on my matrimonial prospects."

"Indeed I did, George, when I wrote to you."

"Did you? well; I had forgotten. I don't know that any very strong congratulatory tone is necessary. As things go, perhaps it may be as well for all of us, and that's about the best that can be said for it."

"Oh, George!"

"You see I'm not romantic, Kate, as you are. Half a dozen children with a small income do not generally present themselves as being desirable to men who wish to push their way in the world."

"You know you have always longed to make her your wife."

"I don't know anything of the kind. You have always been under a match-making hallucination on that point. But in this case you have been so far successful, and are entitled to your triumph."

"I don't want any triumph; you ought to know that."

"But I'll tell you what I do want, Kate. I want some money." Then he paused, but as she did not answer immediately, he was obliged to go on speaking. "I'm not at all sure that I have not been wrong in making this attempt to get into Parliament,—that I'm not struggling to pick fruit which is above my reach."

"Don't say that, George."

"Ah, but I can't help feeling it. I need hardly tell you that I am ready to risk anything of my own. If I know myself I would toss up to-morrow, or for the matter of that to-day, between the gallows and a seat in the House. But I cannot go on with this contest by risking what is merely my own. Money, for immediate use, I have none left, and my neck, though I were ever so willing to risk it, is of no service."

"Whatever I have can be yours to-morrow," said Kate, in a hesitating voice, which too plainly pronounced her misery as she made the offer. She could not refrain herself from making it. Though her grandfather's threat was ringing in her ears,—though she knew that she might be ruining her brother by proposing such a loan, she had no alternative. When her brother told her of his want of money, she could not abstain from tendering to him the use of what was her own.

"No;" said he. "I shall not take your money."

"You would not scruple, if you knew how welcome you are."

"At any rate, I shall not take it. I should not think it right. All that you have would only just suffice for my present wants, and I should not choose to make you a beggar. There would, moreover, be a difficulty about readjusting the payment."

"There would be no difficulty, because no one need be consulted but us two."

"I should not think it right, and therefore let there be an end of it," said George in a tone of voice which had in it something of magniloquence.

"What is it you wish then?" said Kate, who knew too well what he did wish.

"I will explain to you. When Alice and I are married, of course there will be a settlement made on her, and as we are both the grandchildren of the old squire I shall propose that the Vavasor property shall be hers for life in the event of her outliving me."

"Well," said Kate.

"And if this be done, there can be no harm in my forestalling some of her property, which, under the circumstances of such a settlement, would of course become mine when we are married."

"But the squire might leave the property to whom he pleases."

"We know very well that he won't, at any rate, leave it out of the family. In fact, he would only be too glad to consent to such an agreement as that I have proposed, because he would thereby rob me of all power in the matter."

"But that could not be done till you are married."

"Look here, Kate;—don't you make difficulties." And now, as he looked at her, the cicature on his face seemed to open and yawn at her. "If you mean to say that you won't help me, do say so, and I will go back to London."

"I would do anything in my power to help you,—that was not wrong!"

"Yes; anybody could say as much as that. That is not much of an offer if you are to keep to yourself the power of deciding what is wrong. Will you write to Alice,—or better still, go to her, and explain that I want the money."

"How can I go to London now?"

"You can do it very well, if you choose. But if that be too much, then write to her. It will come much better from you than from me; write to her, and explain that I must pay in advance the expenses of this contest, and that I cannot look for success unless I do so. I did not think that the demand would come so quick on me; but they know that I am not a man of capital, and therefore I cannot expect them to carry on the fight for me, unless they know that the money is sure. Scruby has been bitten two or three times by these metropolitan fellows, and he is determined that he will not be bitten again." Then he paused for Kate to speak.

"George," she said, slowly.

"Well."

"I wish you would try any other scheme but that."

"There is no other scheme! That's so like a woman;—to quarrel with the only plan that is practicable."

"I do not think you ought to take Alice's money."

"My dear Kate, you must allow me to be the best judge of what I ought to do, and what I ought not to do. Alice herself understands the matter perfectly. She knows that I cannot obtain this position, which is as desirable for her as it is for me—"

"And for me as much as for either," said Kate, interrupting him.

"Very well. Alice, I say, knows that I cannot do this without money, and has offered the assistance which I want. I would rather that you should tell her how much I want, and that I want it now, than that I should do so. That is all. If you are half the woman that I take you to be, you will understand this well enough."

Kate did understand it well enough. She was quite awake to the fact that her brother was ashamed of the thing he was about to do,—so much ashamed of it that he was desirous of using her voice instead of his own. "I want you to write to her quite at once," he continued; "since you seem to think that it is not worth while to take the trouble of a journey to London."

"There is no question about the trouble," said Kate. "I would walk to London to get the money for you, if that were all."

"Do you think that Alice will refuse to lend it me?" said he, looking into her face.

"I am sure that she would not, but I think that you ought not to take it from her. There seems to me to be something sacred about property that belongs to the girl you are going to marry."

"If there is anything on earth I hate," said George, walking about the room, "it is romance. If you keep it for reading in your bedroom, it's all very well for those who like it, but when it comes to be mixed up with one's business it plays the devil. If you would only sift what you have said, you would see what nonsense it is. Alice and I are to be man and wife. All our interests, and all our money, and our station in life, whatever it may be, are to be joint property. And yet she is the last person in the world to whom I ought to go for money to improve her prospects as well as my own. That's what you call delicacy. I call it infernal nonsense."

"I tell you what I'll do, George. I'll ask Aunt Greenow to lend you the money,—or to lend it to me."

"I don't believe she'd give me a shilling. Moreover, I want it quite immediately, and the time taken up in letter-writing and negotiations would be fatal to me. If you won't apply to Alice, I must. I want you to tell me whether you will oblige me in this matter."

Kate was still hesitating as to her answer, when there came a knock at the door, and a little crumpled note was brought up to her. A boy had just come with it across the fell from Vavasor Hall, and Kate, as soon as she saw her name on the outside, knew that it was from her grandfather. It was as follows:—

"If George wishes to come to the Hall, let him come. If he chooses to tell me that he regrets his conduct to me, I will see him."

"What is it?" said George. Then Kate put the note into her brother's hand.

"I'll do nothing of the kind," he said. "What good should I get by going to the old man's house?"

"Every good," said Kate. "If you don't go now you never can do so."

"Never till it's my own," said George.

"If you show him that you are determined to be at variance with him, it never will be your own;—unless, indeed, it should some day come to you as part of Alice's fortune. Think of it, George; you would not like to receive everything from her."

He walked about the room, muttering maledictions between his teeth and balancing, as best he was able at such a moment, his pride against his profit. "You haven't answered my question," said he. "If I go to the Hall, will you write to Alice?"

"No, George; I cannot write to Alice asking her for the money."

"You won't?"

"I could not bring myself to do it."

"Then, Kate, you and my grandfather may work together for the future. You may get him to leave you the place if you have skill enough."

"That is as undeserved a reproach as any woman ever encountered," said Kate, standing her ground boldly before him. "If you have either heart or conscience, you will feel that it is so."

"I'm not much troubled with either one or the other, I fancy. Things are being brought to such a pass with me that I am better without them."

"Will you take my money, George; just for the present?"

"No. I haven't much conscience; but I have a little left."

"Will you let me write to Mrs. Greenow?"

"I have not the slightest objection; but it will be of no use whatsoever."

"I will do so, at any rate. And now will you come to the Hall?"

"To beg that old fool's pardon? No; I won't. In the mood I am in at present, I couldn't do it. I should only anger him worse than ever. Tell him that I've business which calls me back to London at once."

"It is a thousand pities."

"It can't be helped."

"It may make so great a difference to you for your whole life!" urged Kate.

"I'll tell you what I'll do," said George. "I'll go to Vavasor and put up with the old squire's insolence, if you'll make this application for me to Alice." I wonder whether it occurred to him that his sister desired his presence at the Hall solely on his own behalf. The same idea certainly did not occur to Kate. She hesitated, feeling that she would almost do anything to achieve a reconciliation between her grandfather and her brother.

"But you'll let me write to Aunt Greenow first," said she. "It will take only two days,—or at the most three?"

To this George consented as though he were yielding a great deal; and Kate, with a sore conscience, with a full knowledge that she was undertaking to do wrong, promised that she would apply to Alice for her money, if sufficient funds should not be forthcoming from Mrs. Greenow. Thereupon, George graciously consented to proceed to his bedroom, and put together his clothes with a view to his visit to the Hall.

"I thank Providence, Kate, that circumstances make it impossible for me to stay above two days. I have not linen to last me longer."

"We'll manage that for you at the Hall."

"Indeed you won't do anything of the kind. And look, Kate, when I make that excuse don't you offer to do so. I will stay there over to-morrow night, and shall go into Kendal early, so as to catch the express train up on Thursday morning. Don't you throw me over by any counter proposition."

Then they started together in the car, and very few words were said till they reached the old lodge, which stood at the entrance to the place. "Eh, Mr. George; be that you?" said the old woman, who came out to swing back for them the broken gate. "A sight of you is good for sair een." It was the same welcome that the inn-keeper had given him, and equally sincere. George had never made himself popular about the place, but he was the heir.

"I suppose you had better go into the drawing-room," said Kate; "while I go to my grandfather. You won't find a fire there."

"Manage it how you please; but don't keep me in the cold very long. Heavens, what a country house! The middle of January, and no fires in the room."

"And remember, George, when you see him you must say that you regret that you ever displeased him. Now that you are here, don't let there be any further misunderstanding."

"I think it very probable that there will be," said George. "I only hope he'll let me have the old horse to take me back to Shap if there is. There he is at the front door, so I shan't have to go into the room without a fire."

The old man was standing at the hall steps when the car drove up, as though to welcome his grandson. He put out his hand to help Kate down the steps, keeping his eye all the time on George's face.

"So you've come back," the squire said to him.

"So you've come back, have you?" said the Squire.

"Yes, sir;—I've come back, like the prodigal son in the parable."

"The prodigal son was contrite. I hope you are so."

"Pretty well for that, sir. I'm sorry there has been any quarrel, and all that, you know."

"Go in," said the squire, very angrily. "Go in. To expect anything gracious from you would be to expect pearls from swine. Go in."

George went in, shrugging his shoulders as his eyes met his sister's. It was in this fashion that the reconciliation took place between Squire Vavasor and his heir.

CHAPTER XXXIX
MR. CHEESACRE'S HOSPITALITY

As the winter wore itself away, Mr. Cheesacre, happy as he was amidst the sports of Norfolk, and prosperous as he might be with the augean spoils of Oileymead, fretted himself with an intense anxiety to bring to a close that affair which he had on his hands with the widow Greenow. There were two special dangers which disturbed him. She would give herself and all her money to that adventurer, Bellfield; or else she would spend her own money so fast before he got hold upon it, that the prize would be greatly damaged. "I'm —— if she hasn't been and set up a carriage!" he said to himself one day, as standing on the pavement of Tombland, in Norwich, he saw Mrs. Greenow issue forth from the Close in a private brougham, accompanied by one of the Fairstairs girls. "She's been and set up her carriage as sure as my name's Cheesacre!"

Whatever reason he might have to fear the former danger, we may declare that he had none whatever as to the latter. Mrs. Greenow knew what she was doing with her money as well as any lady in England. The private carriage was only a hired brougham taken by the month, and as to that boy in buttons whom she had lately established, why should she not keep a young servant, and call him a page, if it gave her any comfort to do so? If Mr. Cheesacre had also known that she had lent the Fairstairs family fifty pounds to help them through with some difficulty which Joe had encountered with the Norwich tradespeople, he would have been beside himself with dismay. He desired to obtain the prize unmutilated,—in all its fair proportions. Any such clippings he regarded as robberies against himself.

But he feared Bellfield more than he feared the brougham. That all is fair in love and war was no doubt, at this period, Captain Bellfield's maxim, and we can only trust that he found in it some consolation, or ease to his conscience, in regard to the monstrous lies which he told his friend. In war, no doubt, all stratagems are fair. The one general is quite justified in making the other believe that he is far to the right, when in truth he is turning his enemy's left flank. If successful, he will be put upon a pedestal for his clever deceit, and crowned with laurels because of his lie. If Bellfield could only be successful, and achieve for himself the mastery over those forty thousand pounds, the world would forgive him and place, on his brow also, some not uncomfortable crown. In the mean time, his stratagems were as deep and his lies as profound as those of any general.

It must not be supposed that Cheesacre ever believed him. In the first place, he knew that Bellfield was not a man to be believed in any way. Had he not been living on lies for the last ten years? But then a man may lie in such a way as to deceive, though no one believe him. Mr. Cheesacre was kept in an agony of doubt while Captain Bellfield occupied his lodgings in Norwich. He fee'd Jeannette liberally. He even fee'd Charlie Fairstairs,—Miss Fairstairs I mean,—with gloves, and chickens from Oileymead, so that he might know whether that kite fluttered about his dovecoat, and of what nature were the flutterings. He went even further than this, and fee'd the Captain himself,—binding him down not to flutter as value given in return for such fees. He attempted even to fee the widow,—cautioning her against the fluttering, as he tendered to her, on his knees, a brooch as big as a breast-plate. She waved aside the breast-plate, declaring that the mourning ring which contained poor Greenow's final grey lock of hair, was the last article from a jeweller's shop which should ever find a place about her person. At the same time she declared that Captain Bellfield was nothing to her; Mr. Cheesacre need have no fears in that quarter. But then, she added, neither was he to have any hope. Her affections were all buried under the cold sod. This was harassing. Nevertheless, though no absolute satisfaction was to be attained in the wooing of Mrs. Greenow, there was a pleasantness in the occupation which ought to have reconciled her suitors to their destiny. With most ladies, when a gentleman has been on his knees before one of them in the morning, with outspoken protestations of love, with clearly defined proffers of marriage, with a minute inventory of the offerer's worldly wealth,—down even to the "mahogany-furnitured" bed-chambers, as was the case with Mr. Cheesacre, and when all these overtures have been peremptorily declined,—a gentleman in such a case, I say, would generally feel some awkwardness in sitting down to tea with the lady at the close of such a performance. But with Mrs. Greenow there was no such awkwardness. After an hour's work of the nature above described she would play the hostess with a genial hospitality, that eased off all the annoyance of disappointment; and then at the end of the evening, she would accept a squeeze of the hand, a good, palpable, long-protracted squeeze, with that sort of "don't;—have done now," by which Irish young ladies allure their lovers. Mr. Cheesacre, on such occasions, would leave the Close, swearing that she should be his on the next market-day,—or at any rate, on the next Saturday. Then, on the Monday, tidings would reach him that Bellfield had passed all Sunday afternoon with his lady-love,—Bellfield, to whom he had lent five pounds on purpose that he might be enabled to spend that very Sunday with some officers of the Suffolk volunteers at Ipswich. And hearing this, he would walk out among those rich heaps, at the back of his farmyard, uttering deep curses against the falsehood of men and the fickleness of women.

Driven to despair, he at last resolved to ask Bellfield to come to Oileymead for a month. That drilling at Norwich, or the part of it which was supposed to be profitable, was wearing itself out. Funds were low with the Captain,—as he did not scruple to tell his friend Cheesacre, and he accepted the invitation. "I'll mount you with the harriers, old fellow," Cheesacre had said; "and give you a little shooting. Only I won't have you go out when I'm not with you." Bellfield agreed. Each of them understood the nature of the bargain; though Bellfield, I think, had somewhat the clearer understanding in the matter. He would not be so near the widow as he had been at Norwich, but he would not be less near than his kind host. And his host would no doubt watch him closely;—but then he also could watch his host. There was a railway station not two miles from Oileymead, and the journey thence into Norwich was one of half an hour. Mr. Cheesacre would doubtless be very jealous of such journeys, but with all his jealousy he could not prevent them. And then, in regard to this arrangement, Mr. Cheesacre paid the piper, whereas Captain Bellfield paid nothing. Would it not be sweet to him if he could carry off his friend's prize from under the very eaves of his friend's house?

And Mrs. Greenow also understood the arrangement. "Going to Oileymead; are you?" she said when Captain Bellfield came to tell her of his departure. Charlie Fairstairs was with her, so that the Captain could not utilize the moment in any special way. "It's quite delightful," continued the widow, "to see how fond you two gentlemen are of each other."

"I think gentlemen always like to go best to gentlemen's houses where there are no ladies," said Charlie Fairstairs, whose career in life had not as yet been satisfactory to her.

"As for that," said Bellfield, "I wish with all my heart that dear old Cheesy would get a wife. He wants a wife badly, if ever a man did, with all that house full of blankets and crockery. Why don't you set your cap at him, Miss Fairstairs?"

"What;—at a farmer!" said Charlie who was particularly anxious that her dear friend, Mrs. Greenow, should not marry Mr. Cheesacre, and who weakly thought to belittle him accordingly.

"Give him my kind love," said Mrs. Greenow, thereby resenting the impotent interference. "And look here, Captain Bellfield, suppose you both dine with me next Saturday. He always comes in on Saturday, and you might as well come too."

Captain Bellfield declared that he would only be too happy.

"And Charlie shall come to set her cap at Mr. Cheesacre," said the widow, turning a soft and gracious eye on the Captain.

"I shall be happy to come,"—said Charlie, quite delighted; "but not with that object. Mr. Cheesacre is very respectable, I'm sure." Charlie's mother had been the daughter of a small squire who had let his land to tenants, and she was, therefore, justified by circumstances in looking down upon a farmer.

The matter was so settled,—pending the consent of Mr. Cheesacre; and Bellfield went out to Oileymead. He knew the ways of the house, and was not surprised to find himself left alone till after dusk; nor was he much surprised when he learned that he was not put into one of the mahogany-furnitured chambers, but into a back room looking over the farm-yard in which there was no fire-place. The Captain had already endured some of the evils of poverty, and could have put up with this easily had nothing been said about it. As it was, Cheesacre brought the matter forward, and apologized, and made the thing difficult.

"You see, old fellow," he said, "there are the rooms, and of course they're empty. But it's such a bore hauling out all the things and putting up the curtains. You'll be very snug where you are."

"I shall do very well," said Bellfield rather sulkily.

"Of course you'll do very well. It's the warmest room in the house in one way." He did not say in what way. Perhaps the near neighbourhood of the stables may have had a warming effect.

Bellfield did not like it; but what is a poor man to do under such circumstances? So he went up-stairs and washed his hands before dinner in the room without a fire-place, flattering himself that he would yet be even with his friend Cheesacre.

They dined together not in the best humour, and after dinner they sat down to enjoy themselves with pipes and brandy and water. Bellfield, having a taste for everything that was expensive, would have preferred cigars; but his friend put none upon the table. Mr. Cheesacre, though he could spend his money liberally when occasion required such spending, knew well the value of domestic economy. He wasn't going to put himself out, as he called it, for Bellfield! What was good enough for himself was good enough for Bellfield. "A beggar, you know; just a regular beggar!" as he was betrayed into saying to Mrs. Greenow on some occasion just at this period. "Poor fellow! He only wants money to make him almost perfect," Mrs. Greenow had answered;—and Mr. Cheesacre had felt that he had made a mistake.

Both the men became talkative, if not good-humoured, under the effects of the brandy and water, and the Captain then communicated Mrs. Greenow's invitation to Mr. Cheesacre. He had had his doubts as to the propriety of doing so,—thinking that perhaps it might be to his advantage to forget the message. But he reflected that he was at any rate a match for Cheesacre when they were present together, and finally came to the conclusion that the message should be delivered. "I had to go and just wish her goodbye you know," he said apologetically, as he finished his little speech.

"I don't see that at all," said Cheesacre.

"Why, my dear fellow, how foolishly jealous you are. If I were to be downright uncivil to her, as you would have me be, it would only call attention to the thing."

"I'm not a bit jealous. A man who sits upon his own ground as I do hasn't any occasion to be jealous."

"I don't know what your own ground has to do with it,—but we'll let that pass."

"I think it has a great deal to do with it. If a man does intend to marry he ought to have things comfortable about him; unless he wants to live on his wife, which I look upon as about the meanest thing a man can do. By George, I'd sooner break stones than that."

This was hard for any captain to bear,—even for Captain Bellfield; but he did bear it,—looking forward to revenge.

"There's no pleasing you, I know," said he. "But there's the fact. I went to say goodbye to her, and she asked me to give you that message. Shall we go or not?"

Cheesacre sat for some time silent, blowing out huge clouds of smoke while he meditated a little plan. "I'll tell you what it is, Bellfield," he said at last. "She's nothing to you, and if you won't mind it, I'll go. Mrs. Jones shall get you anything you like for dinner,—and,—and—I'll stand you a bottle of the '34 port!"

But Captain Bellfield was not going to put up with this. He had not sold himself altogether to work Mr. Cheesacre's will. "No, old fellow," said he; "that cock won't fight. She has asked me to dine with her on Saturday, and I mean to go. I don't intend that she shall think that I'm afraid of her,—or of you either."

"You don't;—don't you?"

"No, I don't," said the Captain stoutly.

"I wish you'd pay me some of that money you owe me," said Cheesacre.

"So I will,—when I've married the widow. Ha,—ha,—ha."

Cheesacre longed to turn him out of the house. Words to bid him go, were, so to say, upon his tongue. But the man would only have taken himself to Norwich, and would have gone without any embargo upon his suit; all their treaties would then be at an end. "She knows a trick worth two of that," said Cheesacre at last.

"I dare say she does; and if so, why shouldn't I go and dine with her next Saturday?"

"I'll tell you why,—because you're in my way. The deuce is in it if I haven't made the whole thing clear enough. I've told you all my plans because I thought you were my friend, and I've paid you well to help me, too; and yet it seems to me you'd do anything in your power to throw me over,—only you can't."

"What an ass you are," said the Captain after a pause; "just you listen to me. That scraggy young woman, Charlie Fairstairs, is to be there of course."

"How do you know?"

"I tell you that I do know. She was present when the whole thing was arranged, and I heard her asked, and heard her say that she would come;—and for the matter of that I heard her declare that she wouldn't set her cap at you, because you're a farmer."

"Upon my word she's kind. Upon my word she is," said Cheesacre, getting very angry and very red. "Charlie Fairstairs, indeed! I wouldn't pick her out of a gutter with a pair of tongs. She ain't good enough for my bailiff, let alone me."

"But somebody must take her in hand on Saturday, if you're to do any good," said the crafty Bellfield.

"What the deuce does she have that nasty creature there for?" said Cheesacre, who thought it very hard that everything should not be arranged exactly as he would desire.

"She wants a companion, of course. You can get rid of Charlie, you know, when you make her Mrs. Cheesacre."

"Get rid of her! You don't suppose she'll ever put her foot in this house. Not if I know it. I've detested that woman for the last ten years." Cheesacre could forgive no word of slight respecting his social position, and the idea of Miss Fairstairs having pretended to look down upon him, galled him to the quick.

"You'll have to dine with her at any rate," said Bellfield, "and I always think that four are better company than three on such occasions."

Mr. Cheesacre grunted an unwilling assent, and after this it was looked upon as an arranged thing that they two should go into Norwich on the Saturday together, and that they should both dine with the widow. Indeed, Mrs. Greenow got two notes, one from each of them, accepting the invitation. Cheesacre wrote in the singular number, altogether ignoring Captain Bellfield, as he might have ignored his footman had he intended to take one. The captain condescended to use the plural pronoun. "We shall be so happy to come," said he. "Dear old Cheesy is out of his little wits with delight," he added, "and has already begun to polish off the effects of the farmyard."

"Effects of the farmyard," said Mrs. Greenow aloud, in Jeannette's hearing, when she received the note. "It would be well for Captain Bellfield if he had a few such effects himself."

"You can give him enough, ma'am," said Jeannette, "to make him a better man than Mr. Cheesacre any day. And for a gentleman—of course I say nothing, but if I was a lady, I know which should be the man for me."

CHAPTER XL
MRS. GREENOW'S LITTLE
DINNER IN THE CLOSE

How deep and cunning are the wiles of love! When that Saturday morning arrived not a word was said by Cheesacre to his rival as to his plans for the day. "You'll take the dog-cart in?" Captain Bellfield had asked overnight. "I don't know what I shall do as yet," replied he who was master of the house, of the dog-cart, and, as he fondly thought, of the situation. But Bellfield knew that Cheesacre must take the dog-cart, and was contented. His friend would leave him behind, if it were possible, but Bellfield would take care that it should not be possible.

Before breakfast Mr. Cheesacre surreptitiously carried out into the yard a bag containing all his apparatus for dressing,—his marrow oil for his hair, his shirt with the wondrous worked front upon an under-stratum of pink to give it colour, his shiny boots, and all the rest of the paraphernalia. When dining in Norwich on ordinary occasions, he simply washed his hands there, trusting to the chambermaid at the inn to find him a comb; and now he came down with his bag surreptitiously, and hid it away in the back of the dog-cart with secret, but alas, not unobserved hands, hoping that Bellfield would forget his toilet. But when did such a Captain ever forget his outward man? Cheesacre, as he returned through the kitchen from the yard into the front hall, perceived another bag lying near the door, apparently filled almost as well as his own.

"What the deuce are you going to do with all this luggage?" said he, giving the bag a kick.

"Put it where I saw you putting yours when I opened my window just now," said Bellfield.

"D—— the window," exclaimed Cheesacre, and then they sat down to breakfast. "How you do hack that ham about," he said. "If you ever found hams yourself you'd be more particular in cutting them." This was very bad. Even Bellfield could not bear it with equanimity, and feeling unable to eat the ham under such circumstances, made his breakfast with a couple of fresh eggs. "If you didn't mean to eat the meat, why the mischief did you cut it?" said Cheesacre.

"Upon my word, Cheesacre, you're too bad;—upon my word you are," said Bellfield, almost sobbing.

"What's the matter now?" said the other.

"Who wants your ham?"

"You do, I suppose, or you wouldn't cut it."

"No I don't; nor anything else either that you've got. It isn't fair to ask a fellow into your house, and then say such things to him as that. And it isn't what I've been accustomed to either; I can tell you that, Mr. Cheesacre."

"Oh, bother!"

"It's all very well to say bother, but I choose to be treated like a gentleman wherever I go. You and I have known each other a long time, and I'd put up with more from you than from anyone else; but—"

"Can you pay me the money that you owe me, Bellfield?" said Cheesacre, looking hard at him.

"No, I can't," said Bellfield; "not immediately."

"Then eat your breakfast, and hold your tongue."

After that Captain Bellfield did eat his breakfast,—leaving the ham however untouched, and did hold his tongue, vowing vengeance in his heart. But the two men went into Norwich more amicably together than they would have done had there been no words between them. Cheesacre felt that he had trespassed a little, and therefore offered the Captain a cigar as he seated himself in the cart. Bellfield accepted the offering, and smoked the weed of peace.

"Now," said Cheesacre, as he drove into the Swan yard, "what do you mean to do with yourself all day?"

"I shall go down to the quarters, and look the fellows up."

"All right. But mind this, Bellfield;—it's an understood thing, that you're not to be in the Close before four?"

"I won't be in the Close before four!"

"Very well. That's understood. If you deceive me, I'll not drive you back to Oileymead to-night."

In this instance Captain Bellfield had no intention to deceive. He did not think it probable that he could do himself any good by philandering about the widow early in the day. She would be engaged with her dinner and with an early toilet. Captain Bellfield, moreover, had learned from experience that the first comer has not always an advantage in ladies' society. The mind of a woman is greedy after novelty, and it is upon the stranger, or upon the most strange of her slaves around her, that she often smiles the sweetest. The cathedral clock, therefore, had struck four before Captain Bellfield rang Mrs. Greenow's bell, and then, when he was shown into the drawing-room, he found Cheesacre there alone, redolent with the marrow oil, and beautiful with the pink bosom.

"Haven't you seen her yet?" asked the Captain almost in a whisper.

"No," said Cheesacre sulkily.

"Nor yet Charlie Fairstairs?"

"I've seen nobody," said Cheesacre.

But at this moment he was compelled to swallow his anger, as Mrs. Greenow, accompanied by her lady guest, came into the room. "Whoever would have expected two gentlemen to be so punctual," said she, "especially on market-day!"

"Market-day makes no difference when I come to see you," said Cheesacre, putting his best foot forward, while Captain Bellfield contented himself with saying something civil to Charlie. He would bide his time and ride a waiting race.

The widow was almost gorgeous in her weeds. I believe that she had not sinned in her dress against any of those canons which the semi-ecclesiastical authorities on widowhood have laid down as to the outward garments fitted for gentlemen's relicts. The materials were those which are devoted to the deepest conjugal grief. As regarded every item of the written law her suttee worship was carried out to the letter. There was the widow's cap, generally so hideous, so well known to the eyes of all men, so odious to womanhood. Let us hope that such headgear may have some assuaging effect on the departed spirits of husbands. There was the dress of deep, clinging, melancholy crape,—of crape which becomes so brown and so rusty, and which makes the six months' widow seem so much more afflicted a creature than she whose husband is just gone, and whose crape is therefore new. There were the trailing weepers, and the widow's kerchief pinned close round her neck and somewhat tightly over her bosom. But there was that of genius about Mrs. Greenow, that she had turned every seeming disadvantage to some special profit, and had so dressed herself that though she had obeyed the law to the letter, she had thrown the spirit of it to the winds. Her cap sat jauntily on her head, and showed just so much of her rich brown hair as to give her the appearance of youth which she desired. Cheesacre had blamed her in his heart for her private carriage, but she spent more money, I think, on new crape than she did on her brougham. It never became brown and rusty with her, or formed itself into old lumpy folds, or shaped itself round her like a grave cloth. The written law had not interdicted crinoline, and she loomed as large with weeds, which with her were not sombre, as she would do with her silks when the period of her probation should be over. Her weepers were bright with newness, and she would waft them aside from her shoulder with an air which turned even them into auxiliaries. Her kerchief was fastened close round her neck and close over her bosom; but Jeannette well knew what she was doing as she fastened it,—and so did Jeannette's mistress.

Mrs. Greenow would still talk much about her husband, declaring that her loss was as fresh to her wounded heart, as though he, on whom all her happiness had rested, had left her only yesterday; but yet she mistook her dates, frequently referring to the melancholy circumstance, as having taken place fifteen months ago. In truth, however, Mr. Greenow had been alive within the last nine months,—as everybody around her knew. But if she chose to forget the exact day, why should her friends or dependents remind her of it? No friend or dependent did remind her of it, and Charlie Fairstairs spoke of the fifteen months with bold confidence,—false-tongued little parasite that she was.

"Looking well," said the widow, in answer to some outspoken compliment from Mr. Cheesacre. "Yes, I'm well enough in health, and I suppose I ought to be thankful that it is so. But if you had buried a wife whom you had loved within the last eighteen months, you would have become as indifferent as I am to all that kind of thing."

"I never was married yet," said Mr. Cheesacre.

"And therefore you know nothing about it. Everything in the world is gay and fresh to you. If I were you, Mr. Cheesacre, I would not run the risk. It is hardly worth a woman's while, and I suppose not a man's. The sufferings are too great!" Whereupon she pressed her handkerchief to her eyes.

"But I mean to try all the same," said Cheesacre, looking the lover all over as he gazed into the fair one's face.

"I hope that you may be successful, Mr. Cheesacre, and that she may not be torn away from you early in life. Is dinner ready, Jeannette? That's well. Mr. Cheesacre, will you give your arm to Miss Fairstairs?"

There was no doubt as to Mrs. Greenow's correctness. As Captain Bellfield held, or had held, her Majesty's commission, he was clearly entitled to take the mistress of the festival down to dinner. But Cheesacre would not look at it in this light. He would only remember that he had paid for the Captain's food for some time past, that the Captain had been brought into Norwich in his gig, that the Captain owed him money, and ought, so to say, to be regarded as his property on the occasion. "I pay my way, and that ought to give a man higher station than being a beggarly captain,— which I don't believe he is, if all the truth was known." It was thus that he took an occasion to express himself to Miss Fairstairs on that very evening. "Military rank is always recognised," Miss Fairstairs had replied, taking Mr. Cheesacre's remarks as a direct slight upon herself. He had taken her down to dinner, and had then come to her complaining that he had been injured in being called upon to do so! "If you were a magistrate, Mr. Cheesacre, you would have rank; but I believe you are not." Charlie Fairstairs knew well what she was about. Mr. Cheesacre had striven much to get his name put upon the commission of the peace, but had failed. "Nasty, scraggy old cat," Cheesacre said to himself, as he turned away from her.

But Bellfield gained little by taking the widow down. He and Cheesacre were placed at the top and bottom of the table, so that they might do the work of carving; and the ladies sat at the sides. Mrs. Greenow's hospitality was very good. The dinner was exactly what a dinner ought to be for four persons. There was soup, fish, a cutlet, a roast fowl, and some game. Jeannette waited at table nimbly, and the thing could not have been done better. Mrs. Greenow's appetite was not injured by her grief, and she so far repressed for the time all remembrance of her sorrow as to enable her to play the kind hostess to perfection. Under her immediate eye Cheesacre was forced into apparent cordiality with his friend Bellfield, and the Captain himself took the good things which the gods provided with thankful good-humour.

Nothing, however, was done at the dinner-table. No work got itself accomplished. The widow was so accurately fair in the adjustment of her favours, that even Jeannette could not perceive to which of the two she turned with the amplest smile. She talked herself and made others talk, till Cheesacre became almost comfortable, in spite of his jealousy. "And now," she said, as she got up to leave the room, when she had taken her own glass of wine, "We will allow these two gentlemen just half an hour, eh Charlie? and then we shall expect them up-stairs."

"Ten minutes will be enough for us here," said Cheesacre, who was in a hurry to utilize his time.

"Half an hour," said Mrs. Greenow, not without some little tone of command in her voice. Ten minutes might be enough for Mr. Cheesacre, but ten minutes was not enough for her.

Bellfield had opened the door, and it was upon him that the widow's eye glanced as she left the room. Cheesacre saw it, and resolved to resent the injury. "I'll tell you what it is, Bellfield," he said, as he sat down moodily over the fire, "I won't have you coming here at all, till this matter is settled."

"Till what matter is settled?" said Bellfield, filling his glass.

"You know what matter I mean."

"You take such a deuce of a time about it."

"No, I don't. I take as little time as anybody could. That other fellow has only been dead about nine months, and I've got the thing in excellent training already."

"And what harm do I do?"

"You disturb me, and you disturb her. You do it on purpose. Do you suppose I can't see? I'll tell you what, now; if you'll go clean out of Norwich for a month, I'll lend you two hundred pounds on the day she becomes Mrs. Cheesacre."

"And where am I to go to?"

"You may stay at Oileymead, if you like;—that is, on condition that you do stay there."

"And be told that I hack the ham because it's not my own. Shall I tell you a piece of my mind, Cheesacre?"

"What do you mean?"

"That woman has no more idea of marrying you than she has of marrying the Bishop. Won't you fill your glass, old fellow? I know where the tap is if you want another bottle. You may as well give it up, and spend no more money in pink fronts and polished boots on her account. You're a podgy man, you see, and Mrs. Greenow doesn't like podgy men."

Cheesacre sat looking at him with his mouth open, dumb with surprise, and almost paralysed with impotent anger. What had happened during the last few hours to change so entirely the tone of his dependent captain? Could it be that Bellfield had been there during the morning, and that she had accepted him?

"You are very podgy, Cheesacre," Bellfield continued, "and then you so often smell of the farm-yard; and you talk too much of your money and your property. You'd have had a better chance if you had openly talked to her of hers,—as I have done. As it is, you haven't any chance at all."

Bellfield, as he thus spoke to the man opposite to him, went on drinking his wine comfortably, and seemed to be chuckling with glee. Cheesacre was so astounded, so lost in amazement that the creature whom he had fed,—whom he had bribed with money out of his own pocket, should' thus turn against him, that for a while he could not collect his thoughts or find voice wherewith to make any answer. It occurred to him immediately that Bellfield was even now, at this very time, staying at his house,—that he, Cheesacre, was expected to drive him, Bellfield, back to Oileymead, to his own Oileymead, on this very evening; and as he thought of this he almost fancied that he must be in a dream. He shook himself, and looked again, and there sat Bellfield, eyeing him through the bright colour of a glass of port.

"Now I've told you a bit of my mind, Cheesy, my boy," continued Bellfield, "and you'll save yourself a deal of trouble and annoyance if you'll believe what I say. She doesn't mean to marry you. It's most probable that she'll marry me; but, at any rate, she won't marry you."

"Do you mean to pay me my money, sir?" said Cheesacre, at last, finding his readiest means of attack in that quarter.

"Yes, I do."

"But when?"

"When I've married Mrs. Greenow,—and, therefore, I expect your assistance in that little scheme. Let us drink her health. We shall always be delighted to see you at our house, Cheesy, my boy, and you shall be allowed to hack the hams just as much as you please."

"You shall be made to pay for this," said Cheesacre, gasping with anger;—gasping almost more with dismay than he did with anger.

"All right, old fellow; I'll pay for it,—with the widow's money. Come; our half-hour is nearly over; shall we go up-stairs?"

"I'll expose you."

"Don't now;—don't be ill-natured."

"Will you tell me where you mean to sleep to-night, Captain Bellfield?"

"If I sleep at Oileymead it will only be on condition that I have one of the mahogany-furnitured bedrooms."

"You'll never put your foot in that house again. You're a rascal, sir."

"Come, come, Cheesy, it won't do for us to quarrel in a lady's house. It wouldn't be the thing at all. You're not drinking your wine. You might as well take another glass, and then we'll go up-stairs."

"You've left your traps at Oileymead, and not one of them you shall have till you've paid me every shilling you owe me. I don't believe you've a shirt in the world beyond what you've got there."

"It's lucky I brought one in to change; wasn't it, Cheesy? I shouldn't have thought of it only for the hint you gave me. I might as well ring the bell for Jeannette to put away the wine, if you won't take any more." Then he rang the bell, and when Jeannette came he skipped lightly up-stairs into the drawing-room.

"Was he here before to-day?" said Cheesacre, nodding his head at the doorway through which Bellfield had passed.

"Who? The Captain? Oh dear no. The Captain don't come here much now;—not to say often, by no means."

"He's a confounded rascal."

"Oh, Mr. Cheesacre!" said Jeannette.

"He is;—and I ain't sure that there ain't others nearly as bad as he is."

"If you mean me, Mr. Cheesacre, I do declare you're a wronging me; I do indeed."

"What's the meaning of his going on in this way?"

"I don't know nothing of his ways, Mr. Cheesacre; but I've been as true to you, sir;—so I have;—as true as true." And Jeannette put her handkerchief up to her eyes.

He moved to the door, and then a thought occurred to him. He put his hand to his trousers pocket, and turning back towards the girl, gave her half-a-crown. She curtsied as she took it, and then repeated her last words. "Yes, Mr. Cheesacre,—as true as true." Mr. Cheesacre said nothing further, but followed his enemy up to the drawing-room. "What game is up now, I wonder," said Jeannette to herself, when she was left alone. "They two'll be cutting each other's throatses before they've done, and then my missus will take the surwiver." But she made up her mind that Cheesacre should be the one to have his throat cut fatally, and that Bellfield should be the survivor.

Cheesacre, when he reached the drawing-room, found Bellfield sitting on the same sofa with Mrs. Greenow looking at a book of photographs which they both of them were handling together. The outside rim of her widow's frill on one occasion touched the Captain's whisker, and as it did so the Captain looked up with a gratified expression of triumph. If any gentleman has ever seen the same thing under similar circumstances, he will understand that Cheesacre must have been annoyed.

"Yes," said Mrs. Greenow, waving her handkerchief, of which little but a two-inch-deep border seemed to be visible. Bellfield knew at once that it was not the same handkerchief which she had waved before they went down to dinner. "Yes,—there he is. It's so like him." And then she apostrophized the *carte de visite* of the departed one. "Dear Greenow; dear husband! When my spirit is false to thee, let thine forget to visit me softly in my dreams. Thou wast unmatched among husbands. Whose tender kindness was ever equal to thine? whose sweet temper was ever so constant? whose manly care so all-sufficient?" While the words fell from her lips her little finger was touching Bellfield's little finger, as they held the book between them. Charlie Fairstairs and Mr. Cheesacre were watching her narrowly, and she knew that they were watching her. She was certainly a woman of great genius and of great courage.

"Dear Greenow; dear husband!"

Bellfield, moved by the eloquence of her words, looked with some interest at the photograph. There was represented there before him, a small, grey-looking, insignificant old man, with pig's eyes and a toothless mouth,—one who should never have been compelled to submit himself to the cruelty of the sun's portraiture! Another widow, even if she had kept in her book the photograph of such a husband, would have scrambled it over silently,—would have been ashamed to show it. "Have you ever seen it, Mr. Cheesacre?" asked Mrs. Greenow. "It's so like him."

"I saw it at Yarmouth," said Cheesacre, very sulkily.

"That you did not," said the lady with some dignity, and not a little of rebuke in her tone; "simply because it never was at Yarmouth. A larger one you may have seen, which I always keep, and always shall keep, close by my bedside."

"Not if I know it," said Captain Bellfield to himself. Then the widow punished Mr. Cheesacre for his sullenness by whispering a few words to the Captain; and Cheesacre in his wrath turned to Charlie Fairstairs. Then it was that he spake out his mind about the Captain's rank, and was snubbed by Charlie,—as was told a page or two back.

After that, coffee was brought to them, and here again Cheesacre in his ill-humour allowed the Captain to out-manœuvre him. It was the Captain who put the sugar into the cups and handed them round. He even handed a cup to his enemy. "None for me, Captain Bellfield; many thanks for your politeness all the same," said Mr. Cheesacre; and Mrs. Greenow knew from the tone of his voice that there had been a quarrel.

Cheesacre sitting then in his gloom, had resolved upon one thing,—or, I may perhaps say, upon two things. He had resolved that he would not leave the room that evening till Bellfield had left it, and that he would get a final answer from the widow, if not that night,—for he thought it very possible that they might both be sent away together,—then early after breakfast on the following morning. For the present, he had given up any idea of turning his time to good account. He was not perhaps a coward, but he had not that special courage which enables a man to fight well under adverse circumstances. He had been cowed by the unexpected impertinence of his rival,—by the insolence of a man to whom he thought that he had obtained the power of being always himself as insolent as he pleased. He could not recover his ground quickly, or carry himself before his lady's eye as though he was unconscious of the wound he had received. So he sat silent, while Bellfield was discoursing fluently. He sat in silence, comforting himself with reflections on his own wealth, and on the poverty of the other, and promising himself a rich harvest of revenge when the moment should come in which he might tell Mrs. Greenow how absolutely that man was a beggar, a swindler, and a rascal.

And he was astonished when an opportunity for doing so came very quickly. Before the neighbouring clock had done striking seven, Bellfield rose from his chair to go. He first of all spoke a word of farewell to Miss Fairstairs; then he turned to his late host; "Good night, Cheesacre," he said, in the easiest tone in the world; after that he pressed the widow's hand and whispered his adieu.

"I thought you were staying at Oileymead?" said Mrs. Greenow.

"I came from there this morning," said the Captain.

"But he isn't going back there, I can tell you," said Mr. Cheesacre.

"Oh, indeed," said Mrs. Greenow; "I hope there is nothing wrong."

"All as right as a trivet," said the Captain; and then he was off.

"I promised mamma that I would be home by seven," said Charlie Fairstairs, rising from her chair. It cannot be supposed that she had any wish to oblige Mr. Cheesacre, and therefore this movement on her part must be regarded simply as done in kindness to Mrs. Greenow. She might be mistaken in supposing that Mrs. Greenow would desire to be left alone with Mr. Cheesacre; but it was clear to her that in this way she could give no offence, whereas it was quite possible that she might offend by remaining. A little after seven Mr. Cheesacre found himself alone with the lady.

"I'm sorry to find," said she, gravely, "that you two have quarrelled."

"Mrs. Greenow," said he, jumping up, and becoming on a sudden full of life, "that man is a downright swindler."

"Oh, Mr. Cheesacre."

"He is. He'll tell you that he was at Inkerman, but I believe he was in prison all the time." The Captain had been arrested, I think twice, and thus Mr. Cheesacre justified to himself this assertion. "I doubt whether he ever saw a shot fired," he continued.

"He's none the worse for that."

"But he tells such lies; and then he has not a penny in the world. How much do you suppose he owes me, now?"

"However much it is, I'm sure you are too much of a gentleman to say."

"Well;—yes, I am," said he, trying to recover himself. "But when I asked him how he intended to pay me, what do you think he said? He said he'd pay me when he got your money."

"My money! He couldn't have said that!"

"But he did, Mrs. Greenow; I give you my word and honour. 'I'll pay you when I get the widow's money,' he said."

"You gentlemen must have a nice way of talking about me when I am absent."

"I never said a disrespectful word about you in my life, Mrs. Greenow,— or thought one. He does;—he says horrible things."

"What horrible things, Mr. Cheesacre?"

"Oh, I can't tell you;—but he does. What can you expect from such a man as that, who, to my knowledge, won't have a change of clothes to-morrow, except what he brought in on his back this morning. Where he's to get a bed to-night, I don't know, for I doubt whether he's got half-a-crown in the world."

"Poor Bellfield!"

"Yes; he is poor."

"But how gracefully he carries his poverty."

"I should call it very disgraceful, Mrs. Greenow." To this she made no reply, and then he thought that he might begin his work. "Mrs. Greenow,— may I say Arabella?"

"Mr. Cheesacre!"

"But mayn't I? Come, Mrs. Greenow. You know well enough by this time what it is I mean. What's the use of shilly-shallying?"

"Shilly-shallying, Mr. Cheesacre! I never heard such language. If I bid you good night, now, and tell you that it is time for you to go home, shall you call that shilly-shallying?"

He had made a mistake in his word and repented it. "I beg your pardon, Mrs. Greenow; I do indeed. I didn't mean anything offensive."

"Shilly-shallying, indeed! There's very little shall in it, I can assure you."

The poor man was dreadfully crestfallen, so much so that the widow's heart relented, and she pardoned him. It was not in her nature to quarrel with people;—at any rate, not with her lovers. "I beg your pardon, Mrs. Greenow," said the culprit, humbly. "It is granted," said the widow; "but never tell a lady again that she is shilly-shallying. And look here, Mr. Cheesacre, if it should ever come to pass that you are making love to a lady in earnest—"

"I couldn't be more in earnest," said he.

"That you are making love to a lady in earnest, talk to her a little more about your passion and a little less about your purse. Now, good night."

"But we are friends."

"Oh yes;—as good friends as ever."

Cheesacre, as he drove himself home in the dark, tried to console himself by thinking of the miserable plight in which Bellfield would find himself at Norwich, with no possessions but what he had brought into the town that day in a small bag. But as he turned in at his own gate he met two figures emerging; one of them was laden with a portmanteau, and the other with a hat case.

"It's only me, Cheesy, my boy," said Bellfield. "I've just come down by the rail to fetch my things, and I'm going back to Norwich by the 9.20."

"If you've stolen anything of mine I'll have you prosecuted," roared Cheesacre, as he drove his gig up to his own door.